Jagged Dreams

C. C. Saint-Clair

1. Lesbians - Fiction. 1. Title
A823.4

Saint-Clair, C.C.
Jagged Dreams 2nd. ed.
978-0-9803344-1-8
ISBN 0-9803344-1-1

Book design by www.bookmakersink.com

All characters in this book are fictitious and any resemblance to real persons, living or dead, is purely coincidental. Certain real locations and institutions are mentioned, but characters and events depicted are entirely fictional.

Lazy Moon Productions
Moorooka, Queensland, Australia
lazymoonproductions@netspace.net.au

By the same author

North And Left From Here (Take II) (revised edition)
Benchmarks (revised edition)
Silent Goodbyes
Risking-me
Far From Maddy
Morgan in the Mirror

About Jagged Dreams

Emilie finds her lover, Tamara, face down and unconscious near her Jeep. It soon becomes apparent that a violent blow to the head is the cause. Beyond the fear of possible complications not yet ruled out by Tamara's doctor, Emilie and the police need more clues than they have regarding the attacker's identity and motive.

Jagged Dreams is about the disturbing reality that becomes Tamara's during the time she spends in the ward, inside her bed, inside her head, while her thoughts go on, sliding and slithering away from her.

Jagged Dreams is about two lovers on different sides of a considerable age gap, the dreamy sensuality of woman to woman trust. And beyond all that, it's about working out who has aggressed Tamara.

"Saint-Clair is the mistress of capturing emotions and trapping them between the lines of her work … a form of writing both addictive and painful for the intensity of feeling that can be experienced whilst reading."

Elise Archer, Adventurer

"It is refreshing to find an author in the romance genre who can let her characters reflect on their own thoughts, actions and values, in a way which gives rise to insight and self awareness, and which is also done without proselytizing or being didactic."

F. T. Johnson

About the Author

QUEENSLAND, AUSTRALIA – Lesbian romance has a new voice, that of C.C Saint-Clair. She belongs to a rare breed of contemporary lesbian writers who achieve a lot more than mere titillation in their fiction. Her writing is solid, sensuous and evocative. It deserves the tag already attributed to it - that of 'the thinking woman's lesbian romance'.

Born of French parents in Casablanca, Saint-Clair is a native French speaker though she completed her formal education in the United States, at The University of Texas, majoring in English Literature.

She now lives in Australia with her long-term partner, free to pursue her interests in cinematography, computer imagery, and collecting rustic antiques.

With her debut novel, **North And Left From Here**, C.C. Saint-Clair launched a series of trademark romantic and sensual plots.

Since her return from a challenging trek inside the jungles of Sarawak, Saint-Clair has written the screenplay adaptation of *Far From Maddy*, which came at 2nd at the *Rhodes island Film Festival* [GLBT Barren Branches] screenplay competition in 2005, and made it to the quarter finals of the international but stritcly mainstream Scriptapaloosa comp in 2006.

Visit **C.C.**'s website for extracts and choice author cuts:
www.ccsaint-clair.com

Acknowledgements

Five novels later and the same heart-felt thank you and my love to Myahr B., who still is my Ideal Reader.

Grateful thanks are also extended to Joy and Susan for their efforts to search for and destroy malingering typos that make it a game to elude me.

Any errors made in regards to Tamara's medical condition are entirely mine, but I wish to thank Michael Keogh, and Michelle and Gavin Duffy who have helped me with the surface knowledge that I needed to write about concussion.

I also wish to thank Sandy Viney for some information about Queensland police procedures.

PROLOGUE

She stops in mid-stride. No, she thinks. I shouldn't just barge in on her like that and surprise her.

So instead, she has a look around the foyer. She looks at the artwork on the walls, at the large potplants strategically placed in each corner, by the lifts, and by the entrance to each hallway. She runs her hand along the already deserted receptionist's desk.

Her eyes roam over the 'No Bullying' poster and on a notice-board she recognises one of the memos her lover had been working on a couple of nights earlier.

"What if I type Deconstruction Of Hero(ines) Part II and then follow through with the usual pedagogical blah blah blah?" her lover had asked late one night, late because *that* night they had made love at the time her lover would otherwise have been typing the next day's inter-departmental memos and student notices.

"What if you do?" she had answered, unsure as to the real question.

"Well, I don't necessarily want to mention the male hero thing first, right? But it does have to be mentioned because … well, because they do have to deconstruct how male 'heroes' are fabricated too. I mean, *that* comparison *is* the main thrust of that particular unit."

"Mmm?"

"But our students, even the girls, they're really not ready for the *shero* word. Mind you, the *she*-hero term seems somewhat contrived, and now that I think of it, it reminds me a bit of *she*-goat," her lover had rambled on, thinking out loud. "And yet, *heroine* is totally corny. So, without pandering to the males…"

As she hovers near the entrance to the hallway on the right, the impulse to peep into Suite 104 to surprise her lover hasn't yet left her, not totally.

She would like to knock on that office door and say, Hey … Look who's here. *Moi,* she would grin. Not just on time but *before* time. So, you going to show me around or what?

She would like to see her lover at work. She imagines her as she might look up from her monitor or from the contents of a filing cab-inet to answer a knock on the door. Does she keep on working, waiting for *whoever* to open the door and poke their head through or does she peer over her half-moon glasses and call out, Come in! How does she *move* inside that office?

In her mind, she imagines her lover, in one of the offices to the right of the sliding doors, some four doors down. She imagines her tidying up her files, diarising a couple of must-do items. She imagines her organising today for tomorrow or next month. She imagines her, too, glancing at her watch, relaxed in the thought that *she* won't be around for a little while yet. She imagines her smiling at the thought that all is well in their world and that a pleasant evening in a New Farm restaurant lies ahead for the two of them.

She would like to meet some of her colleagues, too, even if her lover introduces her only by her first name without adding, *my lover.*

Knocking on her office door would be fun but she won't impose *that* on her lover. Home and work, different spheres, says her lover. Both private. Differently private. Both for different sets of eyes.

Never mind, she tells herself.

She smiles at a private thought as, with the straps of her backpack wrapped loosely around her wrist, she walks back through the sliding doors and into the fading afternoon light.

As she nears the car something glints at her, something on the ground. Almost behind the front wheel but not quite. She drops her backpack by the car door and leans down to have a closer look. As she does, a blue blur moves across the furthest quadrant of her peripheral vision.

She reaches down but her fingertips do not get to retrieve the glinting object. If they had, she would have immediately recognised one of her lover's favourite ear studs.

*****

ONE

White. White-grey. Grey-blue. Blue-cool. Bubbles. Lots of bubbles. Bubble and rise. Breath choked. No more noisy bubbles. Quiet. Muffled sounds. Thud. Thud. Thud. Heartbeats. Upwards through the breaking blue. Warm-blue. Tam-Darling, really! Just because papa does it when he shouldn't, *you must never jump off from up there*. Bub, you understand? Watery voice. Use the ladder. That's what Old Jacob's for you know, Jamie. I told him that, I know I told him to use the ladder.

Grey. Hard, grainy, nasty grey. Wet against my cheek.

White-blue again. White-blue ice. Cold-blue. High blue white walls. Walls against my body. Tight. Cold. Hard. Blue. So much of it. Why so much blue?

A voice. From inside. No, not from inside me. Outside. Not in my head. One finger in my ear. The other ear tight against the pillow. Mother's voice. Small and far.

A stranger's voice. "Watch that bloody drip. Is she coming around?"

Walls. Soft-hard thickness. Cold ice-walls too tight. Too tightly against me. Can't breathe. Slip. Grip toes! Slip, slip, slip away.

Electric blue. Dildo-blue. Uh … no. Not for me, she said. You *should* know better, shouldn't you? she said. It's just that I never got around to giving it to Solange. That's what she said. Leather-blue blur. Grainy grey. Rough against my cheek. Too weak, no grip.

In the ward, inside her bed, inside her head, Tamara's brain is taking her back to a particular day, though that day is already years old and that's because her thoughts are still not hers to harness.

Tamara tossed and turned as if she truly believed that a show of temper would muffle the exultant sounds that came from the farmyard. The roosters, the frigging roosters, were already awake. She pushed her head further into the downy depth of the pillow and yet the roosters' predawn calls were, in fact, not as discordant as that of the crows in Alex's suburban backyard.

'No sound can possibly be worse than the early morning cawing of the Brisbane crows,' she used to think back home, in Australia. 'Even a flock of chirpy galahs would be softer to the ears.'

The other difference was that Alex's backyard crows cawed *after* sun-up round six a.m., not *before dawn*. And so, what Tamara was craving, at the moment of the roosters' triumphant cock-a-doodle-doo,

1

was a few more hours burrowed inside the warmth of her bed. One finger inside her ear-hole, the other ear jammed tightly against the pillow, she closed her eyes again, willing the receding drowsiness to linger on just a while longer.

She stretched first one leg then the other. Her thigh muscles protested. Again, still, even after eight days. The sole of one foot snuggled back against the calf muscle of the other leg. It's that frigging squat that does it, she thought. It's the hours on end bit that does it. It's a killer.

Screaming muscle aches had not been on her mind when she had let her wanderlust take her to the East of St Emilion and up and down, inland from the banks of the Dordogne River. What thoughts had drifted, while she strode past vineyards and the century-stained walls of low-set farms revolved around the odd ridge one of her socks had shaped inside her hiking boot. Her backpack harness rode comfortably against the length of her back and snugly against her hips. So uncluttered had her backpacker's mind become while trekking through this friendly territory in the central western region of France that preventing the skin irritation from forming a blister had been the sole concern of the past few days, certainly her only annoyance.

Basic physical comfort she had decided, comfort within one's body, was essential. It was the gateway to wellbeing. Everything else was absolutely optional: saving for an old age that may never come, a three-bedroom house in the suburbs, a PDA and a mobile phone, emotional entanglements, tattoos and piercings, other must-haves she either had or wished she had. She lumped them all into an imaginary bag labelled 'Disposable Gadgetry'. It is not the indeterminate leave of absence from her ordinary life as a worker in the Brisbane Domestic Violence cell that had given her that particular insight, but two or three weeks of solitary trekking.

And so, it was the newfound understanding of what really mattered that had prompted her to give into the rub that was irritating the outer side of her big toe inside her Trailblazer boot. She had smiled to herself, face lifted to the soft afternoon sun. She knew that *that* irritation would soon be relieved. And she would, once again, have a totally blank screen on which important things like sunsets, smells and scents, picturesque sights, new and unexpected experiences, would paint themselves. All of that, plus the incredible feeling of being at ease within her young and healthy body, would leave one at a time their clean, uncluttered impressions. That feeling ruled supreme. Sweet. Priceless.

"Alors, la jeune Tamara! On bouge là d'dans?"

Tamara scrunched her eyes more tightly shut and suppressed a groan. Marielle's voice, cheery as usual had, yet again, found a way to sneak all the way to Tamara's middle ear and beyond.

"Oh là. C'est sûr qu' après l' chant du coq y en qu' pour les paresseux à c' t' heure-là."

Marielle knew that Tamara was no longer fully asleep. That is what *she* knew. What *Tamara* knew was that there would be little gained by pretending deep sleep. Marielle's daily wake-up call said it all. The gist of it, as Marielle had patiently explained until Tamara had understood, was that it's only laziness that makes the sleepy head sleepy after the roosters have called in the new day. That's what the winegrower's daughter said adhering, as she did in all things, to the locals' earthy reasoning. And so, Tamara knew that Marielle wouldn't go away. Not before she had seen her soft-pale feet poke from under the *édredon* and grope for the thin floor rug.

"Allez, La Grande! Un bon p'tit déjeuner pour chasser la faim d' la nuit. Et les raisins, y sont déjà à nous attendre, eux."

Marielle liked to refer to the household's only backpacker as *La Grande*, the tall one. Not that Tamara was unusually tall, standing only at five eight, but she was certainly taller than the vigneron's daughter. Though slight, Marielle was much stronger, her body stubbornly enduring, born as she was into daily physical work that went far beyond doing the usual washing-up expected of city children. It was the trekker's slender hips and taut rollerblader's legs that made her look taller than she was.

Tamara yawned silently, rolled over and wiggled her toes. She rotated both wrists and winced again in the darkness. Yep. That ache was still there, too, still deep inside the muscle that snaked from wrist to elbow. It, too, protested, but from the repeated strain of cutting bunch of grapes after bunch after bunch with pruning secateurs. Some two thousand bunches a day she had cut. Multiply that by eight for the number of days I've been at it, she mused, and that amounts to sixteen thousand wrist snips. Awesome.

Grape-picking was a fine thing but Tamara had quickly figured out that vines were not harvested by picking. Only by cutting. Snip, cut, snip, cut, cut. Don't know how she does it, Marielle, topping me by another thousand. Every day. Must be in the genes. Something her mother must've put in her baby formula.

The second part of Marielle's early morning wisdom is about, as she says, not forgetting the grapes. They're out there, already waiting for us, she says, how cute. Quaint, Tamara sighed inwardly, imagining the dark round grapes in their chunky clusters just hanging. Like, they're just waiting for us to start snipping. Snip, snip, cut, cut, snip.

Tamara swivelled her hips slightly to ease the strain she felt in her lower back. The unexpected sweet sensation that spread throughout her body was different from, but not unlike, the pinpoint moment in lovemaking when an indescribable shimmer focuses her attention. The exact second when her body kicks into the pre-orgasmic phase. She moaned softly.

Marielle was sliding the curtains sideways to allow the pale premorning light to filter inside Tamara's corner of the converted barn. The light crept in through reluctant windowpanes, chasing away the bits of night that had been clinging to the whitewashed walls, like Tamara to the warmth of her bed and drifting thoughts.

Tamara seldom understood everything that was said in French but she understood enough to get the general drift of whatever was being said around her. Her precipitously revived A Level high school French could only stretch so far at such short notice.

Marielle liked the foreigner's easy smile. She liked her smile because it made it easy for her to smile back. Besides her unusually green eyes, she liked, too, the traveller's approach to struggles that she, herself, wouldn't have liked to face in a foreign land and in a foreign language. She understood Tamara's determination to keep on cutting, to keep on snipping, even when close to the edge of her endurance.

Marielle knew a lot about determination. About the determination it takes to keep going, teeth gritted, to keep the pain inside and the silence outside, though Marielle's endurance was not at the physical level. She was healthy, strong, used to back breaking- tasks. She was resilient. It was that resilience that allowed her to keep her thoughts silent behind gritted teeth and in a calcified heart. And so, unwittingly, Tamara had successfully completed, in Marielle's eyes, the essential phase of an unwritten rite of passage.

Because of all that, and because they were close to the same age, and because Tamara's presence offered her a temporary break in an otherwise all male environment, except for her mother, Marielle didn't mind repeating things slowly, exhibiting uncharacteristic Gallic patience. And so Tamara knew how knowledgeable the young woman was in regards to all aspects of the vineyard and the farmyard fowls and the cows.

And Tamara had observed the many things Marielle knew to do with her hands. Wide and strong hands, she had. Larger than her below-average height and slim frame would have suggested. They were totally capable, those hands of hers, and one day they would become hard like Madame Dufour's, her mother's. Hard because calloused. Calloused because never idle.

Tamara raised her wrist to peer at her watch face. Just as she suspected, the small hand had crept up to the five but the big hand was lagging behind. It was nowhere near the twelve. She ran a hand over the warm skin of her stomach, up and across her breasts. Her nipples felt her touch. She sighed again but made herself sit up.

"Ça va. Je suis ré-veillée." Yes, she was awake though still fuzzy from the night. Still fuzzy from her recurring dream, but awake.

Will there ever be a time when that dream will just go away? Go away and stay away? *Jamie jumped.* He was not allowed there at all, not even under adult supervision. She had shouted at him to climb down, to get back on the deck. 'Use the ladder. Go very slowly. Old Jacobs is not for little people,' that's what mother says. 'You know Papa says you're not allowed up there. You're never to climb up there, he said that, you know?' Instead, Jamie had pushed off the tiny barrel-like platform of the crow's-nest. He had jumped. He hadn't wanted to. Not at all. His eyes. All he –

"C'est bien, Tamara. Bientôt, c'est toi qui viendra me chercher."

I don't think so, Tamara thought. No matter how often Marielle might suggest the idea, Tamara couldn't possibly envisage a time when she would beat her to the breakfast table. She'd have moved on long before farmlife could alter her in such a drastic way.

As she emerged a little more from the night, Tamara was keen to not let a lurking grumpiness encroach any further. She needed to flush it out of the corner of her head, from whatever corner it was that wanted to revert to her old habit, the twenty-four year old habit of sleeping in. Lazy weekend mornings had always been a sacrosanct ritual of hers.

Tamara ran her hand over the warm fleecy fabric of her pajamas over her still sleepy, still warm sex, and she stretched again. But again, she reasoned, if waking Marielle from inside the huge four-poster bed tucked away in the east side of the first floor was an option, a viable one, that would certainly entice her more quickly out of her own bed. Why, she might even beat the roosters to the dawn and watch the sunrise through the small window tucked under the eaves, the vigneron's daughter's moonlight-pale body tucked into her own.

Chuckling at her own sleazy thoughts, Tamara finally decided the time had come to keep her eyes open and face the wonders of and flatten the sleep-tousled spikes of dark hair that stood up at odd angles, Tamara crossed the paved courtyard on Marielle's heels, quite keen now to stand by the warmth of the kitchen's hearth. On the other side of the heavy French doors, Madame Dufour's strong chicory-coffee blend and *tartines* cut thick would ready her for the work ahead. By then, a little more of the sun would be out. By then, the vines would be glistening with clingy, crystal-clear raindrops. By then, the grapes would just be hanging, waiting to get cut off the vine, just like Marielle said.

Some eight days earlier, Tamara had entered the wide court-yard that she guessed might date back to the fourteenth century or thereabouts. She had knocked on the door that seemed frail, embedded as it was inside the thick depth of stone walls. No one had answered. She had propped her backpack against the age-stained wall, happy to separate herself from the load that had almost become an *excroissance*, a growth, that had latched on to her lean frame. A dog had barked. A voice had answered it. A woman's voice, it had been. Good sign, Tamara had thought.

She had rounded the corner and almost stumbled headfirst into a knee-high, moss-festooned well. The dog had barked again, unpleasantly this time, and the woman who had been feeding the fowls looked up. The dog barked again, clearly suggesting to Tamara that she shouldn't come any closer. Glad the dog was tied up, she nevertheless stayed where she was, the cool moss of the well refreshing against the side of her knee. She waved at the *fermière* who seemed young, about her age. To better see the stranger, the young woman raised her hand to shade her eyes against the slanted rays of the afternoon sun.

"*Bun-jour,*" Tamara had said.

"*Bonjour,*" the young farmer had replied noncommittally, eyes still shielded.

From her position by the well, Tamara had launched her request in rusty French. "*Uh … Je voudrwais … Est-ce possible … un endrwoit pouhr dohrmir?*" she added.

"*Ben, c'est qu' ça dépend,*" the young woman had replied still noncommittally but pleasantly enough. When, pushing back a strand of chestnut hair, she had added, "*Viens un peu. Viens,*" with a movement of the hand that meant 'Come here', Tamara thought it augured well for her toe. It would soon be free from the irritating rub of the sock.

And when, a while later, Tamara had found herself alone in the converted barn that was a lovely high-ceilinged, thick-beamed affair, she almost felt like baby Jesus in the manger. She expected, of course, that there would be some kind of exchange *en nature*, as they say, some work to do in the vineyard, but she hadn't asked what. On the one hand, the task of communicating with strangers seemed, momentarily, too arduous to attempt just then. On the other, she was totally unworried as to what the work might entail. Whatever the vignerons had lined up for her she guessed would be fair and within the ability of any fit young person.

On the first of Marielle's post-dawn visits to her barn, Tamara's only gripe had been the gritty sensation behind her eyelids. She had slept well but not enough. Marielle had ushered her to her place at the breakfast table. Thick chicory coffee, the morning's milk already in the heavy *grés* jug, thick slabs of home-made bread smothered in creamy butter and grape preserve had put her into the right gear for what lay ahead.

She found herself ushered in to join a *hourdon*, a team of cutters, all of them local men of varying ages. Some smiled awkwardly. Some simply nodded. *Les campagnards*, though usually welcoming, Tamara had already noticed, were not by nature talkative people. Though she, herself, was always extremely interested in others, in the human species in general, she didn't mind working in silence, letting the postcard-documentary quality of these moments in the vines fill her senses, before the squatting, the bending, the cutting and the snipping numbed them. Besides, any conversation in French would have had to be reduced to a threadbare simplicity.

Grape harvest in the Bordeaux region is still very much a local males' business though exceptions are made for itinerant workers such as Tamara. However, when Marielle joins the *vendangeurs*, the pickers, she doesn't actually *join* them. It wouldn't be fitting for *her* to take her place inside an all-male *hourdons*. Solitary work at the other end of the vineyard under the late September skies affords her hours of silence as, in her hand, she feels the weight of the bunches of Cabernet-Franc or Cabernet-Sauvignon grapes. Hours of emptiness as her hand mindlessly clenches and releases the secateurs' handles. Hours during which she takes in her fill of that land she loves more than she loves herself. So many hours during which to also hate the code of silence of that land that keeps her walled-in. *Emmurée,* as the French say.

"*C'est Tamara. Elle est Australienne,*" Marielle had said that first morning in lieu of introduction. And she had left, in a swirl of calico skirt above dung and mud-splattered plastic boots, chestnut hair already piled up under a wide-brimmed hat. The mornings were cool, there was no doubting that but, though late in the season, the sun was still able to muster considerable strength as soon as it cleared the low-lying hills. Marielle knew this year's harvest would be sweet and have a high alcohol content.

From the other side of the *rége*, of the row, one of the silent men had handed Tamara a little yellow plastic basket and a pair of sticky secateurs. He had smiled at her but only with his eyes. She had smiled at him with all of her face. He had looked away. She had glanced at an old man a few metres ahead and had imitated his stance, his squat, shoulder to the dusty vine.

The basket, Tamara had figured out, was just the right size to accommodate four kilos of grapes. When these little baskets were full, a porter would come around and empty the *vendangeurs'* baskets into his own, a huge one that he carried on his back. One that, by the time he emptied it on the flatbed of the truck, released some eighty kilos of grapes. At the family-owned *vignoble* of Sainte Thérèse, the vines were always harvested by hand. To the devil may go the mechanical harvesters used by some neighbouring *viticulteurs.*

At Sainte-Thérèse, the Dufour family still did things in the traditional way. Good year, bad year, from the top of the genealogical tree to its lower present branch, the Dufours had struggled with their vines and for their vines since the 1800s. Through the 1886 deadly invasion of the Phylloxera louse that came from the south to decimate thousands of hectares of vines, they struggled and survived. Through spring-times that were as cold as winters they survived, but the grapes were as dried up as old nursemaids' teats. Through torrential rain that brought in a rot that could never be dried out, the Dufour estate survived, though barely. And family feuds tore up more parcels off the *patrimoine* and added none.

The Dufours struggled and the name had survived. But hard times, bad times, bad fortune, bad luck, wars, deaths, and intermittent greed through the decades had seen to it that what remained of the original estate could, at the turn of the twenty-first century, only produce a fraction of its legendary former yield. Still, there were some two hundred hectares of Cabernet Sauvignon and Cabernet-Franc to bring in, ferment, bottle, and more importantly, to drink.

For the French *oeunologues* and local connoisseurs, the *cuvées* Sainte-Thérèse were a delight made thus delightful by its *méthode artisanale* and its limited production. Rare were the smaller vineyards that could produce, year after year, such a balanced, rich, and silky Cabernet at a price that shamed its loftier neighbours who used their chateaux's exhausted name to justify the market price of their *cuvée.*

Anyway, Marielle was only a few years younger than Tamara but, at nineteen she didn't know any other life but that spun out of the seasonal cycles that revolved around the hectares of vines that still belonged to her father. But when all the work was done and dinner over, Marielle would jump on the back of the old rumbling Ducati her fiancé had inherited from an uncle. Hugging the back of the low-lying hills, amber red, Christian's broken tail-light quickly became a lone receding eye.

A red light blinks. A red beacon across the aisle to guide Tamara back to where she needs to be.

"Any second now. And counting."

"Five seconds and I say she'll have come good. One … two … three … four. And … Hellowww? Yes! Here she is."

I can see through water. Far above me. Pale. White. Elongated sounds from the deep. What's up? White again. White everywhere. White walls. Soft walls.

"Tamara, hello. I'm Fiona."

Is this voice for real? It's like, so muffled. Muffled. Someone's talking to me.

Tongue. Move tongue. Tongue, move!

Oh, man …Dry … All dry. Swallow. Wipe the blur away. Water in my eyes. Underwater water.

"Nah, nah, nah!" Fiona says in a staccato. "No, no, no," she reiterates. "Tamara, don't you go moving around so soon."

Bumble-bees buzz all around. Awh … my head! Throb. Contract. Expand. Contract. Crack. Pound. Pound. Pound. *Who is this woman?* Where am I?

"Tamara, I'm Fiona. You have a thumping headache, right?"

Right. A hangover like I've never had in my whole entire friggin' life. What the hell did I have to drink last night? I … uh … Last night?

Two fingers resting lightly across Tamara's wrist, eyes on her fob watch, Fiona started counting each pulse over fifteen seconds and multiplied them by four. Sluggish.

Water. Swallow. Blink. Blink again. A splash of white. A face in my face. Close. Too close. Uh … yes, white. White, more white. No blue. Oh. Back to blue. Close eyes. Eyes! Close!

"No, no. Tamara, keep your eyes open. Good. Thatta girl."

Dots. White dots. White polyps in a storm. Upside down storm. A night storm of white polyps. Dark water. Cold. Clams. Clammy. Sweaty.

Back in the blue. Warm-blue water. No! Not from there, Jamie. You're not allowed. Only my Papa can jump in. Even me, I have to use the ladder *and I live here.* Even if you're older than me, Papa says you can't jump from there. Black Night's a schooner, you know. Schooners are jolly big. They're all big like this one. Big but not always black, you see. They look mean. This one is nice but Mamma, she thought we should still call it Black Night. Too high, says Mamma. Too high for me to jump off the crow's-nest. She's wrong, though. I'm not that little any-more. I'm seven years old, you know. And look, I'm the best swimmer. I'll beat you to that rock out there. That's if you ever get down here. It's nice in here in the warm-blu –

"Hellooow, Tamara. You've drifted off. We've met, remember? I'm Fiona. Tamara, Dr Mac is here to see you."

White Jamie. Too white in the warm-blue. Blurry. Blurry white. White moon. White face. *Fiona?*

"Hello, Tamara. I'm Dr Mac. First name's Gill," says Doctor McIntyre in her usual breezy way. "They tell me you've just woken up. Is that right?" She removes the ball of her thumb from Tamara's eyelid. "Feeling groggy?" Another frown flutters over Tamara's brow but she cannot think of what she needs to reply to the woman's questions. Too fast. "It'll wear off. Did Fiona run past you what info we have?"

Very dirty lenses. Must clean lenses. Hey, I don't even wear glasses. Must see that face on the other side. Mac. Fiona and –

"Tamara, you're at the RBH."

R ...B ... *Why?* "Uh ... what ... uh ... where am I?"

"You're at the Royal Brisbane, Tamara. Ward seven. It would seem that you've suffered a violent blow to the head. You have moder-ate concussion. What is the last thing you remember clearly?"

Fog. Fog's thinning. I can see her now. Like Mamma's face. I could see Mamma's face like that. Upside down looking under the water, she was. Looking down to see me through my puddle of water. Calling out to me. There but not there. *Not where I am.* High up, she was. Up and far from me.

Cold clanks. Thin clanks. Metal against metal. What the fuck is this Mac woman telling me? "Before I got ... *here?*"

Long spidery fingers of pain twitch deep inside Tamara's head.

"No, don't move your head. Keep still. The trauma to your head is not severe but there is trauma. Concussion. No fractures. No haematoma, subdural or otherwise. So do you remember talking to anyone?"

Tamara closes her eyes, hoping to ease the pain away. To ease the pain and clear the confusion. To keep the slide from sliding any-more. To keep everything still and get a grip.

"What I remember?"

"Do you remember walking through a parking-lot at around six?"

"Had coffee … I was early. Concu … *concussion?* Why?"

"Well, Tamara, I can't answer your Why question. I can't say why it looks like someone took to you with something much heavier than a rolling pi – "

"My … my head. When?"

"Earlier this evening, Tamara, some four hours ago. Give or take. But the good news is that you'll be able to go home in a day or two. We'll know for sure by tomorrow. That coffee you mentioned, at what time was it?"

Thoughts slide past but do not connect.

"Tamara, at what time do you think you had that coffee you mentioned?"

"I was early. I … had to meet … I was going to meet … some-one after work."

"At what time were you going to meet this friend of yours?"

"She's not my … uh … At five …I think."

"At five or at six, Tamara? Can you remember? The friend who called the ambulance says she was expecting you shortly after six."

"It's not … I can't get think back to … Can't think. Not clearly."

"OK." Doctor Mac glances at the nurse who tighens her lips, her way to indicate that she, too, understands there might be a prob-lem. "So, you stopped somewhere for coffee because you were early? Your friend said she found you a little after six but she doesn't know how long you'd been waiting or, more to the point, how long you'd been unconscious. It's very important that we know how long you were under. Do you understand, Tamara? No, don't nod. Just say yes."

Too late. Eyes squeezed tight Tamara moans softly. When she opens her eyes they are shiny with repressed tears.

"I left close to six … the coffee shop."

"Good. Excellent Tamara. And where did you go next?"

"Next door. To get … my … my friend. Early. I remember I was early."

"Very good all that, Tamara. So you might have been uncon-scious only a few minutes before she found you and called the ambu-lance. We'll just say ten for now. So, young lady," Dr Mac asks again, "how old are you?"

Light. In my eyes. A flicker. Steady probe. Aawh … fucking hell!

"Tamara, be still," says Fiona firmly. One hand loose across Tamara's forehead, she's holding Tamara's eyelid open with her thumb. With her free hand, she shines a light into Tamara's eye. "The pain's from the blow, not from the light. I just need to look at the back of your eyes. Be a good girl, will you?"

"My head hurts. It's like, so bad." Her heart is beating far too fast. "Thirsty … please."

Glass skittles. Shards bite. Blinding white pain. Red throbbing pain.

"Don't move your head." That's the other voice. "You don't need to. Yes, that's much better. Suck as hard as you want. A little more. Now, Tamara, tell us a little something about yourself like, what's your surname?"

Questions. Too many questions. I hear them now. Not nice. Finger in my ear to block off the sounds. Push back into pillow. Can't hear Mamma. Turn off the light, Bub, she says. Yes, I say, turn off the bloody light.

That sick feeling is in Tamara's stomach. A dark and hollow feeling. Her Adam's apple bobs up and down. Up and down again. Too fast. Saliva is thinning inside Tamara's mouth.

One finger in her ear to not hear. Burrow into pillow. Receding light. Thumping. Throbbing. Oh …not good. No more water. Hot. Too hot.

"Uh … I … uh … I feel … might throw up."

"It's OK, Tamara. It's the sedatives. The anti-emitics will kick in soon. Tamara, please tell me what you make of my fingers … How many? And now? What about this light?"

Light? Yes. Turn off the friggin' light! Where is it? "Uh … yes. Light."

"Where's the light, Tamara?"

Where *is* the frigging light? "Behind … behind my eye."

"Which eye?"

Tamara cannot tell which of her eyes registers the light.

"Tuh … Tamara." Tamara's public school vowels, the BBC accent, as Emilie calls it, come out wrapped around the name. Tahmahhrah.

"Yes, that's correct. Tamara what?"

"Tuh … Tuh … " Oh, for fuck's sake. No, don't cry now. I can do that. I know my name. "Tuh … Townsend."

"Good, Tamara. Very good. Now, what do you remember of voices, sounds? People talking to you? Remember anything of what they said?"

Grey cotton noise.

"It would seem you have a touch of amnesia. Antegrade/retro-grade amnesia. It only affects your memory in terms of what's happened just before and right after the trauma to your head. That's only momentary. What's a bit harder to tell, at this stage, is whether or not there's been microscopic tearing under there." Doctor Mac raps her knuckles on the side of her head as she would on a door. "You've received a violent blow to the head, a nasty one, there's no denying that. But you may have been very lucky all the same," Doctor Mac adds, peering into her patient's face. She pats the limp fingers, just below the protruding cannula taped to the back of her hand. "So, back to the old question, how old are you, Tamara?"

"Twenty … eight."

Aawhh. Rip flash. Mad bees buzz. Chainsaw head.

"No, no. Don't move like that. You must avoid that kind of pain for yourself. You were found unconscious. Someone called the ambulance."

"Someone?"

"A Ms Anderson. Emma-Lee Anderson."

"Emilie."

"Emma-Lee, yes. The ambulance driver confirmed he got to you in under ten minutes. Anyway, all in all, looks like you may have been out for about twenty minutes, twenty-five on the outside. We can't know for sure."

"Not Emmalee."

"Excuse me?"

"Em … ilie."

"And what about Emma-Lee?"

"Her name's Emilie, but … she's not my friend."

"Are we talking about Ms Anderson? Emma-Lee?"

"She's … my lover."

"Ah … yes. Ms Anderson did say something about that. So, you do remember Emma-Lee. Good, Tamara, that's very good."

"Em … I need to call Em … to let her know … that I'm … She'll think I'm … I'm late … again."

"She knows you're here, Tamara. She's the one who called the ambulance and she followed it here. But she doesn't know what's happened to you. There was no one around, you see. Only her, it would seem. Anyway, the good news as I said, is that we've already done a CT. No fractu – "

"Em is … here? She is?"

"No. She's been and gone, Tamara. You'll see her tomorrow."

"Oh."

"You're doing well. Ah, no. No! Don't touch your head just yet." Doctor Mac slips the stethoscope back around her neck.

Tamara opens her eyes again, heart pounding from the reeling pain. Doctor Mac points to the occipital region of her head, in a gesture that parallels her ear. "That's the point of trauma. There's already some swelling and there will be more by tomorrow. But the swelling is only on the outside, Tamara." The stethoscope gleams against the white coat. "That's the good news you want to hear. There's no intercranial bleeding. There's no brain swelling. There shouldn't be any neurological residual. But the pain may be due to some stretching of nerve fibres. We can't tell for sure, Tamara. These things don't show up on a CT scan. These disruptions of nerve processes can only be seen microscopically. OK, I tell you what," Doctor Mac says enthusiastically, as if she's just had a great idea, "you've had a long day. We'll have Fiona give you a little top-up of Midazolan." Doctor Mac turns to the nurse, "If the intensity of the pain persists, we might switch her to morphine by midday tomorrow. It'll depend on how focused she is." The doctor smiles encouragingly at Tamara. "Fiona, when you're done here … "

Tamara closed her eyes and felt the pain well inside her head.

Warm-blue. White-blue. Cold blue. Jamie, white Jamie. Too white. I say, Don't you jump, Jamie Townsend. Wide-eyed. Dead-eyed, Jamie Townsend. Stubborn-Jamie. Wants to impress me because he's older. Being older doesn't make him swim better, though. Or jump further than me.

Heavy jolt on my shoulder. Bubbles. Great bubbles. Blurry bubbles. Breath choked. I keep my bubbles inside to see him better. Dark. Dark water. Dark schooner from under puddle of water. Bad Night. Bad, bad, Black Night. Blurry watery puddle in my eyes. Water in my mouth. In my throat. Mother! Papa! Ma-mah! White. Too white Jamie. Cold-blue. White and wet, all floppy in Papa's arms. Wet inside. Too much wa –

"Tamara, are you awake?" Fiona touches Tamara's shoulder. "I need to look into your eyes, all right?"

No, not all right.

"Tamara?"

That friggin' light again.

"Tamara, I'm going to pull up your eyelid, OK? That's so I can look at the back of each eye."

Blinding flash.

Oh, my brain hurts. My god, what's happening *in there?* Bloody hell!

"Awh…"

Swelling, she said. Con … cussion. Mush. Pulp. Squashed. Squeeshed.

"And who's got the greenest eyes in the ward, then? Puts mine to shame, right? I always fancied I had nice green eyes, but … "

Another flash.

"I'm sorry to be doing that to you, Tamara. It hurts doesn't it?" Fiona asks, though not pausing for an answer. Some degree of photophobia was to be expected.

She knows that Tamara must be feeling her head like a squashed melon. Spilt by a great whopping sledgehammer. That Tamara would be wanting to throw up. That she'd be frightened. That she wouldn't understand the pain in her head. That she'd be asking, *What if it never goes away? What if I'm never the same again?*

Flash … flash.

"I'm just looking at your eyes, Tamara. I'll be as fast as I can."

Flash … flash.

Fiona doesn't much like the chronic talkers, and she doesn't much like the crabby patients who come through her ward. She understands they are in pain, but she doesn't understand *their* pain. Even cute guys. Like, not everyone's old who comes to the hospital. But no matter how cute he might be, if he's crabby, she's just not at her best. She does the best she can to alleviate everyone's pain but when they snap at her, she really has to work hard at her temper. Even after four years as a fully accredited nurse, she still needs to work on that.

The older nurses tell her she'll get used to it. Fiona thinks that if she were ever to get used to it, she'd already *be* used to it.

She smiles at Tamara. "Try not to move your head too much for now. How are you feeling?"

"Like shit."

"I thought you might. Besides your head … any other pains?"

"My cheek."

"You've got a nasty graze there. Hope you weren't planning on seducing anyone here, tonight, the minute I turn the corner, right? You weren't were you? Oh … no! Don't shake your head," Fiona says a little alarmed.

It is true that she needs to think more carefully about what she tells her patients. She must not chatter to them about things that will create discomfort. And for this one, Tamara Townsend, the thing for her is to not let her move her head.

Flash … Flash.

Fiona wonders why anyone would have wanted to hurt Tamara, even if she's gay. And she thinks that, perhaps, it might have been that woman's husband - Anderson, was it? - who might have done it. The jealous guy thing. Happens all the time. Though straight herself, she knows that men don't handle the woman gay thing well.

"Well, anyway," Fiona, cotton ball in hand, is preparing to swab Tamara's cheek, "you got to know you're not looking your best. That cheek's all red. It'll puff up some more but it'll be clean as a … whistle. Keep still. Can't do much about your head and all but, that cheek of yours … that's the bit that's under control."

"Uh … Fiona?"

"Umm?"

"Look … it's not personal … or … or anything," Tamara begins awkwardly, "but like, will you be coming back … soon? Or can I go … like go to sleep now?"

Fiona grins, pocketing her little torch. "No, not tonight, I won't be coming back. We do respect our patients' beauty sleep, you know." Almost as an afterthought, she asks, "Any more thoughts as to what you were doing in that parking-lot?"

"Nope. I … remember going into the parking-lot and maybe I went inside to let her know I was there. I was early … for once. Did Emilie say … "

"I didn't get to talk to her myself, Tamara. She would've talked to the nurses at Resuscitation but from what Dr Mac was saying, no, it seems that your friend was surprised to find you there in the first place. Even more surprised to find you dead to the world. A bit of a shock, I imagine."

Tamara closes her eyes.

"Right," the nurse adds lightly. "Try and get some rest. The Midazolan should kick in soon."

"Fiona … uh … Thanks."

"Not a problem."

Fiona stops by the bed chart to enter new data regarding Tamara's blood pressure, pulse, temperature, saturations as per the oxymeter, her ability to respond to questions and obey commands.

Get some rest, she said. Neck hurts, face hurts, shoulders hurt and my head … I don't know what's wrong in there. Skull's shrunk tight, like a few sizes too small. What the fuck's happened to me? I was going to wait for her to come out by the Jeep. Inside the Jeep. Sprawled on the ground? Like … dead or something?

****

Enormous bunches of dingy, round grapes swirl back and away from Tamara's face. She settles on her side.

Cutting and snipping in the *vendangeur's* squatting position, shoulder to the vines, Tamara has spotted Monsieur Dufour, Marielle's father. Of the host family and neighbours, he's the one person she hardly ever sees. Marielle says that he spends a lot of time at the other side of the village, at the press shared by a few of the smaller estates. He needs to be there at the weighing-in of his harvest and to do some *conjonctures*, preliminary theorising, projecting as to likely quality of the end product, brought in raw, in deep red mounds on flatbed trucks.

"*Une belle récolte, tu sais.*" Marielle said the yield would be full this year again. "*Faut voir le pressoir.*" In the space between them, she had used her hands to draw for Tamara the picture of overflowing vats. Large brown eyes shining with pride, she had puffed up her cheeks to indicate the fat grapes bursting with sticky juices.

They were both companionably seated on the front step of the farm's main door. Dinner was over. Marielle would soon be with Christian, hugging the low-hills, pressed against his back, her face sheltered against his leather-clad shoulder. Tamara would soon be asleep in her barn. She was far too exhausted at the end of these days to sit by the hearth and dream fire-dreams.

The August rainfall hasn't lasted long enough to bring in a significant amount of rot, Marielle had gone on explaining. And though there might be some dilution, it would not be significant. Tamara had asked about the dilution, latching on to a word she had understood on her own. But there are times when goodwill alone is not enough. If Marielle's method-related talks were to make any sense, they soon became too involved; for the one to simplify to such an extent as to be understood by *l'Australienne;* and for the other to do such mental reaches in an area where she lacked basic knowledge that that conversation, too, had soon been abandoned.

As she held the heavy bunches, one at a time, in the palm of her hand to better separate them from the vine leaves before cutting, Tamara glanced at Monsieur Dufour, curious to have a good look at him. He didn't have his dinner at the same time as Marielle and her mother. Not even when some of the neighbours dropped in and chatted to Madame Dufour and her daughter over little glasses of marc brandy.

On such occasions, Marielle always made it a point to find Tamara wherever she might be walking and bring her back to include her in the local neighbourly socialising. And Tamara would sit a little off to the side, in the ancient-looking rocking chair that had been Marielle's great-grandmother's. She would nurse her little glass of *eau de vie*, lost in thoughts by the stone hearth while the others, seated as per the local custom at the kitchen table, discussed or argued (Tamara wasn't sure when one ended and the other began) matters of the vines.

"*Monsieur Dufouwr ... il mange pas?*" Tamara had asked the second time she hadn't seen him at the table.

"*Il mange trés tôt, Monsieur Dufour. Il aime se promener dans sa vigne avant la nuit.*"

"*Ah, oui,*" Tamara had replied, nodding her head vigorously, in an enthusiastic indication that she understood.

Apparently, the man liked to take long and solitary walks around his vineyard before nightfall, so he had very early dinners, no matter who dropped in to visit. Tamara had concluded that Monsieur Dufour had to be a bit of a recluse, even if his wife was content with the idea that Sainte-Thérèse, and its vines, were the man's life, his love.

Mindful to keep up with her picking partner on the other side of the row, she moves the secateur from bunch to bunch. Snip, snip, snip. Gently, she deposits each inside her cutter's basket.

Black beret pushed away from his forehead, Monsieur Dufour is standing legs apart on the flatbed of one of his trucks. Tamara glances up at him while snipping stems. Even under the shapeless cloth of blue drill trousers and his well-worn corduroy jacket, he is, visibly, as gnarly and dry as his vines after pruning. A vertical scar, where eye meets cheekbone, bunches up a web of puckered wrinkles.

Here and there, from the mounds of bunches piled high around his knees, he picks up a dense bunch. He rubs the dust off the taut darkish skin. He plucks a grape at random and holds it up to the sun.

Inside Tamara's head, the sun is only an elongated shimmer that stretches and distorts her memories.

He squeezes the plump flesh behind index finger and thumb till the purple skin tears itself open. His nail slices the flesh further and between his fingers he rolls it to make it yield all its sticky juices. She watches him, strangely fascinated, as he licks his fingers with the flat of his tongue, smacking his lips cryptically. He grunts, nods, and flicks the skin away. Dropping the bunch back into the heap, he gropes deeper inside another of his dark red and dusty mounds, sampling another set of grapes at random. He repeats the sequence.

In this part of the world *l'âme du vigneron* is not learned. It is passed on, Marielle had explained last night, right after dinner. Tamara, back from one of her late walks, had found her seated on the edge of the mossy well, listening for the low, rumbling sound of Christian's Ducati.

"De père en fils. From father to son. *Et moi,* I work like the son as much as I can, for now. *Enfin,"* she had sighed, "one day, Christian, he will be the son at Sainte-Thérèse."

"Et toi, tu sewras la femme du fils, oui?" Tamara asked, doing her best to tighten the naturally loose lips of the English. She needed to clip her syllables more and not let them get drawn out beyond recognition.

"Oui. Je serai la femme du nouveau fils," Marielle had replied. The new son's wife. Pulling a clip out of her hair, she let it drop freely against her shoulders. She fluffed it with both hands before shaking her head to loosen the long strands.

A winegrower's soul, she had explained, is passed on from father to son. And so is the land on which the vines are planted. From her father's estate, Marielle will only inherit the farmhouse not the land. Madame Dufour, herself, has very little to leave her only child besides chests full of lace and a couple of family heirlooms and many notebooks full of handwritten, time-tested recipes for every occasion. But her fiancé, when he weds her, will become the heir of a vineyard equal in yield, if not in reputation, to that of his own parents'. The union of Marielle and Christian Laforge, also because he is her elder by more than ten years, is good for the future of both vineyards.

Apropos of absolutely nothing, Tamara had had the sudden urge to tell Marielle that her skin was pale, as pale as moonlight, though, on this cloudy night, the late September sky above Sainte-Thérèse was pitch-black. In any case, her survival French and the staple questions and answers she had down pat were far from enough to convey even a reasonable attempt at poetry.

"Lumière lune pale," she had said to Marielle.

Marielle had frowned and then she had shrugged her shoulders saying something about not liking the moon, any moon. Then, she had remained silent. Then, impulsively, she had turned to Tamara. With her thumb, she had brushed the young woman's eyebrow.

"It 'urt?" Marielle had asked, the tip of her index finger brushing over the little silver bolt Tamara wore embedded at the edge of her brow. *"Ça fait pas mal ça?"* Marielle had screwed up her own eyebrows, grimacing in anticipation of the pain she was asking about.

Marielle's expression made Tamara laugh. "No, it doesn't hurt. It's like your earring. *C'est comme ton boocle d'ohreille,"* she said, touching the sleeper that bit into Marielle's lobe.

"Ah bon. That's OK then," Marielle said, apparently reassured.

The low rumble of Christian's Ducati meandered out of the low-lying hills. Both of them straightened up on the ledge of the wishing well.

Marielle patted her hair again and as she stood up, she smoothed the cloth of her loose cotton skirt. She wasn't wearing her plastic boots. She had replaced them with chunky white socks and ankle-length Doc Martens. Dark red ones.

Christian didn't enter the courtyard but waited near the gate. Still straddling his bike, he reached inside his leather jacket and drew out a pack of Marlboro Red. Tamara watched him flick the top of a Zippo lighter and inhale deeply. He did not acknowledge her in any way.

Already a couple of strides away, Marielle turned around. She mouthed something that Tamara understood. Something that made her blush in the moonless night. She sighed and made her way back to her barn in the dark. Marielle straddled the space behind her fiancé and wrapped her arms loosely around his waist, ready for acceleration.

Beep, beep, beep. Soft little beeps insert themselves inside Tamara's dream. The oxymetre clamped on her finger is beeping a blind vigil. Too many little noises, Tamara thinks. I don't like little noises. Too many. She rolls on to her other side tucking one hand under her cheek.

Tomorrow would be the full moon. It might rain, Tamara thought, because she needed a thought, other than ones of Marielle, to occupy her mind before she went to bed. She looked up into the night sky, heavy with clouds. It apparently rained often on the night of the full moon. Tamara already knew a few facts about the locals' preoccupation with the colours and the cycles of the moon. She had understood that Marielle had a particular dislike for *la sanguine*, the odd ginger-red moon like the one that had apparently been over the vineyard last April, though she hadn't explained why.

Tamara had found that weird, as a full red moon, low over the gentle hills, though she had never seen one, would surely be a breathtaking sight to behold. Another sight to take away with her when she left Sainte-Thérèse. A sight that would keep her company while, already, another landscape filed past, blurry and unfamiliar, on the other side of a grimy train window two days hence. On the train that would take her to her next stop.

All the harvest would be in by tomorrow night. Then, the following night there would be the *Fête des Vendanges* at St Emilion that she had planned to attend, as a last interaction with the world of the vines. Early the following morning, she would begin retracing the steps that had led her to the vineyard. She didn't want to be too exhausted to miss out on the end of harvest celebrations in the medieval village and so she might hitch a couple of rides now that the locals knew her as *l'Australienne,* one of the *vendangeurs.* She would stay at *La Feuille de Vigne*, The Vine Leaf, a little hotel she had booked on her way up. And the next day, at 9.34 a.m. she would be on her way to the Bretagne region for an, as yet, indefinite period of time. Three days or ten, it was too early to tell.

Tamara was glad she wouldn't miss the spectacle of the full moon. When she turned around to where the road meanders in and out of the hills, the Ducati's receding red eye had already blinked one last time.

The night was dark, the vines still, and the low hills silent. Christian and Marielle had been absorbed by the night. It was with a clear sense of relief that Tamara realised she was far too buggered to hang around under the star and dream fire-dreams ignited by Marielle's whispered last words.

"J' t'aime bien, tu sais. T'es mignonne."

Tamara knew what that meant. It meant that Marielle liked her. The *mignonne* colloquialism implied that Marielle found her endearing.

"Moi aussi, je t'aime bien," Tamara whispered into the darkness. Me, too. I like you well.

*****

The ward is quiet but sleep is not a tranquil affair. Tamara turns around restlessly. She is asleep but small, unfamiliar noises crawl inside her ear and make her heart thump. She is aware of her pain, the dull pain of her brain being squeezed, steadily squeezed like an orange. She is aware too of her burning cheek. And of the various aches that have settled inside her body. She is aware of the cannula and of the annoying sensation of having this thing tug at her every time she moves her hand. But her thoughts are not connected to any of these pains. Drifting and fleeting, they dance on the edge of vertigo.

"Black Night," she said. "You know why? Can you guess why that's going to be her new name?"

Tamara shook her little girl's curls, green eyes wide on Laurel's face.

"Well," her mother began with her soothing, fairy tale-time voice, "for many people, you see, darling, a black knight, that's the one with a K … K as in kite … well, a black knight is not usually a nice person."

"He's scary, isn't he, Mamma?"

"Well, yes. A black knight is *supposed* to be scary but – "

"But our Black Night, she won't have a K. She's the gentle night around us. Did I guess right?"

"You guessed right, Bub!" Laurel exclaims, patting her little girl's cheek. "And so, now, what do I do, huh? I don't have a proper story to tell you anymore now, do I? This clever little girl I know has stolen my punch-line."

Tamara giggles and flapped her little hands. "So, our schooner, she's good, isn't she, Mamma? She's big and strong." Without waiting for Laurel to reply, Tamara added, cat-green eyes shiny with conviction, *"She's got* to be a very nice boat, doesn't she? She protects us from the sea when the sea is bad. She does, doesn't she, Mamma? That's because she's *so* big."

"Yes, she does protect us, darling. And she is rather big. But it would have felt very odd to us, to your Papa and to me, calling such a big black ship something like White Knight, you know, like the one who always saves the princess when – "

"Oh no. That wouldn't have done at all. That would've been a very silly name for our big boat. Besides," Tamara added very seriously, "I don't think only white knights should rescue princesses, you know, Mamma."

"Well, no. There's no reason why – "

"I could, couldn't I?"

"Could what, darling?"

"Could rescue one, a princess, I could, couldn't I, if I found one that needed rescuing? One day?"

"Well … yes. I guess you could. But you'd have to be strong to rescue princesses," Laurel countered, keen to have her little girl go to sleep before she asked her to read yet another princess in distress fairy tale. "And so, to be strong, a little girl who's … only … "

"Only five!" Tamara exclaimed, playing a familiar game with her mother.

"Oh, well, then. A little girl who's only five certainly needs to go to sleep very quickly. As in right now, if she wants to grow up strong and be really alert to rescue princesses. And so," Laurel said, getting up from her daughter's bunk, "we're going to turn that light off, aren't we, Bub? And Black Night will look after all of us."

"Mamma?"

"Yes, Bub."

"Can we go looking for prawns tomorrow?"

"Of course we can. That's what we'll do at low tide. We'll dinghy to shore and we'll walk on the beach. And we'll take our little baskets with us and – "

"And some nets too."

"Ah, yes, and some nets."

"Low tide, Mamma, I think tomorrow, low tide is after my nap, don't you think so, mamma?"

"I think you might well be right, you little clever one. But for now, you must sleep. Say goodnight now. And we turn off the light."

Ah, yes, drift, drift, drown. Drown deep. Sleep. Beep, beep, beep. Soft little beeps. Not nice beeps. There, but almost not there. If only I could, I would, I'd sleep. I'd much rather sleep. Not drown. Drowning's not nice, is it, Mamma?

One finger in her ear, slowly Tamara rolls again to her side. Her brain follows in slow motion. Constricted and pulsating and throbbing, it rolls with her. The other ear flat against the pillow, the soft little beeps don't come in.

There was the siren. The ambulance came. Big men. Big boots. They all boarded Black Night. They scooped up Jamie. Limp, he was, Jamie. But he was dry now. Dry under a towel. An orange and bright blue towel. The big, big towel, it was, the one that Mamma wraps around herself.

"Don't stay here, little girl," one of the big men said as he strode past Tamara. "Go play," he added gruffly.

But before that there had been the piece of twine. Black and curled on itself on the galley counter. Black and curled. Black and tight around Jamie's ankles when Papa brought him out of the water.

"Tamara," Papa said, "This was around Jamie's ankles."

Jamie's ankles are tied. I thought that when I saw him dripping everywhere, in my papa's arms.

"Why did you tie his ankles together, Tamara?"

Jamie is dead. He drowned because his ankles are tied with a black piece of twine.

*****

Swish … swish… White rubber sole on linoleum. A nurse stops by Tamara's cubicle and listens.

Snuff one. Snuff two. Twin swirls of smoke rise from the wicks. Plate one, plate two, one knife, another knife, forks in one hand. Two glasses in the other hand, she wonders whether she can also carry the empty bottle of wine to the kitchen without letting it slip through her fingers.

"Hey, Tam, why don't you come over here a minute? There's something you could do for me."

Tamara looks at Alex who, seated on the sofa, is looking at her from above the rim of her water glass. Alex is yellow, yellow and bulging. Misshapen, as if stretched inside the rubbery skin of a yellow balloon. A dull yellow fish-eye portrait.

"What's up? Feel like a good old-fashioned hug or something?"

Alexandra Delaforêt likes good hugs. Good hugs like the ones Tamara gives her.

Tamara had been surprised when she had first worked out that Alex was into hugs, real hugs. She had found that surprising. At first glance, most would agree, Alex really doesn't look like the huggy-cuddly type. She bristles too much.

"No," says Alex. "Uh … Yes! I mean, I'm always ready for a hug but what I meant is, can we talk about whatever is on your mind? You know, the little *something* that comes and goes but doesn't quite disappear?"

Too intense for her own good is, on the whole, what Tamara thinks of Alex. She really needs to chill, she does. But, Tamara ponders what 'little something' is Alex on about? She stacks plates, knives, and forks and glasses by the sink.

"And what might that be," she asks from the kitchen, wrapping BBC vowels around the question, "that little something that you have detected *on my* mind?"

Tamara's intrigued. Grungy plates gotta wait, she decides. Oh shit! What if she wants to talk about *that* thing? *The thing?*

Standing close to Alex who has plopped herself on the sofa, bare feet planted in the thick pile of a rug, Tamara peers into her eyes. Dark green eyes. Serious eyes that smile all the same. It's not so much her eyes that smile but the lines at the corner of her eyes that do. Laughing crow's-feet have got to be the secret of Alex's smile.

"Have I told you you're looking really cute tonight?" Alex begins, patting the side seam of the young woman's sand-coloured, zip-off convertibles.

"What, only cute?" Tamara asks, mockingly offended. Around Alex, she does the incredulous-offended bit very well. It's a game they play. And they've been playing it for quite a few years. Pretty much since Tamara's return from Europe.

"No, not only. Sexy too," Alex shrugs her shoulders. "Well … sexier than in your faded jeans and shirts. Will that do?" she pats Tamara above her silver belt buckle.

"Uh … well, hell. That might just make me blush, telling me things like that, Al. Maybe it's that desert gear you like, huh?"

"Maybe I do. Maybe it's all about Cargo shorts and the sleeve-less Tees."

"And what … nothing about me?" Tamara pastes on a pretend pout.

Alex is not *really* coming on to her. The two of them go back a long way. It's all under control now.

"OK, Tamara," Alex begins with what Tamara calls her stern teacher's voice. "I'll give you the full treatment, just this once." She sits up and adjusts the emerald-green linen of her shirt over her shoulders.

Tamara had registered the new shirt, urban-western in style, as soon as she had come upon Alex who had been waiting for her on the large wooden deck that overlooks her pool. Nice, she had thought, but on Alex what she likes best are shades of blue. Any of the many shades of blue that make up Alex's wardrobe. Strong blues. Blues bold enough to carry a suggestion, to suggest a purpose. But such blues can be deceptive. Blues are not always safe.

"Yes, that khaki gear does suit you. But … " Alex turns Tamara around to have a better view of her backside. "That is the thing, isn't it? If one wants to strut around in jungle gear or look like she has just stepped out of somewhere on *The English Patient* set – "

"Or *The Mummy*'s?"

"Or *The Mummy*'s. Strong shoulders and good legs certainly help the whole thing hang together." She pushes off the sofa and gets up. Tamara grabs her by the waist as she brushes past and wraps her up against her.

"So, what were you saying about a hug, Al? Huh?"

Alex tousles her hair as she would her kid sister's, if she had one, and uncharacteristically quickly, she moves out of the hug to reach for the book she had been reading earlier.

"So, what? That it?" Tamara asks, turning around to keep Alex in sight. "You're off to read? Didn't you want us to like, talk about some-thing? You said – "

Alex stops in her tracks as if she has just remembered the little something she had brought up. "Ah, yes."

She takes three steps back, flops on the sofa once more, settling into its curve where the back and armrests meet, and gestures for Tamara to sit across from her on the Bentwood rocker.

"Whassup?" Tamara asks, taken aback by the eyebrows arched in an expression she knows well.

"OK, Tam. You look great, I love you to bits and I'm your good buddy. You know all that. But you are ... Uh, how do I say it?"

"Say what?"

"Well, my dear, I would say that you have been a bit flat for quite some time now. Flat, when you come here." Leaning back into the sofa, Alex adds, "In fact, you have not been your normal, effervescent self *for months*."

"You mean, I'm not my bubbly little self?"

Alex nods.

"Thattit?"

"Yes, that is it from *me*," Alex enunciates in full, as per her habit. For some reason, she never takes shortcuts with words. No contractions, ever. And yet, the American overtones that lay sometimes quite thickly over her French accent, in such a way that people who have never been to Canada assume she is Canadian, would well lend themselves to a more casual speech pattern. With anyone else it would. But again, Alex didn't take shortcuts with anything much at all.

She and Emilie are very similar in that respect too, Tamara thinks for the nth time.

"But, hopefully, *you* are going to say something. You are, aren't you?" With one of the frowns that darken her eyes and betray the lack of choice that her question may have otherwise suggested, Alex seeks a confirmation.

"Uh ... yeah."

"So ... how long have I not been ... effervescent, then?"

"Can't say for sure, Tam, but my question to you is, Do you agree that you have been carrying on ... in a flattish sort of way ... for quite some months now?"

"Maybe I have." Tamara shrugs, aware she's procrastinating in a very lame manner. I'm the roadblock here, she admits to herself. I'm the clot in the artery that's obstructing the flow of this friggin' conversation. Alex has already seen through me. I do have *that* thing on my mind.

To Tamara, the idea of being best friends with one of her exes had always sounded putrid. "Gag," she used to say, pretending to throw up, when her other friends were so into creating the-family-they-chose thing.

"You've loved them, those girlfriends of yours, you know, when you were together," they would tell Tamara. "Can't *just* leave them, then. Can you? Not when the worst is over. It goes like that … " they would persist. "Everything you've shared with them, the good memories, the pain, too … All that gets turned into something that's better than family. Better, too, than starting from scratch, with someone who'll only ever be *just* a friend."

But for Tamara, the idea of being queen bee within her little bevy of exes, of surrounding herself with other queen bees and their own bevy of exes, all that seemed a tad too incestuous.

"Limited gene pool," she'd say. "Constricting. And leaves no room for secrets."

Still, Tamara had made an exception for Alex. Besides, she had argued back with the same friends who had questioned her attachment to *that* particular woman, the *older* one, they had never gotten around to know well, "Alex is Alex."

"Look, you're right. There *is* a little something that I should've run past you by now. But it's not like it's a problem." It's not a problem as such. That is quite true. And yet, Tamara should have raised that *non-problem* with Alex a long time ago. It's just that she didn't know how to start without sounding totally inept.

The hard plastic of the cannula cuts into Tamara's cheek but she doesn't feel it. Like a doll dropped neither quite on her side nor on her back, the position of her legs has set her body in an awkward angle.

"Is it a little something that might, perhaps, involve Emilie?" Alex asks gently. "Tam?"

"What makes you think my loss of fizz has got anything to do with Emilie? Why not with work or health? Or with my mother and Lita, down there, in Lismore? Or – "

"Because we've been talking since 7.15 p.m." Alex hooks a finger under the steel watch face to slide it back to where she can read it. "It's now, what … 11 … 23."

She's so extremely precise about time. It's like every grain of sand counts. Tamara can't remember a time when her friend had been more than a minute late in all their time together. She used to drive Tamara crazy. It was as if she was expecting the Red October tanks or a horde of lashing Triffids to block her way, anytime, anywhere, and make her late. That, or get a flat tyre or run out of petrol. Alex was, actually, more likely to run into a horde of lashing Triffids than to run out of petrol. The Triffids were, after all, beyond her control. Emilie too, Tamara reasons only to procrastinate a little more while she still can. Emilie, also, is a bit of a punctuality freak herself.

Stressing about things like time didn't come naturally to Tamara. She only ever tried to be on time for work-related appointments but, again, not to the minute, not like Emilie and Alex. This having been said, Tamara didn't much like the thought of Emilie sitting somewhere in a coffee shop, on the steps of a cinema, or even at her place, wondering what might have delayed *her*.

'Accidents do happen, Tamara,' Emilie would remind her. 'I find it difficult to just hang around when you're over fifteen minutes late and not *even* consider that something, *something unpleasant*, might be keeping you. And if that were to be the case, one day, how … would I get to find out, huh? Like, who'd call me, huh?'

"No, look, Alex. Yes, you're right," Tamara concedes with a sigh. "There *is* something but no, it's not like it's about Emilie. I mean not really. It's more about me."

"All right, so why don't you just get on with it and – "

Hot. Hot. Too fucking hot. Throb. Awh … For fuck's sake. What – Oh. I'm still there, aren't I? Tamara's eyes are open. Yep, still here. Haven't gone away. The white curtains of her cubicle, the metallic table by the side of the bed, the open space above the railing, above the three sides of her white-cloth cubicle. I bet it's got wheels underneath it, she thinks, turning her head cautiously towards a standard-issue, bedside table. A vase. Three flowers. When did they get here? Had they been there all along?

She reaches out to feel the flowers. Her brain contracts and expands violently inside her shrunken skull. Dulled lightning bolts zap inside. Real petals. Cool petals. Tiny but real.

Swish … swish. Swish … swish.

And again. A pale shape floats on by. A cough, somewhere to the left, somewhere on the other side of the curtain. Again the cough. Whispers. Soft sounds.

Swish … swish. Swish … swish … swish. The pale shape returns. The nurse walks past on white rubber soles. By the open curtain, by the open side of Tamara's cubicle, she stops and listens. Tamara quickly closes her eyes. She doesn't want to move her head anymore. She doesn't want to talk.

Swish … swish … swish. The nurse walks away on white rubber soles.

Emilie. How is she dealing with this? What does she thinks has happened to me? Emilie needs to … needs to talk to Alex. They need to …They need to be friends. They do, don't they? They're like so much alike. I have to tell Alex. Emilie had nothing … she had nothing to do with it. Like diz … They're like disygotes. Like twins, I always said that, didn't I?

Tamara is restless. Thoughts tug at her. They weigh down on her. They make her sink into the hospital bed mattress. The mattress wants to curl up around her. It wants to close over her. The red eye blinks and fragments inside Tamara's brain. Red. Orange. Yellow.

I shouldn't be staring at that candle but it really bugs me when she's like that. She frowns. Alex's eyes look dark. I always find it intimidating when she does that. She says it's because I'm an Anglo. People of English stock, she says, scare easily in conversation, with the interpersonal stuff. She's always said that. She's said that for as long as I've known her, probably because she's French *and* passionate *and* adamant about everything.

Passion, it's true, is not really a British national characteristic. She's right about that but, though I'm a Brit living in Australia, I don't think I have the eggshell ego that Alex likes to pretend I have. Anyway, right at this moment, I'm still doing a close impersonation of a tucked-in echidna. Any time now, she will say that that, too, reminds her of her students' staple reflex action when under fire, however gentle the fire. Fire is fire. I understand those kids she's talking about. Even a mild fire burns. Even a blooming candle burns, a match even, a cigarette too. The intensity of Alex's stare could certainly burn. "So, why don't you tell me what you've been leaving out?" she asks again, leaning forward on her elbows.

"Well…" I begin, not quite yet sure as to what will come next. "I don't know that there's anything to say," I add limply.

The big deal fact is that I still feel guilty about the way *I* ended up being the one involved with Emilie. Could as easily have been *her,* Alex, with Emilie. In fact, we can all agree it'd make a damn sight more sense if she had. Emilie said so herself.

She said, "Well yes, Tam, it might've made more sense for me to get involved with Alex, but that wasn't to be, now was it?" Then, Emilie smiled and added something like how irresistible I had been, then. "Still are."

Thank god she added that. And she says it all came about because she liked the way I kind of wedged her against me and another hard place when I wanted her full attention, when I wanted to arouse her like I was *already* aroused. It was instinctive. I wanted her. Just couldn't wait to feel her, all of her. I still feel the same way. I like to come up to Emilie, right up close, and press myself against her as I reach for her mouth. She says that really turned her on in the early days. Still does. So there.

"Not sure about what?" Alex asks again, and I sense her growing impatience. Alex is not a patient woman. Too intense to be patient.

"Not sure there's anything to share here."

"Ah, look, Tam, my question is simple enough. Now, either you do something with it it or you don't."

She is leaning forward as if to get closer to my thoughts. Used to love that intensity when we were together. I still do. It's just that now I find it a little intimidating. I'm aware of the woodpecker, rapid and short, forward and backward movements of the rocking chair under me. Can't sit on that rocker without getting into some kind of manic Woody Wood-Pecker action. Sit still.

"Look, I've been with Emilie for a while now but..." Oh man that shouldn't be so hard, surely. If only she'd kick back and stretch on the sofa or something instead of sitting with her elbows on her knees looking at me expectantly. That rocker's bugging me. I can't sit on that rocker and not rock. "Look, I'll come and sit next to you on the sofa. Relax, Al, stretch out. You don't look comfortable. I'll just sit there," I add, pointing to the empty side of the sofa. "Hey, should I make us a coffee before we spin out ... you know, whatever it is?"

"Sure, I am always good for a coffee." Alex scoots closer up to the sofa armrest and stretches her legs on the cushion. That's better. "Just don't you go skippin' on me, ya hear?" she calls out, whipping up a Southern drawl. "You ain't gonna get off that turnpike that easily, I'm awarnin' you." And imitating the piped voice that, in the Paris metro, too often informs passengers that the traffic, interrupted because of accident to passenger, is about to resume, she adds, "The conversation, that hasn't yet started, will resume ... upon the timely arrival of two mugs of steaming coffee."

"I'll be back in a tick."

Kettle's on.

Alex is a formal type of woman. She can fool around like the best of us but deep down, she's a precise and formal woman. Maybe that's because she's a teacher. An English teacher at that. Who'd have thought I'd ever fall for an English teacher. Never even had a crush on any of *my* teachers, not even the Phys. Ed. ones.

Anyway, that had been a bit of a turn-on when I had come on to her at The Cage. Like she was on her own and looked so totally disconnected from it all that I tried to get her into some chit-chat and was that ever hard work! Found out later that Alex doesn't like chit-chat. Not one bit. She's into real conversations.

"Conversations," she says, "take the mind places. Social chit-chat goes nowhere, leads into nothing. It's like chewing gum. It's automatic and it disconnects the brain."

Coffee grinds lay in the plunger's glass container.

Alex and I lived together for some fourteen months. And then, I took off on a jet plane.

Boiling water floods against the glass container. A dark tidal wave of grinds rises against the glass.

Alex ditched me.

Plunger locked in on the steamy, dark surface rises. A dark tidal wave, it swirls up. Slow motion on an elastic trajectory. Dark wave, dark eyes. Alex's eyes are too dark. Bits of torn paper lie at the bottom of a bin.

She wrote that, being so young and all, I needed to be 'free to explore the sights.' Explore the sights, really! Clever pun. Or was it a euphemism for what she thought I'd be bursting to explore? That's Alex for you. Broke my heart, she did.

Tamara stirs in her white bed. Beep, beep, beep. She hears the soft beeps. And she remembers having heard them before but Tamara doesn't know why she keeps on hearing these soft little beeps no matter where she goes. Her body turns heavily on the mattress. Her face settles against the pillow.

Cups. No, not cups. Mug one, mug two.

When I came back, three years later, I thought that Alex and I might reconnect. I was hoping we would. No go. Very fond of me, she said she was, and all that but she still gave me a cold, "Look, Tam, our time was up when you left. You are lovely, truly you are, but we cannot go back in time. We cannot wind back the clock."

I felt we could've wound back time a lot better than Gatsby had been able to with his Daisy. That's just the type of useless stuff I've retained from my school days. But Alex was adamant; she didn't want either of us to attempt playing god with time. I was almost twenty-eight when I came back but she insisted I was *still* too immature to even think about permanency, let alone take time to spell the damn word. She was right, of course, not about the spelling bit, but about the doing it. Can't think of settling, as in for good. I'm totally into Emilie, though.

I think there was a time when Alex might have been attracted to Emilie. That's what we need to talk about. And the thing is, Alex and Emi do have an awful lot in common, even beyond their compatible age.

Both of them are somewhere past the mid-forty mark. Yes, I own up. I do have a thing for older women. Well, I do since I connected with Alex. Anyway, the conversation I need to crack with Alex is about whether or not she feels that I've stolen her thunder. Got to bite the bullet and ask.

Time to clear the stale air inside my guts. Time to know whether I really need to keep on feeding my little guilt-termite or can I just let it starve to death. I really need to know whether she's like cut up about that or not too much. Or not at all. What if she is?

The plunger plunges through the coffee-scented murk.

"Look, Alex, you remember how Emilie was the one to let you know how she and I had linked up, right?"

Alex's long fingers have encircled the hot mug. Her frown deepens as she considers my question about Emilie. "Uh ... Ah, yes. Actually, that is not quite accurate." She smiles one of her quick smiles. "She didn't give me the news at all, you see. She tried to but I think she was trying so hard to find a clever way to tell me the simple fact that she ended up getting herself all tied up in a major knot. So I helped her out by suggesting that maybe she was calling to tell me the two of you had decided to ... yes, to get it on. To link, as you say."

"Uh ... the point is that I felt it should've been up to me to break the news to you but Emilie insisted she should be the one to do it."

"Tam, you're going in circles here. However it was handled months ago, and by whom, is now quite irrelevant, don't you think?"

"Question: why did Emilie think she should be the one to make that call to you?"

"Why don't you ask her that question?"

"I have. She said that if I really wanted to know I only needed to ask you."

"So, because she won't say, you're expecting me to?" Alex's arched eyebrows are making me feel silly. That's a neat little trick of hers, that.

"Well, you never did say but ... Look, did you tell her you had like a thing for her, or something?"

"No, can't say that I did that. I don't think she and I have ever talked about that. We talked about films a lot, as you know, and ...

about the women issues I'm into but, no, can't say that I ever told her I had … that I had a thing for her."

"OK, but *did you* have a thing for her?"

"I did."

Awh, for fuck's sake! "Why didn't you tell me?" I hear myself ask, already on the defensive. "How was I supposed to know?"

Now that's a bit of a pretend indignation, isn't it? *I did know.* Well, I didn't know, *not for sure*, but I *kind* of knew. For a while I did, and then I forget about it. And I had pressed on with my own seduction of Emilie.

"Al, you should've said."

"Why should I have told *you* anything, Tam?"

"Well, if you had mentioned it, I could've – "

"Look, that had nothing to do with you. It was not *you* I was attracted to, was it? Not this time." Alex drives her eyes into mine. "Been there, done that. This time around, little one, it was Emilie I was … interested in. At the same time you were."

"So?"

"So, what?"

"So, did she know?"

Alex hesitates, frowns again and grins. She can do that all at the same time.

"She knew."

"How, if you didn't tell her?"

"I kissed her."

I'm speechless but I've got to ask, "What d' you mean, you kissed her?"

Sure, *I* can rock up to a woman I fancy and kiss her, maybe not like, full on French, but a kiss is a kiss. But Alex doesn't carry on that way at all. She's a bit tight when it comes to things like that. Self-conscious and all. She'd never risk making a dick of herself.

"Hey, Tam, don't go obtuse on me now. I said I kissed her. I'm a dyke, right? So, hey … one thing I do, on occasions, is kiss women."

"Uh … it's just that … you don't normally – How did you do *that?*"

"How?" she asks again with a new set of raised eyebrows.

"I don't mean *how*, I mean, like where? Not where did you kiss her, but like *where* were you?"

Alex. Emilie. Tamara tosses some more. The wide movement of her hand pulls at the IV line but the cannula is taped securely to the back of her hand. The light inside her head has a jaundiced tinge to it but Alex still looks like Alex.

"OK." Alex runs a hand over her fuzzy head. She's giving up the game, thank goodness for that. "I went to her place." She reaches to set her mug on the leather coffee table and wedges her back against the corner of the sofa. "You're absolutely right. For me, yes, it was a weird thing to do. I hadn't planned on doing it at all but one day, I found myself in her street. I rang her doorbell. She invited me in. I followed her to the kitchen and we chatted about this and that. The usual weather-work-cars chit-chat. You know, loose and fluid, but the type I am not too keen on because, after a while, nothing terribly meaningful has been said. And boom," Alex mimes bringing her two hands together. "Next minute, we're kissing. Wonderful. Like two magnets connecting. Out of the blue. Impossible to resist and … good." Alex grins exuberantly. "Definitely … *good.*" Her eyes shine and crinkle at the corners. "Actually, it was all a lot easier than I would ever have imagined. Must have been the fact that I had not had to work myself up to it."

So, what do I say to that? Had *I* already kissed Emilie by then? Would that have been before or *after* my first walk with her at the Mt Coot-tha Botanic Gardens? "You kissed Emilie. In her kitchen?"

"Helloww, Tam! Yes, in her kitchen and standing up. By the sink I think it was. Or was it by the fridge? What, too daring for someone my age? Too impulsive to fathom?"

"That's … no. I mean, no, that's … great but you're like always so … Well, you always think everything through … so much … usually. True?"

"Absolutely. I do try to, but not this time around. So what? Let's just say that for once I bucked my own MO." Alex shakes her head like she can't believe, so many months later, that she actually did that, ring Emilie's doorbell one day and jump her in the kitchen.

"So, you kissed her and … "

"*We* kissed, Tam. Mutual, reciprocal. We kissed for a long time. Kind of lost track of time, actually. Very, very, sexy. Totally passionate. Mad."

"And then, what?"

"What do you mean, And then what?"

"Well, I don't know … *What* came next?" Bad phrasing.

"Nothing *came* next. Once … once it was over, we did have that cup of coffee. We talked a bit but, strangely enough, not about anything greatly personal. The thing is that … the moment, the kiss, had left us somewhat winded. A little confused. I suspect neither of us had anticipated anything like that happening … Well, at any rate *not there* and *not then*. And though I don't think we felt that awkward about it, we just couldn't launch into anything greatly meaningful."

"Alex … like, I don't know what to say here. If you had told me about that … I would've butted out." Is that so? Would I, truly, have butted out? I think I'm crapping on here.

"Hey, Tam," Alex pushes away from the backrest, settles herself differently on the emerald-green cushions and tucks her legs under her. "The Chinese brain-teaser was not yours to solve … not this time around so … chill." Her eyes are dark again. "The matter was between Emilie and me. She was the one who had to think and decide. For herself, by herself. And I assume that's what she did." Alex's door-shut tone makes it clear that she's not going to debate that particular point any further. Not with me. "She decided to go for whatever it is *you* can bring her for now. End of story. That happens." Alex would have used the same wry tone if she had said, Shit happens. "So, anyway … what does that have to do with you having become *unbubbly?"*

"Uhmm … everything." I feel like shit. "You see, I've been thinking all along that maybe I should've *guessed* that you'd be attracted to Em and, yes, she to you. Like, you have so much in common and all." I can't look at her, not just yet. "But it was just a feeling I had, right? I didn't know for sure, did I?"

"No, Tam, you did not."

I drag my eyes back to hers, tentatively, as I sip the coffee that's gone cold in my cat mug. "Are you OK with that? Like now?"

Alex blinks then looks away and I, by now, I have a wet lump in my throat.

"Sure, I'm OK about it," she begins firmly. "Emilie was not ready for … well, she probably was, but hey, she met you, she changed her mind. Hey, lighten up, Tam." Alex is back to smiling another of her quick smiles. "How could she resist those legs, and that totally endearing personality of yours?"

She's winding me up or what?

"Look, honestly, Tam, you holding back to give me more space in which to make my moves, that would have been really embarrassing, both for Emilie and myself. Surely you can see that for yourself." Alex rubs the tip of her fingers over a temple and with a sigh she settles back against the sofa armrest. "Tam, she was attracted to you *a lot*, and to me a little *less*. End of story. This is not the Bold and The Restless." Pointedly she adds, "We, *older* women, we know when to clamp down on a slide. Practice does that for us. It helps us read the signs."

"The Bold and Beautiful or The Young and The Restless."

Alex is lousy when it comes to pop culture, not just TV soaps. She's doing fine with Limp Biskitt and the occasional burst of the old

Metallica, Moby and Savage Garden but she's definitely more into women's voices.

"Whatever," Alex retorts with a dismissive flash of the hand. "Tam, I didn't know either, did I, that you had been seeing Emilie … that way, romantically." Alex frowns again. Her eyes darken. "See? I didn't tell you. You didn't tell me. You and I weren't very much aware of the other while all that was going on. Doesn't matter." She shrugs. "It was Emilie's call all along. As it had to be."

I know what she's saying. But still.

Swish … swish. Swish … swish … swish.

Another pale shape floats up to the white curtain. Another nurse walks on white rubber soles. By the open curtain, by the open side of Tamara's cubicle, she, too, stops and listens. This one walks up to the IV drip and looks at her watch before fading away on the other side of the white curtain.

Tamara breathed in. Slowly she exhaled. Yes, she will miss this place. She will miss its sober beauty. She will miss its quiet ruggedness. The evening air was cool on her face but she was not cold. She had told Madame Dufour that she would be late getting to the dinner table and that she needn't wait for her.

"Eh ben, La Grande. Marielle, s*he say you go?"* Madame Dufour had asked jovially.

"Ce soihr, yes" Tamara had replied, *"Je veux respirer les vieilles piehrres et le lune. Le lune nouvelle."* Even when she realised too late that she had given the moon the wrong gender, that even in third grade she had known the moon was feminine, that was exactly what she wanted to do on her last evening at Sainte-Thérèse. She wanted to breathe in the old stones and take her fill of the moon. "Tomorrow, I go. Tonight, I enjoy Sainte-Therèse one last time."

Madame Dufour had offered to leave the loaf of bread out along with a terrine of her foie gras preserve and a generous portion of her Clafoutis for dessert.

"Merci, Madame Dufouhr."

Yes, she wanted to be out there on her own to say goodbye and to say thank you to the vines. Goodbye because, in the morning, she would be heading back to St Emilion and would probably never return to Sainte-Thérèse. Moments like those of the harvest, of the past ten days, the thoughts and feelings such as had reached an untapped part of her heart, the incredible beauty of the landscape, the simple purpose of the vignerons: all that had enthralled her was not hers to keep. It was not even hers to return to.

She knew that once gone from there, an anti-climactic reality would claim her back. Back from the suspended moments spent at the Dufours'. Moments when she had been known as *La Grande*. Moments when her body ached like never before. Moments when she would lie in bed, as the cocks crowed, fantasising about Marielle whose only wish was to see her, the backpacker, up-end herself and embrace the day. Moments when, shoulder to the dusty vines, she would look across and over the vast expanse of green furry rows, feel the gentle sun on her face and close her eyes to better let in the mood, the colours and the good-humoured banter in a patois she could not possibly understand.

Thank you, she was going to say to the vineyard, thank you for the memories it had forever imprinted on the blank screen that now lived inside her. Full as it was of unique, unanticipated moments, that screen was always blank. Always able to fit in more. Like an enormous screen but one, too, with an enormous memory stick, one that would never be too full.

Over the familiar trail she strode, her back to the farmhouse, just as the sun slid behind the fringe of trees that sealed off Sainte Thérèse to the west. The harvest was over and the vines which grew in rows, rows and more rows than the eye could hold, lay abandoned and dishevelled. Ravished amid soiled and trampled leaves. Ravished and fenced in, where Tamara stood, by the deep ruts the trucks had sliced in the soft soil, again and again, as they had pulled in to receive the harvest from the porters' huge baskets and left with their sunshine-drenched, dark red bounty piled high on their backs.

Tamara sat at the foot of an ancient vine, one that began the row closest to the trail she had been following. She worked her shoulders around the gnarls and leaned back, ankles crossed. Eyes half-closed to better breathe in the early evening air, she listened for sounds but there weren't any to be heard. None, except for the muted bark of a dog and a rhythmic, ringing clang of the sort, she imagined, a hammer might make hitting upon an anvil. Further away, the diffused sound of a receding tractor engine. This is so good. This place is so beautiful, Tamara thought. I mean, it's like I can pluck a peaceful feeling right out of thin air. Right as I sit here. All I have to do is just … breathe. If only I'd been born into such a glorious life, she wished earnestly. I mean, a life in which *being here* would be life, my life. Like, not just backpacking through the place.

Smoke rose from all the rooftops as far as she could see. Three acres away, three hectares away, three kilometres away, not as the crow flies but as the low-lying hills meandered, from every chimney rose a plume of light grey smoke. A church bell rang to the north. It was only five o'clock but the sky was already shedding its shades of dusk. The night sky was, once again, poised to overpower all around, all but the moon. Tonight was the night of the full moon and it would rise from the escarpment below and eclipse all else. Marielle had predicted it would be *une rousse,* a russet one. A red moon.

Meanwhile, lights like fairy lights in the distance glowed from inside the windows cut in the thickness of the stone-walled farms. Tamara inhaled. The air now had the faint taste of wood fires.

A tinkle made her ear twitch. She turned her head and trained her eyes on the bend in the trail a few metres away. An animal most likely but of what kind? A dog? A cow? What other animal might walk around with bells on? Not goats, this was not goat country. Lambs, rams and ewes didn't usually traipse about on their own. She heard the scraping of hooves and words spoken softly, as if whispered directly into someone's ear, to soothe.

"Allez, La Fleur. Ce soir, tu seras bien la dernière à rentrer au bercail. Ah, la rousse, comme je la haïs celle-là. Elle, plus que lui."

She recognised Marielle's voice. Though Tamara was not able to make out all the words she picked up on the tone, sad and heavy.

She stood up just as Fleurette's great head rounded the bend and dusted the back of her shorts. The cow shied away and Marielle looked up.

"Hey," she said.

Obviously startled out of her homily to Fleurette, she stood still. It was clear that, at nightfall, she had not expected to bump into anyone at the edge of this plateau.

"Ah ben ça, La Grande," she finally exclaimed with a smile, one pale hand still on her throat. "It is a … a surprise." She nudged the big black and white cow that had stopped on the trail when she had. Fleurette ambled, unconvincingly, over the rutted trail and stopped again as the farmer's daughter was not following. She shuffled all four hooves in a different position before turning her large head towards Tamara who went to her. She patted the white patch on the animal's cheek. Fleurette rolled her long-lashed, brown eyes.

Tamara didn't have any problems with patting the cow but she didn't quite dare pat the big rubbery snout that was exactly where she would have liked to rub her hand. Cow snouts are so inviting, to look at, if not to touch, almost like cartoon snouts. They made her smile, and Fleurette had an excellent snout. Shiny as all get out and … big. Do cows have teeth? she wondered briefly. Herbivore, yeah, OK. But what, they chew, don't they? So, what do they chew with, uh, like, wouldn't Fleurette, here, need some kind of teeth to pull –

"T'es pas perdue au moins?"

"Non. Pas pehrdue. J' attends la lune." No, she was not lost. Yes, she was waiting for the moon. And yes, this time she had given the moon the appropriate gender. The moon *could only* be a feminine word. *Au clair de la lune, mon ami Pierrot.* Her mother used to sing that little song to her well before she had begun pre-school.

Marielle moved closer to her cow and leaned against her side, facing Tamara. She, too, patted the animal. Well, she didn't actually pat the cow's forehead as much as she rubbed tight little circles into it. Then she smoothed the short fur on Fleurette's cheeks and pulled a few of the shorter tufts on the cow's wide muzzle. That makes sense, Tamara thought, you pat something delicate, like a cat or a dog even, but a big animal like Fleurette, she'd need something more … more substantial than a cat-pat, she would.

Marielle's fingers brushed against Tamara's. In the encroaching darkness, both hands jerked back too quickly. As quickly as if they had touched hot embers. Fleurette shuffled sideways, pushing against Tamara who thought the cow might step on her foot.

She was thinking about the cow's weight on her foot but only to better cancel out the thumping of her heart. It had lurched as her fingers had inadvertently touched Marielle's and her heart was still beating too fast. She tried to imagine what *that* weight on her foot would feel like because she didn't know how to address the hot, bright flares that had ignited inside her. Well, that was not entirely true. She did know how to address that particular fire. What she didn't know was how to douse it, seeing as it was straight-and-engaged-to-be-married Marielle who had ignited it too unexpectedly.

Tamara had neither been preparing nor prepared for such a touching, an *attouchement*, as the French said. Not when she had stood up to greet Marielle and Fleurette as they rounded the bend, she hadn't.

Marielle spoke in the darkness and Fleurette snorted, twisting her thick neck to look back at her.

"Donne. Donne la main," she said softly, reaching for the hand that Tamara had retracted, the hand that lay flat against the animal's neck. *"Viens. Touche la Fleurette. Là sur le museau."*

Marielle placed Tamara's hand on the cow's muzzle, right where the fur ended and the big and shiny cartoon snout began. Right where Fleurette liked to be touched, she had said.

"N'aies pas peur. Ça mord pas une vache," she added, aware of Tamara's hesitancy.

So cows didn't bite after all. Well, there you go.

Marielle's hand guided her friend's gently over the cow's damp and rubbery, wide snout, back up the wiry forelock and kept it there, under her own. Tamara looked at Marielle who was smiling, waiting for Tamara to look up.

"You go away tomoro, yes?" Marielle said in the best English she could manage. "Tomoro, at zis awer you be in St Emilion, yes? After you be in train, yes? Next day, yes?"

"Yes. Day after tomorrow."

The hand of one under the hand of the other on the warm wiry fur of the cow's withers, the young farmer and the backpacker stood facing each other from opposite sides of the cow's heaving sides. Marielle rested a forearm on Fleurette's back.

Tamara closed her eyes against the cool evening air and even more tightly against the explosion of a desire she needed to keep to herself. She didn't dare move away from Fleurette's side. She didn't want to. She even imagined that if the big cow was to crush her foot, that pain might just about alleviate that which had just ripped upwards from her loins.

She was like a rabbit frozen in the glare of headlights and her heart was beating just as fast from a different type of panic. Then, she felt Marielle's cool breath on her nose. She felt Marielle's night-cool lips over hers. Heart already thumping, Tamara stopped breathing. The cow shuffled sideways and moved forward. Her hooves scuffed the protruding rock embedded in the soil.

The spell should have been broken but Marielle was still there. Still there, still holding Tamara's hand. There was no longer anything separating the two. Tamara brought Marielle in close. Close against her. When she felt Marielle's lips open under hers, she thought she was going to come right there, right there and then, so strong was her arousal. Marielle moved closer against Tamara and Tamara groaned with desire, with an almost out of control, manic desire.

Tamara lost track of time. She lost her bearings totally as her hands, her mouth, overtook her senses. They overtook her senses and moved to make love to Marielle.

But then, something like a retracting rubber band pulled Tamara back. She opened her eyes. She held Marielle so as to peer into the young farmer's face. Unblinking, perhaps unseeing, Marielle was staring ahead.

"Marielle?" Tamara said softly. *"Marielle … uh … Dis quelque chose,"* Tamara urged. She wanted, really wanted, desperately wanted Marielle to say something. Anything.

Finally, Marielle blinked. She seemed to reconnect with the moment. A tear left its imprint down her cheek. She turned on her heels, clicked her tongue and nudged Fleurette forward. She led the cow away, one hand loose on Fleurette's neck.

"No, Marielle, wait. *Je m' excuse. Attends."*

Ahead of Marielle, as if to block off her exit, the full moon had begun rising from below. The enormous half of a diaphanous communion wafer, it was, translucent, *sanguine*. Bad moons, Marielle had earlier said about russet moons. It was her belief that the red moon was always a bad moon. *'La rousse iz a verree bahd moon.'* She had been so adamant about that that Tamara had assumed something about the moon had to affect either the farm animals, or the cows' milk, when it was not only full but red.

She felt disoriented. She felt as if she had woken up from an erotic dream, a very hot dream only to find her arms empty and the other side of the bed cold. Her sex was throbbing and warm. No one to hold. No one to love. She pressed the palm of her hand against the thick seam of her jeans to ease the pain away.

What was Marielle doing here anyway, at this time of the evening, alone with Fleurette? she asked herself. The cows were always bedded down way before sunset. Had Fleurette gone walkabout and Marielle had had to go fetch her back? Then, why walk away from the farm?

With a jerk of the shoulders, Tamara pushed off from the tree. She stepped back on to the trail but she did not retrace her steps back to the vineyard. Instead, on impulse, she followed it up the hill, up to where the wide, transparent moon-disk was still growing out of the lowland below.

Everything looks different at night but she knew she had not yet been near this waterway, obviously a narrow reach of the Dordogne River that snaked over the narrow clearing. If she had, she would undoubtedly have noticed it lap the foundation of a huge and squat rock edifice. Its wide and conical roof seemed made of slate. It and the water glistened darkly. Only narrow slits had been cut into the thickness of the wall to allow a very narrow view of the area beyond. Slits only wide enough to accommodate silent flurries of Norman arrows, she thought, somewhat awed by her discovery. She decided on the spot that the trail had led her to the remaining tower of a ruined medieval fortress.

This was indeed an amazing place, bathed in the eerie moonlight, still and mysterious. She wondered what name the locals had given the place. *La Tour Cassée* for Broken Tower? The tinkle of a bell drew her attention. Fleurette? Her heart skipped. The tinkle again. As she moved closer to the sound, Tamara discerned Fleurette's black and white patches.

To this day, Tamara insists that it could only have been a kinky sort of juvenile curiosity that had pushed her to walk, almost on tiptoes, closer to the ruin.

The moon shrinks to a tight red orb. Tamara opens her eyes. The moon shimmers and then it blinks. It dissolves into the darkness to reappear huge and sanguine above the tower. Tamara turns on her side, legs trapped inside twisted sheets.

The sob rippled inside her brain. Clearly a woman's sob, of that she was sure. Tamara moved to a mound of rocks that turned out to be more than a mound of rocks. It was an enclosure more like a semi-detached cellar.

A new sound bounced through the stillness, the huhh, huhh, huhh of a Wimbledon player returning a powerful volley. She listened again. She imagined Christian straining and puffing and grunting. *That,* she had to see. Why the voyeuristic urge? she didn't know. Later, she put it down to the impulse that has children peeping into their parents' bedroom through keyholes.

Stained by the grubby glow of a dirty kerosene light, Marielle's nakedness was partially exposed, only some two metres below where Tamara stood peering through broken tiles, but at the far end of a deceptively wide room. Hands splayed on a dirty floor, young breasts pointing towards a slab of rough concrete, though Tamara could only see half of Marielle's body, it was obvious that she was also resting on her knees.

How typical, Tamara thought immediately. He wants the doggie position, but doesn't even bother to bring a doggie rug with him. So typically male, that, she almost spat in the darkness. Then her heart lurched. This was so different from the way she had fantasised making love to Marielle. Is she really enjoying this? she wondered, suddenly as flat as a fizzless Coke. Well, again, why not? she reasoned. If she loves the guy … and it hits the spot.

Tamara sighed but adjusted her face against the cold rough-ness of the slate tiles. From that new position she could see Marielle's slender waist, like that of a whippet, and two male hands, wide and strong, around her slender hips, bringing her small buttocks backwards to better meet each of her partner's pelvic thrusts.

"Huhh," went Christian.

Her angle of vision was still too narrow to allow any view of the young man. All she would have on him were his amazing grunts and his preferred point of entry. Kinky all right! But where's the turn-on for Marielle? she mused again. Goes to show. Gotta be another case of the different strokes for different folks thing. But again, she redirected her thoughts, who knows where her G spot's located, huh?

The top band of a pair of cotton knickers, pale blue against Marielle's hips, showed between her lover's hands. Tamara frowned. Knickers? How weird, I mean, the guy's gonna burst any second now. They have any condoms out here, or what?

Christian ranted again, "Huhhh."

Marielle's face, neck craned at an odd angle, turned as if to face the slit behind which Tamara was hunkered. She jerked her face away from the spying hole, hoping the young woman hadn't caught her movement. How embarrassing if she has, Tamara thought, blushing at the thought of Marielle having spotted her spyhole on them at that most intimate of moments.

When she risked peering down again, the breath caught inside Tamara's throat. What the hell is *he* doing here? Straight into her limit-ed line of vision she had recognised Monsieur Dufour, Marielle's father.

Holy shit, she thought, we've just been bounced into the scene where the lovers are busted and the maiden's maidenhead needs to be avenged. There was Monsieur Dufour, legs wide apart, as she had seen him stand that day back at the vineyard, strong on the flatbed of his truck, pressing fleshy grapes between index finger and thumb before testing for sugar contents.

There he was standing off to the side, drill-cloth clad knees level with his daughter's breasts. It was then that the breath caught in Tamara's throat. "Awh … for fuck's sake," she muttered.

Between the index finger and thumb of the one hand, Monsieur Dufour was holding his flaccid penis. In the other hand he held a crum-pled handkerchief. She watched, unbelieving, as he wiped his penis with it. And Marielle was still, still and quiet. Still on her hands and knees. Still but whimpering.

Monsieur Dufour hitched up his trousers. His appendage slid back inside his baggy trousers. His fingers quickly ran up his fly. He bunched up the soiled handkerchief and shoved it inside his right pocket. Horrified, mesmerised, Tamara watched as he moved closer to his daughter. One knee to the ground, he reached towards her. He reached tentatively as if, in his flesh, he still remembered how she had once sunk her teeth into his hand. How another time she had lunged at him, leaving twin trails near his eye that he had simply explained as a barbed wire mishap. That particular barbed-wire mishap almost cost him an eye.

And there he was, patting his daughter as he would have patted a feral animal. Afraid she might scratch at him again. Afraid she might bite him again. But she remained still. She remained still and so he risked patting her hair. He became braver and let his rough, sperm-smelly hand smooth the loose dust-and-tear-stained strands of chestnut hair and clumsily tucked them, the best he could, behind his daughter's ear. He seemed to be whispering something to her.

From where she stood, chest pressed against the angled slate tiles, Tamara could actually see Marielle's eyes. They were wide. Wide and unblinking. Wide and unseeing. I've seen these eyes before, Tamara thought, heart in her mouth. Yes, earlier. Up the trail when a tear rolled down her cheek. Just before Marielle had turned on her heels, clicked her tongue, and nudged Fleurette forward. But even *before* that. Somewhere else. Different eyes but unblinking, unseeing in the same way. Whose eyes? Where?

Monsieur Dufour straightened himself again and moved away from Tamara's field of vision. She let herself slide to the ground. And because she couldn't bear to think of Marielle, her thoughts went to Fleurette, to Marielle's cow. Fleurette would be getting very restless by now, fretting even. Kept up too late out of the familiar warmth and night sounds of her barn.

*****

The slow scraping sound below the door awoke Tamara. Her first eyes-open thought had been that she had dreamt the sound and she had rolled over pulling the eiderdown more tightly around her shoulders. But she heard it again, a very quiet type of a scraping, the way one would scrape if not intending to be heard. Not meant to disturb. Tamara sat up, squinting into the darkness.

Scrape ... ... Scrape.

The scraping stopped but in its stead a softly metallic sound set Tamara's heart in a frantic beat. Insecure little clicks seemed to be coming from *inside* of the lock to her front door.

"What the hell?" she whispered, suddenly uncomfortable with the weight of the cover on her body. It made her feel trapped. She had locked the door, of that she was sure, just as she was sure that it was being slid backwards.

Rooted to the spot Tamara, her mind revving but in neutral, let mad thoughts race around in tune with the erratic beat of her heart. Dufour was on to her. His honour and reputation were at stake. He wants to silence me. In a parallel groove, Tamara had Madame Dufour on the other side of that door. She was loveable but ineffectual as a wife, deficient as a mother. She had known of her husband's gross crime but had failed to move heaven and earth to stop him abusing their only child. And she had come to protect her man.

"Awh, for fuck's sake," Tamara said out loud as the door swung ever so slowly, ever so quietly on its hinges. Eyes tight, eyes squinting into the cold darkness that slipped in from outside, she threw the eiderdown off her legs and held her breath as the door clicked shut. The bolt was being wound clockwise, back to its original position.

"Marielle?" she whispered at the slight shape that moved towards her.

"Oh," was all she heard. A little 'Oh' of surprise mitigated by a little 'Oh' of disappointment.

"J' voulais pas t' réveiller," was all Marielle said. I didn't want to wake you.

Perplexed, heart still thumping, adrenaline still coursing through her stomach and solar plexus, Tamara watched warily as Marielle moved closer to the bed.

And now what? she thought.

"Mais … why are you here?"

"Chut, ne dis rien, je t'en prie." Shush, be quiet, please. Don't ask me anything. *"J'ai froid."* Marielle was cold.

Now that her eyes had adjusted to the darkness Tamara watched as Marielle quickly pulled off, first her cardigan, then a long-sleeve T-shirt. She watched the loose cotton skirt flutter to the threadbare mat by the bed. Marielle stepped out of her plastic boots. They had been scraped free of mud and cow dung. As a reluctant spectator at a happening, as the one, in the front row, who ends up being picked by the performer who needs someone to toy with, Tamara watched.

Marielle held up the corner of the *édredon*, slipped her slight frame alongside Tamara's and pulled the eiderdown back over the two of them. Tamara winced as Marielle's cold hand came to rest on the bed-warm skin of her stomach. Marielle wiggled and snuggled herself into a position so that Tamara's arms and legs ended up enfolding her in a stiff but warm cocoon. Then, she moved her cheek against Tamara's collarbone and stayed still. Tamara realised that she was ram-rod stiff and holding her breath. Why is she here? Why now? Why not last night? What does she want from me? Thoughts whirled around faster than the wings on a dragonfly. She made herself breathe in deeply and exhale slowly. She made herself relax her shoulders and arms, her hands and thigh muscles. She allowed them to hold Marielle in a loose embrace and she focused on the woman, a mere girl, who had crept out into the night to snuggle into her bed.

Marielle's body had been so tightly wound and so cold that Tamara was able to tell almost to the second when she, too, let the taut-ness of her muscles soften, when Marielle's breathing became freer. Tamara eased herself in a more comfortable position, careful to keep Marielle still and she sighed an odd sort of a sigh, almost a sigh of well-being. Her face nuzzled Marielle's hair. It had the clean fragrance of lemon, of wood fire and lemon. Soon, both were asleep.

The tapping on her shoulder is annoying Tamara.

"Wake up, Tamara."

She shrugs the hand away. A tight ball of pain skittles to the other side of her brain. She blinks into the face.

"Time for your medication."

Too close. Too fucking close. She blinks again. The face reshapes itself.

"No, no need to move your head for that. You'll be back to sleep before you know it. But for now, young lady, I need to make sure all your vitals tally up to something reasonable."

"You're not Fiona."

"I'm not Fiona, no. She's been working overtime, Fiona has. Come … drink a little more of that. You need to hydrate."

"Can't." Shakily, Tamara hands the paper cup back to the nurse.

"Je sais qu' tu sais,' Marielle said. I know that you know. *"Je savais que tu m' suivrais."*

Marielle had anticipated that Tamara would follow her to the tower. Someone had to find out, she said when, some time after midnight, they had woken up.

Tamara, her cheek resting against Marielle's chestnut curls, had asked in simplified English, "Why you think I follow you?"

"Because I … *euh* … because I go on the trail without saying goodbye to you."

And so they whispered a little to each other, both careful to avoid the words father, abuse, incest and sex (though three of these words were pretty much the same in both languages), as these would have led to other words that would have pinpointed the evening's event too clearly. More specific words would have made it and every other preceding russet-moon encounter, too horrifyingly palpable. And so, the common memory of earlier lay between them like a sawn-off body part on a pathologist's slab. Only covered, only made decent, by the thin sheet of their combined silences.

Marielle had shifted into Tamara's arms, in between her legs, but she had remained there, her right side against Tamara's left.

How young had she been when it all began, Tamara wondered. Did her mother know? How could she not know? Why hadn't Marielle found a way to stop him? I mean like, how long has it been going on? Did Christian know? Why hadn't she told him? What fucking use is he to her if she won't even tell him *that*? How much longer will she just hang in there and keep on enduring *his* hands, her father's hands, on her? Didn't she know there probably were organizations in Bordeaux that could help her out of Sainte–Thérèse?

And so the only question Tamara whispered in the dark was, "And why, *pourquoi tu restes ici?*"

"Many time I think I…*euh*…I think I must leave. But I stay because I live 'ere. This is my land, *tu comprends?* I love Sainte–Thérèse. I can never go away. It is in my … " She had looked for the right word, a word not so commonly used in high school French.

"Blood. It's in your blood, yes?"

"Ah oui, in my blood. Inside…'ere…" She pinched the skin of her arm. "In my skin. *Oui…je l'ai dans la peau.* I hate 'im but 'e is my father. She is my mother. She does not know. It kill 'er if she know."

Intellectually, Tamara understood what Marielle was saying about her love for the land, her countryside, for the vineyard, but at an another level, lacking a strong sense of her own roots, she could not accept that enduring a father's twisted sexual urges was the right price to pay for living near her beloved vines. She already knew that if anything like that had ever happened to her she would either have told someone, early, very early on, or would have left home, never to return. Screw the vines, screw him. Close the door on that friggin' nightmare and move on, she wanted to tell Marielle but she didn't.

And Marielle shifted inside Tamara's embrace. She snuggled up closer and briefly looked into Tamara's eyes. Unexpectedly, she ran her thumb over and over again the silver bolt that pierced her eyebrow and, like a sleepy child, dropped her head back against Tamara's cheek. When Tamara shifted to peer into Marielle's face, Marielle's lips covered hers and melted all of her. And the mad rush of desire coursed again through Tamara's limbs, through her sex, through her ribcage and, for the second time that day, almost short-circuited her brain. Almost but not quite.

Though Tamara's hand had been resting on Marielle's naked skin, on her hip, she had encased her resolve in concrete; she wouldn't let that hand stir. She wouldn't let it caress Marielle's thigh. She wouldn't let that hand move across the flat plane of Marielle's stomach and down, down to the chestnut curls that she knew she could reach so easily, even from her position.

Marielle's face was nestled against Tamara's cheek but her hand had begun a slow sleepwalk wander under Tamara's pyjama top, electrifying all the nerve endings along the path it travelled.

Tamara did not attempt to stop Marielle's flat-handed, dreamy exploration. It was just too marvellously sensual. It was transporting her to a place she had never known, only comparable, she thought, to the erotic arousal one might feel if bound. Bound, as in hands and ankles loosely tied to the bedposts. Bound, as she was by the silent promise to not take advantage of Marielle's need for warmth and love, for non-sexual love, no matter how Marielle chose to express that need.

So Tamara lay, exposed, vulnerable, hardly able to contain the deep-set arousal, thankful for the obscurity of darkness, unable to touch back, unable to slow down her arousal by a shift of focus while long and beckoning stabs of desire spread and spiralled down her thighs. Unrelenting, as gentle as the ebb and flow of the sea, Marielle, hand flat on Tamara, lit trails of desire, hot and white and shimmery, radiating from her very core.

The memory of Marielle's father, of his two hands pulling Marielle's buttocks against him, of him rubbing his penis against her until he came on the thin cloth of her pale blue knickers, that vision jumped into the darkness of the room but Tamara squeezed her eyes shut against it. And she held Marielle even more loosely, so determined she was to not let *her lust* …

But she came. She came in a syncopated, muffled groan. Led by Marielle's dream- inspired slow glide over the soft cloth of her pajamas, over her thigh, over her stomach, over her sex, over one breast and the other, her hand flat against her ribs and down her thigh again and against her sex again, the wave, a wave laid up by the combined power of the preceding ones, crashed and broke in a million jagged irridescent tongues.

Tamara came, almost in spite of herself. She had sucked in her breath through clenched teeth, and she tried to slow down the manic beats of her heart. And she tried to not let herself be totally swept away, submerged by the delicious swarm that rippled and swirled deep, deep inside her. Her priority had been to spare Marielle yet another 'ejaculation' – orgasms, squirting sperm, sexual release, even her own, less messy, less graphic, yes, but still the same primitive animal release. That night, for Tamara, all were one and the same: affronts to Marielle's raw feelings.

So she tightened her embrace around Marielle, and pressed her cheek into the woman's lemon and wood-fire scented hair and tried to stifle her moan when the wave of ecstasy broke then spread away from her clitoris. And in the darkness, she blushed when she felt Marielle's hand cup her sex, no longer in a sleepwalking meander but purposefully, knowingly, to ease away what sparks of frustrated desire might have remained trapped. Tamara exhaled forcefully and cupped the back of Marielle's hand with her own in a tacit acknowledgement.

Neither woman spoke but, immobile, each clung to the other. Finally, Marielle tucked one leg over Tamara's thigh and draped one arm across her chest, her hand resting over Tamara's collarbone. Tamara didn't dare move. She did not dare touch Marielle as a lover. She didn't think Marielle really wanted that to happen, not even then. She wanted to leave her with a sense of power, with the power of pleasuring another, freely. At her choosing. Soon, they fell asleep together, a second time that night.

When Tamara woke, she was alone in her bed. There was sunlight in her converted side of the barn though the curtains were still pulled. She hadn't heard the roosters' crow. No sign attested to Marielle's presence in her bed. None beside the unalterable memory of Marielle's touch, and the weight of Marielle's head against her shoulder.

She sighed, looking at the whitewashed ceiling, as if for the first time. She scrutinised the heavy beams that clung to it. She had never lain in bed so long, not since she had arrived at the Dufours'. There had always been the grapes waiting, the harvest to bring in. And Marielle to wake her up. But the harvest was in, the *vendanges* were over. Before

C. C. Saint-Clair

the morning ended she would be on the road, retracing the steps that had brought her to Sainte-Thérèse, inland from the Dordogne River.

Aware of a vague ache, she brushed her hand over her sex. She squinted. She crossed her legs then curled up on her left side. She began planning the trek back to St Emilion. And where to find Marielle. And how to say goodbye.

*****

TWO

"Uh, excuse me. Could you tell me…"

The nurse turns away from the lift door to look at the woman, whom she notices for the first time. Momentarily, she is taken aback by the bright colours painted on the woman's shirt and by the silver brush of her hair. She feels as if she should take a step backward to take in all that colour, to take in the inch-wide swirls of cobalt, hot pink and fluorescent green that battle it out on the canvas that is the woman's long shirt.

A frown flutters over her eyes in an illogical expectation that this woman's query is likely to be an all-involving affair that she doesn't have time for.

"Are you right?" she asks, Queensland-style, one finger still tapping the Down button.

"Yes, I am, thanks. I am looking for Tamara Townsend. I have been told – "

The nurse's face lights up. "Tamara?"

"Yes, Tamara," Alex answers, not overly surprised by the nurse's familiarity with Tamara.

"You must be Emilie, her … her friend?"

"Ah, no. I mean yes. I am her friend, which is what brings me here. But no, I am not Emilie."

"Oh, I'm sorry." The nurse fiddles with the fob watch that dangles upside down over her left breast pocket while she surreptitiously slides another look at Alex. "She's already had a visitor this morning, early. The girls said but I wasn't … "

Alex takes in the fluster on the young nurse's face. "No harm done. So which way will I … "

"You'll find her a couple of beds away from that window. Just along there."

The nurse points to a vague spot towards the far end of the room, but before Alex has time to focus on any one of the metallic bed ends that protrude from the double row of partially drawn curtains. She adds with an engaging smile, "Uh, I'm Fiona. I was here when they brought her in last night, fresh from Resus, you know, when she came to." A little bell chimes from behind the elevator doors. They slide open. Two nurses step out on white soles that make a squishing sound on the linoleum. "And well … anyway, duty calls. I've just started my shift. I'll pop around in a little while, just to say g'day to Tamara." Fiona turns again to face Alex. "And to fluff up her pillows," she adds with a cheeky grin.

"I'm sure she will like that. Thanks for the – "

"Not a problem."

Alex looks again at the far wall and moves her eyes a couple of beds back. To the right or to the left of the aisle? That funny little nurse didn't say. She really hates these places. *What is it about them?* she wonders as she cautiously makes her way through the middle of the ward. Queasy feeling. Fear of pain. Ah, yes, it's about being afraid to see the pain in *their* eyes or the wounds on *their* body. Even *imagining* pain makes her terribly afraid of the day she, too, will feel pain, one similar to theirs. It will rake through *her* body and eat at it from the inside and it will squeeze *her* brain like a grapefruit. It will, one day. All of us, healthy people, she ponders sombrely, we're doing the complacent sitting-duck thing until that one check-up that won't add up, the one that will require a second opinion. That's if nothing more brutal gets to me first.

But … it is not so bad here, she thinks, as the initial pounding in her chest subsides. This here has got to be a ward from where *everyone* leaves … on their own two feet. Not on a gurney. Not under a white sheet. No blood. No moans. No body parts altered by illness and distorted by accidents.

Walking almost on tiptoes, as she does on the rare occasions she finds herself inside a church, an empty church she might have gone in on impulse, for its calm, for the coolness within its walls, she asks herself, And Tam … how is she?

A few steps further, she spots her. A sigh of relief escapes from her lips at the sight of her unbandaged head. Once in front of the bed, though, she hesitates. And she frowns in front of the unfamiliar loose rag-doll flop that has arranged Tamara's long body in an odd way under the sheet. She frowns, too, at the unfamiliar stiff curl of Tamara's fingers over the sheet. And she frowns because she is spooked by the tubing that juts out, as intrusive as the-X-that-marks-the-spot, from the band of pale skin etched on the back of Tamara's left hand.

She blinks and steps back. Again she looks at Tamara's body. And Alex's throat tightens because as she looks at Tamara's abandoned but uncomfortable body she thinks that anything at all could be done to her, to that body, while Tamara is not in charge of it, while it is empty of her usual nonchalant vitality.

Alex's throat becomes mushy and coarse at the same time. She has to swallow hard to push the air down it but only feels a lump. Is it any easier, she wonders, when it's an old person whose body lies there in that loose but cramped, unconnected sort of way?

She had expected to find Tamara dazed, possibly bandaged and possibly hooked to … things, to many things. As it is, she is surprised that Tamara is not hooked to anything much at all, only to an IV line and to a gadjet clipped to her middle finger. What she clearly had not expected was to see her, Tamara, robbed of her usual purposefullness.

OK, Alex reasons, she's asleep right? So … who is ever purposeful in their sleep? With shutter-fast speed she remembers what Tamara *should* look like aleep. She should be lying on her left side, one hand, palm up cradling her cheek, hip curved to allow her legs to settle comfortably into the curl. Curled in a cat-curl, is how Tamara normally sleeps, as puposefully comfortable as Anjo, Alex's Siamese, used to look when she napped on the living-room rug.

Alex lets her eyes travel upwards from the young veins that snake from the back of Tamara's hands, to her wrists, up her arms to disappear under the soft rise of her biceps. The quiet strength that emanates from Tamara's firm and lovely tanned arms reassures Alex because *that* is a familiar sight. The familiar hollow at the tip of Tamara's collarbone, just before it meets the round curve of her shoulder, paler than her arms, *that* reassures her too. And she smiles because that lovely exposed shoulder makes the loosely draped, prim and pink hospital gown look a lot less prim than it should.

Strands of her dark hair spread against the white-white of the pillow, Tamara certainly appears asleep, sheet gathered around her hips, but her face is made tight by something that may well be pain. If not pain, Alex thinks, then at least intense discomfort. And on the cheek that had faced away she sees the graze, two red lines embedded in a cushion of puffy pink flesh the size of a fifty-cent coin.

And now what? she asks herself, as she considers her options. Let her sleep or … If I leave now to let her rest, she'll be pissed off when she finds out I was here and didn't wake her.

So she stands in front of Tamara's bed and rests her hands on the thick metal curve, cool against her palms. She takes in the chart, clipped as they always are, at the foot of the metallic bed, the bedside trolley with the usual arrangement of a pitcher of water and one glass, a little vase of flowers. Real or fake? Hard to tell from here, nice enough even if they are made in Taiwan. Well, well, and what have we got here? She grins at the sight of a little pink bear, pink from head to toe, perched on the edge of the trolley, turned so as to watch over Tamara's sleep.

"She's asleep, little bear?" Alex asks softly.

With a start, Tamara opens her eyes. "Hey – Awh … fuck. Oh, Al. I'm sorry. It's like … every time I move – " And more carefully, she asks, "Hey … whassup?"

Alex grins at the spark of quirky energy. "What's up to you, *too*. But *that* should have been *my* line, don't you think?" she jokes. "Considering … well, considering. So, what have they done to your head?"

"Not too good. I mean…Awh…" Tamara shuts her eyes and groans softly. When the green eyes snap open again, Alex notices the tightness around them and over Tamara's high cheekbones. And she notices, too, that Tamara's eyes are shiny, too shiny. "Don't know what … what he did … that creep, but it fucking hurts like hell," she grumbles, trying to raise herself higher up on the pillows while keeping her head still.

"Wait, wait. Let me help you."

Tamara squints at her. "Wicked!"

"What is?"

"Your shirt. Wicked but so bright. Glows in the dark."

"Ah, indeed. You know–" *You know how to pick them,* Alex had been about to reply because Tamara had offered it to her only a few months back. Instead she adlibs in a cheerful pretense, "You know me, Tam. I want to know my students are awake when they look at me. As in, not numb behind eyes wide-open. So … when in doubt, go for bright." But Alex frowns. Does she *not* remember that shirt was her birthday present to me? "Oh, by the way…" she plods on, "Your chatty little friend in white sends her regards."

Alex threads her two arms under Tamara's and helps her prop herself up more comfortably.

"Fiona?" Tamara pulls her mouth downwards. "Tell you what…" she whispers, "… lethal with the flashlight. And then she's like hell-bent to…"

Alex plucks the edge of the hospital gown and brings it back protectively over Tamara's shoulder. "Come, tell me all your miseries, little one."

"Guess she's got to do it…clean this thing on my cheek." Hand on her chest, Tamara closes her eyes again.

"What do you mean, you *guess*? If young Fiona does not do a good job on that cheek of yours, I'll personally – "

"This morning another one … another nurse came, too…" Peeping at Alex through half-closed lids, Tamara is cranky. "They all want to look at the back of my friggin' eyes. Sounds a bit … like warped, if you ask me."

"Look, be nice to them, Tam," Alex says tapping Tamara's ankle where it lies under the sheet. "I bet you the word is out that there is a real spunky dyke somewhere on *this* floor. A new arrival, you see." She squats by the bed to be level with Tamara's face. "They want to check you out, that's all."

Tamara groans but, this time not from the pain in her head. Alex kisses her on her good cheek. "So, tell me about your head." Her hand lingers against Tamara's forehead and smoothes her hair back towards the pillow.

"Well, it's … coming along," Tamara smiles palely. "Good news is that they're not really doing anything to it … to my head. Not anymore … not after all the tests and whatnot. I guess that means I'm an easy fix." She puts on a grin. "Thing is, I don't remember any of that. Like they say … they scanned me and tested for this and for that because…" She stops and shuts her eyes. Alex watches as Tamara's chest rises slowly and falls slowly. "Well … when I first got here, like so out of it … they didn't know why I had passed out. Like maybe I had had … an allergic reaction to … Or maybe I was a junkie." She moves to rub her face with both hands but one hand freezes just above the graze. She gnashes her teeth and curls her fingers into claws to express the annoying irritation that graze causes her. "Good news, no bleeding of the … uh, of the brain lining. But maybe some … what is it again?" she asks out loud. "Awh…for fuck's sake," she exclaims frustrated by her inability to state clearly what she wants Alex to know. "Look, I'm not up to this hospital IQ talk." But she persists all the same. "There's swelling … but … Uh, it's all about tearing or stretching … bruising or not. Al," she sighs, "…ask again tomorrow or … Em will tell you. The doctor's explained it … but it was like so early this morning. I had these awful rushes of nausea and…" she sighs as if what little energy she thought she could muster for Alex is almost depleted. "Maxalon. I remember the name. That's what I get for … for the nausea. Panadol doesn't work … like not at all … so, yeah … Now what I remember, 'cause it's like so weird, is that I got some morphine earlier today. What you make of that, huh?"

"Well, hell." Alex replies carefully. "Maybe that's a good sign. Like they wouldn't give you something that might send you on a loop if they were really worried about … uh, your state of alertness."

"Anyway … nothing to do but wait. Ah … X-rays too, and CAT … scans they did, last night. You've seen Emilie?" she asks, out of breath, eyes shining too brightly.

"Seen her? No, I didn't see her. She called me … That was last night, to tell me what had happened but – "

55

Careful not to lift her head off the pillow, Tamara points to the general area at the back of her head, on the right side, almost at the base of her skull. "That's where I got hit, right there."

"What is the pain like, Tam?"

"Al … you don't want … to – " Another deep frown tightens the skin around Tamara's eyes. Alex's wince in sympathy. Tamara breathes in deeply and holds on to her breath, until the pain subsides. "Comes and goes. I move my head. Hammers clanking down again and again. Then, it's like … my brain's just like squeezed. Like my skull's gotten too small for it, you know? Like shrunk. Or," she adds, the memory of that particular pain making her queasy, "long fingers of … of *pain* that rip through." She flexes her ankles under the sheet and brings her knees up. "Hangovers, you know, I've had some. Real nasty ones. But … like so lame compared to this."

Alex nods and waits for the patient to say more. She looks at the little pink bear perched on the bedside trolley, then looks back at Tamara. "I thought Emilie might be here."

"She'll drop in again after work. Hey … grab a chair. She's been in … already. Soon as the doors opened. Don't know how she managed that."

Tamara smiles weakly at the thought of Emilie, hair twisted by sleep in a way only Emilie's hair gets twisted. She virtually saw her scrambling around to get to the hospital before work while *her* inner clock madly alarmed to get her back to bed, to get her to luxuriate in the thought that she didn't *really* have to get up, not for another hour. "But like, only long enough to check my pulse. Told her Fiona had already done that, checked my pulse. So Emi said that … Uh, some things are best checked … twice."

"Cute."

"Wouldn't be so funny … like if she actually knew how to check for pulse, but … mmmff … She wouldn't find one, I mean a pulse, not even one … on a vibrating … uh … on a vibrating Nokia."

Alex would like to ask someone if Tamara's *non-sequitur* and fragmented thoughts are a direct, possibly a lasting consequence of her head trauma, or are they simply momentary side-effects due to the combination of shock, exhaustion, and medication?

"Ah … but look!" Tamara reaches to pat the bedside trolley without moving her head. Alex gets to her feet to help her but Tamara already has the little pink bear dangling by one paw. "She brought me this little fellow for company."

"*Her* bear, is it?" Alex asks doubtfully, looking at the little pink thing sporting what seems to be a gold earring in one ear. She hadn't imagined Emilie would be the type of woman to have little bears, pink, pierced or otherwise, strewn around the house. No hints of bears in her kitchen, she remembers wryly.

"Yep, that's her little rainbow bear. See? Rainbow flag. It sits on her monitor, at home."

"I see. Cute little thing, isn't it? Looks so serious, almost like it has a bit of a frown on its little face."

Tamara plops the little bear on the sheet near where her other hand, the one with the cannula, is resting. "Anyway," she begins again, "how did you know to find me here? I mean, it's not like it's my fave hangout or anything."

"Emilie called to tell me what had happened. Last night," Alex explains for the second time. "She was quite frazzled by it all."

"Oh … yes." Tamara frowns. "You've said that. So weird for her to find me … dead to the world. I mean, when I meet her at work, it's … in the jeep that I wait, not like, napping on the ground."

"I can imagine," Alex replies, somewhat comforted by Tamara's ability to make little jokes. "I think what really got to her was being so terribly helpless. Not knowing what to do beside roll you to one side. But as she said, if you had stopped breathing, she wouldn't have had a clue as to what to do, let alone in what order." Alex stretches her legs to sit more comfortably on the chair.

Tamara tries to imagine Emilie's panic but a chuckle breaks through. "You know the funny thing? She always goes on about the fact that she's never even done First Aid or any of that. Used to really worry when she was with uh … with Solange.But nothing ever happened to Solange." Alex raises an eyebrow. "Uh, one of her exes. Not the one just before me. Before that again."

"What? A daredevil or a diabetic?"

"Daredevil. Into … a penchant, uh … for risky things."

"Somehow I wouldn't have thought that adrenaline-charged moments suited your Emilie."

"The … moments … no, they didn't suit. Not much. But the woman, Solange … she suited."

"Ah well, in that case, you know how it is – "

"Yeah, yeah. The good with the not so good."

Alex pats Tamara's hand. "Hold on to that thought, little one. You never know when it might come in handy. Anyway, the other thing that had Emilie in a spin, last night, was how she had eluded the police– Ah, no, hold on. Maybe that is too strong a word. Let's just say she stood them up."

"What you on about?"

"Didn't she tell you?"

"Told me? She only stopped to … uh, long enough to check my … that I was still breathing. As I said."

"Have the police been to see you?"

"Yes. A Senior Constable something or other and a Sergeant Detecti – "

"A *Detective* Sergeant?"

Tamara initiates a careful shrug. "Not sure why they came, really, after Em left. Asked if I might've been followed. If I had like, seen anything or heard anything uh, weird in the parking lot."

"That it?"

"Pretty much. They wanted to know why I was there in the first place so … I had to tell them about this *friend* … I'd been waiting for. Then, they wanted to know all about this friend. Name and all. And my head was totally throbbing by then … I was going to throw up. Doctor Mac, she moved them on. I didn't throw up but … Thing is, I really want them to get the bastard but I was feeling like too woozy to think. To talk." Tamara's face is pale and tense. "The police … They seemed to already know about Emilie … *The Friend*. Why you think?" she asks suddenly. Her brain is thrumming again. The oxymetre clamped on her middle finger has picked up her raised pulse. It beeps soft little beeps but, to Alex, they seem to form one long line of beeps. Like dots crowding on one line. One neatly pressed against the other.

"Well … you see, uh, she called the ambulance first…" Alex tries to explain, though she is distracted by the beeps. Shouldn't someone come and check Tam? She makes herself sit back on the chair on a resolution not to interfere with the running of things. Surely Tam is OK for now. "Uh, yes, she called the police, right? And then, when she realised that you had been mugged she – "

"Mugged? *Me?* Not just hit on the head? Awh… "

"Tam, darling, you really must find a way to talk *and* keep your head flat against those pillows of yours. Here," she says gently, handing Tamara a glass of water.

No … Can't drink …Don't know why … I just…"

"What do you mean, you *can't?* You're a two-litre-a-day-babe."

"Before, Al. That was before. Today … I just can't get it down. I think that's why I'm so stuck to this … tube." She lifts her hand to show Alex the line stuck to the back of her hand with transparent tape.

"Right." Alex nods agreeably though she doesn't understand why

Tamara won't drink water. What does that have to do with anything? She wants to ask someone in the know.

"Tamara?"

Both Tamara and Alex look to the source of the voice. Fiona strides to the head of the bed. She turns off the volume on the oxymetre. Thank god for that, Alex sighs, realising for the first time that she had stopped breathing freely since the beeps had picked up.

Fiona prattles as she sets about checking Tamara's blood pressure and temperature. "The old head again, hey? Goes to show. It's not as tough a head as you had thought."

"As I understand it, Emilie found your backpack thrown … somewhere. Behind the car, I think and– "

"My skates? They gone?"

"Your skates? Uh, I don't know. I don't think she mentioned them. You had them on?"

"Duh!" Tamara manages to say without the usual movement of the head that would accompany that exclamation. "I'd know where they are … if you know … like the mugger, whoever he is, he's not gonna hang around … undo, uh, unlace them and struggle to pull them off while I'm, like, out cold and in full view, is he now?"

"Well, in some very dark alley, it could happen or…" Alex suggests, eyebrows raised, "or in an Eddy Murphy com – "

"True."

"Seriously, Tam. Did you skate there?"

"I do often, yes. I walk to the … what … the Pier 1 ferry. I lace up as I wait. After the ferry, it's up Sydney Street and to the I-o-FuK." Alex frowns. "You know … where she works, the Institute of Further Knowledge. A short skate. Only about fifteen minutes. Then I chill in the car or nearby."

"Do you go in and let her know you're – "

"Ah, no. *That,* I don't do."

"Why not?"

"It's the closet thing, Al. You know … *the closet* thing?"

"Ah, *that* closet thing."

"That one, yes. But I think you and her, you both suffer from … from, uh … the same delusion."

"And which delusion might that be?"

"That as long as you're not seen … kissing, uh … French kissing a chick, you're safe with the … you know … the *Don't Tell* part of … of the *Don't Ask* thing."

"Tam, you should rest. You're talking too much for – "

"You always say that," Tamara answers eyes still closed.

"Emilie doesn't think so, though." Alex watches her chest fill with air. When she breathes out, Tamara opens her eyes again.

"So," Alex sighs, crossing ankle over knee. "What you're saying is that we're wasting a great deal of effort, Emilie and I, stuffing ourselves in a transparent closet, not to mention a glass one?"

"Correct." Tamara smiles the best smile she can muster. "Hey, Al ... you're so serious today ... looking at me like I've half-morphed into a Beige ... you know, uh, an alien. I'm an easy fix. I'll be fine. You'll see."

"I know." But Alex's dark look of concern does not match the lightness of her tone.

A chuckle bubbles up inside Tamara's chest but chuckling means moving her head. Moving her head unleashes a pain that skittles against glass. Glass breaks. Broken glass hurts. And so Alex doesn't get to hear Tamara chuckle. When she opens her eyes again, Tamara is focused. She wants to know about her skates.

"There goes some five hundred bucks if they went walkin'." She considers the matter a minute and then, startled, she adds, "It's worse ... I mean if they've been stolen. Emilie gave them to me and– " "Hold on, Tam. Try and remember. First, you get to Emilie's workplace, to the parking lot downstairs, correct?" "No!" Alex says sharply, squeezing Tamara's hand into her own. "No, Tam. Don't nod. It's OK. Breathe, now. Breathe, Tam. Breathe again. Breathe into the pain. Like that." Alex over-inhales near Tamara's ear, holds on to the air and lets it ooze out slowly. "Don't nod. Just blink slowly. OK. So, you remove your skates right there and then and you wait for her to come out. Just blink. Is that how it goes? Good. You stuff them in your backpack? No? So you toss them ... you toss your skates in the car?"

Tamara breathes in, holds her breath and lets it out very slowly. "Yes, that's ... pretty much what I do." She squints again but Alex recognises this particular squint as one of concentration. "Uh ... I remove them and I ... I usually stash them in the back, on the floor. I wait for her. For Emilie."

"In the car?"

"Yeah, I listen to music. Or I have a little walk around."

"OK, Tam. Don't move your head. Nodding is not allowed today. Ready?" Tamara smiles to indicate she is ready. This blinking thing makes her feel like she's paralysed from the neck down. "OK. Look, Tam, I would have thought that Emilie would be the punctual type, the *very* punctual type. You agree? OK. So how come you get there with so much time to spare?"

Tamara interrupts without moving her head. "Not *soo* much time, just a couple of minutes. She knows that I'm not … like, not usually there on time. Sometimes I'm there at six, sometimes 6.15. Like it's not *so* late, right? So she hangs back a bit. I get there, I listen to a couple of sounds and then, she comes out and…"

"How long have you been together?"

"Hey, only eight, no … nine months. Gimme a break."

"Hey, you don't need a break *from me*, that's cool. Anyway, your skates are probably in the back of her car. What she did notice was missing, though, was your discman. And your wallet."

"Oh." Tamara tries a quick mental check of her wallet's likely contents. "So … he's taken my credit card. And a couple of twenties … give or take. And – " A slow blush settles on her face.

"And?"

"A picture of Emilie."

"Ah, well … could have been worse."

"How so?"

"Could have been a picture of Emilie and you."

"It was."

"You and Emilie." Alex smiles at Tamara's embarrassment. "Doing what? Holding hands? Kissing?" she teases.

"Doing nothing. Just smiling."

"So … as I said, could have been worse." Alex sits back in the straight-backed chair that is getting harder, more uncomfortable, by the minute. Could be that visitors aren't meant to stay long. Maybe that is why there aren't any armchairs around. Or anyone to offer coffee to stressed-out visitors. "Anyway," she explains, "last night Emilie thought about calling the Visacard people to report the theft but – "

"She doesn't know my … my … what? Password, code … whatever it's called."

"That's right, she does not. And, basically, she has realised that in times of emergency there is not a lot she can do for you."

"Or me for her."

Alex looks at her hands. With the thumb of one, she rubs the back of the other. When she eventually looks up, her brow is furrowed, her eyes dark. "Maybe it's time you moved in with her."

"And why on earth – awhh … ahh… For fuck's sake, Alex." Tamara squeezes her eyes shut and remains silent for a few seconds while the pain sub-sides. "What does moving in have to do with … with anything?" she asks through half-closed eyes.

"Oh, many things, and mostly good things, from what I have heard," Alex says, thoroughly aware that most of what *she thinks* she knows in regards to the pros and cons of living with a lover has come to her by way of hearsay. That is one other thing Tamara would say she has in common with Emilie.

Both of them have had a great past. Lots of lovers, interesting ones. Variety helped along by many travels for Emilie and by years of travelling for Alex. But in between, whereas most women have fitted in time under the same roof with a lover or two, though not necessarily simultaneously, both Emilie and Alex, for their own personal reasons, have avoided that route almost entirely. Instead, they found themselves looking down the spiral of reflective introspection on their own, in their big and empty houses, in different parts of town.

Until one day, Tamara saw Emilie perched on a barstool, absent-mindedly dangling the long neck of a Corona between her fingers. That was at The Triangle bar. She had chatted up Emilie as she had, some years before, chatted up Alex, and for the same reasons. Both women, so many years apart, had looked so disconnected from the world immediately around them that they had pricked Tamara's interest.

"Of course, *my dear*," Alex says pointedly, "you know damn well I'm not the most qualified to give definitive info on the benefits of entwining one's life with that of another, but you and Emilie would be a little more conversant with each other's … kind of stuff. In any case, Oh Young One, you do travel light." Alex pauses for effect. "And if your skates are already parked in the back of her car … well…" She arches her eyebrows, trying on a lewd and suggestive expression to make Tamara smile, but Tamara doesn't smile.

"Wrap it up, Alex." It's Tamara's turn to frown. "I … I … love her. I love Emilie but, like, living with someone is totally different again." Tamara has a think and a blink. "Well, I did it with you … but – "

"Well, there you go. See, we are the *living proof* that cohabitation can work. It was not the living together bit that put an end to us, was it?" Alex shifts on her seat and lets her eyes settle on the intense little bear still plopped near Tamara's hand. "It was your wanderlust; a lust like all others, I should add, that was *totally* appropriate to one your age," she adds looking up.

"Right, but with Emilie, it'd be different. I'm not planning on go – "

"Oh my, that would *really* be living on the edge, that," Alex chides, not knowing whether she is teasing or serious, "moving in with your lover and not having an escape pod organised ahead of tim – "

"Alex … you're giving me a fucking headache now," Tamara says sharply, eyes already shut tight against her pain. "That's *on top* of that other *fucking* pain I had *before* you started this … this conversation." She breathes in slowly and exhales slowly. Green eyes snap open. "Ease up. I can't keep up. Not today."

She closes her eyes again and makes herself control her breathing by slowly breathing into the pain. To calm it, to coax it into being gentler. She feels the movement of her brain knocking against the back of her head as if bursting to get out, to ooze out, to come out in lumps. She feels the onset of nausea. Eyes closed against it, against the thudding, she hopes that by the time she dares open them again, Alex will have picked another conversation tack. Make it a light one, please. An entertaining one, Tamara hopes.

But she is the one who says, "It kind of kills the thing, doesn't it … this living with your lover."

"It's been known to," Alex replies softly.

Through half-open eyes, Tamara watches Alex spread her hands and shrug, as the French do, to suggest helplessness in the face of Destiny.

"Anyway, Emilie said she felt a little better by the time she hung up last night. So…" Trying to engage Tamara in an easy-glide topic she asks, "How are the two of you coming along after so many months of *serious* love?"

"Hey," Tamara grins without moving her head. "It's all good with me and Em."

Something in her tone makes Alex ask, "Yes, but?"

"Oh, it's just…"

"It's just what?" Alex asks, leaning forward.

"Uh, it's just that … Look, Al, don't do the intense thing again. Please. Not today."

"I'm not intense about anything, Tam. It's just me … being me."

"Look, I can try and fill you in … a little … but only if you promise to ease off."

"I promise, Tam. I'll try and be *less* me. I'll just listen and think … and I won't say much. Is that – Don't you go nodding now. Just blink. Is that OK?"

"Yes. The thing about her is … well … she's into the, you know, the holding back thing in a major way."

"The holding back thing?" Alex peers into Tamara's face.

"Goes back to the first night after we … we made love. When I left her place … afterwards. She said that I needn't call her the next day." A flutter of incomprehension registers on Alex's brow. "She said that she'd call *me* … when she was ready to." Tamara looks away.

"Oh, that!" Alex relaxes into the chair that refuses to adapt to the contours of her back. She knows she is less intense when she leans back but how to lean back into a hard, straight-backed chair?

"Uh … well, yes. She wanted to control our thing her way … like way back then already. Like, to not get attached and so on."

"Very commendable of her, really." Alex says, careful to avoid any particular tone. "Sounds ideal for someone like you."

"Come off it, Alex. I was twenty-three when you and I met. I'm twenty-eight now."

"Almost twenty-nine if I'm right."

"Right, almost twenty-nine and twenty-nine's a lot closer to thirty than to twenty."

"Absolutely."

"So, that's my point," Tamara's tone is decisive but her eyes focus on the edge of the white sheet where it lies against her hips. When she looks up, to Alex's surprise, her eyes are misty. "Uh … It's not so clear cut," Tamara begins again, slowly rearranging her legs under the sheet. "There's *no* problem, not as such. It's just that I'd like her to let go and … open up. You know, just let go."

"Look, Tam. We have been over that terrain before, you and I. Nothing new under the sun, girl. Remember when you came back from Europe? You thought *we* could just … start over. Well … no. No, we couldn't. Remember why *I* thought we couldn't?"

"Yeah, I know. The young and unreliable bit."

"Yes, as you say, but only the 'young' bit." Alex's long fingers draw rabbit ears in the air. "The 'unreliable' bit," she goes on, "is incidental to the 'young' bit. But you are older now … *almost* twenty-nine. But so are we, Emilie and I … older. I was … uh … what, about thirty-six by the time you left?"

Close enough. Tamara nods. Alex was thirty-five-and-a-half.

"The age difference is, if anything, even more palpable now. You, my little one will always be on the *young* side, on the *wrong* side of the age gap." Alex's hand flies through the short silver bristles of her hair. "You see, Tam, *that much* younger, for women like Emilie and for me, it doesn't just mean fun and funky to be with, it implies that you have different needs and, ultimately, plans that are different from our own. Such *is* the nature of the beast." She leans forward to reach Tamara's hand and keeps it in hers. "Look at it this way. There's about a seventeen-year age gap between the two of you, right?" Tamara nods.

"There is," Tamara admits grudgingly. "She doesn't want to *invest* and get hurt, like when I left and you …If I leave … "

"That's right. She rightly assumes you are not going to hang around forever." Alex argues, turning on the accent in another attempt to make Tamara smile. "She ain't no dumb bunny, that gal of yours, but she does want to *enjoy you* … for now. So, you should let her do whatever it is she needs to do." Her dark eyes hold Tamara's in a no-squirming-allowed stare. "I really don't think you are in a position to ask for more, Tam. Hey, who picks up these older women for you, anyway?"

"OK, dump on me." Tamara understands that Emilie should do what she can to afford herself an emotional neutral zone of sorts. But that's what hurts. For Tamara, neutral zones are dead zones. Zones where nothing happens. She wants Emilie fully involved, fully engaged, on full throttle with her. "Look, I absolutley … uh … She makes me hum, Al … as in like, totally! So it's not like I'm about to pack up and … go anywhere. Not next month. Not even in the next three. Not like anytime in the near future."

"'Not any time in the *near* future.' Tam, Darling, hear yourself, will you?" Alex lays Tamara's hand flat on the sheet to lean back into the chair. "*Months* from now or *two years* from now, Tam, for Emilie, it'll only amount to yet another … false start."

"So, OK … but cut me some slack. It's not like there are … ever any … uh, any … guarantees. Like, not even with women of your own age, right?" Tamara feels her brain again. She feels it pressing itself, harder and harder against the walls of her skull. She has to close her eyes and just be still, if only for a few seconds.

"True, no guarantees. Ever." Alex's eyebrows get knotted in a thinking frown. "And it is never painless, Tam. It is never neutral. A failure *is* always a failure."

"And? Like, why is a failure with a younger woman like such a big deal? I mean, a *bigger* deal?"

"Well … I don't know how to put it without falling into the ageism complex. I'll just say ... Off the cuff … I'll just say … Ok, it goes something like this: getting started with a partner of a compatible age, at any age, is like attempting to climb up to the top of a tower. Yes, there are all the risks that we already know about, whatever the age we are at the time of the climb." Again, Alex runs her hand through her hair, a habit she picked up many years ago, though the reason she had then to do it is no longer there. "Now, going for the same height, without that relative compatibility of age, is like taking a greater … uh, a greater emotional risk. It is like … yes, in a way it's like choosing to not use the safety net. Or whatever it is climbers use to keep reasonably safe, even when they lose their … their grip." Tamara remains silent so Alex adds one more little thought on the topic. "And of course when one teams up with a younger partner, there's also the risk, a strong possibility, that the young offsider will complete the climb the fastest and want to move on, leaving the older climber dangling. Anyway, what is in it for you?" Alex can be relentless. "Besides the fact that she makes you hum."

"What about you?" Tamara is not relentless, but she can try and toss the ball back. "Because of what, like the odds in favour of a well-balanced climb?"

"Well, your question is a bit back to front. And your tense is misleading. I *fancied* her, past tense, Tam, because she ... Let's just say that she grew on me. We had quite a few post-movie conversations, she and I, and when she came over to my place for dinner, that one time, we ended up talking till 2 a.m. Not at all about us, though."

It was after *that* dinner that Tamara had guessed Alex's interest in Emilie. Alex had cooked a very exotic seafood dish that Tamara had found, the next day, half-eaten in the fridge. Alex hasn't cooked anything *that* elaborate for anyone in a long time, had been Tamara's thought at the time. Busted by the Ginger Snapper.

"She can be very charming," Alex adds.

"I know. That's one of the things she's got in common with you. So, for you to get on with her, there'd have to be like so many odds stacked in your favour, right?"

Alex brushes her fingertips through the bristle above her temple. "Well, on the one hand, there are never enough odds stacked the ... the right way. And on the other," she continues, no longer looking at Tamara, "I would not have wanted the thing to be too predictable a success either. But for once, for me, I would have said that, yes, there would have been enough *good* odds in our favour. Certainly enough to get *me* climbing that tower."

"So, she ... It's like she chose to go against *good* odds," Tamara asks, feeling suddenly terribly weary.

Alex lets the comment go by.

"I mean ... I'm glad she did ... but why didn't she just choose you?"

"Oh, girl!" Alex is not smiling. "You do need to grow up. Just think about that one all on your own. Please."

A momentary silence settles between them. Tamara has plucked the little pink bear from where it had been sitting all along and considers it from its new position on her stomach. Slowly she rubs the little pink forehead with her thumb. Concerned, tiny, shiny, licorice-black button-eyes that match a tiny, shiny, button snout look back at her.

"Right, OK, I turn her on. She likes my *young* body." Tamara breaks in, tugging at the little bear's earringed ear.

"For sure," Alex rejoins sticking out her bottom lip. "Don't hang up your skates just yet. Keep on doing your laps at the uni pool. But, Tam…" she adds, with a full earnest smile, "the sexual appeal thing, that's only part of it, I'm sure."

Tamara feels the tug of annoyance. It goes beyond the pressure that is building up inside her head, again, as relentlessly as the tide creeps up on the foreshore.

"Oh, come on. Give us a smile, will you? I told her you were wonderful, that you had an honest personality and that you had matured a lot during the three years you had been away and – "

"So, what do I do, O Wise Woman of the suburbs?"

"Why don't you just try the one-day-at-a-time thing?"

Tamara glowers at her. "Alex," she asks tightly, "would you ever … let yourself go, uh … like you've just said? Doing the one day at a time with another young-*er* dyke?"

Alex shakes her head vigourously. Tamara watches her, desperate for that same freedom of movement. She suddenly feels totally wrung out.

*****

THREE

"Tu peux m' toucher. J' suis pas faite en sucre, tu sais." Marielle had used the colloquial expression to remind the tall Australian that she wasn't made out of *sugar*, that Tamara could in fact touch her, that Tamara could make love to her, properly. And Tamara had touched Marielle. She touched Marielle but only with her fingertips. She touched her with the same tentative touch that she had touched her very first woman-lover.

Marielle moved closer. Leaning against Tamara, she reached for her hand and lay it flat against the woollen cables of her red cardigan, flat over her stomach. And she moved Tamara's hand over the thin cotton of her skirt.

Tamara breathed in deeply as slowly, silently, Marielle guided Tamara's hand on a reconnaissance of her body, guiding her hand over her sex and across to her thigh. When Marielle felt it grow more confident, she let go of Tamara's hand. She freed it to explore on its own and, leaning more comfortably against Tamara's thighs, against her stomach, against her breasts, she closed her eyes. Marielle felt the thudding heartbeat and she grinned because it matched her own. Then, she turned to face Tamara.

A heart-stopping moment earlier, there had been a knock on Tamara's hotel door. She had answered it, quite surprised to find Marielle standing on the doormat.

"Eh ben quoi, La Grande, tu m'invites pas à entrer," Marielle had chided. And so what, you're not going to let me in?

*"Uh … Entre, Marielle. S*ure, I mean, come in. I … uh … I wasn't, like, expecting you. I didn't even know you were … But, hey, come in, yes."

Seeming calm, Marielle had stepped inside the backpacker's little room under the eaves. She had closed the door behind her and, without turning away from the tall backpacker, she had locked it with the key that was already in the keyhole.

She had reached for Tamara's hands and, eyes closed, she lay them flat on either side of her face. Tamara stepped closer, right against her. Bodies touching, they swayed together in a tight hug. Marielle had been the first to pull away but only enough to reach for Tamara's mouth.

The red eye blinks at Tamara. From across the aisle, it insists. It wants to make contact with her consciousness but, from where Tamara's thoughts have retreated, she is only aware of Marielle's desire, only aware that of all the things in the world Marielle might have wanted at that specific moment, it was the feel of *her* tongue between her lips. It was the silky warmth of their tongues and lips blending and melting together.

Marielle reaches behind Tamara and lets her hand roam over her jeans. She spreads that hand over Tamara's back pocket, letting her fingers drift over the thick double seam and over the round curve of the backpacker's buttocks.

Tamara's silent response is to press her hips forward and wedge Marielle against the door she has just locked. Sex ignited, Marielle's heart lurches. She reaches under Tamara's sweater to touch the skin Tamara knows she remembers from the previous night. The intensity and focus that emanate from Marielle cleary indicates to *her* that something is different. That Marielle has decided something – she wants to discover the feel of *her* skin and the parts of *her* Marielle hadn't touched, not properly, the night before.

Marielle caresses Tamara's back, her wide swimmer's shoulders, and the smooth skin that covers her ribs. Her mouth melts and dissolves under Tamara's while all of Tamara melts and dissolves around a maddening, blinding ache she has not prepared for. That urge, that ache, go far beyond the dream-like trance retained from the night before.

And Tamara, oblivious to the cannula pressed hard against her cheek, is on the road to St Emilion, a ghost at Marielle's side. She struggles inside Marielle's mind as she struggles under the white shroud that keeps her too tightly bound to the mattress of the hospital bed, too tightly bound to slithering thoughts, and she sighs heavily as Marielle sighs, knowing she has reached the quicksand moment of her introspection. And Marielle knows the truth. Marielle knows she's never touched anyone *so well* as she's touched Tamara, not even Christian. By *so well* she means so slowly, that other night, last night.

But Tamara's not a *woman*, Marielle reasons from inside the swirl of thoughts that melt and disappear only to swell again from deep inside Tamara's slippery dream. Tamara is ...

As Marielle holds Tamara's face in between her hands, as her thumb rubs the little silver bolt that pierces her eyebrow, as she looks into her eyes, Tamara senses that Marielle is unguarded against the searing ache that she knows is spreading upwards from her belly. And when Marielle slides an urgent hand under the demim waistband of her jeans, she is not surprised.

A sunken mooring, the hospital bed anchors Tamara's body but not her thoughts. The red beacon blinks silently in the distance but means nothing to her. And yet, she becomes aware of how Marielle feels *her* breath against her ear, *her* hand under the calico skirt.

Marielle knows exactly how close to touching the elastic of her crotch the backpacker's fingers are. Tantalisingly close. Half a millimetre away, half a millimetre away from touching her arousal. And so Marielle hooks an index finger around the first rivet of Tamara's fly and snaps open the remaining three. And, as she does, Tamara just knows that for the first time ever, Marielle is not primarily accommodating someone else's need.

When Marielle undoes Christian's fly, when his need bulges, so big, so hard against her, she touches it mostly to give *him* the relief he needs. When her hand cups Tamara's sex to know her wetness, she does so out of a need to relieve her own need. Her need is to feel it. Her need is to explore the satiny warmth of Tamara's sex. Her need is to know how it feels when Tamara makes love to a woman.

A few moments later, Tamara covers Marielle with her long body. But she covers her lightly, carrying some of her weight on her elbows and knees and toes. Marielle reaches for Tamara's mouth at the same time as she presses the flat of her hand against her lower back, silently asking Tamara to give up bearing her weight.

Marielle moans softly as Tamara drops more heavily against her, as Tamara's tongue caresses the corner of her eye, the underside of her lip, as Tamara's mouth blends and melts over hers. Marielle moans again, stretching her lithe body under Tamara's hands, under the inquisitive caress of her tongue. And Tamara feels how good Marielle feels. So good naked. So good in her arms. So good under *her*.

Marielle's body pressed against Tamara's, her ankles hook over the backpacker's calves. No heaving, no thrashing, and yet so much, so much. So much, she loses track of her body's boundaries. Marielle melts and blends, becoming one with her lover. She reaches for Tamara's mouth and gently presses her hand against the back of her head. Tamara responds with a more enveloping kiss, a probing, dissolving kiss, one that obliterates all around them, the little hotel room, and the cacophony of sounds outside.

In the medieval village of St Emilion, the revellers were celebrating the end of the harvest. Every vineyard's *récolte* was safe. Everyone's harvest was safe from rain, safe from worms, safe from rot and drought and bugs and lingering acidity. Inside the *pressoirs*, the harvest was safe at the press. As far as the eye could see, from *la Place du Marché* to *la Tour du Roy* et *la Chapelle de la Trinité* revellers milled, grouped, dissolved, and marched, and chanted. *L'hôtel de la Feuille* where Tamara had booked a little room on her way up the north side of the Dordogne River happened to be in the hub of that unbridled mirth.

Later, much later that night, Marielle and Tamara went out into the narrow cobbled streets. They had blended into the throngs that danced, whistled and drank, jostling their way to nowhere in particular. They had shared a plate of *andouilles frites* and they had drunk wine, though not from the Sainte-Thérèse vineyard.

Once bottled, the limited Sainte-Thérèse *cuvée* would not be found in simple bottle-shops, not at the Nicolas outlets and not in supermarkets. Only the ones in the know, the ones with the nose, would know where to avail themselves of a dozen bottles, if they were quick enough and lucky.

Marielle, though, had not come to Tamara's room empty-handed. She had clumsily wiped ten-year-old dust off a bottle hastily plucked from her family's cellar.

'*Pas pratique,*' she had said apologising for the extra weight Tamara would carry in her pack. Lowering her eyes, she added, 'For later. For when you have an occasion special ... *trés spéciale* to celebrate. You think of me then.'

Tamara ran her hand over the still dusty label.

'*Domaine Sainte-Thérèse*', she read out loud.

The classic ink drawing showed the nine-hundred-year-old farmhouse, its great barn, and off to the left the knee-high wishing well into which Tamara had almost toppled the very first time she had walked into the courtyard. She had been following the voice of a young woman talking to a dog.

And then, on the dusty label there was the vineyard. Row upon row upon row of the vines Tamara had helped harvest. Two thousand bunches a day to Marielle's three thousand. Tamara felt her, throat tighten. Her eyes tingled. So she had brought in Marielle, close, close to her and they hugged, Marielle's head on Tamara's shoulder, Tamara's cheek against Marielle's lemon and wood-fire scented hair, the dusty bottle wedged in between.

From their seat at the sidewalk café, Marielle and Tamara watched the sea of faces flood by.

Marielle said, *"Tu sais,* ... what you see in the tower, that night with my father ... it does not 'urt so much, you know. It does not 'urt my body. Many time before, when I was young I want to *emmasculer* ... *Euh,* to cut ... cut out ... to cut off his ... *Castrer*, like for a bull." Tamara watched Marielle become more frustrated by her lack of English but she understood the slicing off movement Marielle made with her hand. "But 'e is my father. And if I say a thing, my mother, she will die from ... *chagrin.* She will cry so much. For me. For 'erself but for 'im also. What she did wrong, she will ask, if I say something to 'er." Marielle sighed and her large brown eyes fluttered briefly over Tamara's face. "Now, it is too late. Many years too late. You understand? I am not a child anymore." Tamara nodded and Marielle averted her eyes again. Almost as if she had sensed the question burning on Tamara's lips she began again, this time with her eyes on the Formica tabletop. "Why I go there? You want to know why I go there with Fleurette? Why I do not stay in my room? Why I do not tell Christian? Or the Police? 'Ow I can explain to you?" Marielle sighed and dropped her hands to her sides. Trying to explain was too huge a task. And yet, she tried a little more. "One day, many years ago, I take *fil barbelé*, you know ... *euh,* wire for fence. With points?

"Barbed-wire?"

"Yes, I think that. Before the day of the moon. I take this to the cellar. I 'ide it. And after ... when 'e finish with me, I jump and I hit 'im on the face with the ... "

"Barbed-wire."

"Yes, with that. He bleed a lot. I 'urt 'im a lot, very bad. 'Is eye was very bad way – " Again Marielle flapped her hands in frustration. She looked up and her eyes stayed on Tamara's. "And *tu sais,* he say nothing. He did not shout, 'e did not get ... *en colère*, you know, he did nothing. Not violent. Slowly he just walk away. I stay in the cellar and I cry again. And, Tamara, *la rousse,* you know, the red moon, it does not come every month. It is not so usual in Bordeaux *région*. I am sure it is why he choose only the nights of the *rousse*. It is one way for him to control 'is ... " Again Marielle shook her head. Tamara knew she wanted to access words that would enable her to talk about release and perversion but she also wanted words to talk about respect and a rock-bottom, basic sort of love from a daughter to her father, no matter what. She wanted words, more English words. She wanted them to help Tamara understand why, for her, it was not so bad.

"Maybe the red moon, it comes two times every year. I 'ate 'im. I 'ate what 'e does but it does not 'urt me. It does not 'urt me in my body. You understand?"

"Yes, I understand," Tamara said wanting to say Yes, I understand he's ashamed of what he does to you. I understand that you think that what he does does not physically hurt you. But what about you? What about your soul? she wanted to shout. But again, if that conversation was to be meaningful, it would require a vocabulary that she knew neither had in the other's language. So she simply returned Marielle to her initial track.

"*Pourquoi? W*hy even go there with Fleurette?"

"*Pourquoi?*" Marielle shook her head. "Yes, I ask me that too. Many time. I remember the first time well. He took me by the 'and and we walk to the *tour* … to the tower. Me and 'im. Not with Fleurette but with another cow. When I was little, I loved my father … much. Very much. Now, I don't love 'im but I am proud of 'im with the vine and with the Sainte-Thérèse wine, too. *Tu vois,* Tamara, 'e has fifty-three years. He work in the vineyard always but he is the boss of Sainte-Thérèse for thirty-two years, after *grand-père* Dufour died. He has *succés* with the wine. Everybody says 'e is very good, very clever with these things. And 'e is proud man. And 'e hurt too. A lot. *That,* I know." Marielle reached for Tamara's hand. "You know why 'e not come to dinner? Why 'e never comes? Why he does not go to village or see people when he not working? You know why not?" she asked again. Tamara shook her head. "He don't see people because *il a honte. Il s'isole comme un chien malade.*" Marielle realised she was speaking far too fast for Tamara to understand. But, her hand tight over Tamara's, she continued with words bursting to come through. "Alone always because he 'urts inside 'imself. Me too, I 'urt inside myself. *Cette chose, tu vois,* he cannot control … that thing … what he does to me. *Alors, tu vois,* I go there with Fleurette, to the tower. *Quand la lune est rousse, je sais qu'il m'attend. Je sais qu' il se déteste.*"

Marielle swept back the shorter strands of hair that had fallen over her eyes, and she stopped, flushed, breathless. She rubbed her pale forehead with her free hand and grimaced. All these thoughts knotted up and locked inside her for so long were stirring like snakes in a pit. She was not teary, her voice was firm. She looked in control of her emotions. She had had, after all, many years during which to work out what was what, for her. But when Marielle's eyes met Tamara's again, when she saw the frown of concern and the palpable incomprehension that floated over the green-green of her new lover's eyes, she felt very vulnerable, very raw. She picked up the tumbler and sipped the wine. Then, she looked at Tamara's hand inside her own and gently she pulled hers away. Leaning back against the chair, she started again in fractured English.

In essence, her father carried so much guilt tied to the depraved need he had of his daughter that he had excluded himself from every interaction that was not work-related, which explained why Tamara had never seen him at dinnertime. It explained, too, why he didn't join Madame Dufour in socialising with visiting neighbours and why he never, ever, left Sainte-Thérèse. His guilt had turned him into a recluse. Like a sick dog, Marielle had said. And she had explained how she was proud of him in regards to what he had achieved and consolidated during the past thirty-two years, since he had inherited the vineyard and all attached responsibilities from his own father. And how aside from that thing he had about her, he was a good man.

She hated that need of his, but more than anything, now that she was grown-up she felt sorry for him. And so when she knows, as every local does, that the full moon will be *rousse*, she takes Fleurette to *la tour* because she knows he will be waiting, sitting on a pile of rubble, his face hidden inside his hands. He will do what he has to do and then, he will whisper to her, gruffly begging her for forgiveness. And he will leave and she will stay there, empty, dirty, soiled, but unable to truly hate him. She didn't hate him enough to truly wish him dead.

"Why only when the moon is *rousse?*"

"Ah … yes. 'E said, many year ago, the first time, 'Not many moon like this one, Marielle.' Later, much later, I understood it is the way he control 'imself. Waiting for the red moon. Like the…alcoholic… wait all year for one drink, one drink on *Nouvel An* –"

"New Year's Eve?"

"Yes, that, after Christmas, yes. New Year. And another drink on birthday, maybe. And so I do not go so many times to the tower."

What a gentleman! Tamara almost spit out sarcastically. Instead, out of consideration for Marielle, she remained silent.

They mingled, shimmied and sashayed amongst the revellers a while longer but, that evening never having been meant to turn into a truncated therapy session, certainly not past the moment Marielle turned the little black key inside the lock of room 8, they returned to the little room under the eaves. What they both wanted most of all, as the night wore on, was to escape, to forget and to go back to the room tucked away, above the *rue du Marché* and taste each other again and again and again and make love again.

The red eye across the aisle woke Tamara up. Was it really the red eye across the aisle or was it the snoring that resonated from the other side of the white curtains? Was it the snoring or the need to have a pee? It might have been any or all of the above but when Fiona checked up on Tamara again, after the snores had momentarily subsided next door, after she had kept her eyes shut against the intrusion of the red eye across the aisle, Tamara hadn't gone back to sleep.

Her head pain just sat there, lurking right under the skull. Like a child in need of attention, it prodded and pierced and lanced and flashed and thudded and seared but it did not rip out in searching fingers of brain-eviscerating pain. Though contained, the pain created a throbbing haze all around Tamara's brain.

"You'll be fightin' fit before you know it, Tamara," Fiona-the-nurse had said while she prepared the medication. "A little morphine…just enough to make you more comfortable."

Tamara had only groaned.

"It is good you do not belong to the earth," Marielle said. She was tucked against Tamara's breasts, against her hips and thighs. "If your *parents* were *vignerons,* yes?" she asked to see if Tamara was following her mind-thoughts. "And if you loved the vineyard like I love it … All would be … *euh* … It would be very *compliqué* for us, *yes?"*

"Yes, more complicated," Tamara nods. "But it's already a bit complicated as it is." Simplifying her thought, she checks, "Now … it's not complicated?"

"No, not so complicated because you do not belong to the life of simple persons, like me. You belong to your other life. Not to the simple life of *euh … paysans,* peasants, yes?"

"Yes, peasants."

"So, it is not complicated to see that I do not belong with you. Not complicated, Tamara. Just sad. I like you very much. Very, *very* much," she added with much childlike enthusiasm as she turned inside Tamara's arms to face her. "But is it better like this. You 'ave a train to take at nine hours, yes?"

"Yes, I do. At nine thirty-four."

"So, Tamara Toonsend, I stay … 'ere with you *jusqu' à* … until it is time for your train. After … well …after that I … " Marielle's voice faltered.

Tamara looked into her young lover's eyes. Large as they were, they seemed larger again, magnified by brimming tears, tears that Marielle was trying to hold back. Tamara kissed those eyes. She kissed, too, the nascent shadows under those eyes. She wiped the tears with her lips and buried her face into Marielle's lemon-scented chestnut hair, holding her more tightly against her.

Tamara rolls over. The flexible tubing tied to the cannula in the back of her hand tugs at her. She frowns at it. The niggly feel of that needle embedded in her vein irritates her. What if I yanked it off? No one ever does, not in films, they don't, she argues drowsily. Lazily, she opens one eye, then the other, aware she has been dreaming again. So much time sleeping, it's not funny. No energy. Just sleep. Sleep and dream weird dreams. Is that the way it's gonna be from now on? she thinks dully.

What if something's really wrong with my head and they don't know yet? Maybe they do know. Maybe I'm the last one to find out. Would they have told Emi? What if that shadow thing Doctor Mac said wasn't there … What if it *was* there?

Tamara is wide-awake now. She can tell she's wide awake because of the soft white blur of the curtains that delineate her cubicle and because of the soft beeps coming out of the machine behind her. How long had it been it since she had thought of Marielle, seriously thought of her?

There had been a period of days, of months even, when Tamara's thoughts always drifted back to Marielle, to Marielle at Sainte-Thérèse, to Marielle warm and soft, tucked inside her arms. Then had come a time when thoughts of Marielle had become more spaced out, like lampposts on a road. As the vehicle slows down, they still glide past but the gap in between lengthens and lengthens some more. Then comes the moment when the car has to stop. The lampposts just don't glide. Not anymore, they don't, not once momentum's lost.

Why am I thinking about her now? Tamara wants to know. Why am I dreaming of Black Night? Of little Jamie Townsend?

All tied up. Yes, *Jamie* had been all tied up but *all* Tamara's dreams and fragmented thoughts, she knows, are also all tied up together. Falling in love with the vigneron's daughter, impulsively as one does when one is young and needs to be impulsive, had left her with a thought, one more lasting, more enduring than any thought of lust could ever be. A thought that had surfaced much later. Later like a bubble breaks the water's skin away from the point of release.

Tamara had left Brisbane for a backpack tour of Europe because she had been at a loose end. By the time she had turned twenty-one, Tamara had enjoyed reading, analysing and writing her way through a B.A in Women Studies but then she had begun drifting. For lack of any clear direction, she had let inconsequential wind whirls push her along into the field of social work and she got herself a degree in that area. She had become unimpressed and dispirited by the amount of paper-shuffling inherent in the responsibility. Frustrated, too, by other repetitive tasks that revolved around women who needed help to move away from the abusive male in their life, Tamara had become a little guilty that she lacked the necessary empathy these women were entitled to from the social worker in charge of their case. And she felt irritated by these women who had, after all, chosen their aggressor; all were victims at the hands of husband, partner or boyfriend. She was irritated by these women who had chosen, not only a male for lover but a twisted one to boot. Two faults against them, she'd say, licking her index finger to better make two crosses on an invisible scoreboard.

Slowly, imperceptibly, particularly during the year that had preceded her trip overseas, she had come to resent being entrenched in a typically female, caring and therefore dead-end, poorly-paid occupation that could never become a career. But she met Marielle, and Marielle's story had moved Tamara to the point where she realised that there had to be hosts of children, hosts of women, who had been as abused as Marielle was. Much more, differently abused than Marielle had ever been. And, at some time during the weeks of meandering back and forth across France, Tamara had made up her mind that, when she returned to Brisbane, she would dedicate her daytime hours to helping the survivors of child abuse.

A worthwhile occupation, she had thought somewhat simplistically. As rewarding as the entire concept was fathomlesslly, repulsively distressing. All the same, she had upgraded her personal file so as to qualify for Child Abuse on-the-job-training. All went well until the day she came across some damning statistics.

She had found a journal article that focused on the incredibly high rate of suicide amongst victims of child abuse, a rate much greater than that representative of any other group of victims. Her heartbeat had picked up as, flipping pages almost feverishly, she had read on. The age at which the victim may opt out of living with guilt and shame varied from case to case. Whether they decided to end their lives while in the midst of an abusive episode or years later seemed to vary according to the peaks and troughs and spikes of the same guilt and shame.

Tamara thought of Marielle's eyes. Her eyes as she had seen them, back on the trail that night of the red moon. Marielle's eyes had been unblinking. Unseeing. And then a big tear had rolled down the imperturbable mask that had overtaken her face. Silently, Marielle had nudged Fleurette and silently, except for the scraping of Fleurette's hooves on the rocky trail, Marielle had disappeared below the orange disk of the full moon. Tamara had never forgotten the look of suspended death, deep within Marielle's eyes. And later, though she had followed sobs she had assumed to be those of sexual release, she had seen that same look, again in Marielle's eyes. Marielle had looked up while her father pounded and rubbed against her buttocks, against the pale blue cloth of her knickers. She had looked up then, unseeing, but straight into Tamara's eyes.

Much, much later, Tamara had remembered where she had seen eyes like Marielle's. She had seen them on a little boy who had been barely older that herself. That little boy had climbed the difficult rope ladder all the way to the crow's-nest. Once there, he sat down, tucking himself in a little ball. He had pulled out a length of black twine from the back pocket of his red shorts. He tied the black twine around his ankles the tip of his tongue between his teeth, so great was his concentration as he tied the black twine into a complicated knot. He had found the bit of twine in a corner of his uncle's workbench below deck. Tamara's father was a great handyman.

"He's got to be, doesn't he, good with his hands," little Tamara used to remind Jamie, "to always be fixing things on our Night."

Be that as it may, Jamie had been pleased to find the twine was long enough to accommodate a Bowline Bend, a knot that, his Uncle Thomas had explained, was normally made with two interlocking bowlines. Tamara remembers how Jamie had taken a sudden liking to that particular knot. He liked the way the two loops made the knot look like twin links in a bracelet.

Jamie had stood upright and had unlatched the side panel of the crow's-nest. He had made sure the knot was tied properly, that it would not come undone. His Uncle Thomas had taught him all about essential knots. Learning to tie his shoelaces had been essential too, at one time. So Uncle Thomas had taught him that knot. The Bowline Bend tight around his bony ankles had become another essential knot. And Jamie had inched his toes towards the edge of the suspended platform. Like an Olympic diver, he measured the distance from the tip of his extended arms to the deep blue waves below.

"Papa says you should not …" his little cousin had shouted at him. But because of the wind in his ears he hadn't heard everything Tamara was saying. But he could see her wave at him from the water below. Jamie had closed his eyes because at that height, the sway of the boat was making him dizzy. He shut his eyes tightly against what had just flashed behind them. He inched both big toes to the edge of the platform so he could feel them stick out. Like the high board diver, he had filled his lungs with air.

"I'll beat you to that rock … " his little cousin had shouted from the water below. And he had pushed his weight down against the wooden platform. The sharp edge bites into the tender soles of his feet and years later, Tamara still hopes that the bite of the plank had been the last thing Jamie felt. A second later, the side of his head cracked against the gunwale below. He was already dead when his body went under the waves only inches from where seven-year old Tamara was treading water.

The train that was going to take her from St Emilion to Bordeaux on time for her connection to St Malo, Brittany, was one that stopped at each little station along the way with the regularity of a dog that had to sniff every tree-trunk he came to.

The train started and the train stopped and the train started again. People shuffled in past the door to her compartment, others shuffled out past the door to her compartment. Someone sat diagonally across from her. Someone else got up and left. Tamara was looking at the still landscape through smudged glass. She was looking at the sliding landscape through the same smudged glass. And the train stopped again. And she became vaguely aware of two men talking in the corridor. She looked away from the smudged scenery and looked at them distractedly, until she heard the one in a neatly pressed soldier's uniform tell the other how he had had to drive out of his way to race to whatever station this was, because the Cahors line on which he had had a pre-booked seat had been temporarily shut down.

"Encore les grèves?" the other man smirked. "Ils en veulent toujours un peu plus pour en faire un peu moins, hein?" He rocked on his heels in a self-confident gesture, visibly pleased with his quick understanding of things. He had said, 'What, more strikes? They're always after a bit more in exchange for a bit less, aren't they?'

"Ah non, not this time," the young man replied flatly, and he repeated what had been told to him by the man at the ticket counter. "… jeune fille… du pont Jaurès… Ah oui, du pays." She watched him nod to the other man's question. "Une fille de la région."

These words connected slowly with Tamara's ear. Then she caught sound of another word she immediately recognised: *suicidée.* 'A young girl … from the area,' the man had just said, and '*suicidée.*'

As soon as her brain had connected the familiar words together, her mouth opened in the shape of a silent O, then she felt blood drain away from her extremities. Her heart thumped madly inside her chest. Her right hand flew to her face, index finger on the tip of her nose, thumb against her cheek, the palm of her hand covering her mouth, she blinked and swallowed. She hurriedly looked away from the men, made herself breathe and looked past the slow moving countryside on the other side of the smudged glass. She made to sit up but couldn't. She made herself breathe again. No, it couldn't be Marielle! Then, with two fingertips of her left hand rubbing over the little silver bolt on her eyebrow she thought, No. It *wasn't* Marielle.

The unfortunate 'local girl' the man had mentioned, the one who had jumped off a bridge and had landed on the railroad track seconds ahead of the inbound train … that girl was not Marielle. Marielle was far too attached to her land, to the vineyard, to leave it whether it be that way or any other way. Besides, Marielle had been very clear. She had been clear about having a battle to wage.

"Non, Tamara," she had said, once again using Tamara's name instead of the nickname she had given her, *La Grande,* from the moment she had offered her room and board in exchange for seven hours of daily work in her parents' vineyard. *"Non,"* she had repeated, teasing Tamara's spiky hair. *"Elle est pas pour toi cette bataille. C'est la mienne toute à moi."* That battle's all mine. It's not yours to fight on my behalf.

Tamara, finally dressed, train ticket sticking out of her back pocket, red backpack propped by the door, had been watching Marielle fluff up her hair with her hands and readjust the waistband of her skirt around her whippet waist. Tamara had suggested, as she watched, that she could hang around either as a lover, as a concerned lover, or simply as a friend, as a concerned friend, while Marielle helped herself organise a different approach to her life at Sainte-Thérèse.

"St Malo, Brittany, it can wait," she had said. "What's over there, anyway? Fish and clams? *Poissons,* yes? Nothing to harvest, right? I can always get there later. All I have to do to exchange my train tick – "

Marielle had to stretch on tiptoes as she kissed Tamara gently on the lips. She had rubbed her thumb, one last time, over the little silver bolt that pierced the outer edge of Tamara's eyebrow and she had left the room shutting the door quietly behind her. And Tamara had jammed her hands deep inside the front pockets of her jeans. If she hadn't she would have reached for the doorknob and would have caught up with Marielle in a few long strides. She would have turned her around by the shoulders. She would have looked into the depth of her brown eyes, but only briefly, for she would have found her mouth. And Marielle, through her tears would have whispered, "Tamara, stay with me. I am afraid now. I was not afraid before."

Instead Tamara had flopped back on the bed behind her, teeth clenched, hand over her thumping heart, counting to one hundred, giving Marielle, Marielle-straight-woman-engaged-to-be-married, the time to decide for herself what *she* thought was best for her.

Anyway, she had thought, no one has ever won a battle, any battle, from under a train. Marielle, with all her healthy, earthy, no-nonsense logic would have known that for sure.

"Fiona, would you know if the police have been around to talk to her?"

"Oh, yes, they've been. The girls were talking about it over morning tea. We're all very … well … we're all a bit concerned by what's happened to her. She's such a nice one, you know." Fiona felt a slow blush creep up her cheeks.

So that's the famous Emilie, had been her first thought earlier that morning when she had heard a woman introduce herself to the Sister-in-Charge as soon as the first visitors had begun drifting in.

Tamara rubs her eyebrow where, in her dream, she still wears a little silver bolt. No, one has ever won a battle, *any battle,* from under a train, she thinks from inside her hospital bed.

"Good morning," the woman had said to the Sister-in-Charge. "I'm Emilie Anderson. I've been told Tamara Townsend has been transferred to this floor. Last ni – "

"One moment, please," had replied the Sister as she picked up the phone that had begun ringing almost as Emilie had stepped off the lift.

And Fiona, who had been sorting out bandages and syringes on a nearby trolley, had turned to have another look at the woman in the neat bottle-green shirt and light linen trousers. And she looked again. What had she expected? A glamour puss from the cover of *Girl* magazine or a prickly, spiky, studded dyke from hell? She wasn't sure. In any case, the woman at the desk was neither. And neither was she anywhere near Tamara's age. Old enough to be her mother, Fiona had almost gasped. Well, not quite, she had reassessed as she had prolonged a surreptitious observation of the woman who, fingertips drumming on the large leather bag at her side, was visibly trying to contain her impatience. A little taller than me … a little heavier than me, but blow me down if she's not well into her forties!

"People here, often you see, they're not at their best," Fiona was telling Emilie, as they stood in the ward near the foot of Tamara's bed. Fiona looked at the woman's face more closely. She considered the strained lines around her eyes and the pale cheeks. It was clear that Mrs Anderson had not had much of a good night's sleep herself.

"They don't like being here all that much, you know. What with their pain and their worries … And so, if she'd been crabby or nasty or not so nice, it'd be easier to imagine someone coming after her. These things, violence, should never happen, of course, I mean not that way, with blows and what nots. So we're all kind of wondering what could possibly have happ …"

"La Marielle n'est plus avec nous," Madame Dufour says into the phone. Tamara's breath sticks to her throat. Marielle is no longer with them.

Emilie wonders about Tamara's restlessness. She sees how the movements of her left hand travel up the IV line. Her eyes shift to the primary and secondary bags, valve and stoppers. She doesn't know what is dripping inside Tamara's vein. She wants to ask the nurse if Tamara's sleep has been that fitful all along. She wants to ask if the IV line is as long as it needs to be but instead she asks, "Did the police stay long when they came this morning?"

Emilie's voice tugs at Tamara's consciousness, but the French voice inside her head is closer. It's so close it's inside her ear where the pain is lurking. "Oh, she gave us a real fright, *si vous saviez.* All night, she disappeared, our Marielle. Even her Christian didn't know where she was. We … "

Words spoken in English have returned to the edge of Tamara's ear. "I wasn't here at the time, but I don't expect they've stayed long." Fiona is still looking surreptitiously at Emilie as if trying to get a better handle on this lesbian thing. She tries to remain casual but an embarrassing blush creeps up her neck. Fiona's eyes move away from the woman's face to dart, a little lower, to the fingers curled up around the wide leather strap of a shoulder bag. No wedding band. No rings of any sort.

Strangely, since last night, another screwed up shift, staff shortage crap, not enough sleep in between, as she came and went, as she gave Tamara her treatment, Fiona hadn't thought much about Tamara's sexuality. These things happen, she had told the girls, the other nurses, at morning tea. And everyone had had a little laugh, each camp straight and gay, careful not to rile the other.

But standing there in the familiar ward, talking to this older woman, to Tamara's lover, somehow *that* made the matter a lot more immediate and sexual than any Rec. Room banter. So much more up front and immediate. "According to Doctor Mac, there's no bruising on the brain ... "

Tamara stirs. She recognises the voice. The nurse. The nurse is talking about her. About her and through a deep puddle. She is aware of a need to stretch but her body is too loose, too far from her. Far away. Only the back of her hand is there, right there.

"She's not drinking enough. Hardly anything at ... "

Tamara had waited three days. Three days after the dreadful news she had heard on board the train. Three days during which she had struggled to better believe that calling Sainte-Thérèse would, indeed, be silly. Of course Marielle was alive.

A grimace of concentration tightens the corners of her eyes as Tamara listens, pressed against the wall, in a corner of the backpackers' hostel lobby. The grey phone is tight against her ear, the knuckles of her left hand tense around it.

"La tête dans les étoiles. Les étoiles dans les yeux qu'on dit par ici, qu'on sait pas pourquoi."

"Plus doucement, Madahme Du Fouhwr," Tamara says to the mouthpiece. More slowly, please. But she's already grasped the gist: Marielle stayed out all night, the night of the Fête des Vendanges. She had returned home with *étoiles*, with stars, in her eyes, her mother has just said.

" ... looks worse than it is. It's the cheekbone ... copped it the most. ... would've hit ... her way dow – " says the nurse's dismebodied voice.

The *thing* tugs again at Tamara's other hand. Go away! she wants to shout, not to the mouthpiece but to the cannula. She wouldn't want to be saying *that* to Madame Dufour, not at all.

" ... with the pain in her head, poor thing. Anyway the police, they had a word with Doctor Mac. Had to fetch her for them. She would've told them ... ... not in a fit state and ... much rather the police wait till the patient ... "

Tamara holds the receiver too tightly against her ear. *"Et maintenant,"* adds Madame Dufour, *"c'est son Christian qui vient nous dire que nôtre Marielle, elle s'en va faire sa vie avec lui."*

And so, Christian came to Sainte-Thérèse. Marielle, he says, has moved in with him. "It's how we do things in our country, *dans nôtre campagne.* For every young woman, there comes a time when she has to go to her man. *Elle va nous laisser un vide à moi et à son papa, ça c'est sûr.* And now that Marielle is gone," the voice goes on explaining, "Monsieur Dufour and me, we're going to feel a *grand vide,* a great emptiness. It's all so recent."

No, Tamara thinks as she emerges from her clingy torpor, no one has ever won a battle, *any* battle, from under a train. Marielle … she's OK.

A second voice penetrates deeper inside Tamara's ear. "Something tells me Blinky Bill and Snugglepot, your *friendly* coppers, are on their way up as we speak. I'm sure it was them I saw in the lobby. Straight out of The Bill."

Emilie! Tamara opens her eyes. "Hey … Em … You're here."

Emilie strides to the bed and gently places her hands on either side of her lover's pale face. She peers into the green cat eyes. Those eyes, when she peers into them, reassure her that the brink on which she stepped when she, Emilie, fell in love with such a young woman as Tamara, might actually be firm enough to keep both of them safe.

For many months, from the start of it all, from the moment *after* they had first made love, from the moment Emilie found herself overwhelmed as much by lingering desire as besieged by her grass-root insecurities, she has been questioning the wisdom of it all. That relentless introspective questioning is not tied to anything Tamara may have said or done. *It just is.* Like a little child's safety light in the darkness of the room, it glowers. It doesn't give off any light. No, not as such. It just is. Constant and permanent inside Emilie's head.

With a lover like Tamara, she knows that not even she can control what has to remain fluid. But regardless of where her questioning may have taken her on any particular day, always, always, one look into Tamara's eyes that hold no deceit and no malice and Emilie knows that all she needs to do is surrender to the Bigger Plan, to the cosmic serendipity that made them connect in the first place.

The problem, of course, is that Emilie does not really believe there is a Bigger Plan that she does not have to fabricate for herself.

She looks into Tamara's eyes. Shiny. Too shiny, still. She lets her finger trace lightly the pinkish shadows that have no business being there, so near the corner of her lover's eyes, near the bridge of her nose.

Though aware of the young nurse behind her, Emilie kisses Tamara lightly on the lips. Tamara grins back, vaguely aware that the breath trapped inside her mouth while she was asleep has gone musty.

"Uh … so … " She reaches for Emilie's hand. "What are the two of you … uh … you know … like, gasbagging about? Huh?" she asks, including Fiona with a slow sweep of her index finger.

Fiona and Emilie look at each other but it is Emilie who tells Tamara the police are on their way up to see her.

"Oh, crap," she grimaces. "I wanted … I … at least a moment on our own before … " Tamara's frown brings her eyes closer together giving her the same perplexed intensity as that of the little pink bear Emilie had left sitting on the bedside trolley. "Been waiting for you all day, you know."

That frown often makes Emilie smile but as she holds her lover's limp hand firmly in her own, her heart contracts. What she wants is to hold Tamara tightly against her, to tell her all will be fine. To tell her she's taking her home, that she'll be safe there forever. Instead, she says, "And me, I've been *thinking* about you all day, Tam. So many times during the day, I've had to stop counting. But hey," she chides, "something tells me … you've done at least one other thing besides wait for me. In fact, I'm sure you've been at it most of the day."

"Doing what a regular pussycat does best," Fiona joins in, "all curled up." And she blushes again, acutely aware of the older woman squatting at the side of the bed, holding Tamara's hand tightly between hers. Back turned, she prepares to check Tamara's blood pressure and check the oxymetre for saturations.

"Damn right. Asleep but dreaming friggin' unpleasant stuff," Tamara rejoins grumpily. The last thing she wants at the end of her first full day in hospital is a chat with the police. And yet, she's very much aware that she needs them to figure out why some sick dick took to her with a two-by-four. Besides, she's not all that much anti-cop. Only when she gets a picture of her car and licence plate in the mail along with a return envelope for a 100 dollar speeding fine.

Fiona rolls Tamara's other wrist towards her on the sheet and casually rests two fingers across it. Emilie arches her eyebrows as the nurse scribbles her observations on the chart clipped at the end of the bed.

"So?" Emilie asks, "How is it? Her pulse?"

"Sluggish but within the expected range," Fiona answers, tallying something else on the chart. "And now we should make ourselves pretty for the gentlemen of the police. Shall we?" she asks in a pre-school teacher tone, without even looking up, falling back on years of acceptable bedside prattle. When she does look up, tucking a stray wisp of brown-dyed-plum hair behind her ear, she finds both Emilie and Tamara staring at her as oddly as if she had just thrown in a Miss Piggy improvisation. "Tell you what I can do, then," Fiona starts again, undaunted, "You ladies relax and catch up. I'll see if I can find our two gentlemen. I'll see to it they don't rush in here too quickly."

"That would be very nice of you," Emilie says. "Thank you."

"Sweet," says Tamara, flashing a weak thumb's up.

"So," Emilie returns her attention to Tamara, "Darling, tell me … how are you *really* feeling."

"Oh, Em … you don't wanna know," is Tamara's despondent reply. Now that Emilie has come to her, she can let herself go. "I've never slept so much in my entire life. I don't want to eat anything. I don't even have to pee. I just doze off and … well, you know, it's pretty freaky stuff, what's been popping up in my dreams." Emilie's hand is cool on her forehead.

"It's OK, Tam," Emilie brings the chair closer against the bed. "How's your head? Tell me about that pain. Is it still thumping and – "

"It … yes. It bloody well hurts. It really, really does." Tamara slides Emilie's hand over her chest. "When the pain comes, like when I move my head, it comes in waves. And I feel my heart thumping like mad and I'm like, all right, this is where I throw up. Like this morning when the cops were here. I'm sure they thought I was going to spew on them or something. Alex dropped in, too, but – "

"Oh good. I was hoping she would. Look, the good thing about sleeping a lot is that you don't move your head so much, huh?"

"Maybe not, but I tell you, Em, I've come up with the weirdest dreams, like nonstop. Unpleasant. Like erratic … like jagged dreams that come out of nowhere but in bits and pieces. Things I haven't thought about for … like, in years. Uh, well, except, you know, for the dream I have, sometimes … about Jamie."

"So you've had another one of those dreams, have you?"

"More than one. Bits and pieces. Flashbacks, but really mad stuff the way it's all coming back to me. All broken up and mingled with sounds and other things. It's like mixed-up pieces of a jigsaw. With sharp edges. Murky. And then, there's Marielle and – "

"Marielle?"

"You remember, the Sainte-Thérèse story I told yo – "

"Yes ... of course I remember, but what about it? I mean, after all these years?"

"Damned if I know. But it's all come up like, just waiting to ... to surface and like Jamie ... his suicide ... How he did it, I mean, tying himself up and just climbing – "

"Hold it, Tam. You said the Coroner ruled Jamie's death as *accidental*. A boy's play gone tragic, that's what he wrote, right? I know you've convinced yourself he ... that Jamie had meant to die, that his jump had been intentional because of your father's thing for him ... But, darling, you don't really know any of tha– "

"Look, Emilie ... " Tamara tries to straighten herself on the pillow. She winces and keeps her eyes tightly closed. Emilie rubs her chest gently with wide, circular movements to appease the accelerated heartbeat. Tamara's heart thuds against her hand.

When the pain subsides, she looks at Emilie with another particular expression of hers. That one means that she's adamant and that nothing Emilie or anyone has to say will make her change her mind. Ever.

"Look, take my word for it, Em. That's not a friggin' theory I'm talking about, please! My father was abusing him, right?" Tamara lifts her hand to brush back her hair and dropping it back on the sheet, glares at the cannula. "I mean, I clearly saw him do it that night. There's no doubt whatsoever about that, right? Just like there's no doubt it was the first time. Couldn't have been a once-off thing. Jamie spent more time with us on Black Night ... more time than with his parents. They were always splitting up. That time I climbed back up to the pilothouse and saw my father. It was ... was like somehow ... Jamie ... he just knew what to do. Like ... stand still and wait for it to be over. I've already told you all about it."

"I remember what you told me, Tam. But you still don't know for – "

"There I was, minding my own business," Tamara cuts in, unwilling to be swayed from what she knows to be a fact. "Going back into the pilothouse to get something for my mother like a ... uh ... could've been her marlin-spike. Maybe she was splicing rope. *That*, I don't remember. But *that doesn't matter*, Em. So, anyway, there he was, my father ... eyes closed. Never even saw me. Never heard me come up the ladder on bare feet. But Jamie ... he saw me. Unseeing eyes, like turned inward. Submissive and enduring. That's what I remember. Just like Marielle's when … when … *you know,"* Tamara is pushing Emilie to remember what details she already knows, urging her to make her synapses make whatever leap they need to make to connect the dots. "My father, right, on his knees behind Jamie. Jamie's board shorts around his ankles. Red shorts. And my father ... with his hand … there he was in the pilothouse fondling or … rubbing, sliding his hand over and over and again, slowly, very slowly over Jamie's … legs and … penis."

Tamara closed her eyes and stayed still. Fuck what the Coroner wrote, she wants to shout. Why don't you just see what *there was to see*, she wants to shout at Emilie. Seconds tick by. For the first time since she's been admitted, Tamara wonders what the persons on the other side of the drawn curtains may have overheard. Who is on the other side of those curtains anyway? She hadn't been awake long enough to be curious about her ward neighbours.

"You see, Em," she whispers, now aware they're not alone. "Unconsciously, I must've understood *enough*. I must've *felt* that something not good was coming down because I remember tearing down that ladder as fast as I could and went to hide right in my mother's lap. Didn't tell her anything. Only later. Like years later. But they had already separated by then." Tamara snorts. "One thing not having anything to do with the other."

"Tam, Darling, you musn't blame yourself. You were only what, six or seven years old?"

"My father fuckin' well knew what he was doing though, didn't he?"

The surge of emotion is not good for Tamara. It only unleashes a relentless sort of pounding at her temples, in the back of her head. Once spent, the pounding recedes slowly like the tide. But unlike the tide, it doesn't withdraw far, not far enough. It just lets go, as a dog lets go of his bone, only momentarily before he tears into it again. "My fucking father, he *knew* all right!"

"Yes, *your father* would have known that what he was doing wasn't right, of course."

Tamara runs a hand over her face. "Awh … shit," she mutters as her hand flies away from the angry graze on her cheek.

Emilie is hot. The first three buttons of her shirt are open but the heat trapped inside the cubicle swirls around her. Tamara doesn't look hot under the sheets. Her hand is not hot, just limp. A tired hand. Who would've thought? Tamara … with a tired hand and crushed rose-petal shadows under her eyes. Tamara in a hospital bed.

C. C. Saint-Clair

Emilie shakes her head. How quickly does a void open up under one's feet. She could've been … killed out there. By that blow or another blow. She could've been stabbed, just as easily. Just as quick. Who the hell did that to her? With what? Why her? Why the attack? she wants to know, far more worried by the parking lot incident than by the story of a little boy twenty-three years dead.

I should've been waiting for her outside. Didn't matter that she was going to be late. So what if I had twiddled my thumbs until ten or quarter past six, until she showed?

Emilie and Tamara close their eyes to better separate the private thoughts that have bobbed up through the thread of their conversation. Emilie listens to the ward sounds. The clinking of metal against metal, a cough here, a quiet conversation further down.

Mike Munro, in a whisper somewhere across the aisle, is telling Australia that "The Prime Minister intends on deflecting the Iraq debate conflict … … Forces would join only if the Australian government judged an engagement in its best national interest and only after hard evidence…" Emilie sighs. Night-time TV pictures of missile exchanges over Baghdad flashback from the past. *When was that, anyway? '97? 98?*

"The US government is still unwilling to take the Saudis' word on Bin Laden's whereabouts." *That's a sensible idea,* thinks Emilie. *Much more sensible than venturing into yet another costly war in Iraq but then again,* she reasons feebly, *a pre-emptive strike might be less costly than…*

Until September 11, Emilie had known so very little about the deposed Taliban regime, past the sensational headlines that, back in '96, had propelled them inside living rooms around the world. And then, there had been that dinner at Alex's. And Emilie remembers how knowledgeable and passionate Alex had been about the plight of the Taliban women. And as she follows the announcer's filtered voice, she thinks that not much, not enough has changed for the women out in Kabul and Kandahar. Yes, some have removed their veil, some have chosen to keep it but many very young girls are jailed for years, denounced by a male of their family, for running away from pact marriages arranged shortly after their birth and due to be honoured after puberty. More women, older ones, are seeking a separation from the men they have been forced to marry under the old regime but most Afghani Muslims are governed by Hanafi principles and the Courts will not allow the women a divorce. The burka was never *all* these poor women had to worry about and now that the visible symbol of their plight is gone,

Emilie suspects that interest in these women's cause will suffer another setback.

During that dinner, Alex had provided Emilie with one of the most informative conversations she had had in a long time. Emilie sighs. *All that seems so long ago now.*

"… Israeli missile attack on a house in Gaza … A sixteen-year-old Palestinian girl who was allegedly planning a suicide attack has been arrested as she was about to cross into …" The disembodied voice of the Channel 9 commentator, like a flea on a dog's back, jumps from one crisis to the next. Through half-closed eyes, a hand flat against the moist skin at the base of her throat, Emilie watches Tamara pluck at her little bear's ears. And she, once again, trains her ears towards the voice. She hadn't watched the news last night either. She was downstairs, at the time of the 6.30 news on SBS.

Unfocused, unseeing, she had stared at the muted TV set affixed high on the wall on the other side of the waiting room, alone, except for the rows of empty plastic seats. This time yesterday, she had been tight as a fist, tight with anxiety. Tamara had just been whisked into the Resuscitation room.

"Police believe a hostel fire which claimed three lives … … before flames quickly engulfed the building."

Lived here all my life and never, not even once, have I had to step inside this hospital. The Royal Brisbane Hospital, my god. Jumping like the newsreader from one connected thought to another she thinks *even the name is unyielding. Must've driven past the RBH a thousand times: to check out the old museum and the national art gallery before the contents of both got relocated to the South Bank complex, or to the show-grounds as a child, with my parents at Ekka time. On the way up to the North coast, to Noosa. Past it and around it, but never inside it. Never inside this hospital. Healthy parents, thank god for that; healthy friends, no siblings, healthy lovers, healthy me. Never inside* any *hospital.*

I just had *to follow that ambulance last night. I just had to.* How else would I have made it here in the state I was? I would've taken wrong turns. Would've gotten disoriented. Would've panicked even more at the thought of not … of not knowing whether … not knowing about Tamara. Emilie forces herself to swallow. Her eyes prickle. That had been the closest she had ever been to personal loss and though she now knows Tamara is out of danger, last night's drama has taken her somewhere unfamiliar. Somewhere where fear lurks and spirals.

Other thoughts, thick with fear and incomprehension, had flooded Emilie from the moment when, last night, some time after 6.00 p.m., she had discovered the body of Tamara, sprawled at right angles to the Jeep. Left cheek against the bitumen. They'll … they'll whisk her away. What if they don't let me see her? What if they don't tell me anything … because … Well, what right do I have to be asking, they'll want to know? What if they're only going to talk to her mother? Who would they know to call, out there in Lismore, if Tamara can't tell them? Of course, in the cold light of day, what can I say? I handled that one badly. I panicked. I screwed up big time.

"Hey … Em. Anyone inside that body what's sitting on that chair?"

Emilie opens her eyes. Tamara is looking at her, a thin smile on her lips.

"Sorry, Tam. First little time off I've had all day. I guess I just blanked away."

"Cool. But … anyway, just to wrap up … you know … that other thing. Don't know why all that's so strong since I've been here. Maybe there's something in that friggin' drip. It started even before the morph –"

"Morphine?"

"This morning. The Panadeine didn't seem to be doing much at all."

Emilie takes Tamara's left hand in her own to have a closer look at the arrangement taped to the back of it, "But somehow, I don't think there's anything in there that's meant to activate … Just looks like a weird transparent worm."

"Oh great! That really helps," Tamara exclaims squinting some more at the tubing. "That's my point, isn't it? It's so gross having this thing in my … in me. Anyway, it's more how it feels *inside* that bugs me. The feel of it, like, you know, just *in* there."

Emilie rubs the skin around the tape. "Maybe you're allergic to it. We'll run that past your friendly little nurse when she comes back."

"Bloody annoying. Every time I go to move my hand, it … it tugs." Tamara flicks the cannula with the index finger of her other hand. "It reminds me of a fish at the end of a line, chewing at the … at the worm. Like it's *totally* gross – "

Emilie is unfamiliar with the new tone, a tone fraught with exasperation, that's woven itself through Tamara's public school vowels. She's only ever known them to carry a sensual, back-throated huskiness. Voices move closer. Hushed voices. Male. A throat is cleared. Soft soles squish to the edge of the curtains and stop.

"Tamara, you do remember Detective Sergeant Johnson from this morning?" Fiona asks, holding up one side of the curtain. "And this is Senior Constable Matthews."

Both men step nearer the foot of the bed, the younger with the boyish grin on his round face, the older with his face muscles arranged around a tight smile.

"I told these two gentlemen…" Fiona explains, deftly reaching behind Tamara, bracing the patient's neck and head between her chest and forearm to prop up the pillows with her other hand, "… that you were feeling a little better but– "

"We won't be staying long, Tamara. We do understand you need to rest." The younger of the two, Senior Constable Matthews takes his position by the left side of Tamara's bed, hand wrapped around the metallic rail. "I'll just perch here for now, if it's OK."

"Ah … *Ms* Anderson, here *you* are," Detective Sergeant Johnson says, in the same insinuating tone he would have used to say, Fancy finding *you* here. He, of the brushed back, flat-topped pompadour hair, reaches inside a pocket to pull out a pad.

"Yes, I'm visiting."

Tamara glances at Emilie surprised by the curtness of her tone and back at the older man in the tired navy blue suit. Her eyes settle on his tie – great swirls of royal blue and gold. Mmmfff. Bit loud but then again, could be worse. She watches as he pulls a plastic pen out of the notepad's spiral. No wedding band. So, the craggy old bastard probably chooses his own ties.

"There. That's better, isn't it?" Fiona says, appraising her patient's refreshed position against the pillows. "Well, I best leave you to it, then." She pivots on her white rubber soles.

"So, young lady. Let's get started, shall we?"

Tamara's eyes flick at Emilie who only raises a silent eyebrow at the 'young lady.'

"This morning, you stated that about 6.00 p.m. you'd gone to the parking lot situated between the Coffee Spot cafe and the Institute of Further Knowledge. Your intention had been to wait for Ms Anderson to get off work. And of course, she's already confirmed that for us."

Again Tamara looks up at Emilie, this time surprised to hear that she has already been interviewed. *We* haven't even had enough private time to even begin talking about it. Like, I haven't even had time to reassure Em properly or to hear how she found me. I mean, her feelings and all that. Wonder what they asked – Oh, shit. Tamara's eyes widen at the sudden thought. What if they ask *me* about us? About our rela – "

" … you recollect about the minutes preceding the attack?"

"Nothing," Tamara says, keeping her head still against the freshly fluffed pillow. "All day, I've tried to come up with … a sound … a feeling, anything but no … nothing."

"Right." DS Johnson presses his lips together and pushes out the bottom one as he considers what his next question should be. "I understand you waited for Ms Anderson for quite a while."

Why, quite a while? Emilie wants to ask. Wouldn't have been more than a few minutes, if that.

"I got there earlier than planned," Tamara begins, her mind clicking ahead to the other moment, any time now, when she will have to pretend she and Emilie are just friends, just close friends. That's what Emilie would rather I did, no question about *that*. The old closet thing. "It was about five to six."

"Do you wear a watch, Tamara?"

Her reflex is to answer with a shake of the head and the pain makes her abort that shake. Eyes closed, she answers through clenched teeth. "The waiter did."

Five to six? Emilie squints at Tamara who is looking at Senior Constable Matthews more comfortably in her line of vision. She was there …*early?* Emilie's heart thuds more heavily against her ribs.

" … had a coffee next door, yes. I was *so* early, like that does-n't happen often at all. So, yes, I removed my skates. Unlocked the Jeep– "

"You had the key to Ms Anderson's vehicle?"

"Well, yes, uh … I do. As spares. In case she, I mean Emilie, in case she loses hers. You know, cheaper than calling the locksmith, right?" A frown and a smile fight for position on Tamara's face.

"Uh huh," Senior Constable Matthews nods absent-mindedly, eyes on his notepad.

Are we already in the 'Please, explain' phase? Is it *so* weird having a friend's car keys? Tamara's mind revs up, unsure as to how best to cover up the sexual element of her friendship with Emilie.

"Right. So you unlock the vehicle."

"And I drop the skates and pads behind the front seat."

"Passenger or driver?"

"Uh, driver."

"Were you going to drive the vehicle?"

"Uh … no, I wasn't going to go anywhe– "

"So, why'd you drop the skates behind the driver's seat?"

Tamara is looking at him perplexed. "Why not?"

"From what side did you approach the vehicle?" the older man breaks in, flipping a couple of pages of his notepad. "A … a Jeep, is it?" he asks the scribbled page in front of him. His hands are large and pale.

"A Renegade. 1971 limited series," Emilie volunteers from her position off to his right.

"Thank *you*, Ms Anderson," DS Johnson replies curtly. "Ah, yes. Here it is … a red Jeep Renegade. Ah yes, '71. Long in the tooth."

Emilie rolls her eyes. "Classics, of any sort, need time to get there."

Students at the institute, boys like Liam, have a sort of fascination for Ms A's 'killer car'. It's not unusual for her to come out of the building during the day and find a couple of boys looking at it from afar. Salivating in full view is not considered cool.

Tamara's eyes crinkle discreetly. DS Johnson moves in closer to her, his back turned to Emilie who has once again seated herself out of the way. Her eyes scan the sphygmomanometer, its grey cuff and the assortment of objects scattered atop the trolley. Emilie returns her attention to the two men.

"… and all would've been very different if she'd left the vehicle at the scene," DS Johnson explains to a befuddled Tamara.

OK, rub it in. Yes, I'm guilty. Bad judgement, *yes!* But at the time, my priority was *her*, my lover, her life, *not* your Scenes of Crime crew.

Emilie has already decided that she didn't like this man much at all. Notwithstanding the fact that she feels foolish enough as it is, he was not letting her forget her lapse of judgement. Besides, he was the kind of man who raised her hackles on sight. On scent, even. Irrational, but real all the same.

Detective Sergeant Johnson chews gum as he breathes. As if he'd stop breathing the second he'd stop chewing. From her position slightly off to his right, she watches his jaw muscles bunch, unbunch and bunch again. And again. Small precise movements like a throbbing pulse misplaced on the side of his face. Unnerving. Has he even stopped at all since he got up this morning? He was already ruminating by the time he had knocked on her office door close to 9.30 a.m. ID flashed and slipped back inside his breast pocket, he had dug out a black spiral notepad and pulled out a disposable pen from its spiral. Hands behind his back, rocking on his heels in a manner that she had quickly found disconcerting, he had asked her to explain why the crew, dispatched after her call on the 000 police extension yesterday after-noon, had found both her vehicle and herself 'missing from the scene.'

The radio dispatcher had clearly explained to Emilie that the Scenes of Crime team might want to inspect *and* photograph her vehicle *and* the area immediately around the vehicle and that they'd be expecting her to meet them at the scene. In spite of her incomprehension of the situation as a whole, as to *why* Tamara was unconscious, as to what life-threatening complications would result from a prolonged state of unconsciousness, Emilie had understood what the voice had said. It had asked her the make and license plate number of the vehicle. She had been able to answer both questions easily as, at the time, hand on Tamara's cold cheek, she had been squatting only inches from the numbers she had just been asked to call out. She had understood the voice was telling her to stay put and wait by her vehicle and to not touch it or anything lying nearby but she had mistakenly assumed that the police technicians would be there quickly, before the ambulance. And the ambulance had rounded the corner, its siren and red swirling lights adding to her confusion.

The back doors had popped open. A stretcher clanked against the bitumen. The paramedic in yellow overalls had positioned a brace around Tamara's neck and deftly he had her lying on a hard spinal board. The stretcher had been rolled back into the ambulance. Emilie had moved to follow but the man in the yellow overalls, the first phase of his 'scoop and run' completed, barred the way. The air-locked pocket of fear that had formed at the moment of her first glimpse of the shape sprawled by her car had had risen closer to the surface.

"Can't let you do that, lady. Safety regulations."

"How am I going to get there, then?" she had asked, brain short-circuiting. Can't let her go out of my sight. Got to be with her. Stay with her. Hold her hand. Tell her I love her. Tell her everything's OK!

"You drive. You get a taxi." Hands ready to pull both doors inwards, he had barked, "Out of the way, lady!" Both doors clanged shut. His job description didn't include holding anyone's hand, the nurse were there for that, he always said. His priority was to check the patient's ABC.

The siren revved up. The swirling lights intensified the fear and the suffocating confusion inside Emilie's brain.

"Where you taking her?" she had shouted dry-mouthed.

"RBH," replied the driver's offsider. "Lady, get someone to drive you." And to the driver he had shouted, "We're outta here. Now!"

Teeth clenched, one hand clamped around the steering wheel, the other jerking away from her mouth to the gearshift and back to the wheel, eyes wide, Emilie had stuck to the back of that ambulance like the ribbon tail to a kite. She had driven on, oblivious of the blurred shapes that pulled up haphazardly, in obedience to the relentless scream of the siren.

Later that night, when they had made her give up her wait at the hospital, "Go home and get some rest: there's nothing more you can do for her at the moment," they had told her, the thought that she had unintentionally screwed up had been the only *other* thought spiking through the night. She could have called the police station then. She could have explained her predicament to whoever was on duty. Instead, she had called Alex, only to tell her about Tamara but she had ended up pouring out the story of how she had "fled from the scene," as well.

And Detective Sergeant Johnson had dropped in on her, at the institute, first thing that morning. She had been in her office, peering blankly at the screen above the half-moons of her reading glasses, when there had been a knock at the door. And there he had been, gaunt and tall. A leathery man with a hairstyle reminiscent of the eighties, sides neatly combed back and the longer strands on top of the head loosely but again very neatly swept to the side. Chewing gum, he had stood assessing her through hooded eyes. Hood-Eyes.

"Yes … Officer, I usually do that." Tamara's weary voice pulls Emilie back to the scene around the hospital bed. "I go to that parking lot on … on a regular basis. Every time Em … Emilie and me have a … feel like hanging about– "

"And what do you ladies do in New Farm when you feel like hanging about?"

"What we *do?* We ... Well, we have … We watch people go by. Uh … we have dinner there … later."

"So you were waiting for Ms Anderson to have dinner with her?"

Aware that Tamara is trying to protect her closet-thing, Emilie tries to make eye contact with her lover who is trying to *not* look at her.

"Sergeant Detective," Emilie begins, getting the policeman's title unintentionally back to front, "as you can observe, Tamara is not feeling her best. So, you might want to direct questions about restaurants and menus to me any time you– "

"Ms Anderson, I remind you that, as of yet, nobody knows anything about the chain of events that led up to this young lady being assaulted."

"My very point. She was assaulted. Whatever we may have had *in mind* to do after … after we met, *that* has nothing to do with anything. She's not here, in this hospital bed, because of food poisoning either. Or are you, perhaps, suspecting the waiter?"

"Em … it's OK. They got to ask what they got to ask, right?"

"Right," Emilie answers tightly, pulse raised, eyes glancing off Hood-Eyes' hooded eyes. Perfect name for him, Hood-Eyes. OK, breathe in. So, what? Someone's got to keep him focused on what's relevant.

"… young lady, besides…"

If he calls her 'young lady' one more time, I'll scream!

"… in *Ms* Anderson's vehicle, besides listening to music and placing a call to…" DS Johnson has returned his attention to Tamara but he is following a different line of questioning. "…placed a call to…" Emilie watches his profile as he scans up and down his notepad, "…to a Miss Taylor, Chris Taylor…to tell her that you would be spending the night at…"

Alarm shows on Tamara's face who, in her present state, is unsure as to how to justify the night spent at Emilie's place.

Emilie didn't know about this phone call, not that it is the least bit important but it brings her back to the fact that Tamara had apparently arrived, not only *on time* but early enough to listen to music and make phone calls.

When Hood-Eyes, during his morning visit to her office, had asked *her* to describe *her* relationship to the victim, she had expected him to understand the word friend. But he hadn't. The way he kept referring to Tamara as her 'young … *friend'* and pausing before the word 'friend' as if tasting it for quality and texture, she could tell the man was having problems with that particular word. So she had inserted the word 'close'. There was no need to be obvious about … about *that* now, was there? No, no need, she had thought back there in her office.

"We're close friends, Inspector." The palms of her hands had felt clammy.

Finally, she had used the words *close* and *friends* one last time but only to give him another word.

"We are close friends, Inspector. *And* we are lovers."

By then, the adrenaline rush had sky-rocketed her anxiety level beyond the stratosphere but she had, somehow, felt freed from DS Johnson's surreptitious and grungy prodding. She felt as if she had cleaned up … No, not cleaned up, *cleansed* the picture, if not for him, then for herself.

DS Johnson had rocked on the balls of his feet, masticating in silence with precise little jaw movements, nipping at the gum, and finally, he had scribbled in his pad.

" … stated earlier the purpose of the call had been to let your housemate know that you'd be spending the night at Ms Anderson's, is that cor– "

"Officer," Emilie breaks in, this time standing up, a finger on Hood-Eyes' sleeve to make him look at her, "Tamara and I *are* lovers. I've made that clear to you earlier this morning. So … as my *lover*, she has been spending some nights at my place. Yes, in fact, it's safe to say that on average she stays at my place two or three nights a week *and* we usually spend the weekends together." Breathless, she stops herself short of adding, 'And we do sleep in the same bed.' Instead, she drops her eyes to Tamara who is beaming back at her a silent, Yes! You fuckin' tell 'em!

Emilie grins back, rolling her eyes and shaking her head too as if to signify, So what's the big deal, huh? But both are acutely aware that *that* disclosure is out of character with Emilie's deep-seated belief that homophobia is alive and well on the streets of Brisbane. Alive and well and particularly rampant in all areas related to the education of young people. She is convinced that, in her field of work, her sexuality is best kept in the closet.

"Hmm…" the younger constable clears his throat softly, before redirecting the interview with another of his lopsided, boyish grins for Tamara, "So, besides making that phone call to your housemate, how else did you occupy your time?"

Tamara replies that, no, nothing in particular had attracted her attention. She only remembers a couple of kids fooling around with their skateboards, doing the usual tail slides and attempting the less usual board-upside-down Casper move. While Tamara does her best to answer further questions for which her antegrade only amnesia provides blanks, Emilie's thoughts meander back to the events of the previous night when she had felt compelled, compelled from the heart, to tell whoever it was that Tamara was her lover.

I came out to that doctor last night, too, didn't I? Emilie thinks, still revved up from her little confrontation with Hood-Eyes. Had to. Couldn't just let Tam go off like that, whisked away. Name, sex and age, nothing else. I did want them to know that someone loved her. I do. I love the woman. Breathe, Em, breathe. She's fine. She's out of danger. No lasting complications, Doctor Mac is positive about that. Bleeding's been ruled out. No drainage. A clear CT. She *will* be fine. The tearing or stretching … microscopic … That's a possibility we might need to monitor … later.

But, hey, coming out to whoever it was, here last night, that's got to be different from having had to lay it out again, nice and flat for old Hood-Eyes. To serve what purpose other than feed his lurid fantasies? I need a coffee. No, I need a drink. Water, yes. Cold water. And then alcohol. Two fingers of whisky ... that's what I really need. So, the police know. Then what? Is telling *them* any different from telling a doctor? Does that make me *more* out and more susceptible to ... *To what?*

"And did you, surprise her?" DS Johnson wants to know.

I can't believe this. Of all times for Tamara to get there early! Emilie shakes her head. I should've waited for her outside. Why hadn't I done just that instead of scratching out some last minute memos that could've waited till – If I had, I would've seen her the moment she had arrived. *Early.* We would've taken off. At the time of the mugging, around six fifteen, Tamara would've been safe. Safe with me, making plans for our evening.

On the edge of the chair, blood pounding against her temples, Emilie sighs heavily, deflated and weary. She's never even come near my office, let alone inside. Not that evening, she didn't. Not ever. Part of that fucking smoke-screen thing I've been *so* keen to keep in place.

"...and I was going to say something cute to rub it in a bit like, Hey, Em ... know *how long* I've been waiting out there? Or– "

"So you did *see* Ms Anderson?"

"Uh ... no. I went inside the building but I didn't see her ... no."

"Are you saying you looked for her and you couldn't find her or– "

"No, I'm not saying that. I said I went into the building ... I thought I might give her a surprise. But I changed my mind."

"And?"

"I went as far as the foyer. Had a look at ... at *it.* I mean, the artwork in the foyer ... and the big plants. Kind of nice really ... as far as foyers go," she says in Emilie's direction. But Emilie is not smiling. Why on earth didn't I just come out of that fuckin' office? What was I doing there that was *so* important that it couldn't wait?

"Checked out some of the posters. Like there was one on ... on bullying, something about it not being tough, and not clever ... I snooped around the notice-board. A blurb from the Head of Comm ... that's Emilie. Something about 'deconstructing' uh ... 'mainstream popular heroes.' Oh ... and heroines, too," she adds, still trying to covertly engage Emilie. "But basically– "

"Basically, Officers," Emilie breaks in, "after 4 p.m., there's no emptier building than a building where *only* youngsters come to learn. They zap out of there before you can say, 'Oh, by the way.' The receptionist goes home at 5 p.m. and switches on the answering machine for the night. None of the teaching staff are required to be there after 4.30. Very quiet. Great moment of the day for uninterrupted thinking." She does enjoy the quiet of the place after hours but she has to add, "All the lights are on but nobody's home, if you know what I mean."

Hood-Eyes swivels his head in her direction. The cluster of liver spots darken his cheek-bone. Uh-uh, back down, girl. Don't wanna go jeopardising Tamara's chances of ever finding out who's done that to her. Don't wanna antagonise the man.

"You sure no one was around that could've seen you?" asks the young police officer, eyebrows knotted in an insistent frown.

"Didn't see any one. It's like she said."

Emilie breaks in with a thought. "There *might* have been a team of cleaners about that time of day. But, of course, they could be anywhere. It's a big place."

Senior Constable Matthews and DS Johnson scribble in their pads.

"Name of that cleaning outfit?"

"Clean … Cleanair … Something like that. Two words in one. No hyphen. They drive a grey truck. No, a panel van. Large lettering on the side."

"What colour letterin– "

"Red, I think. Or cherry. Or Burgundy. I could get you that information from work tomorrow or Graeme might– "

"Graeme?"

Too late. Graeme is about to become involved in the Police investigation. "Yes, Graeme Harrington, the institute's Director. I could give you his number."

"That'd be useful, yes," Hood-Eyes says, implying something like, *Finally* something clever from you, lady. Turning back to Tamara, he asks, "And then?"

"What?" She frowns. "After I left the foyer? Well, that's it. Went back out and … big blank. Next thing I know I wake up here like my brain's too big for my skull." She lifts her hand to backcomb her hair but decides against it, not risking to move her head away from the pillow. Not risking more pain. She won't go looking for it while it leaves her alone.

Senior Constable Matthews nods, "We'll get a handle on this sooner or later."

Oh, well, there you go! Finally some positive thinking's happening here. Emilie feels herself warm up towards the young officer, though she's usually wary of men who have their sideburns cut in a straight line, level with the top of their ears.

"What kind of work do you do, Tamara?"

"Co-ordinator. Domestic Violence Services," Tamara volunteers. Emilie watches her rub again the back of her hand near the cannula.

Then follows a series of questions centered around Tamara's workload, habits and responsibilities.

"Ah, yes. Here it is. So, how much eyeball to eyeball do you do with these cranky husbands?"

Tamara squints at Hood-Eyes.

"All the … the cases I come across, Officer, they … indicate … clearly that the men who've turned on their partners were more … than cranky. And certainly more *bastards* than *husbands* or boyfriends." Cat green eyes flash again. "Domestic violence is a … It's a vicious behaviour. The violent partner lashes out. Simply because he can …because she's there. Like standing by her man. Still trying to make a diff."

Emilie has been listening carefully to what her lover has been saying since the policemen have begun interviewing her. She hasn't just listened to 'what' but to 'how' she has been formulating her answers. She has picked up on Tamara's conspicuously truncated and fragmented sentences. But she also hears a content that makes sense and hangs together reasonably well. She's going to be all right, she whispers silently. And she breathes into the knot that hasn't budged from the middle of her solar plexus.

DS Johnson's jaw muscles bunch and unbunch. Emilie chooses to think it's because of the piece of gum he's still chewing. "Right. But for now– "

"Inspector … it's all about hope, fear, and love." Tamara is not yet ready to let DS Johnson off the hook. And Emilie wonders if Tamara has just promoted or demoted old Hood-Eyes by calling him Inspector. She doesn't have a clue. Neither does Tamara. Maybe if we watched *The Bill* a bit more often we'd know these things. "That's the triangle of emotions. It's what keeps them … battered women unsafe in their own home." Blood rushes back at her temples. *Fuck this for a headache. Thought I could surf through … if I played it short and simple. But … no go.* Like a tidal wave battering a seawall, the blood rush builds up pressure with each repeated assault. "But, uh … to answer your question …" Her heartbeat knocks erratically against her chest. The oxymetre comes alive. Its accelerated beeps rattle Emilie's own heartbeats. Tamara closes her eyes to better breathe in.

Fiona pushes past the curtains and past Hood-Eyes. "That's OK, Tamara. Good girl. You know what to do." She switches off the volume on the oxymetre. "Not like it's the first time, or anything, hey? That's it. Breathe, breathe and relax. Don't mind me while I go about the usual," she adds, barely glancing at the policemen. She is already fitting the cuff of the sphygmomanometer around Tamara's bicep. The edge of the prim pink hospital gown falls back against the grey cuff. "How're you feeling?"

"Like shit. Wrung out." Tamara opens her eyes, leaving to everyone the task of diluting the impact of her words. "My heart's beating too fast …The second I move or like forget … I mean *as if*, right? The pain jumps up and … grabs me. Sorry you had to come again."

"No drama. That's what I'm here for." Slowly she lets the cuff deflate and rips off the Velcro ties. She leans close to Tamara's ear and whispers something that makes her grin in spite of the ricocheting pain.

Back to her ministrations, Fiona asks her, "Cup o' tea?" loud enough for all to hear.

"No, thanks."

"Cappuccino?" Tamara enquires with a shaky smile. "Just kiddin'. Water would be nice."

"That's a good girl." Fiona exclaims, as she enters more data on Tamara's chart. "You probably don't want to know but, by now, you really need to drink enough water to fill up a fishbowl."

"I'll get that." Glass of water in her hand, Emilie is already by her side. She had been poised on the edge of her seat, ready to go to her lover, ready to *touch* her, even in front of the two gentlemen from Queensland Police. Through half-closed eyes Tamara reaches for the glass. Emilie helps her bring it to her lips. The twin shadows of dark pink have spread under Tamara's lower lids. Emilie squeezes her lover's free hand, careful to avoid the plastic tube.

"If you get back on the water," Fiona adds, pointing to the IV line, "we might be able to get you off this thing a little sooner." It's pure bribery but if it gets Tamara to catch up on her liquids, she will be over another little hurdle. One little hurdle at a time.

Everyone remains silent while fingers across Tamara's wrist, the nurse does yet another silent count.

Senior Constable Matthews clears his throat again. "Tamara, we won't keep you much longer, but just before we go – "

Back turned to the two men, Fiona winks at Tamara. 'Works just about every time,' she had whispered in her ear only a few seconds earlier. By that she meant that she had turned up the volume on the oxy, just before the Police had come in, just so that they'd clearly hear it if it happened to pick up. "Makes them edgy and they piss off real quick like."

Tamara returns her attention to DS Johnson to begin again, "No Officer … I don't have … none of us have … contact with the abusive … partners. We only establish the victims' case histories." Dryly, she adds, "We're not there for the *men's* benefit." She glances away from DS Hood-Eyes and, yielding to a need now greater than keeping this interview going, she closes her eyes to better breathe away the onset of nausea.

Hood-Eyes tries again. "Anyone you can think of you may have upset in your line of work? Anyone who might have a grudge against you?"

Tamara begins slowly, "If anyone had a … a grudge, well … anything's possible." She squints ahead, rubbing her brow that no longer sports a silver bolt. She had removed it, permanently, even before her return to Brisbane. Her stomach would flipflop everytime she felt it under her fingers, everytime it reminded her of Marielle, of how Marielle used to touch it, inquisitively at first, then tenderly. "An indiscretion, something the victim might've let slip … Something the partner might've found in a paper bin, inside one of her pockets…" Tamara's eyes widen as finally some dots begin to connect. "Someone might … well … yes. I mean, finding out who I am … where I work's not difficult." She sucks in her bottom lip against the possibility that her attacker may well be someone whose name *is* in her files.

"Tam? What about when you accompany the complainant in front of the magistrate?" Emilie is asking, "You know, for morale support and what not? The fact is that the *other* party sees *you* there. You're in the same room, right? At the same bench, with only the complainant and the Police Prosecutor in between the two of you."

Hood-Eyes' pen is poised over his pad. "Am I right in understanding that although you're not directly involved in these proceedings, you are *in the room?*"

Tamara chooses to not nod. "Sometimes, yes."

Hood-Eyes scratches the side of his neck, just on the inside of his shirt collar. "Well, I'd say that pending confirmation of anything more definite, we'd best hang on to that as a lead. You, young lady, you need to think back…"

Tamara squeezes her eyes shut. This is all getting too much for her.

"Just one more thing before we go," Hood-Eyes says again,

looking at Emilie. "It mightn't be too late to have a look at the backpack and the – "

"It's at home," Emilie says. "But wouldn't it be too late for fingerprints?"

"*Late* but maybe not *too* late. Depends on how many people will have touched your vehicle since 6.00 p.m. yesterday. Or brushed against it. Depends whether you'll have smudged *all* of the perp's prints when you reached inside her pack to…"

Ah, yes, thinks Emilie. I should've done the pen bit, like in films. You don't touch anything. You lift the object with a pen and you bag and you tag.

"Well, that's a job for the dusters," Senior Constable Matthews breaks in amicably. "When you bring in your vehicle and the backpack, they'll go looking for latents. If there's any to be found, they'll keep them nicely labelled for us. Here's my card. Uh, just as an aside, Ms Anderson, when was the last time you washed your vehicle?"

Taken aback by the question Emile's mind goes on the blink. When *did* I wash it? And her mind clears. "I don't wash it myself. Uh … I never feel I have enough time for that. But I took it up the road last time I filled up with petrol … for a wash. That would make it … uh, yes, Tuesday."

DS Johnson stops nipping at his gum. "Three days ago today? But only the day before the aggression?"

Emilie nods. "Why?"

"Better print-opportunity on a reasonably clean car. Here."

Emilie takes the white rectangle of paper from the young officer's hand, noticing the clean and smooth edge of his thumbnail. She's glad this pleasant man should be Hood-Eyes' partner. She'd rather deal with him anytime. She glances at the blue and white checkerboard police motif above Senior Constable Matthews' name.

Maybe there's something enduring about the good-cop, bad-cop routine but, of course, I'm not a suspect. So that leaves DS Johnson on the permanently unpleasant side of life. She smiles at Senior Constable Matthews and nods.

"Yes, I'll drop in the bag and the Jee– the vehicle first thing in the morning. Brookes Street, as it says here?" She flashes the card back at him.

"That's where it all happens," Senior Constable Matthews answers pleasantly.

Hood-Eyes pushes the disposable pen inside his notepad's spiral and lets it drop inside his right pocket. "If anything comes back to you," he says, eyebrows pulling downward, "make sure you give us a call," he advises Tamara.

"I will. And … uh … thanks for anything … For whatever you can find out," Tamara says mustering the best smile she can still muster, a pale and tired one, highlighted by shiny green eyes, underlined by two pinkish smears now leaning towards a more purplish hue.

The ordeal just about over, Emilie remembers her manners and she remembers that last impressions are often lasting ones so, as the attentive hostess at the end of a convivial do, she graciously walks Senior Constable Matthews and Detective Sergeant Johnson back to the entrance to the ward.

The young man stops one stept short of the entrance. "Ms Anderson," he begins turning to look into Emilie's eyes, "as Ms Townsend's close friend, you need to know that the concussion she's suffered in the course of the attack isn't at all consistent with random mugging theories. You see…"

There you go: give them *friend* and *close,* they want *lover.* Give them *lover,* can't bring themselves to say the word within the lesbian context, so it's back to *close* friend.

"…have never heard of a junkie hitting anyone on the head, intent on mugging," the young policeman explains, ignoring Emilie's tucked-in smile, "with something hard enough to cause trauma to the brain but soft enough not to leave a cut or skin graze. And, according to Doctor Mac, what's there to see on the *outside* of Tamara's head is an elongated, a raised sort of thick bump. No blood. So that indicates to us that Tamara wasn't hit with the butt of a gun. Not with the handle of a knife. Not with a piece of wood. Even a lump of wood would leave a particular imprint *and* a cut *and* splinters *and* bring blood. And it's obvious she hasn't been stabbed."

"So … where do we go from there? The angry husband theory still requires a weapon of sorts. And where will we find him?"

Senior Constable Matthews glances quickly at his partner and back at Emilie but sidesteps the first part of her question. "Reality, Ms Anderson, is that we don't have the manpower to put together a decent doorknock of the vicinity. And because the victim is unharmed – all things considered," he adds quickly, "the best we can do is get Media Relations to toss in a thirty-second clip tomorrow, in the Crime Stopper segment, at the end of Today-Tonight. We have reasons to believe that could open us a door."

"Reality is that many crimes are solved once the public gets involved." Hood-Eyes finally looks at Emilie squarely. "Then, we verify whereabouts, ask a few questions, and we get our collar. Can't jump the gun though." Wing-shaped eyebrows beat once. "If you want to help the girl, best thing you can do is go to work tomorrow. A TV crew will look you up. If your boss don't watch TV, you won't even have to tell him anything about anything. Be done in no time." Rocking on the balls of his feet, he continues, "A shot of the parking lot, the vehicle, you walking out of that lobby of yours. Then they throw in a voice-over, summary of the incident, and the usual call for witnesses. There'll be the usual Crime-Stopper number running at the bottom of the screen. Often has immediate impact. All done in a minu– "

"But I won't have the Jeep!" Emilie exclaims.

"Techies'll be done by then. We'll get it back to you in time for the shoot." Hood-Eyes is ready to move on.

"Uh … just one more question. Why there?"

"Why there what?"

"Why attack Tamara there? In that parking lot? Why not at night … somewhere else?"

"Won't know till we grab him but maybe the geezer lives nearby. Maybe he spotted her before. Maybe he's followed her there. Thing is, he knows the place is quiet. My guess is that we're not talking impulse here. We're not talking out of the blue, impulsive behaviour. The bastard's planned it and got lucky. He got his mark without inflicting permanent damage. No grievous bodily harm done. That takes the pressure off him in terms of the law. By the way, know anything about cameras?"

"Cameras?"

"As in surveillance."

"In the parking lot? Uh, no, I can't say that I do … but again, Graeme Harrington … Hold on a sec."

Emilie strides back to Tamara's bedside and glances at her as she rummages at the bottom of her bag. Tamara peers back at her.

"Whatcha doin'?"

"Be right with you, darling. I need to give them Graeme's number. Hey, I ask you, what are the odds that it'd be sitting pretty on the tip of my tongue, huh? His *home* number?"

"Not good, Em. Not good at all."

"You're not wrong." Emilie pulls out her address book. She moves to the bed and lays her hand lovingly over Tamara's shoulder. Only then does she realise that the pink hospital nightie does not manage to cancel the sensual outline of Tamara's full breasts.

But more powerful again is her perception of Tamara's *vulnerability*. And it is the visual vulnerability of the soft fullness of Tamara's breasts under the prim and pink hospital nightie that makes Emilie's heart melt.

"Be right back, darling. And don't you go wandering off."

"Fat chance."

"33 50 49 28," she calls out to Hood-Eyes. "The house that goes with that number is somewhere over in Graceville. Miles away from work. The only way to go, I say."

Notepad slips back in pocket. "When you go back in there," he gestures towards the ward, "she needs to rewind all that she knows. Who, when, compliant, or not compliant at the hearing, overtly aggressive or condescending, and think back to any unusual occurrence. Someone whose Protection Order wasn't respected. We got zip to go on until our Crime Stoppers segment jogs something out of someone. Get her juices going. We'll get back to you," Hood-Eyes says, in lieu of goodbye.

Senior Constable Matthews gives Emilie one of his boyish half-grins and a little awkward wave of the hand.

She leans against the wall and all the air that had not been free to come and go, all the air she had kept blocked in by shallow breathing her way through the day, oozes out in invisible plumes of pent-up anxiety. Head back, she closes her eyes. Her heart beats heavily. It thuds beneath her breast. Quickly, far too fast. Hand over heart, she feels its rhythm. Thump-thump, thump-thump, again and again, piston-like against her hand.

Now that the air is still around her, she realises that her heart has been thumping that way since the previous night. Since 6.15 p.m. on her watch, the time at which she had discovered Tamara, face down on the dirty concrete of the car park. She glances at her watch. Twenty-five hours and twenty minutes. Again she exhales more of the air that had curled up under her solar plexus, making itself safe and stale and oppressive.

In the ladies' restroom, Emilie rests her hands on the edge of the sink. The enamel is cool and wet under her palms. Cool is nice. Wet isn't. She ignores the unpleasant feeling. In the mirror she sees herself, flushed and drawn. Her hair needs a cut. It needs a colour. She needs a shower. She feels sweaty and stale. Like her breath. Cold water on her face makes her gasp but it helps, a little.

"Breathe, Emilie," she tells her reflection as she pats her face dry with a couple of rough paper towels yanked from the dispenser.

"Much worse. All this could easily have been much worse." She blows a puff of air through her nostrils in a little snort and shakes her head. Her reflection looks back at her with tired eyes. The hair around her temples is damp. A dark smudge sits above her right eye where the line of kohl has spread over her lid. She cancels it with the tip of her index finger and leans closer into her reflection. She rubs the top of her lip with an inquisitive forefinger. Round-eyed, she scrutinises the tiny but brand new line that runs upward from her lip.

"Ah, what?"

She moves her face closer again, close enough to almost touch the mirror but too close is too close. Her face is now too fuzzy to reveal the tiny upright line. With a sigh she pulls back.

Another newborn wrinkle. "OK," she says out loud. "How many more to come in the Lipwrinkle Family?"

Suppressing another sigh, she massages her scalp here and there, everywhere, with her fingertips, to ease the pressure that has built up underneath. Before leaving her reflection to the mirror, she hitches the shirt-collar higher up her neck and pats the front of the dark green shirt that is almost a perfect match for the colour of her eyes.

*****

Emilie shifts on her seat and peers again through the spotty windscreen. Nothing stirs, though soft strains of music reach her through the Jeep's open cabin. Eyes open but blind to the outside, she makes no effort to jolt herself out of her irritable reflective state.

Tamara had sent her away to get some rest.

What does the Serenity prayer say again? Something about being granted the serenity to … to what? To accept … *what is.* That it?

"*What is,*" she snorts again.

Then, there's something about having the courage to change … Change what? What is changeable, I suppose. And the … the … ah yes, the wisdom to accept what's not … What cannot be changed. No, that's not right, she reasons. There's something about wisdom in there. Ah, well, yes. Wisdom … which I used to have in at least two molars before the dentist had to go and pull them out. Emilie's mind is idling. Anyway, enough of that. And now what? Home to bed early with a valerian-passionflower combo, that's what.

Tamara sent her away after extracting a promise that if she was intending a hand-wringing session for herself, about how she should have been waiting outside and how this and that was all her fault, then, she'd best give Alex a ring.

Alex, Tamara said, would be a good person for Emilie to be with. She was after all the only person Emilie knew who was close to her lover. None of *her* friends had had much opportunity to get to know her beyond the occasional dinner or party chit-chat.

"Anyway, just think," Tamara had said, "if the situation had been worse, you know, as in like I'd be dead– "

"Tam, please. I'm not in the mood."

"No listen. I kind of fancy the idea … you know … you and Alex like grieving together over– "

Emilie had shoved a finger in each ear. "Tam, you're not funny. I'm not listening."

*****

Emilie thinks she can give it a whirl. If Alex picks up the phone, she might drop in on her. If she doesn't pick up the phone, she'll do a simple two-handed hand-wringing job while sipping on some of the old Dimple.

"I mean, it *is* a special occasion, isn't it?"

Why am I talking out loud? she asks grumpily, but only to herself as she is alone inside the Jeep's cabin. Don't you start losing the plot, Em. You're too bloody young to be flippin'. And she remembers that Merredyth and Joan, *her* closest buddies, still didn't know about Tam being in the hospital.

"I really need to call them," she groans. They'll be upset when they find out I've taken so long to tell them about it. I really don't want to get into a blow by blow, not tonight. So, what do I do? she asks herself, careful not to be doing it out loud. Same thing as for Alex. I give them a ring … and maybe hope they're not there. Just leave a message. Yes, cool.

Question: do I really *not* want Alex to pick up the phone?

Emilie sighs again but grabs the mobile from the bottom of her bag. She punches in her PIN. The mobile beeps. Its tiny black screen changes resolution. She waits for the prompts. Would be good to give her fresh news of Tam. I mean, yes, well, she saw her only this afternoon, but Tamara had had those rushes of head pain. So, Alex might want to know that she's feeling better tonight. Well enough to talk to the cops and well enough to take old Hood-Eyes to task. And she said it herself, she's mending. Emilie grins in the darkness of the cabin. What am I going to do with her, huh? With Tamara Townsend, *my* lover? Who would've thought?

She shakes her head in slow incomprehension of the fact that Tamara is still around, better than around. *Inside* their relationship *and* involved. She remembers how they had made love that first evening. She remembers the searing flashes of desire that had made her throw caution, emotional caution, to the wind. And how they had made love, frantically but tenderly all the same. She remembers how Tamara had talked her into her first protected sex, ever. She pulled out that dental dam and … and I thought she'd last only for that night. One week at the outside. And she's still here. It's not dental-dam protection I need when I'm with her it's … it's … Emilie feels tears of helplessness burn under her eyelids. She closes her eyes and swallows. How do I not get too attached to her? Breathe, Emilie. One day at a time, that's what you've decided to do. No complications. No headache. No expectations of anything else but what is … for now. Live in the present. Get used to the idea of impermanence.

"Ah, hell," she sniffs. "Might as well call Alex. I'd never be able to sleep anyway. Too early. And I hate drinking alone." Aware that she has once again spoken out loud, she sighs in annoyance. But let's do Merre and Joan first.

She punches the first number and enters it. Three rings. Five and … six rings. The answering machine kicks in. Merre's OGM.

'I might be busy. I might not be home.'

Emilie exhales a puff of breath. "I'm busy, I'm not home. Why not *we*, huh? Why not Joan and I, huh?"

Makes no difference. Just leave your message after the beep.

Beeeep.

Doesn't necessarily mean no one's home. Merredyth screens all her calls, every day. Day and night. Could be one of her colleagues ringing and it wouldn't do for Joan, her 'lesbian-live-in-lover', as she refers to her jokingly, to answer the phone, would it now? No, no, no. Not even after four years of living together.

Screens, screens, smokescreens. Tam's right, rice paper-thin screens. We all hang on to our fucking screens! Overgeneralisation. Not everyone does, that's for sure, but *we* do. A slow resentment bubbles upward and sits high and heavy inside Emilie's chest. It's the industry that does it, in one guise or another, the education of Queensland youth.

"Uh, hey, it's me," she says, staring through the windshield. "Look, I need to bail out of our Sunday do. Won't be able to make it. Thing is, Tamara's been admitted to the RBH. She's been mugged and … Well, it was all pretty scary … uh … Well, scary for me and god-awful painful for her. Still is. Concussion. But, yeah, she's coming along just fine. That was last night. Around six. They'll let her come home tomorrow. I'm taking her back to my place. Uh … just for a couple of days. More details later. Oh, hey … Big hug for the both of you. Be well and … yeah, take it easy out there." She terminates the call.

"Over and out," she mutters. Head back against the seat, shoulder muscles tight, she closes her eyes again. What if it had been a knife attack? What message would I have had to leave, for Merre and Joan, on that tape, huh? No, Emilie, don't go there. Totally unnecessary. Tam's been lucky, don't go spoiling it. Breathe. And again.

So, let's try Alex. Do I have her number? Diary, diary … Again she rummages inside her big leather bag.

Now, did I write it in under A or under D for Delaforêt. Nice name that. Sounds so much better than Anderson. Here it is … Alexandra just before Andrea-hairdresser … I absolutely need to call *her* tomorrow about a cut. So, what's Alex's number then?

One, two, three rings. Four … five. And she's not ho–
"Hi, there."
" … "

Emilie had initiated the call to Alex last night, the first since the 'incident' in her kitchen, but only because she needed to tell her about Tam. If she hadn't … who would have, right?

"Helloow?"

"Alex, *Salut*. Uh … it's Emilie here," Emilie says more firmly than necessary.

"*Ah ça alors!* I was about to swing the old crystal pendulum."

"Pendulum? What for?" she remembers now how Alex's unexpected kiss had had her totally humming. She remembers the ache of desire that had rippled upward from *below* her navel. She remembers how strong it had been. So strong, she hadn't been able to open her eyes. Ah, but that had been a long time ago.

"Oh, just to see if you were going to call or not, tonight. That makes it two nights in a row, then. People will start talking, you know."

The air in the parking lot is suddenly too cloying. Emilie's mind is revving but not gripping. A slow blush is continuing a caterpillar walk over her throat, onto her cheeks.

"Seriously, now …I *was* wondering how things had gone for you and the police, you know, after your phone call last night." Alex's voice has lost its teasing edge. "Have you spoken to them or them to you?"

Emilie breathes more easily. "Them to me. And Tam to them. Bright and early this morning at work. And at the hospital, well, that would've been an hour ago. Feels like it was *all* light years ago but … … Uh … I was wondering … Well, not me as such … but *Tamara* thought, well, she kind of thought that I should give you a ring on the off-chance that you'd be hom– "

"Did she say you and I would be good company for each other, tonight, while she is in the hospital?"

" … "

"So as to indulge in some communal commiseration of sorts?"

"Umm, yes, something like that," Emilie admits, aware of how awkward she sounds to her own ears.

"Well … I am home."

Is that what I want to do? Go to her place? "Uh, would I be interrupting– "

"Only CNN and a 'net read of the French press … later."

"Uh … well, then maybe I shouldn't. I did have in mind to go straight home and have an early night."

"Emilie Anderson, you are not calling from your place, right?"

"Right."

"You're calling from your car, *c'est ça?*"

"C'est ça."

"What say you aim that vehicle of yours towards the western suburbs and what say I start us a pot of coffee?"

"OK … Why not?" Can't run from *that* moment forever. Got to face her sooner or later and – "Yes, I could do that."

Just as Emilie was about to pull the phone away from her ear, Alex had another suggestion. Why didn't they meet at a restaurant somewhere convenient for the both of them, somewhere in West End.

"I'll call ahead, just in case. See you there then."

"Right. See you then, Alex."

Emilie punches the End button for the second time and squints through the dirty windshield. Pent-up breath escapes slowly through her lips.

*****

FOUR

Emilie looks around the narrow restaurant. The main room is still pleasantly full though the sidewalk tables are emptying. From where she sits across from Alex, she can see patrons saying goodbye to each other. Conversations hum softly around her. The air is rich with smells. Spicy fragrances mingling with hot oil, mingling with smoke, mingling with the aroma of coffee.

The only thing she deplores about the *Patcharin* on Hardgrave is its lack of decor. Bare walls bar a couple of posters seemingly from the Thai Office of Tourism. Three of them. Her eyes linger on the official portrait of Rama IX, His Majesty King Bhumibol Adulyadej. Still alive? she wonders. He'd have to be the longest reigning monarch in the world if he is.

Emilie brings her attention back to Alex. "So you've noticed too?"

"I couldn't help but." Alex nods gravely. "It really hurt to watch her, or more to the point to hear her strain and … break around what she wanted to say. That and that awful pain she had. Mind you, she would probably say that I'm the one who gave her that massive headache of hers."

"Well … she's doing much better tonight. She's obviously out of the woods but what I'm worried about now are *delayed* side-effects. Alex, did you have a chat with her doctor?"

"Didn't. I would have spoken to the nurse if I had seen her or to the doctor if I had seen her – " With a comical downturn of the mouth, Alex asks, "Him?" to double-check she hadn't too hastily assumed that Tamara's doctor would be a woman.

"Her."

"Happy to hear." Eyes crinkled, Alex raises her glass to the doctor she has neither met nor seen. "Why the question?"

"Well, she said … Doctor Mac … Mac short for McIntyre. Gill, actually. Hey, maybe you know her. Brown ha–"

"Nope."

"Neither did I until last night." Emilie shrugs. "Anyway, she explained something about the mechanical forces that might've been transmitted to the brain at the moment of impact. I hadn't thought much about it but, apparently, the brain moves inside the skull, right, a bit like jelly and of course, it floats in fluid. If it shifted away from its usual position, I mean under the force of the blow, microscopic tearing *can* occur.

Problem is that it doesn't show on a scan … of any sort. *So,*" Emilie wraps up, aware of her lengthy explanation, "in Tamara's case, the gist of what this means is that, though there'll be no permanent damage, she might still have a few difficult days ahead. Possibly weeks."

Elbows on the table, Alex leans forward. "How so?"

"Could be that for a while her brain will process things more slowly." Emilie's eyes lock on Alex's. "Multi-tasking, for example, she might find that difficult. Like, uh, talking *or* cooking. She might not be able to do both simultaneously."

Alex's eyes laugh. "Oh well, *that* will be an easy choice for Tam. No dilemma. Talking over cooking any time."

"Yeah. Mind you, I don't have much of a kitchen life myself," Emillie says with a shrug. "But, now that I think of it … Is it a kind of … multi-tasking that she does … rollerblading plugged to her discman?" she asks cautiously.

"Uh … might be. Technically it is about doing more than one thing at the same time. Just don't know how active or *involving* the tasks have to be to challenge the brain in that way. Seriously now," Alex adds, "jokes aside, any ongoing complication will drive her bananas."

"Well, yes. That's what I'm worried about. You see, Alex, most often the victim of a non-critical blow to the head doesn't remain unconscious for very long." Emilie's hand is arranging and rearranging the knife by the fork near her plate. "Only a few minutes. Most come to before the ambulance arrives." She presses her lips together making a little squeaky sound. "Now, it's hard to tell to the minute but from what we've been able to work out with her doctor, Tamara might've been out anywhere up to twenty minutes. Reacting to certain stimuli, yes, but … *out* all the same."

"Has she been told any of that?"

"Not by me. I'm not sure whether Doctor Mac has had a word with her about it yet. In any case, if she doesn't already know, she will by tomorrow afternoon before she gets discharged. What's the name again for this … uh … *deficits*, I think. Now," Emilie pushes away knife and fork with a sharp movement of the hand, "that sounds like a PC word to me, a euphemism for something that's not so good at all. A deficit … Short of something, a lack." She shakes her head. "Can't be good."

"Six of one or half a dozen of the other, as you said, between deficit and lacking." Alex is thinking ahead of how these deficits might affect Tam. "Is there the likelihood of any other *deficits?*" The crinkled corners of her eyes are not laughing anymore. With a finger, she teases the edge of a saucer small enough to pass as the serving dish in a doll's dinner set. Remnants of a sweet chilli sauce cling, molasses thick, to its flat bottom.

The heavy gold ring she wears on her middle finger glimmers at Emilie who becomes aware that her own fingers are bare. She looks at them surprised at how naked they look. She had left earlier than ever before to stop by the hospital on her way to work. She had been in too much of a flap this morning to remember her rings. Self-consciously, she rubs the length of her fingers with the thumb of the other. Blink-rapid, Tamara's hand, pierced by the cannula, superimposes itself over hers.

"Other deficits? Yes, possibly." She drags her eyes away from her hand. "She might struggle to find the exact word, you know … *le mot juste*, as you'd say."

Alex's finger has stopped teasing the edge of the little saucer. "And so, she would rely on circumlocutory speech to get around that, is that it? Or go on talking in abbreviated sentences to counteract – "

"Something like that … yes," Emilie agrees reluctantly. "And, of course, all that would be exacerbated when she gets tired or stressed."

"Oh boy." Alex looks away. Her hands, one flat against the other, make a steeple, fingers pressed against her lips. Then, one hand leaves the other to rake through the silver-white streak above her temple.

'No wonder it's white,' Tam used to say about the flash of white on Alex's otherwise mostly dark hair. *'I bet it's from raking your fingers through it all the time. Colour's all worn out.'*

"You do know that none of that is going to be easy for her, don't you?"

"I do," Emilie answers tightly.

"When she realises what is happening, *first* she will freak out but that will be short-lived. *Then*, it will drive her nuts. Already when I saw her, she was figuring out something was not right but she didn't let on. If it is short-term, she will find a way to cope but if it hangs around … " Alex pauses on a half-finished thought, dark eyes square on Emilie's. "Is she going to take some time off work?"

"She bloody well should, but I doubt she'll let *any* of us talk her into more than a couple of days on the other side of the weekend." Emilie's hand is back to tease the knife by her plate. Alex watches her slide it length-wise against the varnished wood grain tabletop, again and again, over the tabletop as if to bring on a brighter shine.

"You are not wrong there. But won't she have to pop over there anyway, at the Services, to look through her files and try to ID a lead for the police?"

"Ah, yes," Emilie's hand has stilled. She looks up. "Of course. But again, on the bright side of things, the police might already have a good lead or two come Monday."

"True. If the TV segment flushes out anyone, any witnesses, it's most likely to be tomorrow, Friday. So, yes, they might have enough of a lead by Monday."

"My bet is that if they're still treading water come Monday ... the fuckwit will probably ... end up walking like nothing has ever happened. You know," Alex reaches past the little saucer to tap Emilie on the hand, " ... even after she goes back to work, you should have her at your place for a while. Particularly if she exhibits some, *any,* of the signs, any of these deficits you were talking about just now."

Emilie lets go of the knife handle. "Hey." Her hands jump up, palms outward. "She can stay with me as long as she wants but you *know* how she is." She sucks in her bottom lip.

"How *she* is? Why don't you tell me?" Alex asks softly.

"Uh ... " A slow heat rises to Emilie's cheeks. "I mean at the level of her independence."

"Her independence towards what?" Alex probes gently. "What, not keen on the idea of being momentarily dependant on anyone? On you?"

Emilie shakes her head slowly. The knife slides on the tabletop. In between her thumb and middle finger, it travels lopsided to the left and lopsided to the right. "No, she'll be fine with that ... for a couple of days. She'll enjoy the 'mothering' I suppose. I'm not normally big on pampering." She looks up. "Maternal instinct must've become thwarted, you know, that many years ago. Anyway, with Tamara, it's got more to do with ..."

Alex has to ask, "Is it about her *not* wanting to give the impression that patterns are shifting between the two of you? Maybe getting *too* comforta – "

"Oh, look, Alex, I've got no idea what she really thinks about *shifting* patterns."

"So where is the problem then?"

Back in the ward, starched blouse very close to Tamara's nose, Fiona lifts her patient's chin with her thumb and peers down at her.

"It's coming along very nicely indeed."

Tamara winces as she does each time Fiona swabs the deep graze on her cheek. Three dabs each time.

"Oh, for such a tall and strong girl like you … You've got to be one of the biggest sooks, really!" Fiona looks straight at Tamara's eyes. "Ready? Just two more."

"Ready or not … Not like it'll stop you … or anything."

"True." Fiona dabs the angry red welt with the cotton wad impregnated with antiseptic.

Tamara flinches again. "Awh … "

Three of her fingers still cupping Tamara's chin, eyes on the graze, cotton ball poised between forefinger and thumb, the nurse chides, "For myself, I always reckoned rollerbladers were all tough dudes. Like on TV. They crash, they get up. Ain't it true?"

Tamara's eyes flick away from the cotton ball and back to the young nurse's face. "The *dudes,* yeah, they're … like you say. Tough nuts … all of them. But … haven't you noticed?" She grins a tiny grin. "I'm a woman. I'm not a friggin'–" She stops abruptly, surprised, but probably not as much as Fiona, by the deep blush that has overtaken the nurse's full cheeks.

"Oh … I've noticed…" replies Fiona, letting go of Tamara's chin. She tosses the cotton ball on the bedside trolley. "I meant … It's … I didn't mean…" the young nurse stammers, her back to Tamara doing a fiddle with the IV line.

Unsure as to what might have precipitated Fiona's fluster, Tamara adds with a thin little smile, "So, me, I'm like … a total wimp when it comes to … yeah … pain."

"There you go. All done." Fiona-the-nurse is back in charge. Over her shoulder, she glances at her patient but keeps her attention on the IV bag. She taps the little spigot and watches the liquid in the line. "Now, young lady, time for you to get some sleep."

"How old are you, Fiona?" Tamara asks, wondering where the nurse has picked up the totally annoying habit of referring to a female as a 'young lady'.

"How old am I?" Fiona repeats, sliding her eyes away from Tamara and on to the edge of the trolley. "First year out."

"So you're in your early twenties. A lot younger than me."

Fiona's hesitant nod suggests to Tamara that the little nurse is not wishing to explore her remark. *A nurse with a mission*, she thinks.

No time for idle chatting. "Right. Well … sleep sounds good. Not with the dreams I've been having though. Maybe I should just sit up … wait for tomorrow."

"Nonsense. But it might be an idea to think hard about the name of that guy you said might be in your file. Sooner the cops have his name, sooner you can put the whole thing behind you."

"Yeah," Tamara says, eyes half-closed. "Could be anyone, really. Husband … boyfriend who feels hard-done-by. Like not necessarily some dude who's … eyeballed me at the Courts."

"I'll fluff up those pillows one last time, then." Fiona efficiently brings Tamara's torso forward and reaches behind her. "One little thought at a time. Easy does it. There," she says, helping Tamara settle back against it. "That's better, isn't it? What won't come to you tonight will come to you tomorrow or the day after. And maybe that Crime Stoppers segment the cops want to put on TV for you, that might bring in something too." Fiona adds her data to the data that's already filling half of the chart at the end of the bed. "So, who's the lucky one then? Tomorrow's a big day for you. You get to go home. You wanna be fit for that, surely. Off to sleep then. Dream nice … dreams," she adds quietly.

"Uh, Fiona, in … if I don't see you … uh, later … tomorrow, when I go … Thanks for everything. Hope I wasn't too cranky, you know, like, at first."

"Not a problem." Bending again towards Tamara, she whispers, "It's the old ones I'm not very good with. They're usually real pains in the arse. And some are downright nasty. And some of the old geezers, you know, all shrivelled up but they still want to pinch. You really got to watch your backside, if you know what I mean."

"Gross out."

"You're not wrong there. But … comes with the job, right?"

"Old men need love too? Brave woman."

"That, I am. OK, don't you go hanging around empty car parks anymore, right?"

"Right." Tamara smiles in lieu of shaking her head. "Bad gig all around … car parks."

Fiona clips the board back to the end of Tamara's bed and with a wink and a wave she walks away on her white soles.

Swish, swish, swish…

Tamara closes her eyes. All around is quiet in a muffled sort of way except for the dry cough coming from somewhere further down the ward. The darkness is not dark, not really. When she opens her eyes, she can see her hand in front of her face. And that friggin' cannula is still embedded in it. She can see, too, the frame and the white curtains of the cubicle across from hers, except that the white curtains are more an indescribable shade of dark than white.

She sighs heavily. *Where's Em? Asleep or still out? Where with Alex? Doing what? Will I ask Em about the kiss or is it best to just let it go? She kissed back, right? Got to be that she enjoyed that kiss. Of course she did. Why wouldn't she? So, she fancies Al. So? So …* Tamara sighs again. She sucks in her bottom lip. *So nothing. She can kiss anyone she wants. She's a free woman. What, free? Is Em free to make love? Awh, for fuck's sake, of course, I'll mind if she screws around with Alex. Like she'll mind when I tell her about Zag. So … what? That's it? If I love Em, I can't kiss anyone? Can't have sex anymore … Not with anyone else? Not never? Oh … that's not a good thought. I don't need that. No, not now I don't.*

The pixy-red eye blinks and blinks at her from the monitor across the aisle but Tamara's disconnected thoughts have already taken her elsewhere.

Red lights flash and swirl. The Triangle is in full swing. Jerky movements syncopated by white strobes. Bodies trapped in a false delirium. Teeth flashing. Elbows flailing. Hands waving loosely in the air. Strands of hair plastered on sweaty foreheads. Long hair whips around. Shaved heads and spikes bob up here and there. *Ah, and now, the smoke effect.* The acrid smell of canned smog fills the air as it swirls and wraps around drifting wisps of cigarette smoke.

From her vantage point by the bar, Tamara is shuffling to the beat. *Wonder what Em's up to. Bet she's bored off her nut. Bet she's looking at her watch. Bet she's wondering what I'm up to. Colleagues are important. She should hang about with them more often. Wonder if she minds me being here. Said she didn't. She says things, Em, because she feels she's got to be cool about things like that. She's good that way. She's good.*

Tamara snorts softly: loaded instantly behind her eyes, the video clip, Emilie as she had looked earlier that evening, briefcase in hand, on her way to a work-related dinner. She had slowly, reluctantly, slid her lips away from Tamara's and she had looked deep into her eyes before running the pad of her thumb slowly across her lover's lips, before detaching her lover's hands from the small of her back. Then glancing at her watch, Emilie had kicked into her I-gotta-go-NOW mode.

"Have a Corona for me," she had called out, "but, hey … you remember how you picked me up, right? Because it is what you did, isn't it? That time back at The Triangle, huh?" she had grinned at Tamara's reflection in the hallway mirror. She gave her hair one last pull. "So … maybe this time you try and leave The Triangle empty-handed. Can do?"

"Not a problem Em. Unless, of course, I crack open on the spot, you know, like I did for you, but the odds of that happen – "

"Ah, well, in that case…" Emilie had cut in too quickly, "…if she's charming and charismatic and if it's … uh … karmic," she had added, Tamara had sensed, to pretend a pun, "And you can't help your-self then, hey … A girl's got to do what a girl's got to do, right? OK, gotta go," she had added before Tamara had had a chance to ease her out of her misplaced insecurity.

So Emilie had grabbed her briefcase on the way to the front door. "One thing about Graeme … probably the only *positive* thing about him, now that I think of it …" she had turned to look into Tamara's eyes one last time, "He's punctual." She had run a quick hand through Tamara's dark hair to brush it back away from her forehead, away from her cat eyes. "Be good. Not boring … but … yeah, good."

"I'll get home around one, Em, OK?" Tamara had tried to kiss Emilie one last time but she had already opened the front door and all about her suggested a need, a compulsion, to be on her way to the working-dinner to which Graeme had invited all the Heads of Department.

"Take care out there," Emilie had called out as she drove off with a wave.

Still … Em's probably wondering what I'm really *doing here. Good question that: what am I* really *doing here? Enjoying the music. Enjoying my beer. Just hanging and chillin'. Her mobile's probably turned off, as usual. Should've asked her to turn it on. I'd call just to say, Hey, Em … Just thinking about you and in case you're wondering, I'm only perving, not touchin –*

"Hey, girl. You need to groove."

Cat eyes snap to the right and, by the bar, find a face that had-n't been there before.

"What's up?" asks the girl with hair gelled into tiny volcanic tufts.

"You tell me."

Tamara recognises the girl she had been watching earlier on the dance floor. Actually it's the girl's very short and very red plastic skirt that Tamara had been watching as it flashed in and out between gaps on the crowded dance floor. *Nice ass,* she had thought. *Cute skirt.* She had checked out the legs and the big, red, Mickey Mouse plastic booties that made the girl look leggy in a coltish sort of way, though she wasn't that tall. *Too heavy on the gel,* Tamara had thought, curious as to how the girl's lover might touch the starched tufts. *Or aren't they meant to be touched?* Tamara had looked on but her gaze had dropped away from the hair and with a silly grin on her lips, she had returned her attention to the girl's bopping red plastic butt.

"Wanna dance?" The girl's hand is already closing over Tamara's.

Close-up, she seems to be in her early twenties, fresh-faced and somewhat breathless. Tamara shrugs.

"You're all danced-out."

"Nah. C'mon!" she says, tugging at Tamara's hand.

Tamara puts her beer down on the bar.

"Sweet," says the girl.

And on the opening note of Slow Hand's latest hit, as the slow segment kicks in, the girl steps against Tamara. Her midriff top ends a good hand span before the skirt begins. Tamara's hand settles against the girl's hot bare skin but that hand, Tamara's right hand, the one that had gotten used to the feel of Emilie's softer and thicker body moves away just as quickly, startled by the hard, flat feel of the girl's waist. Tamara brings her right hand back to the girl's waist and, knees touching, they shuffle. Red Mickey Mouse booties in between brown desert boots. The girl snuggles, head against Tamara's neck.

It is at that point in time that Tamara had wondered if what she was doing was wrong. *Is it wrong to dance like that?* she had asked herself shifting both hands against the girl's narrow hips. It's not like I'm turned on or anything. *Is it dancing like that that's wrong or is getting turned on by it? Or is it kissing that would be wrong,* she had tried to decide. *Kissing and screwing, that would be* totally *off-base. Like so wrong. I mean because of Emilie. Dancing's got to be OK,* had been Tamara's final assessment of the situation.

Slow Hand's breathless voice melts around her words. "Show me how to be your lover," she sings.

The girl moves her head away from Tamara's shoulder as she slides her hands up Tamara's bare arms, up and under the ribbed seam of her sleeveless Tee. Tamara looks at the uplifted face. Their eyes meet. Their eyes had met before while they had been dancing facing each other. When they had met, their eyes had smiled along with their lips. But they aren't talking anymore and they aren't a few feet away from each other. Not anymore, they aren't.

The girl's lips flutter over Tamara's. Her tongue teases Tamara's upper lip. *To open or not to open.* A part of Tamara wants to let the girl's tongue play with hers. Part of her does not. The part that does not is the part that, a moment earlier, had been thinking about Emilie and what Emilie, her lover, would consider OK or not OK.

Tamara shifts her eyes away from the lens-blue round eyes of the girl. She shifts her eyes away, too, from the glitter that sparkles up and down the tiny gelled hair tufts on the girl who smiles as she moves closer against Tamara's breasts, against her belt buckle.

The warmth that rises inside Tamara's belly tells her that she's been wrong, at least for a little while. She is properly turned on, full-throttle turned on. And because she is that turned on, she lets the girl's tongue part her lips. She lets the girl's tongue caress hers and she lets the girl's lips nudge hers as they would a Cornetto ice cream. And because Tamara has forgotten about Emilie, one of her hands slides down from the plastic waist. Not the hand that had been startled by the unfamiliar feel of the girl's body. No, not that hand, the other one. Tamara's left hand settles over the girl's round, plastic-sheathed ass and cups it.

And Tamara keeps on forgetting about Emilie until she feels the girl's hand brush against the loose crotch of her Cargo shorts. It is only once she has opened her eyes that Tamara remembers Emilie. She knows, then, that all that is not right. Maybe it is not *wrong* but, all the same, it is not right. It is not the way she had intended for it to go. And she moves her face away from the girl's mouth. And she removes her hand from the girl's plastic skirt and she moves the girl's hand away from her sex though it is very clear to Tamara that *her* sex wants more, a lot more, of whatever it is she has just decided is not right.

"Hey," she says against the blond tufts. "Can't spin this thing."

The girl's lens-blue eyes are not so round anymore. "Can't?"

"That's my stop. I get off right here. Cool with you?" Tamara doesn't wait for the girl's answer. She leads her back to the bar.

"What the fuck!" says the girl.

Tamara smiles. "No fuck. No fuck at all. Not tonight."

As they approach the bar, a woman bumps Tamara enough to make her lurch but the woman keeps right on going through the crowd. Tamara lets go of the girl's hand.

"Wanna drink?" she asks once they make it back to the bar. "On me."

"Wanna smoke?" the girl asks.

"I don't smoke."

"I mean weed?" the girl explains, thumb and forefinger pressed together near her lips.

"Not tonight."

Lens-blue eyes look at Tamara quizzically. "Your old lady's around or something?"

"Not around. At work."

"Ah! I knew it!" the girl exclaims, satisfied to have diagnosed the source of Tamara's reticence. "Gotta live, girl. Need to work yourself a longer leash. Can't go getting the guilts every time you get juicy, huh?"

Emilie had rounded the corner just as Alex was zapping her midnight blue Honda in front of the *Patcharin* restaurant. Alex had ambled towards Emilie, looking fit as usual, one hand in her jeans' pocket, the thumb of the other hooked under the strap of her backpack. Being able to talk about Tamara's trauma face to face with Alex had lifted the level of Emilie's energy.

A first glass of wine, the little Toongtong balls served as appetisers, that and the warm atmosphere of the restaurant, had dissolved some of the earlier tension that had been building inside her head and across her shoulders. But, as she considers Alex's question, the familiar tightness returns to her shoulders like an obedient dog that will not stray far from its mistress. Her eyes tighten to hold back a squint of irritation.

"There is *no* problem, Alex. I was just meaning that after a couple of days at my place, she'll probably be raring to get back to hers and do whatever she does there. You know, the bachelor thing. The total freedom of movement thing," she adds, teasing the little ridge that demarcates the blade from the knife handle.

Sliding her wineglass a little to her right, Alex leans back into her seat. "Like the freedom of movement I have? *That* type of bachelor thing?" she asks, fiddling with one of the tiny glass buttons that dot like dew drops the length of her shirt. Black suits her, Emilie had thought as her eyes had first settled on Alex. It suits her and its suits her hair. Works well with the many shades of pewter and silver that edge the darker layers. The overall effect reminded Emilie of colours in the sea as she had seen it on one particular morning while sailing in the Whitsunday Islands. Hammered silver and pewter, broken unevenly by little white caps that rippled on the surface.

"Yes," she makes her eyes slide away from Alex. "That type of bachelor thing, yes. Tamara will be keen to get back to it as soon as she feels better." *Why didn't I fall for her? Oh!* Emilie sits up stunned by that thought out of left field. *Shouldn't I have?* Her heart lurches.

"Look, I hope I'm not too forward in asking, but have you two ever discussed living together?"

"Discussed it?" Emilie's fingers now move from the knife to fiddle with the thin threads that had been tied around the collar of each of her Toongtongs. She had watched Alex delicately bite around each collar and place the tiny bit of crust to the side of her plate, as one does with olive pits. She notices that Alex doesn't find it necessary to fidget with the food or cutlery. Consciously, she slides her hands off the table and onto her lap. "Uh … no. Can't say that we have." And her mind knots itself more tightly. *What if … what if? What? Again? Hormones decided for me?*

"Then … what makes you think she is not ready to at least *think* about– Wrong question." Alex redirects her thoughts. "Let me put it to you differently, Emilie," she begins again, waiting for Emilie to bring her eyes back to her. "Emilie, would *you* like Tam to move in with you? I mean, not necessarily right now, but … as a near future possibility? Are *you* ready for the symbolic commitment that it would suggest?"

"No."

"No, you wouldn't *like* her to move in with you or no, you're not *ready* for the symbolism of it all?" One eyebrow raised, an almost imperceptible smile trapped in her irises, Alex waits, fingers loose around the stem of her glass.

Emilie answers testily, "Yes, to the first. No, to the second." She tugs at the green collar of her shirt and puckers her mouth, looking very much undecided as to what to say next. *Did I fall for Tam because she's sexy and young … not stopping long enough to consider whether we might be emotionally compatible? Compatible beyond hot sex and caring thoughts?* she asks herself, undecided as to what she can *afford* to say next. "I mean, uh … yes, I would and … no, I'm not." She feels hot again. A fine sheen of sweat has broken out at the base of her throat. Like a hot vapour mist, it spreads under her shirt.

The wineglass against her lips, Alex raises an eyebrow in a silent question. Emilie shakes her head to forestall any further questions. "I'm hot. Hot and tired. I'm not thinking straight," she says, arranging her mouth in a sort of grin while she grips more tightly the topic Alex has raised. "OK. No. No, I'm not ready for the symbolism bit. I'm not ready to suggest living together. That's cool, neither is she."

"Didn't you just say you hadn't discussed – "

"Alex, I don't *need* to discuss it. She's only twenty-eight, for crying out loud. I know she's not into that. Not yet, anyway."

"Well, I'm not so sure about that. I mean, she was into *that* when we were together, whenever that was, even though she – "

What if I have done that, rush in too quickly? Emilie blinks and swallows. "Yes but she knew, uh … it was only temporary, then. It was … from the start, wasn't it? Didn't she already have– "

"Yes, she had. She had already bought herself a plane ticket to Europe. You are right, it was different then. But still, we lived together for some fourteen months or so." Alex's eyes crinkle. "And, true, as far as I know, no, she is not planning another long trip away. Not just yet." Her elbows are back on the table. Again, her lips brush against the steeple of her fingers. Eyes again dark and thoughtful, she asks, "But … Emilie? What is choking you?"

Emilie's eyes brush over Alex's but do not linger. They are prickling, so she breathes in looking for an answer. None comes.

"You *are* quite fond of her, aren't you?" Alex asks again.

"Very … fond. Yes." *Yes, I am.*

"And so?"

"And so," Emilie finally looks at Alex squarely, "that *is* the bloody problem." Tamara is right, she thinks, squinting at Alex, this ex of hers is one *intense* woman. She grins in spite of herself. "The problem … if there needs *to be* one, is that I don't want to make myself even *more* vulnerable than I already am. There, I've said it." *Yes, indeed.* "But hey, strangely enough," she adds, pointing her fingers at Alex, "I thought you, of all people, would understand that."

"Vulnerable? How so?" Alex asks, ignoring the taunt.

"By giving in to … to … love. To the love I feel for … for her," Emilie answers slowly before letting out a groan of frustration. "Awh … look, it's simple really." Her knife skittles forward and clinks against the bottle of wine. "I just don't want to let *all* my defences down, all right?" *Did I choose Tam over her because she's younger? Young? So young?* One hand at the nape of her neck, Emilie quickly rubs the muscles to keep the tightness from settling.

127

And Alex wishes she could do the massaging for her. It could all be done quickly, she reasons, perhaps not just *there* at the restaurant table, but before letting her go home. In one of their cars perhaps.

Emilie straightens on the edge of her chair. "And I'd have to do just that, wouldn't I? I'd have to be prepared to lower *all* my defences if I asked … if I put that … *symbolic* thing to her." Slowly, carefully, she releases her breath in a very controlled, very quiet manner. "Though I doubt she'd want to, anyway. Thing is…" Her eyes skirt the outside of Alex's face but her index and middle fingers tap-dance on either side of the knife. "It's not a desperate need I have, right?" A blush crawls, caterpillar-like, along her neck because her thoughts are still knotted up, snagged. *What the fuck am…* Who *the fuck am I talking about?* "It's … it's only something I don't want to think about … and I'd like to leave it at that … for now." She hears Tamara's frustrated, 'Oh, for fuck's sake!' To which she adds her own, *For crying out loud, Em. Cut the crap.* And she blinks. She blinks because she doesn't dare squeeze her eyes shut tight. Not now, not in front of Alex who is looking at her pensively, her eyes, for once, not intently peering at her as if to read her most intimate thoughts.

And Alex, though she has been suspecting all along that Emilie might be more highly strung than she ever lets on, is surprised by her erratic display of non-verbals and the odd edge in Emilie's tone.

"Emilie?" she calls softly. "Hey? Has Tam told you a bit about what we talked about this afternoon, when I dropped in on her? At the hospital."

Breathe *and* focus, Emilie orders herself. "She … mentioned that you had stopped by. *And* that she had had those awful surges of head pain and nausea but … No, she never got around to …" Emilie reaches for her wineglass and sips too long a sip. "The thing is we've hardly had any time to ourselves. Not since … since last night. The police were already there by the time I made it to her ward but the nurse managed to stall them for a little while. Then Fiona had to reset the drip. Then she brought Tam some sort of dinner but she hardly ate…"

Emilie had been too caught up during the past few months, too enthralled with the discovery of Tamara to think about Alex more than fleetingly, even when Tamara had briefly asked her, in a round about sort of way, about a possible interest in Alex. In any case, thinking about one woman whilst in love with another was not anything that Emilie was really into. Not *while* in love, no, but often at the other end, the downhill end of her in-love phases. In fact, most of her relationships had had a truncated dénouement because, by then, Emilie had had another woman in her thoughts. She knows there certainly had been a touch of that at the end of her relationship with Solange although, technically, it was Solange who had done the cheating. But while Solange had been physically unfaithful, Emilie recalls that she, herself, had been snuggling more and more tightly into an emotional entanglement with a new woman, Roberta, which, when the time came, precipitated the winddown of her relationship with Solange rather than inspire in her a wish to repair it.

"Perhaps," Roberta had said, "you're in this category of early detectors. You've had your time to think and reach a verdict. You're positive your relationship with Solange is…flat line. Mine with Julia is still beeping."

Emilie clamps her mind shut on the *But what if I did do that, fall in love too quickly with Tam?* thought-on-a-loop and tunes into the other reason behind the incipient discomfort felt at Alex's probing. What else is bugging her, she realises, is that she hadn't intended discussing anything, *anything at all*, nothing of a private nature with Alex. And not anything about Tamara beyond her health. Not tonight. Not while she was feeling that tired, that vulnerable.

One had to be mentally fit to keep up with Alex, she knew that. Tonight, she was not. So she had let Alex prod her into a little spot where either a tad of self-disclosure or a touch of tetchiness had been her alternatives. Having opted for the former, and unable to repress the latter, she had stumbled on something. *Something I don't bloody well want to be there,* she thought, needing it to surface like she needed a hole in the head.

But then again, she knows that if she truly hadn't wanted to discuss anything remotely personal with Alex, it would've been easy enough to redirect her. Redirecting Alex is not what requires concentration and an incisive connection to the moment. It's keeping up with her or trying to shoot holes through her arguments that does, once mere conversation upgrades to an intellectual exchange.

I do like being with her. Struggling to keep an honest perspective on things, Emilie uses her wineglass as a time-stalling prop as she tries to scan through what she may have involuntarily overlooked.

I do enjoy her company, she admits. *I do. And* I'm *always moaning about the fact that, with my other friends, we never get 'dirty' and personal. Drops of oil floating on the surface of everything else, that's all our conversations ever are. I enjoy talking with Alex. And, yes, I enjoy … her. Her intensity.* Her. *That's not news. I knew that from before.* Emilie forces a breath deep inside her lungs. *So … what's up now? The last time I saw her alone would've been right after* – Oh my! Startled by the insidious ebb and flow of her private thoughts, Emilie glances again at Alex who, for the moment, seems content just sipping her wine.

Sipping her wine, looking at the congealed sweet chilli at the bottom of the tiny saucer, Alex remembers how Emilie's tongue had felt in her mouth, that day, months ago, in Emilie's kitchen. Imperceptibly, eyes fixed on the sticky orange puddle, she shakes her head. Green cat eyes underlined by high cheekbones break in front of her. Fragile, pain-strained cat eyes. Alex shifts uncomfortably on her chair.

Her only conscious intention, that day, as her hand had reached towards Emilie, had been to help settle the cup she had just filled. She had only wanted to settle it on the saucer. It had been wobbling in Emilie's hand.

She remembers the heat in her belly, that and being aware of her need to go further, to take her … To take her by the hand. To lead her to the sofa. But she hadn't. She hadn't made a fool of herself.

"Anyway," Emilie is connecting back to the present. Alex looks away from the moon of congealed chilli. "Tam sent me away. She said that either I should get home and get some sleep or give you a ring and do something with you, uh … like what we're doing now," She says, teasing the tip of her knife with a fingernail cut short. "I mean … me talking to *you* about whatever *she* thought I needed to get off my chest." She sucks in a breath. "Fact is, I *am* feeling guilty about not having been there for her, you know, in that bloody parking lot and … " Emilie swats the air in front of her. "Never mind."

"Right. So, here we are," Alex replies, an imperceptible strain at the base of her throat. "Hmm. Hey, look at it this way, could be worse. We could be talking about the thing that was in the paper today, the newest amendment to the Brothel Bill, such a hoot, and how the Beattie Government stipulated last year that brothels could not operate within two hundred metres of homes, schools or hospitals. Remember that bit?"

"I remember." Emilie is back in the saddle. She smiles at Alex, eyebrows raised. "Like even a two hundred metre *walk*, right, probably a brisk one at that, is really going to keep the local males on the straight and narrow."

Alex rolls her eyes, hands spread in a shoulder-height gesture of incomprehension. "Makes my eyes water, it is all so ludicrous and, today, there was *more* on that. Do you know how the two hundred metres will be measured, according to the amended Bill?"

"I don't dare guess. You tell me."

"Come on, have a guess," Alex insists. "I don't think you can possibly get it wrong. Ready?" She thought she had read a need, a tremendous need, a need like hers, trapped inside Emilie's eyes. But later, Alex had chosen to think that *that* need couldn't have been all for her. It couldn't have been *only* about her. She squints into a neutral space above the tabletop.

"What's up?" Emilie asks.

"Just blurry eyes." Alex shrugs and rubs her eyes with her fingertips. The heavy gold ring glints under the soft glow overhead. "Too much screen-reading."

"You still doing the insomniac thing?"

Alex nods.

"Spending all these night hours catching up with the world about us?"

"Still do."

"Why don't you … go out more, you know, to – "

"What? At 2 a.m. when I can't sleep?"

"At 10 or 11p.m. On weekends. Out on the scene." Emilie brings a strand of hair back behind her ear but it is not quite long enough to stay hooked.

"Can't be bothered. Nothing has changed in terms of my outlook on this and that and the scene, not since we last talked about that. I still fail to see the attraction … for me … For me, now. Ah," she adds, looking sideways at Emilie, "but you are a good one to talk! You go out on the scene as little as I do. True or not true?"

"True … but I'm not – "

"Even when you were on your own, you didn't," Alex cuts in, "Well, you said you didn't. *But* I do miss the movie-coffee thing you and I had going for that little while."

Until I became totally engrossed with Tamara. "Yes. Me too," Emilie replies with a slow grin but her instinct warns her not to venture down that path. Her instinct tells her to shift her gaze away from Alex's face.

"Right," she says, looking at the little paper flowers stuck in a minuscule pink vase that has been pushed off to the side. "So your question was … ah, yes, how to measure two hundred metres. Wait, wait, don't tell me." She squeezes her eyes shut and scrunches up her nose in mock concentration. She opens first one eye then the other and raises her hand like a polite child in a classroom. "Miss, Miss, the answer is: by the shortest route, yes?"

"*C'est ça!*" Alex exclaims softly with matching mock excitement, still blinking from the rub. "By the shortest 'lawful' route a person can travel … 'by vehicle or on foot'. I swear: I am quoting the law almost verbatim."

The irregular tips of Emilie's bedraggled urchin haircut catch the softer glow of the overhead light. Alex is sure that Emilie's hair desperately wants to be worn short. Much shorter. Goodness knows why she wants it longer, she muses. It's rebelling. Alex tightens the reins on her thoughts.

Emilie scans the room. "And we pay our politicians for the time it takes *them* to think up, draft, legislate, deliberate *and* amend such asinine details?"

"We do. But wash yo' mouth with soap, young lady. Not asinine. This is a hairy health and ethics-related issue 'round our neck of the woods. Queensland ain't Europe, you must have noticed," Alex chides, though her thoughts are connected to an interior monologue that is keeping her from concentrating on the conversation. She only wants to keep it flowing, to keep it simple. She fully understands that Emilie is now out of bounds and that her sexually subversive thoughts are totally out of place. "Fortunes will be made over the legitimisation of brothels in Queensland. Unfortunately, it won't be the sex-trade workers who risk getting rich."

"Right. And if the sex-trade workers or their welfare are not discussed, what's left to discuss, right? So … we could talk about the latest on asylum seekers and whether the Pacific Solution or the United Nations' report– "

"No, look, Emilie! That topic is the opposite of the brothel thing. This one is too serious for now." She pleads, "I don't feel like talking about that, not tonight."

Alex could intellectually argue any of these topics and carry on till the waiter brought the bill but Emilie is only familiar with newspaper-type content. Her guess, though, is that by throwing in her two-cents worth of knowledge she could restrict access to other muddled thoughts that are keen to wedge themselves into the conversation, even if tangentially.

Emilie is once again drawn to Alex's eyes. "OK, you're right," she replies, keeping the sigh of resignation out of her voice. "I'd rather keep it light too. I'm quite tired, really." And yet, afraid to be drawn into a more personally involving topic, she quickly adds, "What's this I heard on the way here about the Democrats and …It sounded like the whole thing had been turned, yet again, into a mud-slinging, back-stabbing match." Aware of the air space she has taken up, Emilie skids to a stop. She sits back in her chair.

"Aren't you asleep yet?" Fiona asks, fingers loose on Tamara's wrist.

"Don't know."

"You don't know if you're awake or asleep?"

"Been drifting in and out. Ever since I got here."

"How do you mean?"

"Weird dreams. Always about things that have happened … things from the past but in these dreams, the … the visuals are totally like, sick. Disconnected. I freak out. I wake up. And I go under some more. And all along, you know, that friggin' pain's just there." Tamara touches the side of her head.

"Well, the morphine will help you sleep better."

"Morphine for Morphean dreams," Tamara replies matter-of-factly.

While the wonderful aromas permeating the little restaurant are working their magic on Emilie's appetite, she takes up the slack. At the best of times she dislikes conversations that run out of puff and 'die' in mid-air. When she's not into specific topic avoidance, Emilie often makes it her duty to keep a conversation going.

"Mind you, I haven't watched the news or read anything, not since Tuesday. Last night, after I left Tam and she was still in the emergency room when – "

Alex heads her off with a grin. "When you called me." Her fingers brush again over her right temple. Some women flick their hair when it gets in the way. Others pat it or hook it behind an ear. Alex did neither. She would weave her fingers through its thickness, above her right temple and, hand flat, she would drive it back, push it back two, three times. Stay! And because she had had to repeat that gesture so many times a day, for so many years, her hand had not dropped the habit.

Emilie shifts on her chair before slowly bringing up her eyes to where Alex's are waiting. "Yes. I called you. I thought you'd want to know about Tam."

"Absolutely. I did. Anyway, there is always that *other* thing we could talk about …" Emilie's heart misses a beat. *Oh, no. Not now! Not after all that!* "I mean, hindsight is a wonderful thing, right?" Alex asks, moving right on. "So … even if we can only look backwards or forwards from the … from the piece-meal, tunnel-vision point of view of the arm-chair-experts-in-world-diplomacy that we are, we might want to talk about…"

Emilie releases the puff of air that had stilled on her lips. She can do this. She can handle this diplomacy talk. She leans away from the table to better stretch her legs, careful to angle them towards the aisle. "You know, back in the ward, I caught a bit of the day's headlines and as I was driving up here I was thinking about John Howard's stance on the possibility of our joining the Americans against a hypothetical …"

Alex wraps her fingers around the stainless steel watchface that hangs loosely on the outside of her wrist and tugs it towards the centre. "Look, Emilie, we've already chatted away some forty-three minutes of this dinner conversation," she teases. "But I think we should really leave *all* these topics totally alone, at least just for tonight. What do you say?"

"Definitely," Emilie finally concedes, aware that this particular strain of conversation needs to be left to expire. "Just for tonight won't hurt. It's not like the headlines are likely to go anywhere in a hurry, is it? I mean, not *these* headlines."

And yet like children keen to postpone bedtime, they linger a while longer on the edge of their conversation. They both agree to agree on this and that but the conversation brought Alex back to the prospect of more terror being unleashed against America and, sooner or later, its allies.

"True." Emilie agrees but her thoughts are vague from lack of focus. "I have this image, you know, in my head, from something I read only a couple days ago." Her eyes narrow on Alex's. "The article referred to some Taliban rank and file in their hometown village some-where in the foothills of the Afghan desert. There was this bearded and turbanned camel herder who, according to the reporter asked, 'You want to see where Osama bin Ladin lived? Why you always want to know about Osama bin Ladin, you and the other capitalists from the West?' By now, they're all pretty safe out there. I guess the Afghan gov-ermnent has never had the budget to seriously investigate these men but…" Emilie shakes her head slowly. "Anyway, back to the camel herder. What he did was raise his stick in the air and shout, 'Look at me. You see Osama. We're all Osama here.' And they all ran around, firing guns at the sky, jabbing the air with their sticks, shouting, glaring and posturing in agreement with what that man had said."

"That which we call a rose, by any other name– "

"Ooh, good one, Alex, yes." Emilie draws one sizzling point on an imaginary scoreboard in front of her. "But can we, please, delete 'rose' and insert 'thorn'?"

"Can do. How about *poisonous* thorn, just for you?" Alex replies expansively, but she is quick to add, "That's the conundrum, isn't it?"

"What is?"

Alex brings up the words old Churchill said about victory at all costs, victory in spite of terror, victory however long and hard the road may be; for without victory there is not survival. And to feed the conversation a little longer, as it seems to be what Emilie is after, her question is about how, in our day and age, might a 'victory' be best and most quickly achieved. She considers Emilie's answer and then she asks again, "Emilie? Hadn't we just agreed to not talk about…" She fans her hands in front of her face in a 'Stop' gesture. "Didn't we just say, at least what, three times now, that we were doing an evening moratorium on that aspect of the world scene?"

"We did. So I'm not going to ask…" Emilie starts, now only to make Alex smile, "But the question really is, isn't it, whether the billions of US and Allied dollars would not get us a longer lasting victory if the West invested them in educatiion and the building of infrastructures that would enable all these people who have learned to hate…"

Forehead crimped, eyes rounded in pretended exasperation, Alex shushes her, "No, *non*. No, Emilie. Tonight, I am not going to make a stand in favour of a peaceful containment of … of anything." The corners of her mouth twitch on a repressed smile. "And no, you are not going to bait me with any other similar topics. And that is a … It is a direct order, you hear?"

Emilie mimes stiching up her mouth.

"So, let's just right here, right now, agree that our moratorium has just been extended to *all* aspects of the world scene, shall we? Whether humorous or serious, please?"

Emilie leans back into her seat with a sigh of resignation. "You're a tough player, Alex, but … yeah, let's."

"Good woman. So, where were we, then, in regards to you and Tam?" Alex taps her glass against Emilie's with an encouraging smile.

Tamara's hand lay flat inside the girl's who lifted it closer to the light coming from the bar. The Triangle is still pulsing all around them. Still pulsing inside Tamara's head.

"What's with the marks?" Zag asked, pointing to the pale strip that cut across the back of Tamara's tanned hand and higher up across her wrist.

"Straps. From my wrist guards. I 'blade a lot. Rollerblade," she explained, before removing her hand from the girl's.

"So what's with the marks on the *back* of your hand?"

"The *guard* part sits there." Tamara's fingers spanned some four inches on the inside of her wrist, from a point above her lifeline to another point where a watchband would probably settle, if she wore a watch. "It's more or less like a hard casing. The marks are from the Velcro strips that keep the thing snug against the wrist. So, what's your name?" Tamara asked, to move the conversation forward.

"Zag."

"Zag?" Tamara asked as, very slowly with her forefinger, the girl began drawing first a Z then an A and a G over the loose cotton of Tamara's shorts. Though the girl's exposed thigh was cool against Tamara's bare knee, for her, the moment had passed.

What she had felt on the dance floor when Emilie had materialised between her and the girl had sobered her up. It had reminded her of the priority she still wanted to pursue.

At that particular moment, priority number one, for Tamara, had been to do what *older* people do. What *older* people do when in love with the one they're with. With the one they're with in their *head*. Priority number one, for her that night, had been *not* to get laid, fool around, fuck around, have sex. And it certainly hadn't been about making love with the girl called Zag. Priority number one had been to disengage from what she had allowed herself and get back to neutral as there was, after all, very little in Zag that had moved Tamara.

Her tongue had but Tamara knew that tongues, in isolation, shouldn't be allowed to count for much. Neither should nice arses even when wrapped in red plastic. *Just as well,* she had sighed, relieved she hadn't actually been doing any hard-core fantasising about the girl, as disengaging from a full-heat-turn-on wasn't one of her strengths.

She would've been quick to argue that she never had had any reason to practise that particular type of self-control. As a matter of fact, she might have added, if pressed, that *that* particular type of self-control was downright peculiar and masochistically kinky. Or so it would've seemed to her in the pre *and* post Alex days that had preceded her involvement with Emilie.

"Yeah, Zag's my posting name, you know, like my code name. Wicked, huh? It's like my friends say. No one's ever come across anyone called Zag, right? So, it's like we all think it's so cool. So, what's yours?" Zag is toying with the side pocket on Tamara's shorts. "Like you got yourself an aka or what?"

"Tamahrah."

"A bit of a Brit, are you? You sound so from the UK."

"Yes, but a long time ago." Tamara undid the girl's finger from the buttonhole on her side pocket and turned to her left.

Patrons were pressing and milling around the bar but none, as far as she could tell, were or had been looking at her and yet she had felt someone's persistent glare tugging at the edge of her awareness.

There are only a few patrons left at the restaurant, now. A couple of nights ago, after a much different dinner conversation, Alex's smile had encouraged Tamara to ease into what had been bothering *her*. Tonight, that smile is for Emilie.

"We've been around the world, in terms of headlines, and back, but tonight what we need to talk about is you, Emilie. And we want to talk about Tam. Together, and / or separately." *And I* also need *to stay clear of that dinner at my place. Emilie was a free agent then.*

Head cocked to one side, Emilie asks, "And when do we talk about you, *chère Alexandra*, or are *you* out of bounds?"

"No, not out of bounds, no.*" Something did click during that dinner. Clicked for me. In me.* "But you know, there is nothing as newsworthy in my life as what has happened to Tam and, indirectly, to you and that brought us … well, it brought me to ask you about what plans you might have, you know, about having Tam settle a bit with you once she is discharged."

"Like hanging, as Tamara would say?"

"Like, 'totally not finished', yes."

"Mahdame." On the upside of a little bow, Chantira Srisai, the owner of the restaurant, is addressing Alex from the edge of the table. "Is everything how you wish it, Mahdame?"

Alex looks up. "Uh … yes." Then she frowns, never quite comfortable with what she perceives as obsequious attentiveness. "Very pleasant." Then she smiles, "Very pleasant, yes. As usual. Thank you."

"Thank you, Mahdame," Chantira Srisai dips her head again. "And you, Mahdame?" she asks, turning to Emilie.

"As my friend said. Very pleasant, indeed. As always." Emilie's reply is somewhat stilted too, but she nods courteously.

"May I ask you, Mahdame, if the Pud Ped Mu is for you or is it the – "

Alex glances from Chantira to Emilie, letting her eyes linger on her face, just while she is engaged with the owner doing her table rounds.

"Uh … that'd be the stir-fried pork in red curry paste, yes?"

"Yes, Mahdame."

The moment will be brief. She senses the '*Mahdames*' are not really Emilie's cup of tea either. *I need to do the moratorium thing on The Kiss, too. Not Rodin's, no. If only! If only we had gotten that far into it … No, don't go there. Leave it alone.*

Alex winces as a flash of unwelcome desire makes her shift uncomfortably in her chair. She sits up, a blush hot on her cheeks. Emilie glances at her but returns a polite attention to Chantira who is intent on explaining the combination of herbs that will have gone into the Pud Ped Mu.

Fidgeting with the bezel of her diver's watch, for no reason but to hear it click anti-clockwise around the dial, Alex slides the watchface towards her once more. Determined to stay within her one drink an hour limit, no matter what, she allows herself a second glass of wine to the halfway mark and refills Emilie's just as carefully. *Should have called her the next day to … just to say something. I thought* she *might call. She didn't. I didn't. And well, we –*

"Thank you, Mahdame. The waiter will bring you the main dishes shortly."

I dropped myself out of the race. Pride. That pride of yours, Alex, makes you do crazy things.

The red light of the monitor blinks red across the aisle. Lights blink red above the bar. Red spotlights ignite the dance floor.

"Zag? That your friend over there?" Tamara asked a while later.

"Could be. Where you looking?"

With a movement of her chin Tamara indicated a spot by the glass mirrors at the edge of the dance floor.

"Near the stage. Pink shirt. Nice face."

Tamara had just become aware that the woman with the pink shirt had, on and off during the course of the night, come inside her line of vision. At first she hadn't noticed, then she had thought the woman might have been contemplating a move in her direction but ultimately she had decided that the woman with the pink shirt and the nice face might be connected to Zag.

Might even be her lover. Past or present. And Tamara had imagined the woman, helplessly hurting and aching, watching Zag hit on someone else though she didn't seem the type of woman Zag would lust after. *Too old for her. Too unassuming.*

"Nah. Wouldn't know her from a bar of soap. Why? You fancy her?"

"She's been looking this way a lot. She probably fancies *you*."

"Won't be her lucky night, then. Not my type. Too old. Maybe she fancies you, huh? Wouldn't be surprised but she's– "

"How old d'you think she is? Late thirties?"

"Wouldn't have a clue. Just too old," Zag shrugged. "What about you, Brit girl?" she asked, sipping her glass of beer. "I know for a fact you're not too old at all."

"Twenty-eight. That's old enough," Tamara didn't resist throwing in. "Old enough to be your *older* sister."

"Phoar! Tell you what," Zag exclaims, lens-blue eyes round and wide. "If *my* sister looked anything like you … I would've been in her nappies a long, long time ago. No such luck though." She leaned against Tamara's bare arm to reposition her glass on the bar counter. As she did, her lips hovered very close to Tamara's ear. "I don't have a sister," she whispered. "But how 'bout I show you what I would've done if you – "

Tamara pulled herself away from the bar rail and gently pulled Zag off her bar stool. When both big red Mickey Mouse plastic shoes stood on either side of her desert boots, Tamara brought her in close. Close to her belt buckle, close to her face. She bent her head towards the girl's face and kissed her fully on the mouth. But it was a closed-mouth kiss. And not a long kiss.

"OK, Zag. You're cute in red. Got a great butt." Still looking into the girl's eyes, she added, "I got turned on out there but, look, that's all there is to it. I'm not looking for a screw. So … that was a goodbye kiss, OK. You be good now," she added, her hand light against the girl's cheek. "Not boring … just good." Cat-eyes flashed and Tamara turned on her heel.

That night, the night of the dinner at Alex's place, close to 2 a.m. when she had let Emilie grab her bag on the way to the hallway, to the door, to the gate, back to the red Renegade neatly parked parallel with the fence line, she knew that she was letting her one chance at Emilie walk past and walk away. She knew that by standing still, she was handing the lead over to Tamara who, she knew from experience, would know how to maximise that lead.

And during the ensuing weeks Alex had spent a great deal of those extra hours that some insomniacs actually enjoy, trying to work out whether she had stood still because of the promise made to herself – not weeks or months ago but years earlier – or because she had been too proud to consider ending up as runner-up to Tamara. Too proud to even attempt positioning herself properly on the starting blocks?

Face it, she had rationalised early one morning, why on earth would Emilie choose an introverted, semi-recluse, already in her forties, far too set in her ways, over ... over Tam's sexy, unencumbered exuberance and easy disposition, huh? Huh?

Upon her return from Paris, still dispirited from the Adrienne debacle, and before that even, (before *that* would make it some time after Tamara's departure for Europe), Alex had made a promise to herself. That promise went along the lines of not ever again, not under any circumstances, taking a woman to bed, on impulse alone. To, never again, give in to a precipitate lust-driven craving. *When temptation comes a-calling,* she had reminded herself many times since, *you'll just have to walk away, Alex, just as simply as you tell your students to walk away from a fight. Just turn your back on her and move on.*

Taking risks didn't worry Alex, not that much. Not as much now as it did when she was younger and lived in Spain. Taking risks didn't matter so much anymore but making a fool of herself did matter a lot. It mattered just as much now as it did then. And when it came to Emilie, in the early days, Alex had simply chickened out. She had not risked her pride. She had kept the promise made and her feelings to herself.

A few days after the fish dinner that she had prepared, she had rung Emilie's doorbell, almost hoping she wouldn't find her home. She had worked up the courage to put pride aside and take her place on the starting blocks, tightly coiled for the starter gun. And she was going to make time away from her books, away from her searches and her researches and away from her writing. She would take time to do things with Emilie, time away from her solitude. She was going to do more with Emilie than just go to the movies and discuss films over cups of coffee or a glass or two of Tulloch's Verdelho.

She was going to do things like Tam was, no doubt, already doing with Emilie. Talks, walks, chats, picnics, conversations and more conversations about all sorts of things. Not just about films and world headlines. Not only after dark. But she also wanted to avoid a courtship period. Ugly concept, that one.

Alex wanted to somehow bypass that period of unconsummated lust when wannabe lovers who give in to the impulse to be transparent spread themselves as thin as rice paper. That's the phase when they open their souls wide, as wide as Venus Flytraps, and they remain in that state of almost absolute disclosure until the bonding deed is done, until the very last of the usual hundred days of grace, before reality bites.

By then, because Alex knew – what she'd known all along – that she did not manage all that comfortably the Siamese twin aspect usually expected by most lovers, that managing a new relationship required work, sacrifices and compromises so that, for her, the Venus Flytrap would snap shut, sustaining itself with what juices it had managed to horde and secrete, knowing there would always be another time. Another one.

Alex had done that too often, too long, like the junkie who each time knows that *that one* has to be her last hit. Till the next. And the one after that. Until all her veins are blown. Until the heart, not necessarily the body, gives out. Alex's heart had almost given out in Paris. What remained of it, she needed to protect and care for. And so, that afternoon she had gone to Emilie's to talk, just to talk.

Emilie had opened the door, surprised but visibly happy to find Alex on the doorstep. They had talked like women poised to slip into a different friendship-gear. They had talked, as usual, about a film or two and about work. They had swapped headlines in a stop-start sort of way while Emilie busied herself with cups, saucers and the makings of coffee. Alex had watched her, in control. In control until she had reached out to steady the cup on the saucer Emilie was holding towards her. It was shaking. And then it had all happened too quickly. *No, it had all happened very slowly.*

The cup and saucer had disappeared and Emilie was dizzyingly close to her, blurry-close. And their lips had met. And their tongues had met in a warm and gentle dance. A dance that they managed to control. For a while. Until it became impossible. Until it became impossible for Alex to keep her eyes open. Until all she could do was dissolve inside Emilie's mouth, leaning against Emilie's sink, Emilie's hips against hers. Not pushing, not pressing. Tantalisingly close, just there against the thick seam of her jeans. She had pressed her hand more firmly on Emilie's lower back to bring her closer in. Emilie had moaned into the kiss. And Alex had needed more, wanting to feel Emilie's sex as intimately as she was discovering the warmth, the softness, the taste of Emilie's mouth with her lips. With her tongue.

But from the tiny, tiny part of her brain that had remained immune to the sensory overload came the reminder of the promise she had made to herself. And Alex had moved back a fraction, sliding her mouth over Emilie's swollen lips, finding shelter against the underside of her lip. Ever so slowly, ever so reluctantly, Alex had begun easing away, despite the searing ache of hot desire. She had opened her eyes. She had pulled away. The ache had stayed coiled upon itself, pulsing, radiating, warm.

But the madness had stopped.

Breathless, Emilie had leaned more heavily into Alex's arms, wedging herself tightly against the length of her body, almost snuggling. Alex had kept her pressed against her thumping heart. Then came the moment when they had to separate their heartbeats. They had to get back to the here and now. An awkwardness had set in. Not the awkwardness felt by two people who regret what had passed.

Maybe it had not even been an awkwardness at all. It had felt more like being disoriented. A dislocation perhaps similar to the one Alex occasionally feels on the way out of a cinema when the film has touched a raw nerve. When that happens, Alex does not feel like talking, not immediately. Emilie hadn't seemed to mind that silence coming out of the movies.

And so, after a moment of unfocused chit-chat, Alex had left without having initiated what she *thought* she had set out to do, which had simply been to usher them into a more sustained pace of socialising, all right, into the courting phase, but staying within Emilie's comfort zone. By being the way she knew Emilie enjoyed her: cool, entertaining, an easy conversationalist.

And so, Emilie had walked Alex back to her car and waved goodbye. Alex had waved back. She had rounded the corner and driven only half a kilometre before she had to pull up along the curb. She needed to close her eyes. She needed to shut them tightly around the persistent bite of desire that had made itself at home in her lower belly. She needed to do that and she needed to settle her heart.

Later, closer to dawn than to night, Alex had realised that because the promise she had made to herself basically went against the grain of her otherwise hedonistic view on life, it had helped that new faces seldom appeared inside her friendship group. And none did who did not come with the New Lover of Someone Or Other tag. Certainly none of these newcomers had ever tugged at Alex's imagination or pricked her curiosity.

She did not mix with a gym crowd as, in her own home, she had installed all the equipment necessary for thorough workouts. She attended neither weddings nor funerals nor christenings and she only went to the synagogue once a year, to celebrate Yom Kippur.

She avoided workshops and when she attended seminars, she made herself *not* arrive early, to avoid the otherwise interminable and inevitable socialising that everyone else seemed to enjoy. Between sessions she would, more often than not, isolate herself in a quiet spot to go over her notes and, once done, she would walk for as far and as long as the perimeter of the venue allowed.

She only went out on the scene when Tamara managed to cajole her into a little foray, usually after a dinner in a nearby restaurant. Celibacy by default, Alex often reminded herself, was yet another way to practise detachment. Only Alex thought *her* celibacy was by default. To everyone else who observed her active non-involvement with people, the fact that she never met anyone new was no wonder.

Trust Tam to drag me to The Triangle that night. Trust her to flush out Emilie. Trust her to bring her back to me, like a most clever gun dog that not only flushes out a quail but also retrieves it. Tail wagging. Green eyes sparkling.

"She looks a bit like you, except for the hair that's longer," Tamara had said. "And all dark brown."

Not in the mood for conversation the night they had met at The Triangle, Emilie had sent Tamara back to the table where Tamara's friend was still sitting. Alex had actually been the first to spot the lone woman casually leaning against the bar but visibly miles away from the activity around her. *She* had spotted her but Alex was not a retriever. If a woman, any woman she had noticed, didn't engage *her* first, Alex didn't even point. The old pride thing.

"And she's got a trace of a French accent, but not like yours. She's only half-French. On her mother's side. She's interesting, Al, right up your alley." Green eyes had the brightness of a child's come upon a surprise. "I'm sure you'll like her."

If it hadn't been for the fact that her car had gone, I'd never have met her. If it hadn't been for her car towed away, she would already have been on her way home by the time Tam and I decided to call it a night.

Alex looks up. Across the table at the *Patcharin*, Emilie is smiling.

"Every time I come here, it's great, I enjoy the food and the low-key atmosphere, no unnecessary airs and graces about the place, but by the time I leave, I feel like I've been 'Mahdahmmed' out. Anyway back to that conversation you had with Tamara. Was it at your place, the other night when she went over for dinner?"

"Yes and this afternoon at the hospital. As it turns out, last Monday night *and* this afternoon we ended up talking about you."

Emilie whispers, "Great, I'm flattered." But drawing in a breath, she asks, "What about, or don't I want to know?"

Monday night, Alex had told Tamara about *The Kiss*. But only in answer to Tam's belated question about stealing Alex's thunder, regarding Emilie. Nine months having gone by, Alex had given up expecting that question to pop up. Eyes downcast, Alex grins to herself remembering Tamara's disbelief while she runs a quick mental check. *That had been Monday. Tuesday night had been Tam's monthly shift at the DV Hotline. Wednesday, last night, the poor thing didn't get the chance to even hug Emilie.* And so, assuming she knew Tam as she thought she did, Alex surmised that she would not have broached *that* topic with Emilie over the phone. So, Emilie's question was transparent.

Alex had found it refreshing in a parallel sort of way, a confirmation of Emilie's integrity, or was it of her sensibility, that she had kept the kiss-moment from Tamara. She liked to imagine that Emilie had sent *that* moment to her *jardin secret*, that little private place on the edge of one's thoughts, not to be shared with anyone, not even with a friend, not even with one's lover.

"Hellowww. Anyone home?"

Alex drags her eyes away from the reflected ceiling light trapped inside the hollow of her teaspoon to find Emilie peering at her.

"Ah, yes," she begins again, now eager to move the conversation away from that *other* conversation. "Where was I? Ah yes. So, this afternoon, at the hospital, Tam and I had a serious conversation about you. Hmm." Alex clears her throat quietly and takes another sip of wine. "And … it would seem that our *young* friend," Alex begins with a stress on the word *young*. "It would seem that Tam thinks you're holding back on her."

Emilie blushes. "She told you that?"

"She did, but that's OK. Good friends do talk about these things with each other. Tam and I go back a long way."

"It's not that. It's just that … I'm just surprised, that's all. I mean, it's all a bit personal."

"Umm … personal?" Alex raises an eyebrow. "To her, yes, that's why she has entrusted me with her thoughts on the topic but … uniquely personal? No, I don't think it is. You see," Alex tries to explain, "she and I have … well, in a way we have already been through a similar phase … I mean the phase you might be going through with her … if you're going through the … the age discrepancy phase." She pauses and waits for Emilie to look up from her glass. "Are you? Emilie?"

Emilie shrugs and leans away from the table. Taking Emilie's non-engagement as licence to continue, Alex continues. "Unlike you, I did not go through that questioning phase when I fell in love with her."

"Alex, you were a lot younger then than I am today."

"I was but, for us, a twelve-year gap was there all the same. I did *eventually* question that gap. A few months after she left, I wrote her that I was cancelling my plan to join her in France. And so, I thought the hardest part of our relationship, the pushing-her-away part was behind me. But by the time she made it back here, she had decided that we could just pick up where we had left off. No sweat. The old easy-peasy thing as they say in England." Alex's finger taps the side of the tea-spoon. The light trapped inside the silver hollow rocks from side to side.

Great hands, Emilie can't help but notice again. Wonderful, long and strong fingers that would have no problem at all spanning from Ctrl to F5 and N on the keyboard.

The shutter-quick image of Alex's hands poised over the curves of her own ergonomic keyboard hits Emilie. Annoyed by the persistent intrusion of such thoughts, she straightens up on her chair and frowns. *The day's been too long. I need to get home. Two Sleep-Ezy pills and sleep.*

"She thought we could have another go because she had grown up."

"My very point. Some are growing up, Alex, while some of us are growing old. A lover on each side is what the age-gap is about. And how did she handle that rejection?" Emilie asks tightly, not at all in the tone she had intended using. "No, don't answer. She got over that by getting involved with me."

Alex's eyes flit over the almost bare walls. They settle on the poster of Wat Pho, home of the Reclining Buddha, forty-six metres of horizontal gold and mother-of-pearl inlays on the soles of his feet. When her eyes go back to Emilie's, she says, "I don't think you need to go there, Emilie." Her tone is controlled and firm. The teacher-in-charge-tone. Emilie's familiar with that tone. She, too, used to be a full time high school teacher. When *her* insides are in turmoil, the tone kicks in for her too. Still does. Hard and fast. "Tam doesn't deserve that and you don't need to short-change yourself. She fell in love with you, full stop."

"Tell me why the 'possibility' that she got involved with me on the rebound seems so unreasonable to you…" The lump at the base of Emilie's throat is mushy and watery, "…when according to her, we, you and I, are so alike? One little difference being that *me*, I'm older than even you."

Alex's eyebrows are knotted tightly under the silver forelock that has fallen over her forehead. She bristles at Emilie. "*Because* Tamara does not think that way. And because…" she adds more gently, "…because despite *some* similarities, you and I are not at all alike."

Emilie snorts softly but does not reply. A little man in Thai dress is approaching their table with two dishes and a silver bowl. She displays a smile for him though she is not yet sure whether he picked his moment well or badly.

"Ganddang?"

"Ah, that's mine," Alex answers flatly.

"And if that's Pud Ped…uh…Mu…" The waiter inclines his torso slightly. "That'll be for me. Thank you."

"And rice?"

"Yes, and rice. For two." The Thai waiter retreats with a slight nod.

"Look, Emilie, the only reason I brought up the topic is because, I think I know something about what you might be shying away from."

"Right. Alex, let's keep that simple. What are you trying to tell me? What's your point?"

"My point? My point … Good question, that. What is my point?" Alex asks, pointing to Emilie's stir-fried pork in a red curry sauce. "How is your dish?"

"No idea but I suspect it will be as it usually is. Good."

"Right." Alex's eyes flash an amiable smile before settling on to the morsel of green curry chicken speared by her fork.

Poker-faced, Emilie looks at her, undecided as to whether she should feel annoyed or not. And if so, what about? *Take your pick,* she grumbles to herself.

"I don't know, Emilie," Alex says without looking up from the next morsel of chicken. "I don't have *a point*. I'm just trying to suggest that you probably do not need to put the brakes on."

"Right."

"No, this is serious. Want to know why I did … put the brakes on?"

Emilie grins and shakes her head. "You'll tell me anyway. Why ask?"

"Hey, rhetorical questions have a right to exist, you know." Fork down, Alex shifts her attention away from her dish. "I did simply because a little voice had told me that if I didn't break it off with her, she would end up dumping me, sooner or later, intentionally or not, most likely for someone more her own age."

"Not necessarily. I mean, not necessarily with one younger."

"OK, it should not have made a difference but, if I'm to be honest with you … it would have uh, made a difference." Alex waves her hand to suggest the futility of explaining what she knows to be irrational. "In fact, it is *that* fear that precipitated the letter I sent her, you know, the Dear Jane letter. Weird," Alex agrees, "but I would much rather lose out to someone my own age." She momentarily absorbs herself in the intricacies of the thick gold band she wears on her middle finger. Emilie lets her.

Gisèle: thirty-three. Emilie: twenty- two.

Her first older-woman love. Her first massive heartbreak. They had kissed and kissed and just about made love, frantic love, in a narrow street, hidden from view by the arch of darkness of a deeply recessed doorway. When they did make it to Gisèle's flat, high above the street, they had tumbled down on her bed. That is how their affair had begun.

It ended one morning. Emilie, who had bounded down three flights of stairs, had found herself breathless and alone on the sidewalk. Alone with the pigeons and the homeless in a post-dawn grey light. That same night, she had made herself go to Mikael's *vernissage*, under the arches of Place Des Vosges, not because it had been planned that way but to see Gisèle one last time. One last time. *Just to confirm the morning's pain.*

It was the shine of her silken black hair, alight under the ceiling spotlights that had caught her eye as soon as she pushed through the glass doors of the art gallery. It was swaying gently from side to side as Gisèle turned her attention from one in her entourage to another.

From where she was standing, Emilie could see her, striking in a simple, black, backless dress that ended just above the knees. Well-defined calves and thin ankles led the eye to black, flat-heeled shoes that matched perfectly the tone and feel of Gisèle's raw silk dress.

Heart beating like an erratic metronome, Emilie had walked back into the night, hot tears down her cheeks. She had vaulted over the hip-high entrance to the garden quadrangle. *Hmmph,* she snorts at the memory. *Yes, I could still do that at twenty-two.*

Forehead against knees, hands flat against her head, she had curled up on the ground, her back against the fountain's wet lip. She had cried quietly. And the moisture on the fountain's curved lip spread through the thin weave of her shirt. She had cried until the steady tinkle of the tiered fountain behind her penetrated her tear-swollen thoughts. Until the insistent murmur of the fountain's light drops, one by one by one, unclamped the hold those thoughts had on Emilie's heart. Until the fountain melted them away like so many crystals of sea salt sat on its ledge. Until it made her breathe again.

Across from Emilie, at the *Pacharin* on Hardgrave Road, Alex is pensively rolling the wide band of gold in front of her plate. And Emilie, though she no longer remembers the pain of those long dead days, knows where to feel for ridges of scar tissue.

So young, so head over heels in love, she thinks to herself as she follows the roll of the ring on the table and the play of Alex's fingers. *Head over heels love doesn't know how to shrink itself. It doesn't know how to make room for … for anything else.*

Emilie looks away from that memory. "Alex, what's the diff whether Tamara's new lover was going to be younger or older?" Emilie asks this to shut down the hologram of Gisèle as she remembers her the last time she saw her, all eyes, all sensual, all into games of the senses. But Emilie's thoughts pull her back to the little café near the Opéra where she and Gisèle used to meet.

In a corner of the glassed-in terrace, her back to the aisle, her back to the door and to the world, Emilie was glancing at the passers-by on the other side of the glass but she regularly dragged her eyes back to the magazine she thought she ought to be reading. She needed to keep up with the world out there.

In the vibrations contained in the turn of a page, her senses went on a sudden sensory overload. *L'Air Du Temps* de Nina Ricci. The memory of the perfume, invisible in its presence, flooded her senses. Gisèle! The silky caress of *her* Hermes scarf against Emilie's ear, the brush of soft-silk hair against her collarbone, *her* lips cool against Emilie's neck.

'*Aime, je t'ai retrouvée.* Let me look at you.' Gisèle always pronounced the short version of Emilie's name, as the French say the word love. *Aime.*

'I wasn't lost.'

'No, but *I* thought I had lost you, *tu sais.* You left that morning and you didn't come to Mikael's *vernissage.* I miss you, *Aime.*' Gisèle had stepped around the bentwood chair to look into Emilie's eyes. '*Tu me manques, tu sais –* '

"It would have made a difference to me," Alex is saying, breaking into Emilie's thoughts. "I guess it's the idea of not being able to, you know, uh … to fight back, of being helpless in a weird way. I would much rather she left me for a woman my own age." She frowns at her glass, unconvinced by her own argument.

Emilie didn't want to hear that Gisèle was missing her. She wasn't going to invite her to sit down. She couldn't. Her heart was beating too fast. The inside of her head had become a shimmery hollow. She was feeling the panic of the bird that hits its wings against a window-pane while the trees, the sky, life are all there. *Just there.* Inaccessible.

Gisèle didn't sit down. She only squatted by Emilie's chair, gathering the folds of her *gabardine* over her lap. She spoke, slowly, gently, as if to a child who had to be reassured. And after she was done, she said, "*Viens. Là … maintenant.* Come." She had stood up to reach for her brown Vuitton wallet. With one finger she had slid the cashier's ticket from under Emilie's saucer. With two fingers she had lifted a fifty-franc bill from the fold of her *portefeuilles* and let it flutter on the table. Enough to pay for two coffees, though the cashier's bill only covered the one coffee Emilie had ordered. Gisèle's wallet had slid back inside the large pocket of her raincoat and she wrapped Emilie's hand with her own. Emilie's breath caught in her throat. The image of a butterfly, wings spread, pinned to a board, crowded the inside of her head.

"*Viens, Aime. Tu veux?*" Gisèle's eyes were brown. They were warm. Emilie, once again, thought of dark amber.

Yes, she had wanted to follow Gisèle, that she did want to do, right there and then. She knew Gisèle's car would be parked nearby, that she would drive them back to her flat, high above *rue de Rivoli* and that they would make love.

Emilie knew that once again, she would dissolve into Gisèle, as she had each time they made love, losing her sense of self, losing the edges of her body when Gisèle wrapped herself around her in that particular manner she had. Emilie's outer core just dissolved into the older woman.

"Et l'autre ... alors?" Emilie had asked as a voice test. "What about her, then?"

"Ah. Still upset by that, *Aime? Dis, regarde-moi?"*

Emilie had not done as asked. She had not looked at Gisèle. Her eyes had returned to the magazine she thought she ought to have been reading. But she did answer. *"Ben ... oui.* Yes, I am. Still upset by that."

"Mais, chérie, ça ne fait rien, ces choses-là. It doesn't matter *si je fais l'amour,* if I made love with her, or someone else. Even if I make love with her again, it doesn't matter. You are you and she is ... well, *elle c'est elle.* You need to grow up about *ces choses-là,* about things like that. *C'est la vie, Aime.'*

Emilie didn't want to grow up to understand things like that. She never wanted to grow up enough to love one woman and make love to another as well. Or to love so little that she wouldn't mind that her lover occasionally also made love with someone else. "It matters, Gisèle. It matters to me. Please, *laisse-moi.* Just go."

Gisèle had not left. She had sat opposite Emilie who could not bear the sensual pull of Gisèle's amber eyes. She could not bear to look at them because she desperately wanted to drown herself in them. She wanted those warm amber eyes to be the last thing she'd see before she closed her eyes and dissolved, one last time, inside Gisèle's embrace.

Across the table, Alex smiles sheepishly. "Oh, look, I guess it's simpler than I thought. No denying it, it's that age insecurity thing. The way I see it, if I have to be dumped for someone else, I would much rather it were for someone more accommodating than me, richer than me, sweeter than me, more intelligent than me, but not *younger* than me. I mean not five or ten or twelve years younger than me. OK, that's me, right? So, I don't always make sense." The smile Emilie sees is the smile of a little girl, disarming and honest.

Back at *le Café de l'Opéra* with Gisèle, that day, Emilie had sprung to her feet, making the cup and saucer tremble on the table. She had yanked her well-worn leather jacket off the back of the chair. The chair had bucked but hadn't fallen backwards. Emilie strode through the glass door and into the *Boulevard Des Capucines.* And she had walked blind until the *Boulevard Des Capucines* intersected the *Boulevard*

Montmartre. And then she had stopped walking. She had stopped running. She had stopped keeping pace with the frenetic beat of her heart. Alex and Emilie are the only patrons left at the *Patcharin*. From the other side of the wall comes the clanging of plates and pots being washed and stacked. Alex pulls on the collar of her black shirt. The little dew-drop buttons sparkle. "What I was going to ask you, before I got discombobulated, just now, by what you asked … What I was going to ask is, what did the little voice, the one that whispered to me about Tam, what did it actually *know* about her, huh?" Alex reaches for her glass of wine but only to slide it further off to the side. "Nothing at all, that's what. OK … here is my point, Emilie. That kind of little voice is simply a … a hodgepodge of preconceived ideas. They're instilled and picked up along the way. We activate it when we want…" Alex's hands shoot out, palms up, waiting for *le mot juste,* the word she is after to fall into them. "We do that, we listen to that voice when we want to *dissuade* or … encourage ourselves about something or other. The way I see it, it acts as a validation of … of sorts. It momentarily takes the burden of decision or indecision away from us. It serves to absolve us from having to…" Alex's long fingers move through the air to punctuate her words and finish her thought for her.

Emilie is still fascinated by the myriad of expressions at play on Alex's face when in full flight. Her exuberant 'Europeanness', that quick energy, the precipitate flow of words accompanied by a whole alphabet of non-verbals are so un-Anglo. *So* un-Brisbane.

"Alex … Your point?"

"Coming. Either way, that little voice gives us the trumped-up reasons we need to bail out and *not* feel like a shit. And," Alex adds, looking squarely at Emilie, palms together, "I suspect that *that* little voice is now whispering into *your* ears. It is scaring you away from what you and Tam have to share." She moves the wineglass further still, away from the movements of a right hand that might add this glass to others that have toppled, cracked, and spilled over the tabletop. "Don't you see? And so what *if* Tam should happen to fly the coop next month or some time during the next thirty years, you'll just have to remind yourself that … that it's all *already* happened to you, many times over, right? She won't be the first woman ever to leave you. Life's a bitch. Love hurts. Everything sucks. All my students know that already. Emilie, haven't *you* ever done the 'Ciao, Baby. This gig's gone flat' bit? Or the 'I'm off. But, Baby, you look after yourself now, ya hear!' routine?"

Emilie sticks her bottom lip out to camouflage a smile but her eyes betray her. "I've done it, yes. Many times, too many perhaps. But that doesn't make me more ready for a payback. Not from Tamara." *Alex,* Emilie whispers inside her head. *So adamant, so intense. Too bloody prickly to ever be ... cute. And yet what is it about her that I find so–*

"Then, you don't want to precipitate a premature ending either," Alex says directly into Emilie's eyes. "Maybe you should give her a better chance to ... to thrive ... with you. A better chance than you're giving her ... if you are holding back on her. More credit." She stops, eyes wide open. "Wow!" she exclaims flopping back against her chair, "I think I need another glass of wine after this. Don't you feel like clapping or anything?" she adds, visibly quite pleased with the role she has just improvised for Tamara's sake. *For her sake because I can't believe, not for a moment, that Tam is not totally into her, into Emilie.* "But tell me something." She taps the back of Emilie's hand. "Honest answer, OK?"

"OK." Emilie breathes in again.

"Uh ... right then. Here goes: is part of your hesitation due to the thought that you perhaps you ... you *might* just break it off with her ... first? Like I did?"

The thought hurts like a glancing dart and Emilie shrugs the sting away. "As you said, life's a bitch."

"Ah, what? Look at us, will you." Alex's hands are in front of Emilie, waving almost in her face, seeking a more secure connection. "We've survived, haven't we? It does not mean we have to search and destroy what – "

"Yes, we've survived. Jaded but ... alive." Emilie straightens herself in her chair to straighten her thoughts. Straightened thoughts are clearer than slouched thoughts. "Look, seriously ... I really can't see a reasonably long term with Tamara. The gap, this time around, yes, the bloody gap is just too wide. So, all right, so what if she's almost twenty-nine. Me, I'm about to turn forty-seven." She stops, thinking her point made. She doesn't know how to interpret Alex's silence. "So, no matter which way we turn it, there's that gap that's eighteen-year *deep*. Not a mere ten or not twelve, don't you see?"

Emilie's hot again. Hot and annoyed. Annoyed with herself and, just as definitely, annoyed with Alex. The weariness of earlier has returned and so has the tightness across her shoulders. She's annoyed because what Alex has touched on is exactly what she's been grappling with, on her own, for the best part of nine months. *You'd think that by now I'd have a grip on this thing.* "Alex, don't go obtuse on me, please. I'm tired." Wearily, she adds, "I've had two very long days. Look, I was already well into my first year at uni, not even still at *school,* when she was born, right? Doesn't *that* say it all?" With her thumb, she slides the knife forward and backwards near the side of her plate.

"Tell me something then. If you were involved with someone closer to your own age, for example say, hey, why not, someone like me … right?" Alex argues tensely, aware she is skating too close to the middle of her own frozen pond. "Would *that* automatically have granted … us a … a perpetual, uh, a perennial Disneyland of the heart? I don't mean in isolation of course, but combined with all the positives that we already know or sense about each other."

Emilie stops fidgeting with her knife. Her eyes flick over Alex's face but settle a hair's breadth away from her cheekbone. "Like what, similar interests up to a point? A genuine liking for each other? And, uh … as a bonus, only a little gap of a few years? You're asking me if *I* think that would be enough to … but you're not serious, are you? You're having me on."

"I am serious."

"Are those essentials enough to keep both players in situ for what, the next thirty or forty years? Till death through old age did them part? No, even all that would still not be enough. There'd always be the intangible, the unexpected, the– What's your point?" Emilie asks even more irritably because she shouldn't have asked that question as she already had the answer. And yet she continued. "Never been good with riddles. Not at the best of tim– "

"Well, this *particular* point is a simple one, Emilie. Have you ever had any assurance, at all, that you wouldn't be dumped? In the past? Even in your youth, when you were full of *joie de vivre*, exuberant and sexy … Just as our Tam is at this particular moment in her life?"

Emilie knows she has to forfeit on that argument. "Well, no," she answers, deflated but still feisty.

"Well, then. I rest my case."

"Right. OK. I've heard you, Alex." Emilie leans back against her chair, shoulders drooping, arms dangling in silent surrender. "I *am* tired but, it's OK. I hear you. I'm closed but not totally *hermétique*."

The red light of the monitor across the aisle blinks and blinks, but Tamara's eyes are closed. Uncomfortable with her thoughts, she tosses and turns. The top sheet tangles and tightens around her hips.

The door that had let her out of The Triangle swung back on its hinges, choking the thumping sounds of the music and trapping inside the billows of smoke. Keys in hand, Tamara turned away from Ann Street and walked towards her car parked at the end of the lane. She lowered her head and sniffed the thin cotton cloth of her Tee. *Phew! Foul.* She crinkled up her nose. *Just as well I'm only going back to my place.*

Jiggling her car keys, she grinned as she strode past the parking spot from where Emilie's Jeep had been towed away on that night when they had first met. *If it hadn't been for that drama, she and I would never have connected a second time.* She looked at the driveway to her right. Still overgrown with weeds, it did look totally abandoned and still too narrow to accommodate a car of any description and, yet, whoever lived in the shabby chamferboard house at the other end of the narrow driveway had called to have the Jeep removed. She shrugged and glanced at her watch. *OK. Shower. Wash hair. Still early enough to grab a video on the way.*

Rapid footfalls filtered through the plans Tamara was making for the next phase of her bachelor grunge night. She glanced over her shoulder.

A woman had just turned into the lane. Another escapee from The Triangle, Tamara thought. *No cooking. No washing up. Crap food and self-indulgence.* Bachelor grunge is Emilie's euphemism for the nights she and Tamara spend separately. Something made Tamara turn around again. Yes, it was the woman with the pink shirt and the pleasant face who was walking a few metres behind her. Tamara simply acknowledged the woman's presence in the deserted lane with a casual, "Hey," as she tossed the keys in the palm of her hand and carried on walking.

I'll pick something nicely trivial, dumbed down. Veg out time. Her flatmate, Chris, and her lover were out of town. Tamara would have the house all to herself. *Bliss. I'll pick something like what Em for sure wouldn't want to watch. Like a Jet Li film.* And with a bit of a start, she wondered what Emilie would make of Zag. *And now, what? To tell or not to tell? Nothing to say. No ... not true,* she reasoned honestly, lacing the keys through her fingers. *Plenty to say but not enough to ... Not worth upsetting Emilie. It's all cool, like totally under control. I don't nee –* "What the fuck!" she cried, as her head was snapped back.

Reflexes slowed by the surprise of the attack, Tamara tried to turn around but she was slammed against the wall. Winded, she dropped her keys.

"You fuckin' mad or what?" she shouted at the twisted face that had grabbed her by the V of her T-shirt. "Let go of me!" She tried to pry the fist loose. "Piss off!"

The woman twisted the T-shirt higher up against Tamara's throat. "Fucking cunt," she spat. "You just fuckin' leave us be," she snarled, lips tight against her teeth. "Fuckin' leave us alone."

The woman in the pink shirt, the one with the pleasant face, the one whom Zag had said was not a friend, *that* woman no longer had her face arranged in a pleasant manner.

Mouth level with Tamara's nose, she hissed, "You come around again, bitch…" The woman's breath was hot and sour. "You come visitin' her again …" she added, shaking her other fist in Tamara's face, "I'll be shoving *that* up your posh little arse." Angry spittle was flying out her mouth.

"You're off your friggin' face or what?"

Everything had happened too quickly for Tamara, too quickly and far too violently. *Time to get rid of the bitch,* is all she reckoned. She had had enough of the woman's foul breath. Forcefully, she brought up her wrist from under the woman's, who still had the V of Tamara's T-shirt bunched inside her fist. The woman's hand flew open and Tamara crashed the heel of her boot on the top of her aggressor's foot.

The woman's eyes popped open wide and she gasped, "Fuckin' hell … Cunt!" Then she grimaced. Tamara shoved her backwards with a quick jab to the shoulder. The woman maintained her balance but only to hop on one foot, like a lame bird, keeping her weight off the other.

"You're fuckin' lucky I don't fight," Tamara couldn't resist throwing back at the woman who, though she was sucking air between clenched teeth, glowered back, propped against the red brick wall while Tamara unlocked her car door.

By the time she had left the restaurant and made it back to the Jeep, Emilie was tired, dog-tired. Knackered even, but exhilarated. Not unlike every other time she had been alone with Alex. She exhaled forcefully through rounded lips. Head back, motionless in the dark cabin, she listened to the noises of the night.

Something caught her attention in the foot well of the passenger side. Leaning over the gearshift, she brought up two CDs. She peered at the faces trapped under the plastic casing and blew a little puff of air through her nose. Slowly, with the hem of her shirt, she wiped the top CD.

Strapped in, she turned on the ignition. She turned on the headlights. She slipped the disk into the slot and waited for the intro that she knew would surge through the speakers, strong and powerful. And it did, powerful and uplifting. Yes! Tam's rollerblading sound. Tamara.

An image of her lover as she had appeared that day at Emilie's front door flashed over the windscreen. Tall and straight, she had stood there in the fading light and there had been an air of quiet assurance about her, wide shoulders loose and unencumbered. Later on that afternoon, they had made love for the second time.

When she's finished mending, she won't have any of these deficits. She'll go on bladin' and she'll go on groovin'. Tomorrow morning, I buy her a new Discman. Tomorrow afternoon, I bring her home.

By the time she pulled up at the first red light Emilie was humming along, beating the tempo on the steering wheel. *"You always make me smile ... ... You give me such a vibe ... ... Ain't the way you walk ... Ain't the job you got that's keeping me satisfied. Oooh ... ooh ... oooh."*

Tamara's eyes snap open, wide-open, long before she thinks about moving. Long before grey, wispy impressions and pixelised fragments of memory are able to cluster into a thought.

By the time the fog clears the whorls of her brain, by the time that fog dissipates enough to turn into mist, Tamara realises she's still marooned in a hospital bed and all she can say about it is, "Awh ... for fuck's sake."

That realisation makes her lie very still. Still enough to feel her head from the inside. The pain in there *is* still there, she can tell, but all its nails are blunted. She feels that pain as a presence that's filled all the spaces under her skull, a bulging, heavy and cumbersome presence that presses itself against bone, but it's no longer clawing to get out. It's not hurtling itself around like a rabid rat in a cage. It's not squeezing her brain out. It has simply overtaken it. It has numbed it.

It must be night-time because all's very quiet except for the snores that are still coming from somewhere beyond the curtain and the dry-coughing patient is still there, too, somewhere upstream. And the fluorescent lights are falsely reassuring in their softened night hue.

Once every spot and dot that were weirdly elongated, fuzzy and oddly coloured when her eyes had first snapped open have resized and adjusted themselves, the red monitor blinking across the aisle like a beacon across the bay helps her get her final bearings.

That's what she screamed at me. I'm totally sure of that. No doubt! Visiting her. That's it, isn't it? Whoa, slow down!

Tamara pauses wide-eyed on that flash of insight. Having automatically assumed all along that her aggressor back in the lane must have been Zag's lover, past or present, jealous or jilted, despite the young woman's denials, Tamara had found it quite convenient to forget all about this post-Triangle ambush of six days earlier. And because, in her mind, the incident was linked to her flirtation with Zag, she hadn't mentioned it to Emilie.

Too difficult to manage that story without lying to Emilie. And *not lying* to Emilie, in turn, would have meant striking some sort of pain, some self-doubt in Emilie. Tamara was sure of that. And during the few days that had followed the lane attack, she had reasoned that she really didn't want to upset Emilie, not over something as silly as the 'Zag thing'.

That's gotta be what made the woman flip, is what Tamara had concluded later that night, at her place, while she had vigorously rubbed her scalp and scrubbed her body to wash the last particles of bar-sweat, second-hand smoke and canned smog.

Concerns about Zag had frothed up, though, while Tamara had covered herself in suds. Violent irrationality is part of what can make a relationship abusive and dangerous. Zag, she thought, was too slight, too young, to handle out-of-control physical outbursts and live by the cycles of the love-fear-hope triangle. Why would Zag even *want* to hang around such a plot?

Even after so many years of talking to survivors, it was only at the intellectual level that Tamara understood what kept these women at home with their abusive partner. Not even her own resourceful and independent mother had known how to leave in time.

The hot jets of steamy water dissolved the tightness that had been creeping across the base of her neck. Eyes closed, palms flat against the white tiles, Tamara had let the water fall across her shoulders. *It's back to the old 'What Seems' versus 'What Is, or 'Appearance' versus 'Reality'. Sucks big time.*

It always did.

Then, as she had wrapped her body inside the large candy-striped bath towel Emilie had left behind, Tamara had considered how she might be able to help Zag … *if* Zag wanted to be helped … *if* they ever bumped into each other again. And yet, all along, something kept tugging at the back of Tamara's reasoning.

Zag only shrugged that she didn't know the woman. She hadn't carried on like a victim. And yet, Tamara wondered, had Zag overdone the seduction act as one straddles railroad tracks knowing a train is fast approaching? If only to jump aside at the last minute? No, for Tamara that didn't make sense. And it couldn't have been that she was *that* desperate to get into my shorts either, she had thought with a shake of the head.

And she had grinned, thinking back to that point in time when, eyes closed and led by the singer's slow voice, she had totally disconnected, dissolved even, until she had felt Zag's fingers against the loose cotton of her shorts, over her sex, searching. *No, something's not right there,* she had argued again with herself. *Victims of domestic violence seldom, if ever … They just don't go out of their way to antagonise their lover.*

Petty teasing intended to whip up some sort of jealousy that triggers a forceful reaction some women interpret as a token of love, those games are not what DV is about. Women on the receiving end of real pain do not seek, do not nurture *that* violence. They don't provoke it because they are damn well afraid of it when it hits. They are afraid of it because they are familiar with the different pains it inflicts and because, in many cases, there is nothing *they* can do to make it stop. *So … where does that leave Zag, then?*

Unable to give herself an answer to that question, Tamara had given herself *another* set of more personal questions while she brushed back the black strands of her hair and smoothed them against her head, behind her ears but fluffing them away from her neck. She let those questions simmer around makeshift answers while she brushed her teeth, thoroughly, methodically, around and over each tooth, over the gums, and the back of each tooth. She spat pale blue spit and rinsed her mouth with flowing water cupped in both hands.

As she had been about to turn off the bathroom light she went back by the sink. Back-combing her hair again but with her hands this time, she leaned closer to the mirror and peered at herself.

As a child, she had been most unhappy with the colour of her mother's eyes. Well, no, that wasn't quite true. It wasn't so much the green itself, the green in her mother's eyes she objected to, as she liked it very much *inside* her mother's eyes, bright and light against her ever-tanned face. It had more to do with the fact that she didn't like that green in *her* eyes.

"Leaf-green, Bub," her mother used to say each time little Tamara complained about not having dark eyes like her father's, like those of her cousin Jamie who spent more and more time with them on board Black Night.

"His parents are not happy with each other," Laurel had said one afternoon as Black Night had been anchored close to shore. "So little Jamie's going to become your little brother. For a while … or longer, OK, Bub? We'll play it by ear."

"Why my *little* brother?" five-year old Tamara had been quick to query. "He's older than me."

"He Well, yes, he is. You're absolutely right, you know," Laurel had answered, a little taken aback. Jamie was such a slight little boy. Tamara was so much more agile, sturdier even, that Laurel often forgot he was already one year older than her daughter. And such a quiet little lad too. Very quiet he had been, loosely draped across her husband's chest that day they had pulled him out of the dark blue water.

White face. Red blood. Black twine.

"Mother? I would never have wished for leafy eyes, you know."

"Your eyes are not leafy, Tam. Spinach is leafy. Bushes are leaf – "

"Nothing's leafy on Black Night, is it?"

"No, not on the boat, no. But everywhere on land, in all the parks and the gardens. The trees and the plants and … hey, you do know what leafy means. So, you pay attention now," Laurel would say, squatting near her daughter, the pink and turquoise sarong Tamara remembered best stretched against her slender thighs. There were often little traces of sea salt on her mother's knees so Tamara would brush them away.

"Imagine tender new leaves in Springtime, tender-green as they open up for the first time. As they see the sunshine, and the blue sky, and they see *you* for the first time. So who's the little girl who would want dark eyes when she could have baby-leaf-green eyes that make everyone smile, huh?"

So Tamara had looked at her green eyes in the bathroom mirror and shrugged. She had shrugged but she felt weird. Like sad. She had frowned at her reflection and had peered more closely into the mirror. More closely still, until her forehead had bumped against the glass. Its coolness felt good against her skin, still hot from her shower.

By the time she had pulled away from the mirror, the questions she had let loose in her head had, magnet-like, pulled in answers, but none she was happy with. So she let them reshape themselves as *more* questions and she let them blink at her from behind the shield of their brand-new question marks.

In the meantime, though, she had figured out that this business of letting herself go with Zag, this business of wanting, if only for a moment, to let go and be … and be … sensual– "No, not sensual, for fuck's sake! Sensual's something else," she had burst out loud, "I'm thinking *sex* here, right?" she had glared at the face in the mirror who glared back at her through slitted green eyes. "Like as in *wet*. Wet, as in turned on by some chick who's not my lover." She was surprised by the effort it had actually required for her to be honest, if only with her-self. "So it's sexual all right. No two ways about it."

Why has this become complicated? She drew in her top lip. *OK ... so ... this business of getting sexual with someone else, someone other than Emilie, just because it's ... Well, yes, just because it's like,* there, available, *and it feels so good,* that *business is gonna happen again. It is, isn't it?* She had moved away from her mirror-self because even *two* of her were failing to make simple sense.

Nine months into her relationship with Emilie and not once had Tamara doubted that she was in love with her, that she was *still* hot for her. Short-term had begun stretching itself first into less short, then into longer-term. Plans had begun taking shape in her mind. *And now what?* she had wanted to know. *One night on the scene, alone, right? It was-n't even like, wow! at first sight or anything.*

She had walked to her bedroom and tossed aside the bath towel. *More like not attracted at all, not at first.* A cool breeze came in through the window, barred, but not against the breeze, and Tamara had run a hand over her breasts. Her nipples registered her touch. *And yet, I let her. I let Zag do whatever and then, yeah, I got like,* so *turned on.* She moved her hand across her stomach where she had felt the breeze caress it. *Too turned on! And yes, I kissed her.* Feet on the brushed-wood floor, Tamara had flopped backwards on to the bed, arms akimbo. *So what?*

Eyes wide, eyes as wide as the white-plaster rosace that clung to the ceiling like a limpet on a rock, she had forced her thoughts to push further into the trail they had only begun to clear. Cautiously she moved as if that path had been strewn with sharp-edged blades.

I enjoyed it. It felt good, she thought, trying not to blink in case she lost her focus, *I could've kept going.* And what she had known all along, but hadn't wanted to identify, broke through the surface. *And it's going to happen again. With someone else. Isn't it? Maybe with some-one who really, like really turns me on, like from scratch.* There was nothing at all wrong with what she had done. *It's like Em's been saying all along. There'll be a time when I might want to go all the way. She's right, Emilie, I'm too young not to explore all that's to be explored.* Only she knew that it would cause Emilie great anxiety and confirm for her that Tamara was indeed not ready to commit.

So? *Is that a problem? What about Em? Will she ever need to … Will she get, like, tempted too … one day?* Tamara had wanted to stop probing further than the edge of an awareness she hadn't expected to bump into so soon. But like the irritating and addictive sensation that some derive from running a fingertip ever so lightly across one's eyelashes, the itch to question what she had never questioned kept her riding the onslaught of doubts that assailed her. *So … because I love Emilie, that's it? No more of that rush with anyone else? Because we're together* that *becomes the line-in-the-sand thing?* Tamara had closed her eyes against those thoughts to better breathe in the night, pulling it inside through the barred window that was not barred against the breeze and not barred against the night and not barred against tortuous thoughts.

If I love Em, I have to make myself never *do that again.* Tamara swallowed hard. *Or if I want to be free to … to do that and … screw around and all, then what? Em and me, we have to break up? Is that how it works with women like her and Alex? With older women?*

Tamara had sat up, loosening her shoulders. *Not good. Bad scene that. Bad all around.* From the heap of clean clothes that rose from an old cane armchair, waiting for her to do something with them, she had pulled on a pair of very faded jeans and a very crumpled T-shirt. Comfort clothes.

Ensconced inside her too-narrow bed, marooned inside the floating white curtains of the cubicle, Tamara shakes her head and regrets it immediately. The blunted claws have grown sharp while she was lost in thought and they rake against her skull.

She had been so sure that the woman in the lane had to be Zag's lover, past or present, jealous or jilted! Squinting in concentration, breathing more freely once the rush of pain has subsided, she makes herself struggle backwards through dates, meetings, and sift through phone calls during the workdays that had preceded last Saturday night, and the days that had preceded the second aggression, that one in the parking lot of the institute, exactly three days after the first. But Tamara's thoughts do not want to get organised, on command. They want to be left unfocused, free to drift in a kaleidoscope of dream-altered images, and so they slide and slither away from her.

It is in a journal article focusing on the incredibly high rate of suicide among victims of child abuse that Tamara reads the damning statistics. Her heartbeat picks up. Pencil clenched between her teeth, she scans the paragraphs almost feverishly.

Part of what she read that day, months and months away from that bed where she is now marooned, related to victims of child abuse who opt out of living. Whether they decide to end their lives while in the midst of an abusive episode, the article said, or whether it was years later, varied according to the peaks, troughs and spikes of the guilt and shame see-saw.

The memory of Jamie who had taken his young life, re-animated by what Tamara had felt that *other* day, months and months earlier, whilst in the train that had taken her away from Marielle and Sainte-Thérèse, had kept Tamara pacing, journal in hand. She thought about Marielle. What if she does suicide, one day? Could it be that she already has? Questions for which she might never have answers swirled around in her head until someone had knocked on the door to the interview room.

Liz ushers in a teenage girl dressed in a big baggy yellow sweatshirt, big baggy black shorts, and cross-trainers. As Tamara looks at her inquisitively, Liz raises her eyebrows in a cryptic silent message to her colleague who represses a questioning frown that would mean, 'tell me more.' But, with the girl already in the room, a private word about her is out of the question. So, Tamara smiles at the young person and silently encourages her to come further into the room.

"This is Jodie," says Liz. "Jodie, this is Tamara."

Liz says that Jodie feels that there might be some aspects of her life at home that she needs to talk about. Liz, hand on Tamara's sleeve, reassures Jodie that Tamara is a wonderful listener who, when the time comes, will be able to suggest a few avenues that Jodie might want to think about in her own time. So if Jodie doesn't mind, Liz should leave the two of them to get better acquainted.

"Would you like a Coke or maybe a lemonade?" Liz asks, halfway to the door. Jodie shakes her head. "Coffee for you?" Liz asks Tamara.

"No, thanks," Tamara shakes her head. She casually tosses the pencil she had been clenching between her teeth and the journal she had been reading onto the desktop. The pen skittles across and bumps against a box of tissues. "I'm coffeed out for today. Jodie, why don't you grab one of the seats over there while I get a proper pen, and … You don't mind, do you, if I take a few notes while we like, get acquainted, as Liz said?" Tamara asks, head bent over a drawer but all the while actively maintaining eye contact with the girl.

Jodie shakes her head again and flops on one of the two green chairs, picking at the cuff of her yellow sweatshirt. By the frayed looks of that cuff, Tamara estimates that the unravelling of the threads would have kept Jodie's fingers busy for a couple of days already. She smiles at the girl who, though blonde, pale and thin, reminds her more of a little leprechaun than a fairy.

Fairies are fair and slight while leprechauns, for Tamara, are usually darker in colour, sturdy, with ruddy cheeks.

Tamara smiles, working out that it might be the little creases underlining Jodie's eyes that give her serious face a leprechaun's twinkle. Jodie cannot see Tamara smile because she is busy dislodging yet another distended row of her rat-chewed cuff.

As Tamara gently leads the girl through the series of baseline questions, she learns that Jodie is only thirteen, not as old as she had initially thought, that she lives with mum, dad, her little brother and a spotty mutt, called Twirly because Twirly likes to jump for a stick that Jodie holds up for her.

When Twirly jumps up, she does funny twists in the air as she goes to grab the stick from Jodie. Jodie's little brother's name is Peter. Peter is seven years old. The family name is Little. The Littles live in a house somewhere in Milton. Jodie caught the bus to come here. She knew where to go because 'there was the address on some poster at school'.

Mr Little owns and runs a corner shop. Mrs Little helps him with the deliveries, the accounting and 'that sort of thing.' No, Jodie's mum and dad do not know that Jodie has come here today to talk to someone from the Child Abuse Division. No one knows, not even her best friend Amber.

To better ease the girl into the next, much more personal, segment of the interview, Tamara comments on the hair colour that Jodie has applied over what seems, from the blunt strands that have been missed out, a warm shade of sandy blond.

Pointing at the top of the girl's head where the Cherry dye is still quite dark, Tamara says, "So, you're into a little colour? Looks good. I'd like to fool around with a little colour myself, but, you know, there's not a lot you can do with black –"

Across the low set table that separates the two seats, Jodie's answer is categorical. "It's not meant to be pretty. Pretty sucks."

"Oh. Well … You might be right, of course," Tamara replies easily, now ready to explore what might have prompted Jodie's snap retort.

In the ward, inside her bed, inside her head, Tamara's brain has taken her back to that particular day, though that day is already years old. That's because her thoughts are still not hers to harness. She wanted them to bring her back to a specific moment of the *previous* work week but they've gone on, sliding and slithering away from her.

Like cats into trophy mutilation bring home bits of mangled baby possum and torn- off bird parts, her thoughts bring back to her unwanted bits of twisted violence, jagged edges of violence and their many shades of pain: violence she has known in her heart if not *her* mind, if not *her* flesh. The only act of violence she has ever felt inside her head, inside *her* body, is the one that brought her to this bed at the RBH.

Sexual violence. Emotional violence. For most of the thirty-odd hours since she collapsed on the ground of the parking lot, her thoughts have been a shaken and stirred cocktail of patches, stretched and distorted by the warped, time-controlled reality of nightmares. Father to daughter, uncle to nephew, woman to woman, the violence she has intellectualised only makes her restless in her sleep. Other moments that her psyche has not yet processed successfully, no matter how dated, are brought back distorted by thoughts that slip away from her.

Jodie's left upper arm is scarred by a neatly criss-crossed arrangement of healed skin. "That was last year," Jodie explains, disconnected from whatever pain these cuts would have occasioned her. "Messy. A lot of blood."

"I bet."

Tamara is new to the business of working in the Child Abuse Division of the Services. She had arranged a switch to that division, upon her return from Europe, thinking that she would be more empathetic towards *these* victims than towards the women who come to grief at the hands of an abusive partner they have, after all, chosen.

So far, due to bureaucratic quirks, the only 'cases' she's been involved with are those of older victims, women who, for the most part, are considering pressing belated charges against an abusive uncle, a friend of their parents, a brother, a father, or a baby-sitter. Not yet against a grandfather. Not yet against a mother.

It was after she met Jodie that Tamara understood that it would be almost impossible to distance herself *enough* from her cases' personal stories of child abuse not to burn out early. It was then she understood that the pre-Marielle approach to her previous responsibilities, in the Domestic Violence Division, had been all wrong, that there was more she could do for women in crisis besides move their files from one department to the next.

And with this insight, she had decided to do what she could, back in her original area of training, for the survivors of domestic violence. For women. Grown-up women. Victims all the same, but less likely to choose suicide as their escape route.

Jodie is Tamara's first child victim, the first child victim to whom she was not personally connected. Not like Jamie. Not like Marielle.

While Tamara was recording the girl's personal details, information that starts off all interviews, it dawned on her that she had never found out how many red moons could be expected to grace the Sainte-Thérèse sky in any given year

Moments later, Tamara had found a reasonably unobtrusive way to bring Jodie around to the reason behind her visit. In lieu of a verbal answer, the girl had lifted her sweatshirt to show Tamara her upper arm. She said it hadn't hurt much.

"Well, I'm glad to hear you say that, Jodie, but surely like, all these lines would have caused you considerable pain. Who else has seen these sca–"

"That's the point! It *has* to hurt."

Tamara keeps her voice steady. "Jodie, who did that to you?"

The tick-tack-toe grid cut into Jodie's matchstick thin arm, near the shoulder, has taken Tamara by surprise but Jodie only shrugs and pulls the sweatshirt back down over her blue singlet, over the square Band-Aid that is glued to her wasting biceps, a couple of inches lower.

"Jodie, you need to be patient with me here, like I'm not quite following. Why does anything have to hurt?"

Jodie shrugs again and the fingers of one hand return to teasing the remnants of her cuff.

A while later, Jodie finally opens a little more under Tamara's careful prodding. She explains that the cuts are self-inflicted, that the cuts make her feel better.

Tamara has read a little about victims of abuse who find release through various aspects of self-mutilation but she has never come across any such person. She has only come across bored teens who thought it cool to scratch at the skin of their arms and 'tattoo' in a little cross, a swastika, or a couple of initials inside a wobbly heart.

"OK, I can understand that," replies Tamara, looking concerned but not going ballistic like the girl thought she would. "But what is that other pain? You know, the one the cuts make you feel better about? Tell me about your *other* pain, Jodie."

Reluctantly, fingers tugging and pulling at various loose threads of her cuff, Jodie finally gives Tamara a new piece of information. "Terry. He gives me that other pain."

Who's Terry? thinks Tamara. Her little brother's Peter. There's no stepfather. What, a neighbour? A relative? A friend of the family? "Jodie, tell me about Terry?"

Jodie slides one short fingernail over a couple of horizontal threads on her frayed cuff. To the right, to the left and back.

Tamara waits for her to add more on her own but, before the silence in the room becomes a barrier to the communication she needs to have with the girl, she asks, "Why does Terry give you that pain? Jodie?"

Tamara is leaning forward on her chair but when Jodie peers at her from under her lashes, Jodie finds her pretty. Not intimidating like Mrs Noel, last year's German teacher who demanded that Jodie explain how she could be so clumsy with a hammer as to turn up, yet again, with a bruised thumb and blackened nail.

Jodie didn't bother telling Mrs Noel that she wasn't clumsy at all. It was her thumb she had aimed the hammer at. What a lame thing to think, Jodie had thought at the time of Mrs Noel's questioning. But Tamara, she looks cool and nice, but she knows she shouldn't trust her to keep her secret *secret* because Jodie knows that Tamara and people like teachers and Guidance Officers at school cannot keep her kind of secret secret. They have to tell other people. And because Jodie is thirteen, she understands why it is so.

But Jodie knows that she has come to this building in the city, today, on her own, to have someone make her secret not so secret anymore. Before that can happen, though, she understands she has to tell someone. And Tamara looks like a good one to tell.

"It was the fourth time I cut myself, you know, the criss-cross. Before that, I was scared so I didn't cut well at all. But one day, I was not afraid anymore. I just knew I had to do it slowly and well. Not like messy and all over the place."

Tamara nods.

"But if it's gonna work, it's like it needs to be different each time."

"Each time?"

Jodie nods. Her leprechaun eyes hold Tamara's. "It's like each time I have to plan it. The way to cut. Can't have people know about it. So I have to plan what I'll do."

And Tamara asks Jodie how she plans the cuts she makes on herself and Jodie explains calmly that it's really about deciding where to cut so it won't show. And how deep to cut so she won't require medical help and how long the cut needs to be to deliver her the kind of pain that she needs to override that other.

Jodie says that she has to be very careful not to bring attention to herself. That's partly why hitting her fingers with a hammer or catching them in doors couldn't do anymore. It hadn't been a good idea.

"Jodie, where else have you cut yourself? Would you mind, like, showing me?"

Jodie considers showing Tamara her arm again because obviously she hasn't seen the Band-Aid there that covers three other cuts, all close together, each close to one inch long. But instead she lifts up the loose leg of her shorts.

On the front of her thigh, a row of Band-Aids, each one next to the other, side by side. No gaps in between the five Band-Aids. A little higher up, another little grid already well into its healing process. I guess, being so young, she heals pretty quickly, Tamara thinks, preferring to think about the healing than the cutting.

"OK, Jodie," she says gently, but without a pretend smile. "You've got plenty of guts, that's for sure. And it's like that *other* pain of yours must be real big if you, like, need that many cuts to make up for it. I understand that. But I'm not guessing well, am I?"

Jodie turns away from Tamara and away from the moth-eaten cuff that drips curly threads over her bony wrist. She looks out of the window. There's nothing to see out of the window. It's too high up in this old building. Too high to see the trees, she thinks quietly. And they don't have any neighbours. Only the sky. It's not sunny out there. Not today.

"Jodie? The thing is that, in fact, I'm not allowed to *guess* at all, you understand?" Tamara leans closer to Jodie but stops at the boundary of the girl's personal space. "If you want us to help," she says slowly, looking at Jodie's unravelled cuff, "If you'd like me to try to do what I can about that *other* thing, you need to tell me what it is."

Jodie does not look up. "Being ugly. That's what did it."

"Uh huh," Tamara says, sounding unfazed.

"It's when I made myself ugly that he stopped. Before that he didn't, did he?"

So, Tamara toils away with Jodie to help her clear more of the bramble that clutters the slight opening she's worked out for herself. It then becomes clear that Jodie thinks that the unwelcome touchings stopped a short while after she had started making herself ugly.

She had begun by chopping at her hair because he said it was very pretty. "'Not like mine,' he'd go. His is a rusty colour that he's always said he didn't like much at all because it comes with all those freckles. And he'd go, 'You know how girls are.' Like, they wanted to know if he had them, the freckles, even on … his … *Down there*," says Jodie looking away, out the window. Then she wouldn't eat. If she ate, she'd throw up.

Jodie thinks that it's been her decision to throw up every day, sometimes more than once.

Tamara thinks that maybe, by the time the throwing up began, Jodie's body had decided to help her along in her silent fight and anorexia had set in. And then Tamara asks Jodie about her monthly cycles. They had begun, too, around the time she had started making herself ugly. A little over a year ago.

"Did Terry know you had reached puberty, like you know, your menstrua –"

"I know what puberty means," Jodie says, eyes wide on Tamara's face. The two little creases that run as an underline from the inner corner of her eyes give her face a natural smile that her lips don't have. She probably doesn't smile much, anymore, Tamara thinks. What frigging thing would she have to smile about?

Tamara feels a sort of resentful anger rise inside her. It is not so much a rush of blood or a building heat that she feels. It's more like a tightness that first settles in her jaws. Then in her shoulders. In a tight, cold slab, inside her gut. That anger is there because of what Jodie has already said. It is also for what she hasn't yet said but that Tamara knows is a part of the girl's reality. Then she realises her anger is also for Jamie. And it is for Marielle.

"How did Terry know you'd started your periods?"

Jodie slumps a little. Her fingers move to return to her cuff but instead she turns to Tamara and her fingers remain idle, dangling between her knees. Tamara notices the girl's elbows angled towards the inside of her legs are clear of the cut on her thigh.

"That one night I was on the rag, he came to my room. So … like, that's how he knows."

"So … what did Terry do then?"

"Nothing. I could tell he was so pissed off but for the first time he … well, he just went away."

"For the first time since…"

Jodie's eyes and fingers have yielded to the magnetic pull of the shredded cuff.

"Jodie?"

Jodie answers but she does not look up. "Since kindie."

Tamara doesn't need to ask for more precision. Past a certain point, precision becomes irrelevant. Since kindergarten is *precision* enough.

"Jodie, tell me about Terry. Who is he?" Tamara doesn't need to know *precisely* how Terry abuses the girl. At this stage, though, she needs to know who he is.

"He's my … brother. That's why he got the red hair. Like my father. I'm more like my mother."

"Who's Peter then? You only mentioned one – "

"He's my *little* brother." Jodie swallows hard. "He's not a red-head or anything. He's blonde just like me, like my mother." Jodie's eyes stay insistent on Tamara's, almost expectant. "My parents say he looks *just* like me only *smaller*. That's because he's only seven years old. I'm thirteen." She stops and she glances out the window. "Terry … he's twenty-two. He's shacked up with his girlfriend."

Tamara would like to ask Jodie what kind of parents she has who are so unaware that they haven't noticed that their oldest son has been a chronic abuser of his little sister, and that *their* daughter is turning herself into a Lotto grid because the only friend she can trust with her pain is a razor-blade. But she won't ask that question. The moment has to remain focused on Jodie and Terry.

And at some point Tamara uses the word *abuse* for the first time. Jodie needs to begin internalising the word. Jodie nods hesitantly. She looks out of the window. There's a cloud there now. She can see the cloud because the sky behind has more blue in it than before so the grey cloud stands out more. Maybe it was there all along and she hadn't seen it because the sky had been the wrong colo–

"Jodie? Will you tell me a little more about Peter? Your little brother."

Jodie lets go of her breath. She lets go of the grey cloud on its new blue background. Wide eyes fly to Tamara's face. She blinks and she bites her bottom lip. And she picks at the stitches that hem the right leg of her baggy shorts, right above her knee. When she looks up again, she looks straight at Tamara.

"That's why I cut myself."

"What is?" asks Tamara, though she feels she might already have an answer.

She looks away, out of the window. "It's because of him." The cloud is not out there anymore. Or maybe it still is, but she can't see it because the sky is grey again.

"Who? You mean your little brother?"

"Because of what Terry does to *him.* That's why I need to cut myself. I can't stand it otherwise."

"Jodie, are you saying that now Terry has stopped abusing you, he's on to your little brother?"

Jodie nods, eyes welling up with tears.

"It's all my fault."

Tamara sits and waits.

"It's all because ... because I made myself ugly. But ... Peter, he was only five and a half. I was already twelve. I should've let him go on – "

Tamara's fingers rake back her hair in frustration. "Awh ... for fuck's sake," she exclaims, no longer able to exert the professional detachment that is supposed to go with the job. She squints at Jodie. Because Jodie is holding her head bent, the big round tears fall directly on the cloth of her shorts.

"It's all my fault," Jodie repeats in a watery voice.

Tamara goes to the desk for a box of tissues that's there for just such occasions. She kneels near the girl's chair. Jodie accepts the proffered tissue without looking up and blows her nose noisily. She runs her frayed cuff across her eyes, careful to avoid Tamara's. So Tamara chooses to disregard another rule. Gently, she taps a finger on the girl's knee. Twice, just twice, softly, hoping she will look up.

Leprechaun eyes magnified by more welling tears, Jodie does look up.

"Jodie? It's like *I* need a hug just now," says Tamara very gently. "You?"

Under the watchful glare of the blinking eye, inside her hospital bed, hampered in her movements by the sheet that's wound itself more tightly around her hips and legs, Tamara feels the anger rise red. She's too hot now. She wants to kick off the top sheet but her hands don't find any part of it to pull. Her heartbeat picks up.

Jodie's voice is distorted, muffled and hoarse like she's all screamed-out. And from deep inside the side pocket of her shorts she retrieves a broken piece of razor-blade. And Tamara watches as the girl makes a fist of her left hand. Mesmerised, though her heart is pounding, Tamara watches as Jodie slides the broken razor-blade across the smooth back of her hand. She watches as the tight skin yields to the sharpness of the blade. She watches as the angled tip of the blade disappears below the skin.

Tamara thinks there should first be a white line across the back of Jodie's hand, a line of fatty tissue perhaps, but there isn't. The thin red line gets wider and wider. The red line overflows its banks and spills on the back of Jodie's hand. It runs in between her fingers. Tamara watches as the big red drops fall on the linoleum. They are dark red and plump when they fall in slow motion towards the linoleum. Tamara has to blink. When she looks again, the big red drops of dark blood are thin, flat and frayed on the linoleum.

Tamara can't breathe. She wants to grab Jodie's hand. She wants to apply pressure to it, to stem the blood that goes on oozing and oozing out. She wants to call for help. She wants, she wants. She doesn't want Jodie to die.

Tamara's nightmare wants her to feel the thick stickiness of Jodie's blood between her own fingers, under her palm as she presses Jodie's hand under her own. Her nightmare needs to feed off her helplessness, off her adrenaline waste before it releases her.

She didn't even know why this nurse was shaking her. It had taken her forever to go back to sleep and the voice was not comforting.

"Look at what you've done to yourself!" the nurse was saying. And when Tamara finally opened her eyes, when she blinked open a small keyhole of a gap from which to peer out of her drowsiness, she saw red.

A lot of red stuck to her, to her nightie and to the sheet she had pulled off the bed. Later, as the nurse kept a vigilant eye over the proceedings, while warm shower jets rinsed the red smears off her face, off her neck, off her arms, off her legs, Tamara grappled with reality. She had, apparently, wanted to get up in the middle of the night, "To pass water, I suspect," said the nurse, "and you must've slipped."

I didn't tear off the frigging thing, she had wanted to tell the nurse who was not Fiona. But she hadn't. She couldn't. She was too light-headed to think, too light-headed to talk. But it was true, she hadn't ripped it off.

The gap that, a moment earlier, had allowed her to peer out of her drowsiness had closed up again, tight as a clam. The gateway into reality, into what had been real had simply disappeared.

The cannula had busted its way out of her vein. Nightmare celluloid blood had become one with real blood. White cloth. Dark red. Deep dark red. Black. Shut down. Some time later the oxymetre had alarmed.

The nurse had found Tamara semi-conscious on the floor, head jammed against the base of the bed, the saline solution dribbling out of the tubing, making a proper mess of the healthy red blood that was still oozing out of Tamara's vein.

By the time Tamara reconnected to the here and now, the nurse was already applying pressure to the back of *her* hand as she had applied it to the back of Jodie's hand, feeling her blood thick and sticky between her fingers. She had been laid back against the pillows.

And a lot of red still stuck to her nightie, to her, and to the nurse's uniform. But on the linoleum, the red was not so red. It was more like pink, more like a diluted red. Like rosé, she thought. It looked far less sticky out there than against her nightie. Less sticky than against her skin. Less sticky than in between her fingers.

"No, you don't need to be looking at it." Deep dark red still on white. Dark pink. "It's a bit of a mess, that's for sure, but we'll get you cleaned up soon as we get a dressing on that vein," the nurse had said, fingers of one hand tight against the gauze pressed against Tamara's hand, the fingers of the other on the bedside buzzer. "Looks a lot worse than it is." The nurse had prattled on as she tended to the back of Tamara's hand. "A shower and you won't even know it's happened."

*****

FIVE

Emilie looks at the lavender-pink shadows under her lover's eyes, wondering how long it will take before Tamara's dreams vaporise, never to return.

"Ooo-aah," Tamara exhales softly as she leans back into the dark green water of the jacuzzi. "Wick-ed! Can't believe I was in so much pain and like, *sooo* in hospital. Totally weird being in that narrow bed like, uh … there for all to see … exposed, like on display for … for everyone who passed by and if they wanted to have a look then … And hooked to that friggin' cannula. And then, what with those … those sick rushes of pain. And dreams weird, like sharp … like glass splintering, like jagged. *Old* stuff," Tamara adds, eyes wide. "*Old* images from … whenever. All broken up …They'd surface in that freaky … distorted way, like the Jodie thing last night. I mean, really! And that friggin'… The pain in my head – " Tamara again skids to a halt. Again that puzzled expression that makes her eyes more round, less like a cat's.

Emilie holds on to the surge of tenderness that is making her all soft inside. She senses that Tamara is meandering through her thoughts as she might through a field of wild flowers. The path is direct enough but the picking of the correct signal is not instantaneous. Her mind doesn't just pluck multiple thoughts at a time. It has become hesitant, like the hand that hovers over a Tibuchina in full bloom, unsure as to which flower to pick as they all kind of look the same in their particular shade of deep purple.

"Tell you what," Tamara says, directly into Emilie's eyes. "Even a … two-day stint in … locked up, uh … in confinement, as in hospital confinement, well … it's enough, more than enough, to make me realise how great not being in a hospital really is. I mean how great…" Tamara frowns again at the circumlocutory echo of her words. She runs a hand over her pale cheek, the one that doesn't sport the still angry graze.

Emilie wants to know if this not getting straight to the point confirms the delayed side effects Dr Mac had warned about. Maybe it's not the *deficit* as such. And that thing last night!

Emilie makes herself breathe against the vision of Tamara smeared with blood. Blood on her arms as she had rolled in her sleep, blood on her face as she had tucked her hand as she does, under her cheek. And blood on the sheets and more blood on the floor. So Doctor Mac had kept her in the ward half a day longer than planned.

"Just to be sure." Doctor Mac had broken the news of the midnight incident to Emilie, who hadn't been there to see anything and whose imagination took off, quicksliver quick, to bring back a horrifying vision of Tamara as Carrie, the girl in that old horror flick, drenched in blood. "But these things always look more frightening than they are. It's just that we can't tell yet how her head's hit the bed frame."

The jacuzzi water is deliciously warm.

"For a while there, like when Alex came..." Tamara muses, "Well, you know ... when she like, stopped over and when the cops came that morning ... When was it?" Emilie holds her breath. "What, only two days ago?" Head back, Tamara sighs again. "Anyway, it felt as if I'd have to stay there forever. Permanent booking," she adds, grinning thinly. "Thought that sick head pain would like, never go away. That I'd be hooked up to that cannula forever. And then, of course the mess because of that friggin' thing. T'was like so freaky weird. In a way, it..." She glances at the dark bruise that's spread on the back of her hand. Emilie wonders whether it has finally ended its upward crawl towards Tamara's wrist. "Like it was bound to happen."

One sharp, clear and throaty laugh rings through the air. It's instantly picked up by another voice, and another. Staggered cackles, in an off-key a cappella, reach a crescendo; the kookaburras are playing in the nearby gum tree.

Eyes shut tight against the ruckus, Tamara waits for the mad cackling laughter of the kookaburras to stop. The thin blue thread of a vein is freshly tattooed across her eyelid. She sighs again after a little while but, this time, in contentment. She lifts her face to the late afternoon sun. "That's the life, isn't it?"

"This is the *good* life, yes." Emilie slides closer to her lover. "Hey, Tam," she says, noticing for the first time the hair-fine lines at the corner of her eye, very thin lines that were not yet real lines, though the last time she had seen Tamara in daylight, they had only been silk-fine threads. "Got to tell you..." She leans against her lover's shoulder to leave a light kiss near Tamara's cheekbone. "I'm glad you didn't kick up too much of a fuss."

"About what?"

"Oh, you know."

Tamara opens her eyes wide in exaggerated innocence, turning her head carefully.

Emilie runs a hand over the top of Tamara's smooth thigh, pale and distorted under the swirling water. She rubs it gently before squeezing it just above the knee to make Tamara grin.

"You bloody well know what *I'm* happy about."

"Maybe I do. Don't know for sure, do I? Then again…" Tamara grins a Cheshire cat grin. "Maybe you should tell me … just so I know you're … uh … we're talking about the same thing."

Emilie scrunches her eyebrows and, pretending deep thought, she taps her temple with a forefinger. "Hmm. Well … Let's see. OK…" she begins, eyes smiling "Let's just say that I'm happy you've agreed to stay here, I mean with me … for a few days. Very happy actually." Her eyes smile at Tamara.

"Oh … that!" Tamara grins.

"Yes, *that*." Emilie brushes her lips against Tamara's ear. "See?" she whispers. "I'm quite easy to please." She moves her face away to better see Tamara's. "No, don't!" she urges, as Tamara cranes her neck wanting Emilie's lips. "No, Tam. You can't move your head like that."

"Who says I … I can't move my head like … that?" Cat eyes are once again elongated by the squint of pain.

"I do … for now. Please." She waits till Tamara opens her eyes again. "So, here's what we'll do…" She stands up in the foot-well and sits sideways across Tamara's lap, one arm behind her neck and around her shoulders. "There," she says, lips brushing Tamara's. "If you can't get to us, we'll get to you. Not a problem, right?"

"Right." Tamara's tongue is warm. It is warm and soft. Emilie's lips only nibble, determined to keep desire from surging, determined to have Tamara keep her head still.

"Don't you get too used to this preferential treatment, kiddo. It's as I told Alex over dinner … My mothering instinct's a bit flat, as in non-existent … usually."

"Well, hey … these are not usual times, right?" Tamara's wounded hand is flat, fingers splayed over Emilie's chest. "Like, how often have you had a lover pass out, like stone cold on you, huh? Comatose?"

"Can't say that I have. Well … not since my uni years."

"Oh … and there I was thinking I was the first."

"Well, let's just say you're the first to pass out in a parking lot," Emilie chuckles, lips against Tamara's forehead. "In those days, you see, poor struggling students that we were, we had a special thing for wine."

"Oh … come on," Tamara groans.

"No, hold on, not as in *Grange Hermitage* or a genuine Bordeaux. We're talking about the days when dinner out meant going to the local fish and chips shop and spreading our greasy papers on our lap, usually somewhere overlooking the river, like at Kangaroo Point. Oh … sometimes, too, we'd be cool and sip on the old Jacob's Creek at what, in those days, maybe only three dollars a bottle, and do the pizza bit." She lowers her gaze to Tamara and smiles against her lips. "But more often than not we'd get into this mulled wine thing."

"As in the Bavarian thing?"

"Oddly enough, yes. Kind of. Basically it's for sure the cheapest way to stretch the cheapest wine we could get our hands on. We'd heat it up, add sugar, orange juice—What?"

Tamara's mouth is set in such a clear expression of disgust that even the old *Mime Marceau* could not have been more expressive in his silence.

"Hey, give it some credit … as a winter drink. We'd positively glow from … well, not just from the heat of the hot wine but from the alcohol mixed with a high sugar content. And blood vessels totally dilated, blood pumping thin, we'd … well we'd just … uh, buzz through the night. Shit-cheap."

Emilie chuckles as she remembers the many ends of parties when, come dawn, everyone was fairly zonked out, sleeping the sleep of the dead. And then, she frowns at a much less pleasant memory of the night when she had let a friend, a straight one, talk her into going out on a double date.

"OK … yeah alright … Still, I don't think that the hot wine thing or the Cinzano and Coke mix would be as efficient, I mean as like, to the point, as the good old Tequila slammers of *my* uni days but … Did anyone actually *pass out* from that sweet-wine?" Tamara asks dubiously.

"Well … maybe not pass out as such but just as good. Shake 'em all you want, no one stirs."

"Cool. I mean, yeah … imagining you like so not in control. Young and wild."

Carefully, Tamara nuzzles Emilie's neck, under the wet mop of hair that was in desperate need of a cut and equally desperate for its monthly fix of *Brazilia* by l'Oréal.

The surface of the water is in turmoil. It flicks up at Tamara's face. An upward drop catches the corner of her eye. She wipes it off with a wet hand.

"So anyway," Emilie says, sliding away to lie more comfortably on the lounge moulded on the other side of the jacuzzi, "back to the conversation you had with old Hood-Eyes." She settles against the jets, one at the level of each shoulder and two twirling along her spine. "I guess you would've had to explain something to him that you still haven't explained to me, right?"

"Hey, when did I have time to explain anything to you?" Tamara answers too quickly. "I mean … it's like I called him just before you came to pick me up from the hospital. And … well … by the time we made it to your place … uh … here, uh, what, we've only been here not even an hour, right? Like you still haven't told me about your dinner with Alex." She lifts her chin out of the water. To the south, low above the horizon, one lone cloud, a pink one, hovers in the shape of a half hollowed jelly bean.

"Tam," Emilie answers, eyebrows again tight with concern, "I *have* told you. You've forgotten?" she asks softly, worried that *this* might be the early sign of one of the possible deficits.

"You went to the *Patcharin*. The woman, uh … You had been Mahdahmmed to death, as usual. You … The two of you talked a lot…" Emilie lets out a breath of relief. Tamara could remember recent information. "But that's not saying much. How did you and Alex talk … uh, get on?"

"Well enough, I suppose. You know how she is." Emilie moves on quickly. "We talked about this and that and local politics, what with the election hype that's gathered momentum and of course, you know, the – "

"I can imagine: A united stand with America against … uh … what's-his-name … in Iraq … and the National budget blowout and what, containment's better than aggression … That kind of thing?

"Hmm." Emilie clears her throat softly. "Well, yes. It's almost like you were there. But we also managed to talk about a film or two once we were saying goodbye … on the footpath."

"Why only then?" As she lets go of the jelly bean cloud to peer at Emilie, Tamara's frown is not set around a grin anymore.

"Because of you, Tam. Alex was most determined to talk about you."

"Oh."

"So we did. But you were right about politics being her fave topic."

"Hey, I like to think I kind of know her well."

"Like she knows you?"

"Like I'd like to know you. Em … can you come back here, closer?" Tamara asks softly. "Too far away over there and if you're not going to let me move on my own…"

With a tilt of the head and a rise of the eyebrows, Emilie asks with mock incredulity, "You'd like to know *me* that well, would you now?" She scoots back closer to Tamara.

"I … uh … yeah. I would." Tamara reaches for Emilie's hand.

"I'm not sure this is such a good idea, you know, for lovers to second-guess each other all the time. Or to be *that* transparent." Her eyes have found the spa thermometer bobbing across from her. "Things might be *guessed* that might not need to be – "

"I know that. It was just wishful thinking what I said … about knowing you. Like having a real … uh … a reliable form of ESP."

"Sounds pretty boring to me, that. What, no room for surprises or anything?" Emilie teases.

"Surprises?" Tamara shifts on the smooth fibreglass bench. "Ah … Only room for good ones. For the bad ones, I'd like to know … uh … Yeah, like know you so well that they wouldn't be surprises anymore, right? That way, I'd always be able to handle –"

"Nah. Doesn't happen that way." Emilie wipes off a splash of water from her face. "Surprises, good ones, bad ones, they keep us on our toes. That's what surprises do."

Tamara looks at the back of her hand over Emilie's and blink-quick, the cannula strobes in front of her. In its place, an innocuous waterproof dressing protects the busted vein that got torn when she got tangled up with the IV line.

Tamara looks away. The jets of water against her back and the ones that nudge the muscles of her shoulders feel good. The blowers would have shaken and rattled her too much, but the jets on their own and the hot soak are just the thing to unknot what in her body is all kinked up. She leans more into the jets to rub away the tightness that lingers. More of her muscles ache now than from any rollerblading spill.

"So, you going to tell me about that flash of insight you had this morning, or do I have to call old Hood-Eyes myself to find out what you told him?"

"OK," Tamara begins, chin level with the water-line. "It all began when I remembered … uh … it's like I remembered that Del called me at the office. You know, I've … On and off … I've told you a couple of things about Del Russell and that partner of hers who hasn't stopped giving her grief."

"Yes, I remember. In fact Del is the first of your 'clients' you ever told me a little about. The first time we had lunch together at the Coffee Spot, remember? You had just paid her a visit and – "

"And back then, you didn't even know that lesbians could get into the DV spin as well as … uh, common variety hets." Tamara's cheekbones rise. She grins a wet grin. "I was already in love with you by then." She leans forward to reach Emilie's cheek with her left hand. "Did you know tha – " She pulls up short.

"No! There you go again. Tam!" Emilie says quickly. "You've got to be careful with your head. You don't want to overdo it too soon."

"Ah. And you and whose … army's gonna put me in a cocoon, then?"

Emilie looks at her, at the eyes that have already wiped away the pain that had dulled and pulled at them two days running. "OK, you're right," Emilie agrees with a sigh of resignation. "I'm not your mother. You decide what you can and can't do."

"Got news for you, Em. Even my mother … she knows to let me do what I think's best for myself."

"Right. So, about your twenty-fifth hour insight?"

"Right. Goes like this." Tamara swivels a little to face Emilie more easily and takes her hand inside both of hers. "I worked it out that it was Monday, last week, that Del called. Her lover … Beth, she'd been around again in spite of the Protection Order that clearly spells it out for her. She's not to come close to Del, like not even within shouting distance, right?" Emilie nods. "And not close at all to anything that belongs to Del. Like not her car or … cat, and obviously not her house."

"But she does."

"She does. She *still* does it. The PO's been written up to last for two years. And it's only been ten months."

"But didn't you say that the workers, you, didn't make house calls?"

"We don't, no, not in the middle of a crisis, not as a rule. But we … Well I do, sometimes. I don't ask if I can, I just do it. And what I do is visit, you know, women like Del who are really struggling because there's really nothing more they can do at this stage, like Beth is not physically harming her anymore. She just stalks her. Regularly. You see, she's like, moved into the emotional power play thing. And Del's like so fed up and scared too that one day, Beth will be waiting inside her house. And she's convinced that … uh, Beth on a bad day is capable of just about anything. Del's afraid that even the … in spite of the PO, something could turn really bad, for one or the other of them, even if only like an accident gone … wrong."

The PO? Where else had she heard that bloody, useless, token piece of paper simply called a PO? Emilie searches her memory, itching to snatch out a name.

"And I suppose that until that happens there's nothing that can be done to protect her."

"Not a single friggin' thing. Not until Beth does something that'll bring her up, you know, in front of a criminal court. So I visit her ... Del, when she phones. From time to time. To cheer her up. I listen to her ... to her woes. She usually feels better for a while but last week, I couldn't make her lighten up. Four cups of tea she insisted I drink with her."

"Better you than me. Four cups would've killed me."

"I did think about you. You've got to be the only Aussie I know who doesn't like her cuppa."

"I take after my mother's side of the family. We're all bean people, as in not into leaves at all." Cat-green eyes question silently. "As in beans ... Coffee-beans. Not leaves, as in tea and stewed infusions. Not much into lettuce eith – Never mind, Tam," Emilie adds in a decided tone. "So, Del called you last week and a of couple days later you went to see her, yes?"

"Wednesday, it was. I've already worked that out."

"And?"

"That's pretty much it."

"Right. So ... what does that have to do with anything? Why ring up Hood-Eyes?"

Tamara spreads Emilie's hand in the palm of her own and traces the length of her fingers. She rubs her thumb over her short nails, one fingernail at a time, as if combined, all these small movements afford her time to think. "Uh ... Em ... listen. Last Saturday night, you remember, you had this dinner-meeting thing for work and – "

"Sure, I remember. The only good thing was that Mary and I sat together and well, she kind of did enough chit-chatting when we weren't actually working, like over dinner, enough for both of us. She's really good that way. So ... what's the connection with last Saturday night?" she asks, looking up.

"I went to The Triangle that night, right?"

Emilie nods, perplexed as to why this conversation is so lumbering.

"And I didn't tell you ... I didn't want to worry you or anything but..."

Emilie slides her hand away from Tamara's to study the water-shrivelled swirls of her fingertips. "You didn't tell me what?" She's very much aware that she needs to sink back into the hot water and just wait for Tamara to get on with whatever it is that needs such a long lead in. So she settles back against the side of the jacuzzi. Tamara is hovering on the edge of something, she's sure of that. But what?

"I didn't know how to tell you but…"

"C'mon, girl, spit it out," she says lightly, to belie the anxiety that's already stirring in the pit of her stomach.

"Well, remember the lane where your car was towed away from? And the overgrown driveway?"

"I do. Bad night. Oh, except that that was the night we met. Well, the night you tried to pick me up, uh?"

"OK. Don't rub it in. Thing is, I played it your way and the end result's the same as– Just took longer to get you where I wanted you, that's all."

"What can I say, huh?" Emilie smiles with her eyes. "Couldn't resist you. But what about last Saturday night at The Triangle?"

"Well … that's the thing. You're not going to believe this but … I was walking back to *my* car. About midnight. And out of nowhere some woman grabs me, slams me against that brick wall – "

"What? Last Saturday night? While I was – "

"That's the thing, yes. She had me by…like that." Tamara shows Emilie how the woman had held her, fist tight against her throat.

"My god! Tam … What did you do? Did you know what she was on about? Like what, she took you for somebody else? I mean – "

"I did kind of work it out. First, it kind of came to me at the hospital, you know, the night of…" She lifts her bruised hand. "I was like all drowsy but I couldn't sleep. Like my thoughts were all over the place. Don't know anymore how I ended up with that god-awful nightmare about little Jodie. So … anyway, I tried again this afternoon, feeling better and all and … I didn't have nothing … uh, anything to do while I was waiting for you. So yes, that woman did scream quite a few things but I distinctly remember her having said something about me having to stop visiting her."

"*Visiting* her? But you didn't know her. Did you?"

"Ah … no. Never seen her in my life, but that's it, isn't it? That's when I realised. She would've meant like me visiting someone she knew. *Her*, as in someone she didn't want me to hang around." Emilie looks at Tamara blankly. "Em, like Del!"

"Say what?" Emilie sits up, eyes drilling into Tamara's. "Some nutter jumps you, the same woman who's been terrorising Del and you don't say anything? Not to anyone? OK … she didn't hurt you but really, Tam!" Her disbelief is palpable.

"Uh … yes. I've just said. I didn't want you to worry."

"Screw that, Tam! You don't have to tell *me* anything you don't wanna tell me but for crying out loud, you've got to tell someone. The cops? Did you at least tell Alex? I mean, last week? Did you?" And there she had it.

Emilie had the name she had been trying to retrieve from a past conversation: Hood-Eyes. He's the one who, back at the hospital, had said that Tamara should try to remember 'Someone whose PO was not respected.' He did say that. He did, Emilie was adamant.

"No." Tamara shakes her head slowly. "Didn't mention it to Alex, no. When was I there last?"

"Monday night."

"Well, I wouldn't have mentioned *that* to her. She's like you. She would've worried just the same. And the police, besides taking down my … declaration … my deposition," The frown of confusion that flutters again over her brow is not lost on Emilie. "There's nothing they can do about it. That woman … she didn't hurt me, you see. Even if she had, unless I was all bloodied up … At best, what?" Tamara is playing with the water. She squeezes it between her two palms. As her palms meet, they belch a small amount of water, a little geyser that spills over her thumbs. "They would've asked me to warn her in writing that she had to cease and desist stalking, uh, following me and … well, stop all other forms of contact. Like, maybe I'd send that registered mail, right?"

Tamara doesn't know what to do about the concern that is still scrunching up Emilie's face. "Look, Em, It's OK. I did the cool thing, like I didn't try to punch or kick or slap or whatever." Her eyes connect with Emilie's and she grins the grin of a clever child. "I just prised her hand loose, caught her off guard with my boot and crashed the heel hard on the top of her foot. That would've been like so painful. Anyway, yeah…" She floats her hand flat and firm over the broken water. She watches it as the water edges higher and higher up the side of her hand. "Well … that's it really. I left her there. Hopping on one foot, she was." The gap between forefinger and thumb is the first to get submerged. "I drove home. Took a shower and chilled with … with … uh … a film." Unable to remember that it is *The One* she had rented from the video shop, she draws in her top lip.

Emilie rolls her eyes. "I bet you got yourself another one of those Martial Arts-special effects-comedy combo films. You did, didn't you? OK," she says, distractedly shifting the sole of her foot against the jet directly opposite her. "So, some lunatic jumps you in an alleyway in the Valley, and you don't tell me because… Because what?"

"Because you might've thought that she might…" Tamara tries not to squirm too noticeably but she's increasingly uncomfortable with the line she has finally opted to follow. "Hey … you would've thought that if this woman jumps me once, she'll jump me again. I mean, you know, because of Del." She lets her shoulders slink below the water-line. That much closer to her ears the water trapped between the side of the jacuzzi and her shoulder pops and gurgles like bubbling water on a soft boil.

"Well, as it turns out … maybe she has," Emilie says carefully. "Is that what you're thinking? Not something random at all? Not like you being in the wrong place, at the wrong time?"

Eyes on the mist-fine effervescence that skims the surface of the water, Tamara shrugs carefully.

"Two aggressions in what, three days … that's not common, Tam. They might well be connected. How weird, really. Surely that should interest old Hood-Eyes and young Matthews. But … how did she know who you are? How did she know of your visits to Del's?"

"Don't know. Maybe it's like the police said. You heard them. Someone can follow me easily when I'm on foot. Or maybe even in the car. Not so easily when I'm on skates, though. On flat ground I'm like faster than a runner but slower than a bike … right?"

Emilie nods, unsure as to why Tamara is seeking confirmation of something she knows to be true. "It'd be difficult for a car to trail me and me not notice. Uphill or on uneven footpath surfaces, can't reach the speeds I clock up along the empty … deserted stretches of river pathways, right? My point is … it'd be hard for a car to tail anyone at such low speed and not be noticed." Made breathless by one of the longest utterances made since Wednesday night, Tamara leans back against the headrest. Eyes closed, she begins again, "So let's say that this Beth, she sees me coming out of Del's front door, right? Last Wednesday that would've been, I'm pretty sure of that. She stalks, remember? Been doing that to Del for the past ten months. She's a stalker and she sees me come out of Del's place. She gets upset, resentful. She gets all steamed up." Tamara's eyes snap open into the blue sky. She blinks. "Then, she figures out that I'm with the Services and I'm the one who did the paperwork for Del's Protection Order. So she decides I'm getting up her nose and she stalks me, too. Feasible, no?"

"Uh … feasible … uh, yes. I mean, some people *do* do these things, yes. Where does Del live?"

"Sydney Street, why?"

"Sydney Street, as in New Farm?"

'Yeah, close enough to the Sydney Street Ferry."

"Oh."

"Oh what?"

"Well, it's silly but … all this time you were telling me about Del … I … well I assumed she lived somewhere like … well … like Kedron or Morningside. Not in *that* part of New Farm."

"Why not?"

"I just assumed she'd live in a workingclass suburb of sorts."

"What, in a chamfer-board boarding-house like … yeah … those that are still there on the un … not trendy part of New Farm?"

Lips pulled in as if to bring back her careless assumption, Emilie is looking sheepish.

"Well, hey … New Farm *is* a working-class suburb, so you're not too far off." Tamara grins at her.

"You having me on, Tam? It's become trendyville. Condos, coffee shops, restaur –"

"Some bits of it have, but what?" Cat eyes squint into the blue sky. "You think everyone there contemplates the river from their balconies? Drinking iced tea, uh, calling their brokers with … newspaper in one hand, mobile phone in the other?" Tamara's tone has picked up and yet, as she brings her eyes back to Emilie, she looks more amused than sarcastic. "Goes to show where your middle-class values take you, huh?"

"OK, I hear you."

"Pretty much everyone out there … like everywhere … who's not a pensioner or unemployed, they all get up around 6 or 7 a.m. every working day. They go to work. So, hey … *that* makes New Farm a *work-ing*-class suburb, right? Get it?"

"Ha, ha. Funny," Emilie retorts flatly, annoyed at her own recurring middle-class assumptions.

"And some like you actually drive *there*, every morning."

"OK, I said … my mistake. Preconceived idea and what not. I confess. So … Del works?"

"Used to be a Certified Accountant. She was doing pretty well for herself … until Beth came along. Then Del had to give up her job. Couldn't keep fronting up with … you know … black eyes, busted lips and whatever. Beth … But … yeah … she probably doesn't have to …

like go and work…" While she talks on, Tamara observes Emilie drown her faux pas in her own water play. "Like she did inherit the house from her parents and what with her own savings … But you know how it is … the sense of purpose thing, the working for your dollar, old world values…" Emilie snaps her hand out of the water and absorbs herself in the cords of elastic water that stretch from her fingers before snapping into nothingness. "She works in a much lesser position … Too old, right, to get back to where she left off, like she's in her late forties." One minute the lines of water are there, thick and stretching, the next … nothing. Not even a drop left to run off Emilie's hand. "Actually, we didn't have a chance to talk about that, being in the hospital and with the cops and the pain and all, but the reason I was *that* early, you know, like, waiting for you that day in the parking lot was because Del wasn't home."

"I didn't know you had planned on…"

"Well, no. As I said, we haven't had a chance to talk about anything that's happened the day before or since, have we?" Tamara says softly. "I went to see her after she called me. Middle of last week. Still looked down in the mouth by the time I left … I thought I'd pop over like unexpectedly … uh … so that'd make it last Wednesday, right? I ring the doorbell. Not home. So I skate around the area. Have another look at that house at the corner of Sydney and Moray streets, you know, the one with the … architecture? Looks like it could be Moorish … in an odd way – "

"The one with the colonnades and the arches and the leadlight on every single window, top and bottom?"

"Yeah, that one. It's like so fascinating I always stop by and have a look. Never see anyone hanging around though."

"All at work, no doubt," Emilie rejoins with a little grin. "So Del lives near that intersection?"

"Not far from there. Behind the Nimbin Nursing home. So I skated back to her front door. Still no one home, so I made my way up to the institute, had a coffee and waited in the car … Well, the rest's history, right?"

"Right. That woman, Beth, she didn't see you in court, then?"

"No. Del had someone with her, her sister I think, and so we didn't do the Court Support thing for her."

"But – "

Tamara turns her eyes to the plant nearest the jacuzzi, a tall tree-fern, like the one Alex has by her pool except that this one, like all the plants on the patio, has its roots bound in a huge clay pot. "But what?"

185

"Just thinking. So that's what you told DS Johnson this morning?"

"Absolutely. His first theory ... one angry dude riled because of some DV related interference into his private life ... So I pitched my story of a woman, mad as a cut snake, totally into the DV spin herself, not respecting the PO, so it kind of hangs." She chews on her bottom lip waiting for Emilie to say something. "Got to admit I'm quite amped on the idea." As Emilie remains quiet, Tamara returns her attention to the tall fern, to its furry trunk and stems, to the long, green reach of the thumb-thick fronds.

"Tam, you really think that this Beth is tall enough and strong enough to put you out with one single blow? Doctor Mac was adamant about that. Your concussion was caused by something blunt. So this Godzilla, she hits you with what, a bare hand and, just like that, you're out? Assuming she's mad enough to attack you twice. At a three day interval? And that suggests she tailed you while you were on skates. You just said that it wasn't likely tha – "

"I'm not always on blades when I meet you after work, am I? Sometimes I stop by Del's ... I mean, driving. So ... hard to tell *when* that Beth got herself all kinked-up about me. For all I know ... might've been last month." Tamara straightens out her legs. An odd tint under the turbulent green water, the skin ripples and wavers over Tamara's muscles. "Hood-Eyes confirmed what Doctor Mac told them about the shape of ... of this." She points to the swollen area at the back of her head. "The weapon had to have been on the hard side of soft but ... like uh, wielded with great strength."

"Something like a karate chop?"

"Yes, a very powerful one. Apparently." Tamara brings her knees up to her chin and wraps her arms around them, mindful to keep her damaged hand out of the water, having perhaps forgotten that it has already been wet. "He said that they had considered that idea ... like at first, but because I'm a female ... you're going to love this bit, Em ... they just didn't think that a guy would actually do that to me, I mean, the karate chop thing." Cat eyes sparkle with humour.

"Ah ... but the butt of a gun would've been what, more female-friendly?" Emilie shakes her head. "Give me a break. Tam, do you really think that this ... Beth ... Is she tall enough and strong enough to have decked *you*? She did more than just deck you, didn't she? You were out for quite some time. If the doctor says the blow would've had to be quite a violent one ... I don't quite see it myself."

"Why not?"

"Because I think that whoever attacked you would've had to be a lot taller than you for the … to give the blow maximum thrust on the…" Emilie executes a chop that cuts into the water and splashes back onto her face. "…down…ward mo…tion." She splutters. "Wet. Very wet."

She wipes her eyes, cheeks, and her grin with both hands but, fingers on her lip, she remembers the new wrinkle discovered back in the hospital restrooms. She feels for it but it is still too young to register under her forefinger.

"Don't know. All I can say is that she's about my height, so maybe that's tall enough. And she's certainly got a strong arm. Not afraid of body contact. Like, she didn't tackle me like a girl … Know what I mean? Like leaving so much space between us, and like going for the face … pulling my hair. Right up *against* me, she was, and literally in my face."

"Mmm. Other thing is that in the parking lot, maybe you weren't standing ramrod straight when … when she crept up behind you."

"True. Now that you mention it … I've been trying to bring it back, you know, the specific moment but … Em … who'd know, right? I might've been bending down to pull up my socks or to pick up … But it's all gone. I mean the friggin' moment's like all gone! I still can't remember *that* or anything really of what happened *after* I came out of the building to wait by the car. Not even sure I went *directly* back to the car. And … not remembering what I did for what, some ten minutes … before you found me, it's freaking me out in a major way."

"How's that cheek of yours? Still looks a bit nasty." Emilie pats her lover's knee. Tamara's kneecaps, jutting out of the water, burnished and smooth, are almost dry. Her fingers leave a moist trail on the cool sheen of Tamara's skin. She feels their shape just as she feels the brittle edge underscoring Tamara's outburst. If she concentrates on the angular shape of Tamara's kneecaps, she might forget that she doesn't have anything reassuring to tell Tamara regarding her persisting ante and retrograde amnesia. So she rests her cheek against them. One feels hard but it fits snugly into the hollow of her cheek. "Maybe the water's not good for it."

"Nah. Almost all healed up. Thanks to Fiona's administra – Uh, Fiona's ministrations."

Plumes of fizz shimmer and twirl in a transparent dance over the water surface. Tamara pats the top of Emilie's head. *This is the good life,* Emilie thinks to herself. *Just as Tam said.*

"You certainly worked that nurse hard – "

"Irony is that she's missed out on my last ... On the big mess I made last night."

"No doubt she'll have heard all about it by now."

Absentmindedly, Emilie reaches for the thermometer and reads the vertical blue line. Thirty-nine degrees, the blurry blue line says. Without her glasses though, she can't tell for sure. "But tell me," she asks as an afterthought, "hadn't you noticed that woman inside the bar? She would've been inside at some stage, surely, if only to better spot you."

"Inside ... uh..." Tamara bites on her bottom lip. *I have to tell her. Can't omit the Zag thing forever.*

Even if Emilie is not ready to hear what's coming, temptation, lust and sexual weakness have got to be topics mature lovers need to talk about, particularly if one's partner is not the source of that temptation, or so Tamara has finally decided.

"At The Triangle?" she asks, doing one last quick unscrambling of the thoughts she is now ready to present to Emilie.

"Yes, at The Triangle. Were you at the bar? You would've been there at least for a couple of hours, right?"

Tamara nods carefully.

"So, that woman who wants to jump you, why would she prefer to wait outside if she followed you there? Maybe she was already there when you walked in. So she recognises you and then she follows you out. So ... anyone acting a bit suspicious ... in hindsight?"

"Actually yes. At some stage I did feel like someone was watching me, like so close, like glaring, but I didn't see anyone. A lot of people around but no one like just standing there, transfixed."

"By the bar or dancing?" Emilie asks, eyes fixed on the bobbing thermometer.

Tamara leans into the side jet for something to do. Her swimmer's shoulders bank above the swirling waterline. "At the bar. I was talking to some chick I'd just met. That's when I noticed a woman like in her thirties."

"What made you notice her?"

"Her pink shirt maybe. I thought it looked a bit like, old-fashioned or something. Then I noticed her face, like pleasant. By the dance floor. Then I noticed her glancing in ... in our direction." *There we go.* "Thought she might've been Zag's friend or lover, though Zag said she wasn't and..." *Any second now.*

Emilie makes herself be very still in the turbulent water. Very still inside herself to better hold on to her breath while she waits. Still as a sphinx listening for tremors.

"Em?"

Emilie reluctantly looks away from the bobbing thermometer. Cat green eyes meet hers.

"Em … look." Tamara can't think of how to backpedal. "At first, I thought that woman, the one I had noticed, because of her pink shirt, right, at first I thought she was that girl's friend. I was talking to a young – "

"You've already said that."

"Okay. Anyway, so this girl, she came to sit by me at the bar. Zag. She was only like about twenty-two or something and she talked too much. I didn't think much at first. She was cute in a … like out of a magazine ad, maybe in *The Face* or something like that." Tamara peers more closely at Emilie who, top lip drawn in, eyes unfocused, is visibly not going to interrupt. Tamara knows she's on her own to finish what she's had to finally begin. "It's not like we had a proper conversation or anything but she… "

"Tam, is all that lead up to tell me that some spunky, young dyke's chatted you up?" Emilie is too late aware of the terseness of her tone. "And that she shouted you a drink? Or you her?"

"I kissed her."

Emilie leans back, just as slowly, just as carefully as if she was the one with the sore head.

"Right."

"She kissed me and I kissed her back."

"Well, there you go." Emilie's hand flashes out of the water. "*That* is relevant."

"And for a few seconds I forgot about you."

Tamara inches deeper into the water to let it lick her chin and her bottom lip, as she waits, eyes almost level with the surface turmoil of currents, swirls, spray and miniature rips that clash and collide at the whim of the blowing jets. When she pushes herself up again with her good hand, she brings her eyes around to Emilie who is once again absorbed by the movements of the bobbing thermometer. Like a boat at its mooring, it tugs and strains. *But even if it managed to break loose,* she wonders, *where would it go?*

"When she … uh, when Zag like, shifted gears … Well, I pulled back and that's all there is to it but yes, I kissed her, Em."

Emilie closes her eyes. She makes herself slide under the surface of the turbulent water. Her hair fans out like a dark brown sea anemone agitated by contrary currents. And under the water she stays. Holding on to her breath is a natural thing for her to do. When her head finally surfaces, her hair clings to her skull in a soft sheen, almost like that of a soft leather helmet, down to her eyebrows, around her ears, against her neck.

Eyes tight, Tamara is intent on Emilie's mouth. It's oddly puckered in a sort of tight but enigmatic smile. Unable to read anything from it, Tamara frowns, undecided as to what needs to happen next. Emilie raises her chin. She gauges the distance separating her from Tamara. The water she had been holding in her mouth squirts and arcs right smack-dab in front of Tamara's chest.

*****

SIX

The morning light filters through the veiled windows of Emilie's bedroom. Tamara sucks in the air in short bursts but not enough penetrates deep inside her lungs. All of her has shrunk to almost nothing. All of her, all her thoughts, all her needs, and she, as a being, have all been minimised, reduced to half a centimetre, to a minuscule region that has become charged with an electricity that is becoming uncompromising.

It shimmers and it is all invasive as hair-thin lashes of electrified ache search, find and ignite. Her body is tense with a desire that has wrapped the room around, the bed around, her body around the swirls of iridescence loosed by her lover's tongue, by her lover's lips. All has melted and blended into sparks and plumes of obliterating desire.

"There can't be any riding of the storm, Tam," Emilie had admonished earlier, referring to something Tamara said to her, months ago, before they were to make love for the first time.

During one of her early dissertations on the merits of having sex as opposed to that of making love in a controlled and attentive manner, Tamara had explained that there were times when she liked to totally surrender to sensual cravings, temporarily losing the focus she'd otherwise have on her lover.

'It's like being in a lightning storm,' she had explained. 'I don't want to tame it. I want to ride it. I want to be selfish, then. I let it suck me into its vortex.'

The conversation they had had that evening in Emilie's bed, intermingled with hot foreplay and intimate self-disclosure, had left Emilie with a permanent freeze-frame memory.

Tamara had scooted even closer to Emilie, the side of her knee resting against her hip. Her sex had been dark pink in the soft glow of the candles, close, tantalisingly close to Emilie's hand and, at that moment, the dated, stylised, feminist representation of the female genitalia had finally made sense to Emilie. The iris. Petals of the iris, indeed.

That morning though, the morning that followed Tamara's discharge from the hospital, the crows and the lorikeets had already been up, deep inside the trees when the alarm beeped. The dry-throated ha-hacking of the crows and the high pitched chatter of the lorikeets pushing forward the faint rays of pale light filtering through the curtains, signalled very strongly that dawn had let in the morning.

Tamara, who had had another restless night propped up against pillows, had watched Emilie fumble with the alarm until her thumb found the OFF button. She smiled at the customary grumpy groans that came from Emilie's side of the bed and watched her pull the sheet over her head.

"Hey, Emi, wanna snuggle up this way?"

Emilie opened her eyes at the sound of Tamara's voice. She blinked at the clock that indicated the same time it did every morning of the working week. She turned under the sheet and inched against Tamara's side to settle with her cheek on the crook of her lover's bare shoulder. And Tamara rubbed her back as one does to ease a child out of a little mood.

Emilie was not truly grumpy, she simply had honed a lifelong resentment of having to wake and get up against the grain of her natural biological rhythm. So, one arm draped across Tamara's stomach and hips, she welcomed a way out of her customary early morning irritation. Together, they had lay in silence, contemplating their respective days ahead, the first Monday after the parking lot aggression.

They had lay in companionable silence, snugly pressed together, Emilie chasing the last of the cobwebs left behind by the night's too hasty retreat until Tamara shifted her hips, moving Emilie's hand a little back so that it covered her sex. A warm and melting sensation unfolded itself under Tamara's ribs. She shifted a little more and rearranged her legs under the sheet.

Emilie lifted inquisitive eyes towards Tamara who had simply smiled. Then, she briefly peered into the green of Tamara's eyes before parting her lips with a sleep-mellow tongue. Tamara closed her eyes as she had closed her lips around the warmth of Emilie's tongue, keeping it inside her, making it hers. One hand against the small of her lover's back, Tamara guided her onto her hips.

"So, it's a deal, Tam? You just lie back and close your eyes?" Emilie had added, as she helped Tamara settle herself against the pillows, "If I had a four poster bed, I'd bind your wrists with a couple of silk scarves, just to make sure you keep your head still."

"Oh, yes!" Tamara replied, still warm and loose from the night, cat green eyes bright with lustful anticipation.

"You got to promise. If you don't … I'll just have to resort to some old-fashioned blackmail. You don't keep still, I'll just have to stop and you'll just – "

"OK. OK. I promise!" Tamara was quick to give in, easing her head and shoulders into the pillows.

She lay back, letting Emilie's hands rove the length of her body. Emilie's lips and Emilie's tongue did the final convincing.

Resisting the urge to respond in a physical way felt marvellously sensual to Tamara. It transported her to a state of arousal she had experienced only once before when Marielle, back at Sainte-Thérèse, made love to her so dreamily that Tamara had thought her to be in an altered state. *From behind a screen of self-preservation*, Tamara had thought. One behind which Marielle could cleanse herself of what her father had again done to her earlier that evening of the red moon.

Inside her bed inside the barn, Tamara had made herself lie very still. Back then, she had been afraid that the ache she felt for the young woman might break the spell. Unable to touch back, unable to slow down her arousal by a shift of focus while long, invasive slivers of desire spread and spiralled down her thighs, Tamara had lain, exposed, vulnerable, hardly able to contain the deep-set arousal, thankful for the pitch-dark of the barn.

The curtains fluttered against Emilie's windows. Tamara had been, for a very brief moment, worried that the quickly intensifying ache would stir up the pain that was still asleep, curled up inside her head. Now, propped against a set of pillows, as the familiar feeling overpowers her, as her lover moves against her skin, all awareness, even that of her lover, has melted away. All there exists for Tamara is the nuzzling of Emilie's lips, the caress of *her* tongue over that tiny hardness of pleasure that has become *all* of Tamara. She sucks in a breath, moaning softly.

Emilie looks up, letting her eyes roam over the plane of Tamara's stomach, over the rise and fall of her chest, over the full curve of her breasts, over the tawny sheen of her arms. And she slides upwards, making herself heavy against her lover's body. Her fingers settle where her tongue and her lips had been. She nuzzles and caresses Tamara's tongue the way she had nuzzled and caressed her sex and Tamara's ribs expand under her. Perhaps in an attempt to anchor herself against movement, Tamara clasps Emilie tighter against her breasts, tighter against her sex as she gives in to her desire.

*****

A knock on the door.

Emilie's eyes and fingers dance over the rows of clear plastic tabs.

"Come in."

She pulls out a folder, flips through its contents and slides it back. Fingers poised over parallel lines of thin metallic rails and more plastic tabs, she frowns at the door, annoyed by whoever might be that timorous person who is not adventurous enough to stick their head in. *What, afraid I might frag them with green goo? Or pop them with a Nerf ball?* Peering over the half-moon of her glasses, she calls again, louder this time.

"Come *in*."

A dark head appears in the space cracked open but it stands higher than Emilie had anticipated. Red cheeked, blue-eyed, goofy-looking Liam is looking at her.

"Uh ... I'm ... uh ... Sorry to bother yo – "

"Ahhh, Liam," Emilie says on a sigh. "If it's about that extension you're after ... Could we talk about it a little later? Now's not a good time."

"Uh ... Miss..." Liam's large T-bone sized hand inches higher up the door jamb.

Another head pops close to his shoulder.

"Erin? What're you up to? Don't tell me our Liam here's brought you along as his bodyguard?"

"No ... Miss. I don't reckon it's like he needs one but ... In a way..."

Emilie glances at her watch and confirms her reading by the clock above Mary's desk. "Look guys, as I said, why don't you pop back after your last lesson. I'll have more time to – "

"I ... well ... you see," Liam stammers, "I might like, not be here later."

"What he's got to say is like so important, Miss ... uh, for once," Erin throws an upward grin towards Liam.

Something about that grin suggests to Emilie that these two are new lovers. Sweet for him, but what's in it for her? Emilie puzzles while her student unravels more of an obscure lead-in, on Liam's behalf. "It's not like it's about school or anything. Uh ... It's not like it's about that extension. And well ... Liam, he asked me to come ... with him, I mean – "

"OK, guys, you win." Emilie pulls the glasses off her nose. "Meet me in the classroom in five. There shouldn't be anyone there this time of day. Will that do?"

Liam's curly mop nods vigorously. Erin's already slipped away.

What's with the tandem act? Emilie wonders with a frown. Liam's a harmless gumbee, a sweet enough dork, when puppeteered by the right hands. However, ever since the day he had called out in class asking if the rumour that, she, Ms Anderson, was a lezzo was correct, Emilie has been wary of him.

"Liam, your question?" she had asked that day in her usual pleasant-but-we-don't-have-time-for-any-nonsense tone.

"Well, it's like, some of us, Miss …"

She had nodded, encouraging him to fast-forward his thought.

"There's talk, Miss. It's like *everyone* says – "

Uh-uh … here we go again, had been Emilie's pull-on-the-alarm thought. She knew *exactly* how the young man in front of her was going to finish his sentence. She had recognised the signals, the vibrations from the group in front of her. She had been there before. Another time. Another place. But the same cocky assuredness. The same expectant vibrancy about the group primed for what they knew was about to come down.

"Well, it's like we … everyone says you're a lesbian." He had smirked. *"Miss."*

And Erin-of-the-many-ear-rivets might not be an overly keen student but what she lacks in terms of academic motivation she more than makes up for with what Emilie perceives is a healthy attitude, not only toward the cardboard authority of teachers but toward authority figures in general.

At nineteen, unlike many of her contemporaries, Erin doesn't need to press flanks with those of her classmates who, from the anonymity of their pack, get a kick out of whispering slyly but well within teachers' earshot, that 'He who can, does. He who cannot, teaches.' Of course, none of them would have been able to name George Bernard Shaw as the 1903 originator of that line and not one would have even heard of cigar-puffing H L Mencken and his paraphrased, '*The ones who can, do. The ones who can't, teach.*'

Erin is not one to freeze, either, in mid-stride at the sight of a teacher. And smarmy obsequiousness doesn't seem to occur to her. Besides, Erin and her silver discman have been contributing to the education of Ms Anderson's microscopic understanding of modern pop music.

"It's like … it's like so … arrested, Miss," Erin had blurted once when, at the end of a lesson, the conversation had somehow drifted to the teacher's musical preference. "You can't just, like, listen to Classical and pretend the rest is total crap."

"Mmm. Well … there might be a few good tunes out there but on the whole, since the innovative seventies and some great '80s tracks, not much seems to have happened besides Rap and Techno – "

"You're just like my mum. It's like unless I sit her down and make her listen she's like so not aware. She goes – "

Emilie had been secretly comforted by the thought that, unlike Erin's mum, when *she* came home *she* had an oasis of calm all to herself from where to tend to her private thoughts and look forward to intimate moments with Tamara. She didn't, first, have to argue about this, that, or something else with a teenage child and lock herself in the bathroom for a little peace and quiet. Maybe she should occasionally *borrow* a teen to get to know the species differently.

So eyes teasing, Emilie had said, "Granted, Erin. Maybe I've become a bit of a troglodyte … Hey, what the hell … Educate me."

And Erin had tuned Emilie to a few singers, fortunately mostly females who, more often than not, she agreed had spunk, voice appeal and lyrics that even she could get into. And occasionally, Emilie had been able to surprise Tamara with a fresh track, compliments of Erin who, of course, had no inkling as to what use Ms Anderson was making of her budding knowledge of Generation X's better music moments.

Well, I'd better go see what these two are on about. Another glance at her watch confirms that she'll have to keep on working through lunch if she hopes to have her submission ready for her afternoon meeting with Graeme and his men in grey, the directors of the board.

It's that time of the year when they frown and hedge and hum, grumble, object, and interject, fingers sliding up and down the column of her Annual Operational Plan. It's the time of the year when the board directors feel the need to remind her of her obligations as a Corporate Card Holder, of her need for probity, of threshold-safeguards and economic risk-assessment. And it's all said so seriously, as if her Communications Department depended on her buying huge pieces of machinery costing dollars in the tens of millions.

We do need a couple more laptops, this and that software, stationery and oh, yes, I've budgeted for the purchase of half a dozen recent-release videos. But no, gentlemen, we won't be needing a combine-harvester this year, not even a bobcat, is what she's been yearning to tell them, at that time of the year for the last five years.

Emilie walks the length of the corridor to her classroom. Whispers greet her as she steps through the threshold. Erin, who had been sitting on her boyfriend's lap, arms around his neck, stands up, drags a chair to his side and flops on it the way she usually flops behind her desk.

Liam spreads his knees in a careless, young male pose, the wide Vee of his legs inevitably drawing the eye to the dropped crotch of the homeboy pants that reach mid-thigh. Emilie notices that his knee nearest Erin cuts into the young woman's space.

"Right, guys. What can I do for you?"

That's got to be the ugliest male fashion that's ever been invented, Emilie often ponders at the sight of these young men who do the stunted droopy-drawers dawdle inside accordion legs or who exhibit toothpick-scrawny, hairy calves that protrude from oversized baggy shorts.

"Miss, Liam's so worried about what's come down."

Emilie arches her eyebrows, waiting for more.

"Uh … to be honest …" Liam begins, still chasing after his voice. "It's Erin's that's talked me into it."

"Into what, Liam? Erin?"

Erin slides a glance in her boyfriend's direction but doesn't say any more.

"Liam? What is it?"

"It's like she thought I should like, talk to you first and…"

"So, here you are, indeed." Emilie leans forward. "And what can I do for you … now that you are here?"

"It's about this mate I have."

"One of *my* students?"

"No, it's not like you know him or anything."

"Right. So…?"

"Uh … well, that's the hard part. Let's just say I have this friend and it's like he's really … He thinks your car's like so sick."

Emilie lets out an offended "Whadda you mean, sick? *My* car?"

"It's OK," Erin breaks in, visibly amused. "It's a compliment. He means like really cool. You know like rad? Like mad?" And with a grin she adds, "You're just like my mum. You gotta keep up with the talk, Miss."

"Oh. Right. So this *dude* you know likes my Jeep," Emilie is puzzled by Liam's stop- start release of information.

While he twists little finger over ring-finger, visibly pondering what he should volunteer next, Emilie processes the first sound bites of information with the speed of an anti-virus update zipping through every nook and cranny of a hard drive. Click-rapid comes the thought that *this* friend of Liam's might be harbouring the fantasy of scoring a ride in the Jeep. Or of having a go at driving it around the block. Oh no! No way, no rides. Or, worse still, maybe he's already hot-wired it to take it on a spin. Shit. If he's damaged it…

"Liam, is my car still out there in the parking lot? In one piece?"

He shrugs. "Yeah, I reckon."

"Well, don't tell me this friend of yours is actually saving up his pennies to make me an offer or anything, is he?" Emilie grins under a frown. "That little baby's not *at all* for sale."

Liam grins back a lopsided grin that somehow complements his beanstalk, goofy looks but probably belies his age. *How old is he anyway? Been with me for the past what, three semesters.* She tries to recall the facts on Liam's personal info sheet because, now, Erin's involved with him. Misplaced, protective mother-hen behaviour, she chuckles to herself.

"Buy it? Uh … no."

"Right," Emilie exclaims in mock relief. "So … what about him and my car, then?"

According to his file, Liam had been a non-committed student up to and including his senior year in high school. That, in itself, justifies his enrolment at the Institute of Further Knowledge. For some, tertiary establishments act only as a buffer, a last outpost between high school and unemployment, while for others the time spent there is a redeemer that provides struggling youths with a few more academic skills before time runs out for them.

Besides his mediocre high school transcripts, his personal file had Liam living with his father, a groundsman at a local bowls club. Emilie remembered that particular piece of information because at the time she had pulled up Liam's file, after his attempt to big-note himself by exposing her (Who *is* that dickhead?) she had wondered how two men fared on one groundsman's wages. Liam, as far as she knew, only worked part-time at one of the Pizza Dens. DOB 19 …80. So, that'd make him twenty-one and a bit. Adult.

"Well … it goes like …" Liam casts another glance at Erin who nods encouragingly. "See, one day I was telling this … mate I have about school and all, like he only has a Year 10 pass, right? So sometimes he goes like, 'How they doing you at that place? What they do is take your dough,' I mean, that's how he carries on, right? And he goes on like, 'All that does is fu – ' Uh sorry, Miss." Liam clears his throat and starts again. "So, yeah what this guy says is, They mess your brains and make a limp dick outta you." Liam shrugs. "That's how he talks, right? So like one day I tell him about well, you know, the usual, and then, … Well, thing is … he already knows about you. Goes back to last year when …uh …" Liam looks about to derail. "Yeah so, he asks about you and so, like I make conversation, right?"

"Right. And?"

"And so … like not long ago, he asks again and I don't know but I tell him about the car you drive, like he's a real petrol head and like your car's the best, right? So I gasbag with him. Like, he lets me hang around but like he really treats me like his junior, right? And the deal is, he's sure he's spotted your car … somewhere. Like he knows all about it."

Emilie frowns. "He does, does he?"

"Yeah, but it's like he didn't know it was yours, right?"

Erin steps in. "He's a real wanker, Miss. Like he says he would've gone to fight in Kabul, right, if he had had the money to get there. And Liam says the dude's like all fired about what's happening in Baghdad or like, going to some boot camp he says that's somewhere in the Hamas or wherever. Like action, right?" Out of Erin's mouth comes a 'prruuttt' sound, like a small fart, as she turns both thumbs inward in the double loser's sign.

"So the thing is … it's like I tell him a bit more…" Liam is faltering again, "…a bit more about you because, like he's really asking because of the Jeep and then…"

A tingling sensation has begun rippling under Emilie's skin, across her shoulders, up the nape of her neck. "Liam? Would you please go on with your story?"

Erin glances at her boyfriend and shaking her head adds the punch line to Liam's agonisingly slow account. "Uh … Look, Miss, it's not like he meant it nasty or anything but it's like Liam, like a while back, he told this guy you were gay or something."

"And?" Emilie asks on a suspended breath. She had just been thinking back to that grotesque email she had found in her inbox some time the end of the previous school year. *Anderson. Your cunts on fire … Fucking lezzo …*

"And … Well…" Eyes downcast, Liam attempts an explanation. "That's why we're here, isn't it?"

"I'm not sure I follow, Liam. Why are *you* here? Why are *we* talking about this friend of yours and *my* Jeep and local gossip. Like, why *now* when…" Emilie hears her tone. Too brittle. Her words, too rushed. Her teacher's tone hasn't kicked in yet. She's not projecting total control. "…there are so many things I need to get done by 3.30. I have a meeting I must absolut…"

"It's about the Crime Stoppers segment, Miss. On the Teev. We kinda know what came down."

Emilie blinks. She turns to Liam. She turns to Erin. "You do, do you? *Erin?*"

"It's like we're pretty sure about it, actually."

"So … you've already told the police? Yes?"

Erin answers on her boyfriend's behalf. "See, Miss, what happened is that after he saw the *Today/Tonight* segment, Liam calls me and he tells me things about that loser buddy he's got and so on. See, I don't know the dude. Don't care to either. So Liam, he calls to tell *me* what he knows. It's like he can't possibly dob in his bud, right? But then, we get to talking some more and he agrees that … yeah, like you say, the police need to know. But then, Liam, he's really like cut up about the whole thing. Like he feels a bit responsible so … yeah … It's his idea to come here and tell you firs –"

Emilie takes in a deep breath. "OK, I hear you, Erin." She makes herself lean back into the plastic chair. "Liam, what are you here to tell me?" For chrissake, she's dying to add, get on with it and spill the fucking beans!

Breathe Emilie. Breathe. Pace yourself. Don't go spooking him, now. He needs to take his story to the Brooke Street station and he'll be going nowhere if you break his balls too soon.

Erin releases another little grain of information. "See, this guy, he hangs around a gym, some dump in the Valley and…"

"Is this mate of yours into … Uh, does he use his hands in any particular way?"

"How you mean?"

Emilie takes in another breath. "Is he into Martial Arts or something like that by any chance?"

Liam averts his eyes again but he answers, "Yes, he is."

"Actually," quips Erin, "He's a fucking … " this time Erin only squints a silent apology at Emilie. *Oh, for fuck's sake,* she'd like to tell the girl, borrowing Tamara's favourite expression, *if you want to say fuck … Fucking hell, just say it and don't let's apologise every fucking time.* "Well he's like… like *really* into it. Big time into the shit. He's like, right into the Iron Palm stuff."

"And what is Iron Palm stuff?"

"It's … uh … it's like a special discipline." Liam sits up and Emilie watches him rearrange his feet - two enormous and partially untied skater's Globes. "Not the usual Karate fool-around stuff like a Kata here and a Kata there. It's a … it's a special thing, a technique. It's all about striking with the *palm* surface of the hand, that's where it's different from the brick-breaking stuff. It's done with like a long whipping move. Not a thrust, no, not really."

Emilie walks back to her office. Mary looks up. "What's up? You look all wrung out."

"I am … all wrung out."

"Want to tell me about it?"

"No." Emilie is startled by the curtness of her own answer. "Ok, look … Mary, I'm sorry. I didn't really mean NO. It's just that I'm terribly behind in the AOP submission that's due this afternoon. At 2.00. It's one hell of a lucky day all around. But, tell you what." Emilie picks up the phone and begins punching in numbers. "Let's do the two-birds, one-stone thing. Why don't you listen in while I talk to Tam? No, really, Mary, hey!" she calls out in answer to Mary's hurt look. "I'd like you to."

Having pasted over Mary a dry scholarly gloss based on nothing more than a first impression, Emilie had purposefully bypassed the colleague with whom she's had to share an office space year after year. But also, Emilie reminded herself, there had been her assumption that Mary, being straight, was likely to be judgmental about alternative sexualities. And so Emilie had opted for a pleasant, professional, but aloof and private manner. More recently, though, and much to her surprise, Emilie had found that Mary was a genuinely good woman to have as a colleague. To have as a friend.

When Emilie had finally disclosed that she was a lesbian, all Mary had said was, "And … what about it? Is this where I'm supposed to come in and exclaim, Oh my God!?"

As she had explained later, she and her husband had already surmised during a pillow talk moment that Emilie had to be a lesbian. And, last year, Mary had come in on the tail end of Liam's staged confrontation of Emilie and knew, too, about the offensive email she had received anonymously, so as Emilie dialled, Mary did as invited and prepared to listen in on Emilie's conversation with her lover.

The phone rings in Emilie's house. At which phone point will Tamara pick up? she wonders. She hears her OGM and thinks it might be time to update it. And she thinks of the words she needs to explain to Tamara what has happened to her.

Eyes on Mary, Emilie begins her preamble. "Hey, Tam, it's me. You around there somewhere? Got news that – "

"Em ... Uh, yeah ... I'm here. Wasn't sure if I should pick up or not, you know, in case ... Like Merredith and ... so I thought I'd wait – "

"Yeah, that's OK, darling. It's whatever you're comfortable with. Now, look, as I was saying, I ... uh, well, something's happened this morning and ... and maybe now I know why you got targeted ... last Wednesday."

Silence on the line. Emilie arches her eyebrows at Mary who, now keen to hear Emilie's piece of news, smiles back with a hunch of the shoulders.

"Tam?"

"I'm here. Just trying to anticipate some of what you might say, like what ... you've heard from the cops? Uh ... yeah, never mind, you tell me."

"Tam, you remember me mentioning a student who, uh, before you and I got together, like at least a semester earlier ... Anyway that student had kind of cornered me in front of other students of min – "

"Yes, I remember. He wanted to know if you were gay and – "

"Right. So his name's Liam, right?" Emilie confirms for Mary's benefit. She is rewarded by a pop-eyed stare of disbelief and a silent shaping of the name Lee-ahm? that Emilie meets with a shake of the head. Palm up, she gestures to Mary a silent Hold On.

"Right. So what has that little drip got to do with anything?"

"Well, that's the thing, Tam. Look, Tam, as it turns out, it's not Del's stalker who decked you in the parking lot."

Silence and then a whispered, "Who did, then? Don't tell me it's your Liam boy."

"No, not him but close. Well, that's the scoop." Emilie slides the reading glasses off her nose and, wearily, she flops on the swivel chair behind her. "Looks like it's a skinhead by the name of SS. SS stands for Street-Sweeper and Street-Sweeper is one who fancies himself as a bit of a vigilante. He keeps the streets clean by – "

"You have *got* to be kiddin'!"

"No, not kidding, Tam." Emilie glances at Mary who looks back at her, a clear question mark in the arch of her eyebrows. So, for her benefit, Emilie adds, "Gay bashing."

One of Mary's hands flies to her mouth. Then she pats the top of her head, as she does when she is involved with something difficult. Then, eyes riveted on Emilie, she drops her arms to her side in a gesture of utter dismay.

"OK, so here goes. Liam knows this guy … You're with me, Tam? A low-life who hangs around a gym in the Valley and Liam kind of thinks he's cool like, you know, a serious dose of misplaced hero-worship. Anyway, comes a day like a few months back, end of last year, when Liam talks to this guy who kind of lets him hang around. So he gets to talking about school, blah, blah, blah and … about that teacher of his who piles all that shit work on him, right?"

"I follow, but what's that got to do with me getting clubbed?"

"For now ... nothing but, Tam, you remember that really sick email that came in just *after* we met? It had me as a lezzo with a cunt on fire…" Emilie glances sheepishly at Mary though she, too, already knows all about that offensive piece.

As it happened, she had come in a few minutes after Emilie had opened her mail, and had found her staring at a blank screen. She had already deleted the message and shut down Outlook, as one flushes an odious item down the toilet, trusting that, from the bowels of the earth, it would never surface again.

"I remember. You were in a total flap about it."

"Yes, well, guess what? If Liam's truthful about this…"

"Don't tell me Liam sent it."

"No, not Liam. That guy … It looks like that guy did."

Silence and then, "Well, better a stranger than someone you know and trust. I mean, like a colleague or a student. Uh … but what's that got to do with – "

"Look, more recently, a couple of weeks ago, Liam has another yarn with the SS dude, right? The lads end up talking cars, as they would, and for some reason the guy asks about me. And the weird thing is that somehow, Liam mentions the Jeep and the dude gets him to talking about it some more and it turns out that guy's already spotted the Jeep somewhere, like he knows all about its specs and so on. Well, you know how it's quite hard to miss – "

"What, your Jeep?"

"Yes, mine. And then, one thing leads to another, the guy carries on how it's an effing shame to have a dyke at the wheel of such a mad rig and well, maybe I own the damn thing but I certainly don't have what it takes to *drive* it, get it? Like not really working the guts out of it, and how something needs to be done about these bitchin' cunts who always end up with what, rightfully, should be *his* and how they get away with … Look, Tam, you got the picture?"

"Got the picture. One sick puppy, but why attack me when it's not even my ca– "

"Tam, you were in the wrong place at the wrong time. Mistaken identity, kiddo."

"Awh, for fuck's sake, Em! Tell me you're making this up."

*****

EPILOGUE

Hand flat against the grimy tiles, Craig Baker heaves a great sigh. He accelerates the pumping of his shaft and adjusts his weight more evenly on the balls of his feet. Higher up the shaft, a nip right under where the head bulges out. All the way back to the root and again. Nice and snug, his dick rides inside his fist, and again. Pull. Pull back. Nip. Faster. Faster. Faster. A squirt of cum splatters against the back of the urinal.

Craig Baker wipes both hands on the back of his black jeans, slides his still wet penis inside his jeans, does up the fly and runs his hands over the month-old stubble on his head.

Hours of palming kilos of round river rocks in a canvas bag, that, and palming queers, make his cock go hard. Nothing sensual, nothing sexual. No fantasising. Just hard.

Craig Baker is a believer in superior conditioning. One strike, certain death, if he chooses it to be so. After he batters his callused hands, hours on end on the rocks, practising the flowing motion of water crashing that gives the Iron Palm its devastating effect, there are only two things he needs to do, today, before downing the first long neck at the pub.

He needs to crack his knuckles both hands together, fingers intertwined, in one mighty crack. Then, fastidiously, he cracks the top ones and the middle ones, one by one. First the knuckles of the one hand, then of the other. And then, he needs to jerk himself off. Only then is Craig Baker ready for his Thirsty Dog at the Ball Bearing pub.

Craig Baker likes to do things in the right order. Discipline. Perseverance. Nothing's ever happened overnight, he knows that. Well, most things don't, but he remembers that story a mate of his told him about how Rome had been burning all fucking night while this dude, Nero, a king or something, he just fucking looked on. Playing a fucking violin.

Craig Baker liked that story. He could actually visualise the whole thing, again and again, just as if he had been there. On that hill, but in a weird way close enough to feel the heat scorch his eyebrows and blister his lips. So, yeah, that shit happened overnight but Craig Baker knew that the kind of cleaning up *he* was into, he knew *that* took time. Just like the calluses on his hands. Time. Courage. Dedication. That, and a brain like his, he often bragged, a fuckin' brain that don't register pain. Man, it's like the fucking gauge's stuck on fucking zero. You can pump it all you like. Zilch. Not a fuck. Not a spark of life.

Tamara turns again in her sleep. Emilie's sleep-soft body is only inches away but she doesn't know it's there anymore. She'd like to wake up but the sick wisps of her nightmare cling to her breath like the folds of a wet sarong.

"Officer Matthews, look … uh … I need to know."

"Fire away."

"Look … uh … how safe is she, Emilie, I mean? Like, is the dude going to be put away for some time or … What I'm asking is, seeing as he got the wrong woman the first time, right, is he likely to come back … like because he's riled or to … do better what he screwed up the first time?"

"Can't say for sure but you got to understand that, at this stage, his only prior is a DUI. We now got his prints *and* we got his DNA but all I can say for sure is that with nothing more to go on than the two or three days he put you in the hospital … that won't cost *him* more than two months. Three at the most. As little as probation … that's entirely possible too. And he'll be out on bail by tomorrow morning."

Hard inside Tamara's subconscious, Craig Baker comes out of the hole in the wall. Senior Constable Matthews' words wrap around her tightly; cue prompts no one has cued in.

Rusty letters peel off the sooty grey entrance to the basement gym. Combat fighting. Bare hands. Muai-Thai. He blinks as he steps onto the bright sidewalk. Heat radiates off the bitumen. Hot tar and hot exhaust fumes. He swivels to his right and, loose-limbed, he ambles past a fish and chip café.

Senior Constable Matthews makes him first. He nudges old Hood-Eyes, except that when he gave Tamara the account of how they had collared the "low-life" that had attacked her in the parking lot, Senior Constable Matthews hadn't said Hood-Eyes, he had said DS Johnson.

So he had ID'd the jerk as soon as he stepped into the street. They'd been waiting for him because Liam, in his statement, had said that this guy was a stickler for routine and that he always finished his workout and went for a beer around 10.30 a.m. Senior Constable Matthews had verified the month-old stubble on the guy's head and the little goatee under his lip. "Just like the Turnbull kid said." That's when Senior Constable Matthews nudged old Hood-Eyes.

"What's with the tat, then?" he had asked as the suspect came closer. "Look like a mermaid to you?"

"Could do. Just hang on a sec."

They let the suspect walk right past them and the SS tattooed on the side of the man's neck, that, and a clear eyeball of the huge tits on the mermaid curled around his biceps, confirmed ID.

Senior Constable Matthews stood up, crossed the street and once the suspect had cleared the busy section, doubled back, whipped out a black leather fold-over wallet and flashed his badge in Craig Baker's face.

"Senior Constable Matth – "

Craig Baker wheeled on the ball of his feet and had old Hood-Eyes right in his face, badge at the ready.

"DS Johnso – "

"Why you in my face?" Craig Baker asks, teeth clenched, chest thrust forward. High on energy, he dances on the balls of his feet. Senior Constable Matthews watches him through slitted eyes. DS Johnson watches him through hooded eyes. All three men stand their ground.

"Craig *Baker*," says the old guy.

"Who's asking, huh?"

"I'm not asking, mate. I'm telling," snaps the fuzz, flashing his badge for the second time. "DS Johnson, Brooke Street Statio – "

"Yeah, yeah, whatever! Who gives a fuck, man?"

"We're investigating a complaint of serious assault on a female – "

"You deaf, old man? I said, who gives a fuck? Right?" Craig Baker's fingers twitch at his side. "You're barking up the wrong tree. You got nofin' on me that can stick. So, what say you stop dancin' with me, huh. What say you piss off and I get myself that beer I need to get in me, huh?"

"Take a breath, Junior," the old cop says, eyes drilling.

"Tell you what, Craig, seeing as you're already treading thin ice, what say *we* do you a favour before that lip of yours puts your arse in a sling, huh? What say *you* come, peaceful-like, and ride with us and you tell us what you got on that aggression that took place last Wednesday. Around 6 p.m. New Farm time."

"You ain't listening, Off-eecer," Craig Baker replies, contempt wrapped around his politeness. "I'm hoofing it for a beer. Got zip to tell you about what you're screeching in me ear." Craig Baker goes to push

C. C. Saint-Clair

past Senior Constable Matthews who's already whipping out a gleaming set of handcuffs.

"Peaceful or painful," he states coolly. "Your toss."

"OK. One for the drones," Craig Baker replies, nonchalantly tugging at the hair under his lip. "I'll fuckin' answer any fuckin' question you want. It's not like anythin'll fall on me. None of your mangy fleas gonna stick to my arse."

In Emilie's bed, Tamara is still sleeping listlessly. Her mid-sleep thoughts, screen-saver-like, churned and poked around and beyond what news Senior Constable Matthews had been able to give her about the arrest of a Craig Baker.

"…a low-life who began by denying everything. Standard. That one needed a serious wake-up call. But, look, you've been through a lot, Tamara, so I won't give you the blow-by-blow … uh, bad choice of words. Look, my message to you is that you can consider yourself lucky that this thug's a coward."

"How's that?"

"Too chicken to use his skill to the max. No doubt he can seriously kink up the wiring inside anyone's brain. Permanently. But he knows the penalty *that* incurs and for all his bravado and big man talk, he's a gutless jerk. He won't walk his own talk, if you know what I mean. So, what that means for you, in real terms, is that you're alive to tell the tale. *And* you're not in a wheelchair."

Senior Constable Matthews had paused to allow Tamara to ask questions. She didn't have any she could ask, not at that particular moment, because too many were whirling inside her head, like butterflies in a butterfly hive. So he continued with what he thought she needed to know.

"We *know* you're not his first hate-crime but we can't pin anything else on him, not just yet. That's because…victims of hate-crimes are slow coming forward. And for what he's done to you, my point is that he won't find himself in front of a judge, not on a GBH charge. See, he knew to stop short of that, of a grievous. It'll take a while," Senior Constable Matthews added, "but we'll keep talking to doctors like your Doctor Mac. And now that we got his latents – "

"Fingerprints?"

"All five of them, real beauties. One on top and one under the flap to your backpack. And three on the side of the vehicle."

As Tamara's subconscious mind attempted to process the events that could have altered the course of her life permanently, viscous and untethered jagged thoughts began a swirling descent into the deepening murkiness of her nightmare.

Today is the day Craig Baker has a mission. Another clean-up mission. That's the least he can do for the Fatherland. Today is the day he goes deviant-palming. So, he makes his way to New farm. The parking lot is vacant, just as he's expected it to be from his earlier reconnaissance. Vacant except for one vehicle.

"Hot, that one. Real hot," he whispers, running his fingers lovingly along the side of the Jeep.

No cunning ambush to plan, so he squats behind the dumpster that's just there at the edge of the parking lot, some fifteen steps almost directly behind but to the left of the Jeep.

Tamara tosses and turns but as a photographer to a light-metre reader, Tamara's nightmare wants her right against Craig Baker.

Right against the ridge of his forehead. *What the fuck's the target's name, anyway.* He tries to conjure up the name the college kid gave him. His teacher's name. Right against the day old stubble on his cheek. Fuck the name. A dyke's a dyke. Dyke's fine for a name. Right against the corner of the mouth that twitches sardonically as it moves around an impromptu lullaby.

"Hey, dyke! Dyke, pike, dyke, tyke, psyc, tic-tac. Here comes a dyke," Craig Baker singsongs with a simple grin, very softly, before his thoughts turn and he rubs the thick ridge of calluses that run over most of his palm. 'Cunt smelling cunt.'

Tamara cannot wake from her nightmare.

Craig Baker is in no hurry. Squatting and waiting's the other part of the discipline. Patience. Timing. While he squats and waits, tweaking the tuft of hair under his lip, he imagines himself at the wheel of the stripped down Jeep. Toss the side panels. Brace a fuckin' M-203 to the back and … Sweet fuckin' Jesus! Sand churning, missiles screaming above his head, Craig Baker's off the Khyber Pass on his way to Jalalabad. He could be a warlord out there, any time. A legend, if only he could score a ticket out of OZ. Gnome-like, he waits until finally the lobby doors slide open. And there she is walking briskly down the steps. His jaws tighten. His eyes close on a squint, that of a sniper on a rooftop.

Look at her, like hot to slide inside and go cruisin' for pussy. All bitches. Fuckin' look at her looking so fucking smooth.

And Tamara, inside her nightmare, is right inside his mind when Craig Baker wishes he had her against him.

Suck my dick, bitch, he'd hiss, *if* he had her. He'd push her face right against his open fly.

And while, from behind the pock-marked steel walls of the skip, he follows Tamara's progress through the parking lot, his thoughts whirl back to the limp-dick who hangs around him like a lost pup, the kid who put him on to his *Mz* Anderson. *Ah, that's her name,* he remembers. A smirk curls up his top lip. "Cunt-sucking *Mz* Anderson."

If I had her in my face day after day after fuckin' day, paying good money for an education, I'd have me a bonus. Miss Anderson. Tight-ass, cool-chick. Arse up, on her fuckin' knees, and drippin'.

Tamara groans in her sleep. The shape of the man's thoughts come to her distorted, but sharp like a broken piece of twisted glass.

You be civil to her, Craig Baker reckons, teeth clenched, *and wham, before you know it, she's got her tongue right where you want to ram your cock. Right inside another bitch's pussy.*

So, he waits until Tamara comes right next to the Jeep. He watches as she reaches inside the backpack that she's rested on the Jeep's hood. Something slightly behind the front tyre catches her attention. She steps back to have a better look at it. Like the white bull at the sacrificial altar, Tamara lowers her head. A blur, the blue snub toe of a Doc, breaks in at the edge of her peripheral vision.

Craig Baker's palm comes crashing against the back of Tamara's head. He could've cracked that head and have his knuckles come out the other side, if he'd wanted to. But he knows the penalty for making pulp out of a brain that's not animal. And years in jail or worse just ain't a price he's ready to pay, not even as a due to the Fatherland.

So he palms her with the fluid but restrained motion of crashing water. Trims down the follow through. Down she goes, all the same.

He gropes through the red backpack that's dropped on the

ground, feels inside, slips her wallet in his back pocket, palms the dis-cman, chucks the bag out of sight and, because he's not in a hurry, he slips back behind the dumpster. One hand flat against the discman, flat against the scaly blue paint of the skip, Craig Baker heaves a great sigh and releases his cock.

Palming queers, that, and hours of palming kilos of round river rocks in a canvas bag, make his cock go hard. Just hard. Nothing per-sonal. Nothing sensual.

Higher up the shaft, a nip and another, right under where the head bulges out. All the way back to the root and again. He accelerates the pumping of his shaft and adjusts his weight more evenly on the soles of his feet. Nice and snug, his dick rides inside his fist –

Swwuush.

He glances up past the steel edge of the dumpster. His fist goes limp around his dick. A woman's walking briskly through the slid-ing doors. He watches as she strides directly towards the Jeep. Who the fuck's *this* bitch? he muses, gnawing on the hair under his lip.

Craig Baker hadn't given much thought to this thing at all, had-n't needed to. On the one occasion he had sussed out the place that time of day, same gig. One day same as the next. Nothing around, nothing moving. He had simply assumed that when the place looked about buttoned up for the night, with only the one vehicle remaining, the ID of the target couldn't be simpler. Like whichever bitch stuck her keys to the Jeep was his target.

So the appearance of this other woman, older than his vic, had him flustered, but only briefly. After all, he didn't give a fuck who the dame was. Could be that cunt's *mother* for all he cared. *Miss* Anderson, like the little punk says, respectful and all, like she's the king's right ball or something.

And then Tamara did have the one question to ask Senior Constable Matthews.

Senior Constable Matthews answered awkwardly but to his credit, Tamara thought later, he gave her an honest answer. "Look, if I can be frank with you, the guy's obsessed. He's fixated on the idea that lesbi – uh … gay women like yourselves, you spoil the good life for him. The way he sees it, his world would be a better one if … Hmmm," Senior Constable Matthews cleared his throat. "He did use the word *exterminate*. Supremacist talk."

His cock's still stiff, stiff and waiting so, while he keeps his eye on the woman who's just broken into a trot, Craig Baker adjusts the callused ridges of his palm so they feel just right around his shaft. Just right, like a RoughRider worn inside-out 'for maximum stimulation' as it says on the box. He spreads his weight more evenly on the balls of his feet. Higher up the shaft, a nip and another, right under where the head bulges out. Nice and snug, his dick is back to riding fast inside his fist.

The woman's on her knees. He glances at her but returns his attention to the knot of turgid flesh that's bursting to burst.

From deep inside her nightmare, Tamara sees the man's neck muscles thicken and how the vein bulges under the double S tattooed on the side of his neck. She wants to run away from the man. She wants to close her eyes to stop seeing but her nightmare does not allow her that. The best it allows her to do is let her eyes shift to the grazed skin of the man's middle knuckle. Inside her nightmare, Tamara can only struggle, she cannot escape.

"Tam? Darling? *Tam!* "

Emilie. Emilie is here. She's dropped her briefcase. Tamara whimpers in her sleep but the cloying fear that had stolen her breath is not yet ready to relinquish her.

Craig Baker glances over the edge of the dumpster one last time. The woman's still on her knees, fingers across his vic's neck, her face touching hers. He lengthens the motion on his shaft.

"Tam ... for crying out loud ... what's happened to you? *Please* ... Tam ... Wake up!"

Fuckin' bitch reckons she's gonna wake up like Sleeping Beauty. Dream on, he smirks. Down for the count. Nice ... nice. One ... more. Ejaculate splatters and runs down the side of the skip. Craig Baker wipes both hands on the back of his jeans. He slides his still wet penis inside his jeans, does up the fly and brushes the palms of his hands on his head stubble.

His eyes still on the woman who's now rummaging inside a big bag, Craig Baker steps back from the blue dumpster, wheels around, vaults over the hip-high wall and is once again an insignificant part of the street's life. The silver discman, earphones dangling, is light in his hand.

By the time the ambulance siren reaches his ears, Craig Baker is perched on a stool at the bar of the Ball Bearing pub, sucking on his long neck, because things must be done in the right order. And after palming a queer and jerking off, because that's what he's had to do, the next thing he's gotta have inside his fist is the long neck of an ice cold Thirsty Dog.

"So anyway, after listening to more of that supremacist crap," Senior Constable Matthews explained as he reached the end of his account, "we ended up charging him for the assault on your person."

Craig Baker had been fingerprinted and he had had to empty his pockets. Three condoms came out of his back pocket followed by a square of white paper.

Senior Constable Matthews asked a rhetorical, "May I?" and since permission was not needed, with two fingers, he lifted one of the condoms and flashed it at the other officer.

"RoughRiders, huh? Looks like our boy here wants to make sure his ladies feel … something," chides the officer at the desk.

"58 mm, hey? Size of his brain, you reckon?" Senior Constable Matthews called out to the cop on the other side of the counter.

"Nah, too big. I'm not a betting man on account of the missus and all, but I'd wager it's how far he can shoot his little pecker."

Senior Constable Matthews chuckled. "Word of advice, mate. If you know how to read numbers … you should really stick to the expiry dates on these little balloons. Unless of course you're desperate for some little maggot to call you Daddy."

Craig Baker just smirked, absent-mindedly pulling at the tuft of hair under his lip.

Senior Constable Matthews picked up the piece of white paper that had also come out of Craig Baker's back pocket. The moment he turned it over, he knew he was looking at a picture that had to come from Tamara's stolen wallet.

Two women standing on inline skates. Shoulder against shoulder. One taller than the other. One older than the other. Both padded up with elbow and kneepads. Both wearing a cap. A red cap for the young one, a blue cap for the other. A rainbow badge in the shape of a heart against the black cloth. The two women are holding hands. They are not smiling at the camera. Only at each other.

"Nice," said Senior Constable Matthews with a grin. "Your girlfriends? Nah. Out of your league. But again, maybe you'd like to get inside the tall one, anyway. You would, wouldn't you? Tits to die for," he adds awkwardly, in spite of himself, remembering the soft curve of the young woman's breasts under the hospital gown. His dick had noticed too. "Thing is, I reckon, *that* smile right here, you see it?" He taps the glossy photograph, "That's a smile that'll never be for you. I reckon women like these two, they get right up your nose. They do, don't they?"

"Freaks," said Craig Baker coolly. "Dickless freaks. Nuthin' more. Nuthin' less and, left up to you, limp-dicks," Craig Baker riles, "they'd all take over, them and the poofs. And they spread their disea – "

Tamara gasps and her eyes snap open. Open like saucers. She has found a way to break through the shock waves of her pounding heart. Disoriented and nauseous, she dares not move. She doesn't even blink as the icy, nasty, now disembodied voice of Craig Baker continued to drift inside her head.

"They leave us the dregs. Like they're everywhere, right? Like lurking to stick their fingers up your woman's cunt. Or your daughter's," Craig Baker snarls, one finger jabbing the policeman's chest.

Tamara blinks rapidly. She makes herself swallow and the bedroom around her reshapes itself. She recognises the paintings and the curtains and the chest of drawers that are familiar to her, familiar inside Emilie's bedroom. She sits up, still dazed and struggling for breath because the thumping of her heart is still knotted around the lingering images and the words that cling to her, unwilling to be banished so soon, back into their non- existence.

It's OK, she reassures herself. *A friggin' fucking nightmare.* She makes herself inhale more of the air that is floating around her head. It's there. Just breathe it in. Let it go. Let *him* fuckin' go away.

One by one the strands of nightmare loosen their grip and recede, and Tamara becomes aware of Emilie's soft breathing, of her body curled up next to hers. And a lump forms in her throat. Slowly, so as not to wake her up, she rests her hand on Emilie's warm hip but she dares not yet close her eyes again in the darkness of the room.

She needs to get up. She needs to make herself breathe better. She needs to splash cold water on her face. She needs to drink a tall glass to splash cold water on her insides. Then she will slide back into bed. She will snuggle right close against Emilie, one arm around her waist and curl up. And, eyes wide open, she will confront her nightmare. She will show it that it no longer has any hold on her. That it is spent, thinning, and transparent. Vaporised. Tamara knows she is safe inside Emilie's bed and she knows that she will be fine once her breathing surrenders to her lover's, once she lets it lead her back into sleep.

****

Dear Reader

If you have enjoyed ***Jagged Dreams***, it is my pleasure to offer you sample pages from ***Far From Maddy***, my latest novel in progress, that explores the impact of unresolved childhood issues on the relationship between two young women: Jo, a twenty-three year old who 'self-medicates' her emotional wounds by choosing homelessness as a way of life, and Maddy, her lover, who tries to rein her in.

The backdrop for this gritty, urban tale of love is the inner city park of New Farm in Brisbane, Australia.

I would also like to invite you to visit for more extracts and the free serialisation of key novels, such as ***Benchmarks*** (revised edition), a venture that I plan to keep going for your enjoyment.

Warm regards

C.C.

Far From Maddy © by C.C. Saint-Clair 2003

"A distinctive voice … unusually poetic for lesbian grunge. Though I usually prefer characters who are a bit more highbrow, I fell in love with Saint-Clair's two young protagonists: Maddy, achingly at a loss to understand why her lover has dropped out of sight, and Jo who needs to find self-love before she can ever be any good for herself, for Maddy, for anyone. *Far From Maddy* is a sheer delight." Veronika Clayton

"Tender and raw. My heart goes out to Maddy but it's Jo I'd want to make whole."   Charlie Baker

Excerpt beginning p. 57

Note:
Maddy and Jo are respectively 25 and 23 years old. The events told in this extract are locked inside Jo's memory.

Jo is fourteen. She comes home from school, drops her bag at the base of the stairway that leads up to her room and goes looking for her mother. She doesn't call for her because Isabel doesn't usually like it when her daughter calls out. Eventually Jo finds Isabel at the bottom of the garden, where no one ever goes anymore, peering inside the much-neglected pond. So as not to startle her Jo, still a little distance away, says softly but clearly, "Hey, Mama. What you up to?"

Still on all fours, Isabel turns her head to meet the voice, "Oh good, Little Jo's home. Come, come," she gestures with her hand. Isabel sits up on her haunches to make room for her daughter. She pats the space in front of her. "Here. Sit right here."

Jo crawls into the space opened up for her on her hands and knees and, with her back to her mother, peers cautiously into the algae-green water. She peers into the water and her mother leans over her shoulder and finally Jo exclaims, "But there's a fish in there, Mama. A fish! A big bugger of a fish." She turns to her mother and meets her mother's oyster-shell eyes.

Smiling eyes. "I knew it would make you happy, seeing a live, healthy, fish in this pond. No idea what it is though."

"Well, it's not a gold fish, that's for sure. It's not even orange at all," Jo says, scrutinising the water for another glimpse of the fish that's no longer visible. "It's a grey thing, isn't it? A *real* fish from the deep. It lives in the dark caves beneath the water of *our* pond," Jo adds following her own narrative. "And *you* found it. I'll make you a plaque like they do for … uh, for discoverers of things." Again, she turns sideways to look at her mother. "What brought you down here anyway?"

Isabel smiles and brushes the loose strands of hair away from her daughter's cheek. "Well, if you really must know," she says smiling gently, "I just got up from my nap wondering whether that pond was still full of water or whether it had … dried up. Jo, would you believe that I couldn't, not even to save my life, remember if anyone had done anything to it, like you, or the gardener. Or even your father."

"Cool but what made you think of the pond?"

"No idea. But I knew you would be home soon and that, eventually, you would find me here. What I didn't know is that I'd end up finding our dinner at the botto– "

"Mama, don't you dare!" Jo exclaims but not too loudly. "He's too gorgeous to even make frying pan jokes within *gill*-shot." Jo squints at her mother. "Get it? Gill-shot, earshot?" Her hair is cut in a smooth, young lady-like bob. It is black and shiny under the late afternoon sun.

"Mmm ... " Isabel pretends to think. "Uh, ah, yes. I get it." Grey eyes sparkle. She tousles her daughter's hair. "Now, do you think that this grey creature that lives deep inside the pond might appreciate a little bread? You know, as a reward for having grown so big all on his own."

"Oh yes. Of course, it couldn't have been easy for him. It's quite lonely out here." Jo's already up on her feet. Dried bits of grass cling to the back of her navy blue uniform. Isabel picks off a couple of the larger ones before her daughter starts back up towards the house. Abruptly, she has an afterthought. "I'm sure he'll like the bread," she says, "but Mama, ... d'you think it's OK to give him people food?"

"Ah, yes." Eyebrows screwed up in thought, Isabel turns to face her daughter. "I mean *no*. I mean, you're right, if it got that big on its own, it probably doesn't need our help now. Didn't have that mean and hungry look about him anyway, did he?"

"Can't say that he did," Jo chuckles.

"Why don't you come back here then, and we just see if he'll come back up for air. Or to have a better look at us."

Mother and daughter peer back into the dark pond. Isabel's arms are around Jo's thin shoulders. Under her hand, she can feel her daughter's heart beat. She nuzzles Jo's black hair. Two peas in a pod.

Jo is fourteen. The light from the garden is trapped inside the glass. Jo watches the refracted light as it spins, as the spray of transparent liquid curves outwards and back. She's already traced its path. She won't have to duck for *this one*. In her mind, she snap-freezes it in mid-air for half the time it takes to blink.

In rapid-fire impressions she thinks, *Would hurt real bad but won't connect. No excuse to invent for school.* So she watches the glass spin in slow motion. She watches it spin free of its transparent content wishing that, before it crashes at her feet, she could truly freeze its trajectory and rewind the last seventy-nine seconds.

The thing is Jo doesn't know, not fully, why her mother has hurled the glass at her. And it is the *not knowing* that makes her a bad daughter. A bad daughter who precipitates her mother's bad moods. *Bad girl. I'm a bad girl,* she reprimands herself silently.

Jo is convinced that she *and* her carelessness are the triggers for her mother's erratic behaviour. It is she who, after all, had chosen the moment, though she knew that mornings weren't necessarily the best times for her to approach her mother, if she was awake, since the medication she still has to take before bedtime often leaves her with a terrible headache and an upset stomach.

Nighttimes she knows, too, were best avoided in the sense that, like the mornings, they were not the best time in which to sidle up to her mother to ask her a favour although, of course, *most* mornings and *most* evenings were fine. It's just that she was too dumb to avoid picking the *one* bad one.

The glass splinters on the brushwood floor. Jo jumps backwards. Shards skittle and scatter, some fly upwards. Isabel is beside herself with rage.

"You, idiot!' she screams. "Don't you know that I could die while they're here? How would your little friends like it, huh, if one of them found me asleep?" Isabel's smile is nasty. "Asleep right here on the sofa. A-sleeeep forever. Forever dead. Sleeping the sleep of the dead, huh? You think you'd be Miss Popular after that, do you?" Once launched, Isabel is relentless. "I've brought you up to think. I've been paying good money after bad to have people, all your fucking teachers, teach you some common sense. A little common sense is all I ask of you. And all you're thinking about is a fucking slumber party?" Mouth twisted she glares at her daughter. "Now, don't just stand there like a retard. Pick up the fucking glass. No!" she yells at Jo's retreating back. "You just get on those hands and knees and you pick up it all up. To the last shard, you hear me? To the last shard!" Strained muscles, tendons and arteries entwine like cables along Isabel's neck. "Let's see you do one fucking useful thing with those hands of yours. *One* single thing that goes beyond holding a pen or a fork. Go on! Show me! And wipe that stupid look off your face, you hear?"

*****

Excerpt beginning p.165

Jo – a solitary figure by the great rose garden. Earphones dangling around her neck, arms at her side, she was undecided. Last night had been rough. Last night, she had had a panic attack and, as she stood motionless in the morning light, her indecision stemmed mostly from *not* wanting to focus on why she had been thinking so hard about Maddy. So hard ever since she had come out of last night's bad trip.

Three bongs in a row had left her zonked in a weird way. And so in the morning light she stood by the rose garden, itself looking like the bad side of a bad trip, mangy-brown and headless, except for a couple of thin stalks dubiously crowned by wrinkled roses. She looked at them dully wondering whether their sad state was because these were way too early for the season and had died before their time or because the season had already come, gone and left them behind.

"When?" she asked perplexed. "When do roses bloom?" She tried to remember the roses her mother used to tend to with loving dedication but her mind had lost the scent of her mother's roses. So Jo flicked a dried-up rose with her fingers. *Dead rose standing*, she thought grittily. ***Dead rose loses head in New Farm Park***. That little headline made her chuckle as she watched the few remaining petals flutter to the ground.

That small diversion over, Maddy popped back inside Jo's head. The thought that Maddy was holding on made her frown. She decided Maddy was just like those roses. She was like the roses in the sense that their season had come and gone and, yet, neither Maddy nor the roses seemed to have cottoned on. Teeth clenched, one by one, Jo's long fingers pulled at another rose's petal. Deliberately slowly she did it, one parched petal at a time, with the same nasty intent as the little boy who pulls the wings and the legs, one by one, off a grasshopper.

Once the rose's petals lay on the dirt totally separated from their heart, Jo resisted the urge to bruise them under her rubber soles. She resisted the urge to trample them pricked by the realisation that, if Maddy was on *her* mind, it could hardly be Maddy's fault.

If the white-flash of insight gained from last night's bong-blaze had dissipated as rapidly as the morning dew that had gathered around her during her fitful few hours of sleep, *if* thoughts of Maddy were back in her head, it was simply because *she* hadn't yet successfully exorcised the dependency she represented. *More's needed. More time's needed. Was never meant to be easy,* Jo reminded herself.

Jo settled on a thought from the past – no long-term illness ever gets cured over night. Miracles didn't exist. Touch-healings weren't miracles, she insisted, only hoaxes for suckers desperate for an illusion, desperate for something to hold on to. She reminded herself that her self-diagnosed illness was no different from the one that had sparked such debilitating pain inside her mother's joints. In her legs mostly, but in her arms, too. Jo went on arguing with herself.

She was not different from the douche-bags who bought false fireplaces just to watch fake flames dance rigidly over a fucking fake log. That gave them the illusion they needed, and being with Maddy gave her the illusion she needed, the illusion that a woman's love was a safe place for her. Safe, in a way her mother's love had not been.

To hammer in that thought further she connected further with the rule of thumb she was familiar with back in her St Joan days, in the days of her mother's illness. If a disease has been allowed to settle and progress for a few years, it will take at least one year of intensive treatment, not just to control it but to wipe it out.

If her illness had been left undiagnosed, she reasoned, and untreated for so many years, then surely it would take more than a month, more than a year, more than two or three even to zap that crap out of her guts. Her sick thoughts needed to shrivel up like a cancer inside radiated cells, that much she knew. In fact, she agreed, they needed to shrivel up and die like those bloody mummified roses she was still looking at.

The malignant degeneration of her mother's bone cells had slowed down. It had become controllable but it had left her emotionally damaged. Permanently scared, all through remission, that it would return. That it would cause her to lose a limb or two. An arm and a leg, literally. Jo snorted at her own *humour noir*. Permanently scarred by that fear and by the fear of her husband tossing her on a refuse heap.

Isabel had died but her suicide had been motivated by one or both of her two fears. The irony was that it was one of those fears that had fed the other, the one that drove *her* away from her husband. That same fear had driven her away from her young daughter, too.

If she *discarded* herself, if she rendered herself unusable, Isabel must have reasoned, the fact that it would be a result of *her own doing* would take some of the consequential pain away. And Jo remembered, as she stood still by the rose garden, the gradual receding, the ebbing of her mother's pain giving way to a drug induced lethargy, only broken up by repeated patterns of melancholy, only broken up by erratic mood swings exacerbated by alcohol.

Jo returned to her initial thought and that was the thought that centred around Maddy still pushing her buttons. The idea that she, Jo, was actually doing active pain management, pain management for a deep-seated heart-wasting disease suited her for the moment.

"Protect the heart. Protect the heart," she repeated to herself. And then, "Maddy, please, leave me alone," she enunciated clearly, carefully as she would an affirmation. "Please," she added so softly the word failed to reach her ears. She looked away from the rose garden, jaws clenched on the determination not to ever allow herself to be made vulnerable. Not by Maddy. Not by anyone else. Not ever.

Jo shoved aside the image of Maddy with her hand. Disbelieving, she stared at the back of her hand were a rose thorn had just scratched her and shook her head. Even *dead*, they still fucking bite. Tiny beads of blood stood diagonally across the back of her hand, pale under the delicate fork of raised veins that was always vulnerable to knocks and grazes.

She frowned at the angry red mark not because it hurt but because she had already decided that the hardest thing to keep clean were her hands. She knew it was from sitting on the ground so much, from spending so much time around grass, dust and dirt. She looked at her fingernails. The thin crescents of grime were wider under the nails of the index and middle fingers of her right hand than under any other.

A few days ago, Jo had slipped on the indian cotton skirt that Maddy had brought her that first time they connected in the park. Jo had been on her way to the Centerlink office to register for the Newstart Allowance, the unemployment benefit she thought she might qualify for, being over twenty-one and unemployed. She had a cake of soap in her bag that she kept wrapped inside a plastic bag, the same supermarket bag that had contained the mangoes she and Maddy had shared as dessert, seated at the little picnic table that faced the apartment block on their last night at Burleigh. Jo had washed her hands thoroughly, scrubbing with her new nailbrush under and around the cuticles. Distracted and tense, she had forgotten the little brush on the wash-basin of one of the public park toilets.

She was distracted and rattled by the prospect of having to hem and haw about her present circumstances. She was rattled because she knew that, away from the park, away from the Brunswick, Sydney, and Merthyr Streets area that had become her turf, she would-n't be safe. Not safe from the eyes of others. Not safe from their *know-ing* eyes. She knew she no longer looked right. She knew that, though her skirt and T-shirt were clean, there would be something about her, even if her fingernails were clean, that would make her beep – unhinged. Feral.

And she was edgy too, because she knew they'd give her a form to fill in with boxes she wouldn't be able to complete. Like, for starters, the home address and phone number boxes. Like the emergency contact box. Like the box in which she'd have to write her tax file number. She did have a tax file number. It's just that her tax file number along with her driving licence and the few personal papers she had brought back to Brisbane some thirteen months earlier, along with her most recent pay slips, had been jettisoned at Fairfield House. Seconds later, though it didn't solve her predicament, she remembered that they were, in fact, safe at Maddy's.

And, later, Jo had gone back to the toilet block hoping that the little pink nail brush that had become so important to her would still be where she had left it, on the edge of the wash basin but, no, the little pink brush was no longer there. Jo hadn't bought another one because when night came, she knew that the ganja she'd be scoring behind the derelict Twin Cinemas would, after all, do a lot more for her than a little pink nailbrush could ever do, at least in the short term. And though a nailbrush only cost a few dollars, every cent she had, she needed to save and shell out for another stick.

So Jo looked again at her fingernails, graphically gross in the strong morning light. Stuck, like under laminating plastic. She had always worn her nails short but since she had lost her nailbrush, she cut them almost to the quick with the nail clippers she had had with her all along, in the bottom of her rainbow bag.

Standing still by the rose garden, she had frowned wearily at the tiny beads of fresh blood that dotted the back of her hand, wondering how she could keep the scratch from getting infected without the help of an antiseptic and Band-Aid combo. The idea that she'd have to shell out at least a 10 dollar bill for the two didn't sit any better with her than forking out whatever it would cost to replace her lost nailbrush.

When Maddy had again found Jo in the park, she had led her to the other side of the park, to the other side of the Powerhouse Entertainment Centre. Alone on the grass, away from prying eyes, Jo had let Maddy take her hand in hers. And Maddy had gently rubbed the soft veins on the back of Jo's hand. And she had held that hand in hers as if it had been a dead bird, still warm to the touch but dead all the same. Like a dead bird that might be revived if she kept it still, if she were able to instill some of her warmth into its feather-light body.

Maddy had looked at Jo's hand. She had let her fingers trace the inverted trident of blue-grey veins that spanned the back of her hands. The main vein snaked backwards from her middle finger to cruise over her wrist and the inside of her forearm.

"You know, Jo, it's weird, that," Maddy had said, caressing that one vein that stood out the most with the ball of her thumb, "but *that* vein is one of the first things I fell in love with. From the start." She was not looking at Jo. "I thought those veins made your hands like, *so* … sensual."

What Maddy really wanted to say was that the veins that coursed the back of her lover's hands made them, made *her* seem vulnerable. Long, thin, and vulnerable. Exposed. So vulnerable that her heart ached to protect her and them. Way back then and, even more so, at that moment.

That afternoon, Jo had looked at the back of her hand. She didn't see the attraction but it was true that for as long as she remembered, the veins on the back of her hands always stood out. Even Amber, her best buddy back at St Joan's, used to tease her about them.

"Most of us have our palms read," she said one day. "But any fortune-teller will *pour* your life out just by looking at these veins of yours." And Amber had looked at Jo. "You get it, don't you, the joke? *Pour*, like from veins. And *pour out*, you know, like gush out too much information? No? OK. Weak joke. Rewind. E-rase." Though she had killed off the joke, she noticed how her friend's half smile had lingered.

And then, another day, Amber came up with a different thought about the veins on the back of Jo's hands. "OK, so most everyone would know to slash their *wrists,* right? I mean, if they kinda wanted to top themselves, right?" Jo had nodded cautiously, unsure as to where the conversation was leading. "But you, girl, you'd only have to just slash the *back* of your hands and that would do it, wouldn't it?"

"Guess it would," Jo had replied non-committally. "But vein slashing isn't the way I'd go about it, uh … if I wanted to waste myself."

"Oh, right. So how would you?" Amber had asked, her tone daring Jo to talk seriously about the *untalkable*.

"Well, that's the thing. I haven't figured it out yet."

Amber's eyes opened wider on the *yet.* Had her best mate been entertaining some thoughts about the taboo topic?

Jo, for whom the topic was neither remote nor taboo since she was living almost in daily dread of her mother's suicide, had indeed spent many a moment thinking about how she would like to handle *her* last seconds of consciousness. And in all simplicity, she had unravelled a little more of what she had worked out for herself. "I know I wouldn't use a razor, that's for sure. Too gross. And I know I wouldn't use a gun. Too sloppy. And, yeah, messy ... like for the cleaning lady," she added, attempting a little humour to make Amber smile. "Wouldn't use rat poison and wouldn't use a noose. Same reason. Nasty to find, right? And I think the rat poison thing would be *so* painful you'd want to rewind for sure, just because of the pain, but it'd be too late and– "

The way Amber had cut her short with a "Oh! Right. You're *so* funny, Brenner!" had kept Jo from confiding that her mother actually had her own suicide kit well prepared. Even after her mother's death, Jo never told Amber about the vials of morphine Isabel had been collecting in the cigar box in the corner of her wardrobe. She had not referred to Isabel's death as *suicide*.

*****

Excerpt beginning p. 157

Dark, rust-red hair standing on end, round blue eyes made more round by mocking incredulity, Maddy is angry.

"I mean, fuck! What gave you the right to spy, huh?" she glowered. "I thought I could trust you, like, you know, TRUST! And what you do? You go abusing your power and– "

Christen frowned. "I didn't abuse my power," she retorted. "I didn't abuse anything." Maddy's blue glare was ice cold. "What?" snapped Christen. "I didn't do anything to her."

"Right. Nothing at all," Maddy said frostily, bottom lip split by her gleaming lip loop.

"That's correct. Nothing except shadow her for a while."

"To spy on her," Maddy snarled.

"Well, no, Maddy, I ... I wouldn't say spy. I'd just say followed and watched."

"Oh, big difference!"

"I think there is ... at least some difference. Spying implies –"

"Spare me the dictionary session, Chris." Blue eyes glaring, Maddy walked away. She didn't want to see Christen's face anymore. Not just then. "Oh, hell, you don't need to make me the bad guy." Christen pushed her sun-blond hair away from her face. "There was no nasty intention on my part." Maddy ignored her.

"What I thought was that if I had a look at her, I might come up with an idea … Something that might help her come around and ... and reinsert. I mean, it's difficult to – "

Maddy glared back at her from the deckchair where she had flopped under the overarching poinciana tree. "Yeah, sure," she grumbled cantankerously. "And how did you even connect with her, huh?" she asked belligerently, twisting her neck to look at Christen who was still standing outside the back door.

Christen had phoned to see if it was alright for her to drop by as she was once again in the neighbourhood and Maddy had replied,

"Yeah, I'm home. Not doing anything much. Just fiddling under the house with Jo's bike."

When Christen had walked through the squeaky back-gate Maddy, squinting into the the sunlight, had popped her head from under the house. "Grab a beer," she had said casually as she would to an old friend. "I'll be up in a tick. Just need to spray a second coat of chrome on the handlebars."

"OK. Don't go inhaling the fumes. They're vicious," the older woman had replied. She had reached into the fridge, popped the cap off an ice-cold beer and had returned to the patio where she sat at the wooden table under the kitchen window. She stretched her legs, crossed her ankles, and sighed. She took a sip from the bottle and ran the tip of her tongue over her lip. She smiled to herself, closed her eyes to listen for the tiny sounds and flutters that filled the air inside Maddy's backyard.

A short while later, when Maddy dropped a hand on the woman's shoulder and said, "Hey," Christen opened her eyes and smiled at the young redhead.

The loose turquoise muscle-shirt Maddy had thrown over a pair of faded low-waisted jeans enhanced the width of her shoulders. Its open sides clearly revealed that Maddy was not wearing a bra and the firm slab of the back muscle that curled gently to touch her ribs made Christen smile differently.

Maddy's hair, near her temples, was flattened damp with perspiration. As if a tribal tattoo, a double smudge of dark grease crossed her forearm. Her hands were stained by silver chrome and black paint.

"I've finally reached the fun stage of this thing," she said, grinning broadly. "Sanding and de-rusting and undercoating all the small bits and the frame, that wasn't great fun but now, it's all hanging well. I'll take you down for a look later."

Christen answered enthusiastically, "I'd love that."

Maddy went inside to scrub her hands clean and came back to the patio, with a bowl of olives in one hand, a bowl of cashews in the other, and a beer caught between two fingers. All traces of grease smudges had disappeared but, as Maddy sat across from Christen, the angled sunlight that bounced off her cheekbone revealed a faint trace of glittery chrome. Christen made herself look away and the two women chattered on easily until the blonde one said, "I saw Jo."

Maddy startled and blinked. She drew in her bottom lip and she stared at Christen. "Jo? My Jo?"

"Yes," Christen smiled. "Jo Brenner, your Jo. I don't know any oth– " she caught Maddy's suspicious squint. "What?"

"How the hell did that happen?" Maddy asked too sharply but Christen went on to explain how a couple of evenings ago after her shift, she had driven up from Burleigh to visit her mother who, at the moment, was not at all well. About to turn her car towards the highway, Christen had hesitated. And on impulse she had turned the car around while she still could.

"I thought that … well … you know," she said focusing on the long spiral of clear perspex that, hanging from a low branch, was spinning swirls of light. "Well I thought about it, you know, as I was driving back on Cornwall … and then I thought it'd be best not to, I mean not to call you. Better if I didn't try to see you. I mean on the off chance that … "

And it had only been then that the connection had happened. If she shouldn't see Maddy, Christen thought, maybe she could see Maddy's lover. Maybe she could hang around New Farm Park and see if she could spot her. Christen admitted that she had been curious as to what young Jo looked like but she also thought that seeing her in the park, or in the streets, might help her think of something constructive that could be done to help her leave the park and resume a more practical lifestyle.

"To be honest," she shrugged, "I can't say that I connected with her at all. It's not like I talked to her or anything. She didn't even see me."

"So how you know it's her, huh?" Maddy asked, not yet ready to let her anger drop.

Christen looked at her incredulously. "Oh, like you think she's hard to spot, do you?" Maddy lowered her eyes. "How many young chicks looking like her have we got hanging around the park area, you think? Like here in Brisbane?" Maddy shrugged. "Anyway, from your MP report, I knew I was looking for a dark-haired twenty-three year old, about five-eleven, wearing army greens and carrying a rainbow cloth bag."

"Ah yes, the report that no one but you took seriously."

The blonde woman waved her hands in front of her chest. "No comment."

"Right."

"What?" Christen asked again in return to Maddy's hard stare.

"Nothing. So, uh … when was it, then?"

"That I followed her?" Eyes away from Christen, Maddy nodded. "Two nights ago. Last Wednesday. Why?"

Maddy shrugged again but this time she turned her attention back to the policewoman. "I haven't seen her for almost a week. Last time wasn't too good."

Silence settled between them. Directly in Maddy's line of vision, dangling from its low branch the long spiral that Jo had given her, on the night of their sixth month's anniversary, twirled under the soft breath of the breeze and the dappled sunlight rippled and shimmered on its curved acrylic surface. Elongated discs of transparent light materialised out of the air below to rise languorously in slow succession only to die and disappear back into the nothingness at the other end of the long spiral. Again and again, on an upward travel, on a downward path, sparkling light cascaded and rippled the length of the spiral. Maddy pulled her eyes away from the magnetic attraction.

"Chris," she said softly.

"Mm?"

Maddy patted the deckchair next to hers. "Come here."

Until recently Maddy had only had one garden lounge but for some reason, though there were a couple of tubular plastic seats scattered in the backyard, one particular afternoon when she had been thinking of Jo, she had decided to buy another lounging chair. For Jo.

Silently, Maddy snorted. Leaning back, she closed her eyes and sighed. She heard Christen's footfalls move towards her over the tiles. She heard the frame creak as Christen settled on the striped mattress at her side. Neither woman spoke. Not for a long time. Anyone peeping inside the garden would have thought them asleep.

Finally Maddy shook her head, slowly, sadly. "I just don't know what to do any more," she began wearily. "When I see her, sometimes we talk but … it's not about it. It's not about why she's there or what she thinks she needs to do before she can come back." She let her eyes be drawn again by the spiral and Jo's voice flooded her eardrums.

'I'd like you to hang it right there,' Jo had said, pointing a few feet at the low-hanging branches of the tree. 'Just so that … when you're out here, gazing into space, the spiral, you know, the way it catches the light, twirling it around and all, well, I'd like to think that it'll bring you … your thoughts back to me.'

Maddy pulled her eyes away and sat up on the striped mattress. "It's not even like I've ever said that she– that we need to carry on as Oh, let's pretend nothing's happened. I mean, what I do tell her is that she can get herself another room. That's to help … if it's the idea of the two-lives-joined-at-the-hip thing is what's making her flip. I tell her she needs to start using some of the money she has at the bank for … for basics. I tell her she can go back to her sister's. I tell her I'm there for her, even if she doesn't want me … Well, yes, even if she doesn't want me as a lover anymore. And all she tells me is that she can't go back to her old life anymore and that means no to a room, no to Jarrah, no to regular work, no even to the dole." Maddy shook her head and nibbled on her bottom lip. "So, I'm like, So … what, Jo?" She frowned, intent on her flashback. "So I ask her if all she wants out of life, like now, is to work one hour a day, sit on a park bench for the rest of her life? And sleep on the ground? And all she gives me is, 'Look, Mad. You don't understand and I can't explain. So just leave me alone.'"

Maddy turned her face towards Christen's. Hurt and incomprehension in round blue eyes. "She says, 'Just walk away and leave me be.'"

For a moment, Maddy remained in silent contemplation of her knuckles. The middle one was skinned but it had begun healing over. She ran the thumb of her other hand over the scab and frowned again. "Jo looks like shit. Like totally wrecked and she's gonna get sick, it's like I just know it. So what does she do, huh? She mops the goddamn floor at some fucking four star restaurant by the river? Cool! So what does she do the rest of the time, huh? Used to be so active before all that. What does she do with her money? Obviously she's not spending it, not even on a fucking nailbrush," Maddy spat bitterly as if Christen's silent presence allowed her to finally think outside her head. "And she's such a hygiene freak. Having dirty nails … That'd be driving her … crazy. And well … I don't know where she washes or showers. Where do you wash? I mean, how do you fucking wash when you don't have a fucking bathroom, huh?" Maddy glared at the spiral. Her hand raked through her hair. "I just can't work it out anymore," Maddy finished in a big sad sigh.

Christen hesitated. She looked at the young redhead feeling her confusion, feeling for her. She opened her mouth and leaned forward to speak but she changed her mind. Instead, she let her eyes be drawn by the mesmerising swirls of sunlight that spiralled in and out of the air ahead.

Still thinking out loud, Maddy broke the silence. "OK, so even if it takes her like one hour … or two, you know, to clean and mop the floors at that restaurant, she must be getting at least the minimum hourly rate, right?" she asked, waiting for Christen's nod before continuing. "What's that then? What, about fifteen bucks?"

"Was, last time I checked."

"So she makes about twenty dollars a day, give or take. She doesn't spend it on food. She's even thinner than before. She doesn't spend it on laundry powder, I mean like, she doesn't do the Laundromat thing, that's pretty obvious by now. Anybody looking can tell her clothes are not– " Maddy heaved another great sigh. "So … what does she do with what she gets every day, huh? I mean, by now, she probably shouldn't be carrying that much cash around, right?"

"She's not."

Maddy eyed the blonde woman. "She's not what?"

"She's not carrying that money on her person."

Maddy opened her round-blue eyes wider. "Oh, right. She's depositing it at the bank, then?" she asked superciliously.

"She deposits it but not at – "

"Oh, fuck it, Chris." Maddy swung her legs on to the ground to better face the woman. "What does she do with her money?"

"Spying sucks big time," Christen replied with a smile that crinkled up her nose, "and now you want me to– "

Maddy ran her freckly fingers through the short length of her hair. "Oh, fuck it," she said in frustration. "Look, I'm sorry about … about before. I was out of line … in a big way," Maddy replied with a quick apologetic grin. "I … look, Chris, what do you know?" She sucked in the silver lip loop and waited, an apprehensive squint tightening her eyes.

Christen pushed herself up on the mattress and gave the redhead a measured look.

"Look, Maddy … " She hesitated one last time. "It's not good … uh … You don't wanna go there – "

"Spit it out, Chris. Tell me! Please."

Eyes turned away from Maddy, Christen replied flatly, "She spends it on drugs."

Silence. "On drugs?"

Christen nodded "On shit. Grass. Weed."

"And?" Her hand raked through her short hair.

"And … nothing. That's it." Christen shrugged. "You wanted to know what she did with her money, so now you know. She blows twenty-three dollars a day."

"Twenty-three?" Maddy bit on the lip loop and considered Christen. "How do you know it's twenty and not what, … fifteen or … five? I mean, I'm asking a simple question here…"

Christen chuckled. "Maddy, you can't buy dope for five bucks, this is not Bolivia. Besides, I've been spying, remember?"

"Yeah. I've apologised for that." Maddy snorted and looked away. She nibbled the inside of her lip.

"Ok, I've tailed her, yes and– Well, I've found that garden hideout where she hangs at night, and I spotted her connecting with a small-fry dealer, one James Mirren who operates from Oxley Lane behind the Village Twin Cinemas." Christen looked at Maddy.

"The boys at the New Farm station know all about him, that's how come I know who he is, but they don't want to make an arrest. No long-term benefit in it," she explained.

"Another one would be standing at the exact same spot in a matter of days. Same old stor– "

"Jo buys from this jerk?"

"She does. A foil. Twenty-three dollars."

"Twenty-three? Like what? They don't do even numbers? Would be simpler."

"They do. Twenty-five dollars is the going price for a two-gram deal but for his … " She considered Maddy. "He gives his regular customers a bit of a discount."

"So … she's a regular."

"She is. Has been for about six weeks."

Jo. Back on drugs. Abruptly Maddy stood up and paced. What was it that Jarrah had said about it, about her sister's habit at the time of their mothers' suicide.

Jaw muscles bunched, Maddy squinted from the effort of bringing back the words Jarrah had used. And when those words came back, she winced. She felt winded. She shut her eyes against the unsettling image. 'She attached herself to the bong like a mare to a feeding bag,' is what Jarrah had said.

Harsh words, Maddy had thought at the time, but at the time she knew Jo had turned her habit around. Jo was clean. And Maddy hadn't had to see what Jarrah had seen. She hadn't had to put up with what she had had to put up with during the year that followed their mother's death, the year Jo spent with her older sister. But as Jarrah's words overlapped with Christen's, Maddy felt sick. Sick with apprehension.

"So ... uh, what does she ... What does she get for twenty-three bucks?" she asked slowly, voice faltering.

"Enough for three or four joints. Depends how she packs them. One killer joint or three or four smaller ones."

"A day?"

"A night. Jo's clean during the day. She only lights up at night. After midnight."

"You know this, do you?" Maddy asked acidly.

"I know that."

"You'd better tell me all of it, Chris."

*****